DREDA SAY MITCHELL

running hot

DREDA SAY MITCHELL

running hot

Published in 2004 by
The Maia Press Limited
82 Forest Road
London E8 3BH
www.maiapress.com

ISBN 1 904559 09 3

A CIP catalogue record for this book is available
from the British Library

Printed and bound in Great Britain by Thanet Press

Dedicated to the one and only Tony
& the original Dreda

Big thanks to Anastasia. Thanks to Maggie, Jane
& David at Maia, and to my consultation crew of
Tony, Exley, DJ, Quincy, Stephanie, Roberta,
Tolu, Adam, Mary, Matt, Ella, Henrietta & Hugo

1

Mehmet Ali lay in East London's number one outdoor spot to die. He lay two doors down from Kwame's Hotshot Barbers and three doors up from Rosaman's Cabs. Over him rocked the bodies of two men as they stomped, twisted and sliced their shoe heels into him. An hour earlier his attackers had been jerking their bodies to the pounding energy of Judge Dredd's Nightsound. Now they continued their dance by fucking him up. At first their movements had been light, verbal in nature, with the need to find what they were after. But their tactics had changed once they realised his lips weren't going to tell them anything. After they had found him, as they knew they would, they'd dragged him to Cinnamon Junction, right on to the main road. They had known that this spot was too notorious, too in-your-face, for any of the cars passing on a Monday at 2.23 a.m. to stop and help. Anyway, any car cruising the Junction at that time of morning had its own business to attend to.

Benji, the more bullish of the two, stopped, tipped his corn-rowed head back on to the wall and breathed, allowing the greatness of power to balloon within his body. His leather-gloved hand grabbed the forearm of his partner.

'We'd better stop and find it . . .'

'Whatever,' Josh responded, his dark brown skin spinning on too much booze and barbs.

'Let's see if the fool's hurting enough to spill,' Benji continued loudly, wanting their victim to understand the next move.

So they demanded from him. Yelled at him. Shook him so many different ways that the only music serenading the new day was the cooing pain from Mehmet's throat. But their dance had been too synchronised, too perfect in its damage, as he only heard the blood draining and drying around his ears. They demanded from him one last time. He wasn't giving it up and they knew it. Frustration intensified their blows. In the middle of a slanted heel movement, Benji wobbled as his head snaked towards the road.

'I can hear Bluebottles,' he whispered, as his black shoe meshed with bone.

'I can't hear a thing,' Josh answered, slowing his attack.

'He's made a total mess of your Clarks,' Josh continued.

Benji quickly glanced down at his shoes. The leather was now polished with the richness of blood.

'Forget about my shoes. We can't afford to get caught so let's settle for 10,' Benji continued, 'and then check back, because let me tell you, if we don't find the ting – this'll be us soon enough.'

As they scattered, their victim had already decided he would never tell them. Better to be dead at the Junction than at the hands of his own people. He shouldn't have gone for that drink. He should have gone straight there. He used his trainers to scrape into the pavement and push himself back and away from the road, needing to check that the merchandise was still secure in his trainer.

Mehmet Ali died at 2.31 a.m., just as the last anonymous car had blown by, throwing a Tennant's can from its window, which rolled like the softest lullaby on to his still stomach.

Schoolboy, known to the criminal justice system as Elijah Ray Campbell, stepped off the X66 bus as it hit the Junction and hit 2.33 a.m. He tensed as a police car screamed past, carrying its hysteria long into the distance. His ear strained against his locks, waiting for the shrill of the Bluebottles' siren to fade. He relaxed. He moved, shoulders curving forward, head swinging low, a posture he had long ago perfected in his twenty-nine years to hide himself from the glare of life. His hood weaved and glided against the bones and ridges of his face like a skateboarder in concrete paradise. He shuffled back from the peeling metal rail, which guarded the pavement from the road, needing to sort out his thoughts. Only a few people realised that 2.30 to 3 was the Junction's serene zone.

No people.

No aggravations.

No unexpected moments.

The ideal place to think. Also, he knew that most would wrongly mark him as a crackhead too worthless to trouble, too useless to know better than to flaunt himself there at that time of the morning. His brisk, brown eyes grinned with remembered freedom at discovering this time.

His eyes shut down as the weathered stench of one too many slashes against the wall streamed by. Nothing like touching other people's lives to spoil a pure moment. He slipped sideways, as he reached The Raven, a club that beat out a rapid 'come and check me' pulse and stood so dark in its skin of black paint that night-dwellers were either enticed into going inside or taking up its offer of using its street shadows to hide in. Schoolboy slid into its shadow. He re-focused. He'd already made his decision. He was going whether anyone liked it or not. Michael would expect to see him and commitment on Sunday. And commitment meant bringing his own knives. Knives he didn't have. Forty quid, that's all he needed. But being a giro-slave and opening his home to the wrong people meant he had no silver to spare. He dismissed doing a residential or a commercial. He hadn't been part of the burglary brotherhood for years and wasn't about to renew his membership. He took a breath. Deep. He was going and if that meant haggling with his nearest and dearest until their loose change converted into knife money in his pocket, then so be it. He needed to gather the cash quickly because in a week's time he wanted to be tucked on to the West Coast Mainline headed for Michael. Headed for Devon. He shook his head. He still couldn't believe it. Bloody Devon, the type of place where those that thought they were in the know would assume his middle name was either Winston or Delroy. But it would be worth it. It had to be worth it.

As the voices of the passing car engines scatted high and low, Schoolboy began running through schemes and names which could get the knife relief fund started. Option one was Terri-baby, his current. She'd do anything for him. Well, nearly anything. But he was too fucked off with her. Too fucked that Little-Miss-Middle-Class-Self didn't think he was good enough to meet Daddy and Step-Mommy. Good enough to shag on their sofa, though. Option two was Emmanuel, who had been one of his main boys. The only trouble was four months ago Manny had become Mr Ten Days Church of the Living Lord, standing on the corner of Dalston Lane and Kingsland Road pleading with the punters at Ridley Road market to get into the rhythm of the Resurrection. Which left Evie. Option number three. Evie his up-and-coming sister. He knitted his fingers through his dreads, massaging his scalp, needing to get his story straight. Evie wasn't stupid. She knew the street, but every now and again her chosen life made her forget. Made her so radical, she wanted to help people like him. He spat a large gob on to the pavement. She was so full of piss sometimes.

His whole head whipped away from the melting spittle as his stare fixed on to what looked like the upward palm of a naked foot and accompanying leg, the only visible sign of a body sandwiched in the gap between The Raven and an estate agents that only sold homes worth a quarter of a million plus. He shuffled around and forward, knowing it wasn't a Raven resident, as anyone and everyone knew The Raven took care of its own within its walls. He wasn't shocked. This end of the Junction was the most popular for advertising new brands of killing. The Junction was angry and it didn't care who knew it. Even the Bluebottles understood this and buzzed right by it. Its anger had become so biting and bold that it was the one pitch in Hackney where the community passed through or around. They used it to move quickly from Hackney to Islington. Islington to Hackney. From living to dying. He returned his attention to the leg. It was covered in the same make of stepping-out trousers he had himself bought last week. Same flair. Same style. Sharp with the tailored swing of someone ready to move on. Shame they were spoiled by the wayward pattern of blood.

He moved his vision to the side, not willing to move it up, more comfortable looking at the collection of sagging bin-bags. Besides, his first time in prison had taught him that when you've seen one stiff you've seen them all. He followed the bags' defeated shapes around until his eyes were stalled by a trainer. Black, cheap, market-stall fodder. Right or left, he couldn't tell. It pointed at him, lying on its side, the space left for the placement of a foot, wide open, dark, gaping at him with the helplessness of a permanent scream. He moved towards it, knowing someone else would have missed it. But not him. Since the age of fourteen he had trained his eyes to observe, catch everything, because he never knew when he might need something. Never knew when he might need to hold something in someone's face, just as a reminder.

The trainer's very poise and look made him squirm. He had enough grief in his life without some trainer thinking it could join the flippin' queue. The pile of misery in his life wasn't so easy to move but he could do something about that trainer. He booted it backwards, scattering glass from the broken street lamp. As the trainer nose-dived towards the ground, it spat something bulky and big towards Schoolboy. Schoolboy leapt back. The object knocked on to the ground and awkwardly rolled to greet him. This time Schoolboy didn't move but stilled himself. His neck jammed down and forward, peering at an object that resembled a half-brick. He knew he shouldn't get involved. Only seven more days to keep his fingernails clean. But when opportunity has been the most influential instigator in helping to decide which corner to turn, it wasn't that easy. He folded his legs at the knees to get a better view of it. He settled on his haunches when he realised what it was. A mobile phone. A relic. A reminder of an age when there was no pay-as-you-go, just pay or get cut off. The type of mouthpiece the average street thief used to give back to his victim in disgust. That was until some Shoreditch-based artist made them fashionable again. The artist had won some national prize called Peace In Our Time, which was a circle of old mobiles standing erect around pictures of dead people from the Congo. Schoolboy had seen it on the telly and had no idea what the bod from Shoreditch was going on about. But he did know that the trendy set were all hunting for old phones to put in their homes as a sign of peace. Option number four took hold and began to tell its own story – sell mobile as a piece of retro for thirty quid to Mikey and fleece Evie for another thirty. That way he could purchase at least the knives and also some fine home-grown Amsterdam he'd heard was doing revolutionary mouth-to-mouth resus. Nothing like leaving London with the aroma of something special flossing his teeth.

He scooped the phone up. It was too bulky to fit in his hand, too wide for his fingers to fit across. He wiped the watery dirt from its backside and forced it into the pocket of his fleece. He stood up and began heading for the traffic lights at the end of the Junction. He knew he should be feeling guilty – stealing from the dead and all that – but the man didn't need it where he was going. Going? The geez was undoubtedly already gone. But whether he was smoked or just well-done was none of Schoolboy's business. Now he needed to decide who he would go to first. Mikey or Evie? Evie or Mikey? Mikey would be easy, just a simple business transaction. Goods for money. Now Evie would be harder. She could easily afford thirty sovs but she wouldn't want to give it up. At least not without running her mouth all over him for a minimum of half an hour.

Abruptly, one of those unexpected moments crashed into his stride, making him stumble. He was shaken. Shaken by the sight of two men coming his way. Shaken, because maybe he didn't know the Junction as well as he should. His shock let go as he marked them for what they were – a pair of freelance amateurs. Only amateurs masqueraded in leather gloves and matching lengthy coats, unbuttoned to create flow and drama as they proceeded down the street. The only drama they played out was pure Shaft. Pure panto. London's freelancers were now marketing themselves as consultants, all tooled up in cottons and linen.

But Schoolboy recognised that even amateurs knew how to use a 9mm or create some other type of life-altering moment. As he passed them he cast his eyes downwards, letting them have their illusion of fear and respect. Life had also taught him that if someone didn't catch a glimpse of your eyes or stare directly into them, they were unlikely to remember your face. His gaze was caught by the gleam of the shoe of the shorter one. Shiny and slick with slime at the edges, as if the man had already trodden in too much of the capital's muck. He brought his head up as they went past him. He didn't look back. 'Keep your face forward' were the last words his mum had sternly soothed him with before she'd boarded the plane back home to Grenada. And he did just that, with his new friend snug in his pocket until his gates came into view.

Schoolboy was long gone before Benji and Josh realised they wouldn't find the phone. Long gone before they realised that they might have been ripped off. Long gone before they realised the only street parasite they had seen had passed them a good ten minutes ago. They tipped out the word on to Hackney's major highways to find him.

2

The word chipped into the dawn of the Monday morning streets two hours before Wahid was told his delivery had gone missing. The woman on top of him was riding his body, but it wasn't hard enough for him. He placed his palms over her backside and dug the edges of his brown-baked fingers into her pink-kissed skin, beginning to almost tear and re-mould her. She understood and began to circle into him faster, pressing his body into the folds of the chair and stamping her hands into the tattoo on his broad chest. The tattoo was huge, but simple. A thick black line curved with the edge of his left pec like a snake, getting thinner as it slithered into the groove between both chest muscles. The tempo of indigo-inked tattoos once again marked him above both pecs. Above the right was the word 'number' and above the left the word 'one'. Because that's who he was and had been for the last four years since he was thirty. Number 1 from the Dalston-based Numbers crew.

He grabbed the woman closer, needing this intimacy to be fast. He needed to remind himself that people still respected him. Would respect him even more when he got the phone. Would welcome him like a brother when he hit America's shores because there was nothing US citizens liked more than slinging their arm around the shoulder of someone with bills peeping from their pocket. He smiled. He began sliding his teeth over the woman's breasts. He loved the feeling of flesh on a woman, all smooth, rolling and rich. He didn't understand this Western thin thing. Bones just reminded him of those bad times back in Lagos in the early 90s. He twisted his tongue under her breast. Now America was going to be fantastic. His breath began to stall, to speed up as he imagined himself in a plush new office in New York. Plasma TV to the left, wide-screen TV to the right, with the aroma of big, fat cigars and an even bigger PA.

His teeth began to pinch the woman's right nipple, making her jump. She knew better than to make any noises. The only sounds he liked were those of himself driving forward. He shut his eyes against the fever pitch of exchanging what the phone had for cash with the buyer. He had made this deal, not anyone else. He thought of the years spent with Number 8 when he had let them run the show. Him, Number 8 and Number 10, what an outfit they had been. But now it was just him and Number 10. Number 8 had long been discarded in the rubbish with all the other no-hopers. He gripped the woman's flesh tighter. This was not a time to think about losers. This prestige would be his and Ashara's alone. He felt the rush of pure sexual surrender displace the woman's manufactured scent. She knew the drill. She jumped off him and got on her knees. His mobile started ringing, ripping the room with one of the latest hip-hop tunes and he knew that was Number 10 with the good news he'd been waiting for. Wahid quickly stood above the woman, his body stretched, making him look much taller than he was. Her small hands lifted her breasts forward as an offering. His clean-shaven head fell back as he groaned. That's what he loved about his life. The ability to see his power displayed before him.

'Get the phone,' he ordered, and his companion rushed to retrieve it from the mock-marble mantelpiece.

As she passed it to him she tried to caress him with her acrylic nails. He had something else in his hands now, so he didn't feel her touch any more. She sulked off and left as he answered the phone. Wahid's attention pulled to the voice at the other end.

'It's me,' the voice paused, then carried on. 'We have a problem . . .'

'A problem?'

'Yes. Our friend didn't show.'

Aneurin Bevan Tower and Ernest Bevin House stood back to back on the south side of Hackney. The side of Hackney that bumped boundaries with Bethnal Green. In the late 80s the Council had floated the idea of calling them after a couple of Latin American revolutionaries, but tenants and subletters moaned that they had enough trouble trying to wring their tongues around English and Welsh without adding Spanish to the list. So the community had taken charge and unofficially rebaptised both houses Eric and Ernie. Eric was tall and slim, Ernie wide and fat. They should have been a double act, but they weren't. Eric played out the stories of 'I'm giving up tomorrow' junkies, wall scribes and anyone else the Council knew wasn't going to cut it with the rest of the population. High in the sky was the best place for them, some said. Nearer to God's divine grace and as far away as possible from the rest of us. Ernie told a different tale. It dared to be caring, clean, a community.

Flat 24 was on Ernie's second floor. Eighth door from the right, the last door on the left. A one-bedroom flat with a rent book that stated it had enough space for three occupants and a layout that held no surprises. A typical T-shaped passage that led to a bedroom, front room, kitchen and a bathroom tucked into a corner. A bathroom that did not deviate from public housing requirements with its sink, standard radiator and a toilet that almost kissed the bath with its nearness.

Monday midday found its resident, Schoolboy, lying in the bath. Naked. With vulnerability squeezed in beside his slender frame. The problem with vulnerability was that it opened the way to the truth. And the truth was he'd been falling for a long time. He folded his back up and tensed his stomach muscles to reach the taps. The water only covered the cheeks of his backside, testament to the sticking stopcock in the tank. Just because there wasn't enough water didn't mean that he couldn't ease back and remember what relaxing felt like. He used the length of his fingers to turn on the taps.

Right tap.

Left tap.

Mix.

He held the shower attachment to deliver water when he wanted it and where he wanted it. He folded his back down allowing the warmth from his flesh to melt against the crawling cold of the enamel. Tiredness was clawing across his skin, trying to pull his eyes shut, but relief kept them open. Relief that it was the Junction, of all places, that

threw up the answer this morning to his immediate probl[...]
as he exchanged the Nokia for dosh he could purchase the k[...]
move out of London for good.

Nostalgia began to scratch him, right across his chest and nipp[...]
in exactly the same way it had since the day he had decided to leav[...]
Moving from Dalston to Devon should have been simple but swapping one place that began with a 'D' for another was not as easy as it
sounded. Evening chats over pints instead of over patties and Turkish
pizzas? He just couldn't see himself kicking his heels in a pub. Devon
he suspected was full of waves of scented hillsides and frolicking
blades of blue sea. Michael said it was all caves, coves and quaintness.
Schoolboy cringed.

Quaintness.

Sounded like some drug that no one wanted to do.

What worried him most of all was the ability of a new place to turn
his tongue flip-side up. Instead of saying, 'you check me' or 'so them
say,' would he be rolling his r's every two seconds? He couldn't
imagine that, but just hearing Michael made him realise this might be
waiting for him around the corner. It wasn't going to be so easy to
leave. It never was. It wasn't going to be easy to cut and run from a
city that crafted the knowledge to bewitch him. From friends who
were addicted in their need to lime with him. From ladyeez who
needed to fuck him and fuck with him. From his own self that had got
used to wallowing with him.

He lifted the shower attachment high and squirted water in his
face. He shook the droplets of nostalgia from his skin. Reminiscing
was such bollocks. Not his style. He specialised in the future. And the
future equalled mobile, dosh, knives and no looking back.

But that wasn't going to happen until he started connecting to the
right people. As he gripped the edge of the bath to pull himself out, the
front door began pounding, with the energy of anger he just was not
in the mood for. He played it silent for a while, but the banging
continued.

'Come on, I know you're in there,' growled a voice that was female,
held high on the back of the tongue, rocking with tones grafted in

ient scuffing of small feet enforced the voice's

ver into the bath. That's all he needed. Jackie
The self-appointed Ms Fix-it of the building,
off your backside and sort yourself out'

ow you're in there because you never bloody well get up before twelve,' her voice continued in its manic march, making his rising times sound like the next crime the bring-back-hanging brigade would debate. He couldn't understand people, especially when, like her, they were from the same generation as him, always complaining because you didn't fit into some type of preordained box. He was a p.m. man. Greeting the world before midday was a no-no. Why didn't nine-to-fivers get it that life was always so much more tuneful half-way through the day?

He watched her small outline skip to the right, past the bathroom window, and guessed that she was hunting him through the curtain-free kitchen. He heard the noise of puffed air, no doubt the same noise she'd made as a child defending herself in the school playground.

'Come on Schoolboy, you promised Mr Prakash.'

Fuckrees.

He sank lower. His breathing started shooting from his chest. He didn't want her or anyone else talking about Mr Prakash. That was sacred ground.

'Jackie, can't a bloke have a bubble-bath moment in peace?' His husky, steam-damp voice echoed against the window.

He heard her skip to the left, planting herself firmly in front of the bathroom window. The top of her head tipped just above the middle section of the window pane. He smiled. That was the best way to see Jackie, all frosted over, blurred in the middle, blurred at the edges, leaving her definition incomplete so he didn't have to deal with all of her.

'Don't worry, I can't see anything.' Her voice grew calm now she'd found what she was after. 'Not that you'd interest me anyway. You promised him that you'd keep up his side of the rota of washing the balcony. The bloke's not been buried a week and you're already pratting around.'

He knew that if he started washing that balcony he'd have to start grieving and he didn't have time for that now. Not with business to attend to.

'When I want a priest for confession I'll let you know about it, Father Jarvis. No can do today, Jackie girl,' he cut in, stepping out of the bath and reaching for the blue towel on the radiator. He folded it around the middle of his body.

'So when?' Her eyes strained against the window.

Schoolboy didn't reply. He just wanted her to go away. To take her busy five-foot-no-inches self and piss right off and stop reminding him of promises he couldn't keep. But he knew that Jackie was like a bedbug, sucking until her belly was full, so it was better to face her now than later. He pulled the unsteady bathroom door wide and padded on to the unvarnished floorboards of the passage. Everything stuck to the wall and ceiling was about the last residents, not him. The walls were pasted with bumpy cream wallpaper and the ceiling was white polystyrene heaven, covered in the type of tiles the Council warned tenants were a fire hazard. He'd never stamped his own mark in this area because he'd convinced himself he'd be passing through. He'd been passing through for twelve years. As he approached the front door, Jackie's voice whined, 'Mr P was really good to you. Don't forget that.'

He knew she was right and that she would never know how right she was. He stood in front of the royal blue door. He shook the damp from his locks as he twisted the door open. The daylight burst against his wet skin and towel as he shifted to stand on the threshold of stepping outside. His eyes hooked into Jackie, taking in her doll-like structure and green eyes that throbbed with the look of someone who had learned to fight to get her way.

Leaning into her track-suited tummy was a neatly wrapped package. Metallic blue, the type of paper he used to wrap a box of chocolates in when he was giving a girl the push. On top of the package lay a folded piece of white paper, covered in different patterns of writing and a picture he couldn't make out.

Jackie bowled up to him, her red hair and freckles beaming in the light. She stopped when the parcel squashed straight into his towel-shrouded pubes. Her hands fell from the package. The parcel held them together. Her head tilted up to stare at him. His chin dropped to stare at her. One of her hands shot up, hovered, then touched his bare stomach, above the line where the towel cut into his navel. Her fingers curved, soaking into his skin, then began a slow kneading motion like they were trying to wipe the water away from his cooling body. He could have stepped back, letting the parcel fall, along with her hand. But he didn't. The aroma of her touch felt too genuine for that. The type of frank touch that had been missing from his life since Mum had gone back home three years ago.

'Don't get any ideas,' Jackie's voice rasped, her hand still stroking him. 'This parcel belongs to you, so just take it.'

No apology for touching him without asking. He lived in a world where treading on someone's footwear could mean being permanently taken out of this life. But that was Jackie. She didn't give a stuff what other people thought. If you didn't like it that was your problem.

The wind flicked the paper sitting on top of the parcel, drawing his eyes to it. His lips fell open when he saw the picture. A photo of Mr Prakash as a young man, underneath the words 'In Loving Memory'. The wind came stronger, tugging the paper. Schoolboy's hand grabbed it, steadied it, then lifted it up.

'I thought you might want this because you never came to the funeral.'

Her hand fell away from his body. He didn't respond to her words. His eyes flapped over the photo, transfixed. He stepped back, leaving Jackie to rescue the parcel quickly before it fell. He forgot about her, retreating further inside, finally kicking the door shut with his bare foot.

'Oi! What about this package?' Jackie screamed from outside.

His stare left the photo and moved up to the door.

'I'll come for it later . . .'

'One of these days . . .' her sentence thrust in, hanging, nasty in its implication of where people like him should really be.

Schoolboy had already forgotten her and her disappearing footsteps as he slow-stepped across the passage into his bedroom. The only furniture he allowed in the room were items that helped him function on the outside. A king-sized bed to make sure that he got enough shut-eye so that he looked relaxed in the world. A wardrobe that sorted the styles of his clothes so that he could interact naturally with different sections of the world. A mirror to check that he was primed and preened for the world. A bedside table to rest his mobiles for instant access to the world. Anything else was a luxury and luxury wasn't what he'd been after. That's until now.

He slumped on to the bed, clutching and staring at the picture of Mr P, his neighbour for the last five years. The man who had taught him about the wonder of knives. The man who had taught him that different knives did different things. The man who had taught him that there was no point holding on to dreams, you had to go out there and get them. He placed the funeral service sheet on the bed as he remembered that his only way of holding on to a new future was to buy the knives.

He coiled himself towards the bedside table where his MBs lay. Some said MB meant Mo-Bile, others said it stood for Mouth Box. Whichever way he looked at it, he was living in a community that created its own language to keep outsiders at a distance. He kept two MBs, one for business and one for personal calls. His business handset was a sturdy, reliable silver flip-top, with a monthly line rental and price plan so that he maintained 24-hour availability with his business contacts. His personal phone was the complete opposite. It was petite, delicate, with a camera and video lens set in the silver-and-black back like a clear round jewel. This phone was not designed merely for talk but as something meant to be enjoyed in the hand. He used it on a need-to-talk basis so he kept it topped up using pay-as-you-go. Now the phone from the Junction had joined his Mouth Box unit. He probed the newest MB on the table, which was also the oldest. He'd christened it 'the Brick' because of its bulk and block shape. Now, poised from the side, it cast off the image of a brick and looked like a black slipper, bringing old-fashioned comfort into his life. It was from an age when a phone was just that – a phone, not an accessory, not a toy. He leaned over, plucked it up, feeling its weight. Feeling the forty quid it would bring into his hand.

He smiled, knowing the sweetness of a new life was coming his way.

Abruptly the phone's screen flashed on, pus-green, making him loosen his grip and smile. The screen blinked twice, then flashed off. The upper half of his face screwed down in curiosity. Then his nose screwed up in irritation.

'Fuckrees. Bollocks,' he whispered, and then kissed his teeth.

He didn't need to be selling faulty goods. That got you a bad reputation among those that mattered. But what did he care? He'd be long gone before the buyer realised the phone didn't work quite the way it was supposed to. He chucked it back down on the table, replacing it in his hand with his business phone. He flipped the top up with his thumb and dialled.

First on his list was Window, the owner of the Minus One Club, which punters just called –1 for short. He pressed its buttons until his address book appeared. Scrolled down until Window's name came up.

'Hey, what a go on G?' Schoolboy greeted his friend, scrunching back on to the bed.

'The usual tricks and tings.'

'This is a quick one. Seen anything of Mikey at your place?'

'No, 'cos my boy is doing love I understand with a woman with seven kids in Stevenage, so he's out of the picture.'

Schoolboy twisted his mouth and looked at Mr Prakash's photo.

'I need some dosh pretty lively and have a piece of merchandise to sell.'

'G, I hope that don't mean you're back climbing through other people's lives again.' Window's tone was packing disapproval. Schoolboy knew he was referring to his teenage years of breaking in to other people's homes.

'Nah, nothing like that.'

The blood swelled in Schoolboy's face, staining him with guilt for the first time about where the phone had come from. He wasn't sure which was worse, stealing from the dead or nicking from the living.

'Let's just say it was a mutual exchange.'

'Still sounds like you swiped it.'

'Well I didn't . . . well, not really. '

Window answered with a huff.

'Anyway, it don't matter where I got it from, have you got any other potential market stall holders who might be interested?'

'I may have by the time you come down. I got a few people to check so come down between 2 and 3.'

He clipped off the conversation, but kept the phone in his hands. Now he just needed to make sure the knives were still available. He started rapid texting with his thumb.

```
c u in Vicky Park @ 2
```

Schoolboy placed the phone on the bed and picked himself up. There were two things he took his time over. Doing business and putting on his garms. Dress to impress was no cliché on his side of the road. If your garms didn't fit it could mean the difference between a completed deal or being out of pocket. The difference between getting a nod of the head or a straight stare. The difference sometimes between natural life and death. He dropped the towel, moving over to the wardrobe, and began to sort through, picking out a pair of solid black riders and matching-coloured loose vest that looked more like something that belonged to a fisherman than something he'd haggled for at Ridley Road Market. He strolled over to his bedside table to pick up the only accessory he ever wore, his timepiece. Rubbed leather strap, bland face, but always pitch-perfect on time. He always fitted it through the third hole, loose enough not to get in his way, tight even to remind himself to check a business appointment. Most people from his world liked to be iced with jewellery from eyebrow to teeth, from teeth to toe. That was too over-cooked for the way he wanted people to remember him. He finished his look with a three-quarter two-tone satin sheen leather coat.

His gaze caught the newly acquired MB. He smiled, the appearance of his dimples speaking louder than any words delivered by his mouth that his luck was on the way up. As his mum used to say, *God was surely walking with him.*

24/7 Cabs
All day, All night
No job too much
Airports
Weddings
Special deliveries
We go out of our way to please you!

Benji studied the card in his hand. Marbled grey background, black script like the miserable Monday afternoon sky above him. The card had been a gift from a G back home, who had tucked it into his palm with a bag of Colombian C and whispered, 'If you ever need a helping hand in London town.' They needed that extra help, right now. They had been riding around, diving into clubs, handing out cash notes like they had been hatching from their pockets since three this morning, trying to pick up word on the phone and face they had seen. They hadn't even given themselves time to bleach. So far they had come up dry. Now they needed that helping hand.

Benji had left Josh soaking with the car on a connecting street, so he approached the railway arches on Bakers Lane alone. 24/7 Cabs stood two doors down from Ray's Auto Repairs and one up from Sayed's Shipping Services. It ranked in the top three of most-used cab services in Dalston. But it wouldn't be winning any consumer prizes. Its ability to dispense cars and crack was not what gave it the edge –

plenty of other businesses were doing that around here. Its reputation hung on the special offers it occasionally pegged out, where drugs blew so cheap that others just couldn't compete. With the special offers came more bodies. With more bodies came the passing of mouth-to-mouth information.

Benji hassled the thick door open and sauntered into a room that held another room. The room he breathed into was all curled carpet, yesterday's oily stench of chips and a fruit machine that blinked and belched colours in the corner. Two chairs provided for customers were backed against a wall. Previous customers must have had razors in their backsides because the seats were slashed, with soiled stuffing spilling out. A transparent wall created the second room. A transparent wall that was rumoured to be bullet-proof.

The one thing Benji had realised moving over Hackney's borders was that it rotated on rumour. Their mistake had added to that collection. The controller's desk was the main feature of the inner room. Benji hustled closer, his lips in rock-steady position and hands ready to address the controller, whose head was hooked down, writing. His dark hair was so closely trimmed that it appeared that every hair had been created by the strokes of a fine paintbrush.

'Hey, bro' . . .'

'One minute, my friend,' came the reply. Soft, gliding, a voice that could hold a tune.

Benji knew that accent. Half his family were from Lagos, the other half from Cork. He didn't see much of either side. He saw even less of his dad. The controller's head didn't move. Benji wrestled some twenties from his pockets, his hand shaking with a desperation he was trying to deny.

'Fancy adding some Eddie Es to your cash in hand this week?'

The controller lifted his head, presenting Benji with a face that was somewhere between twenty-five and thirty years old. A face that was broad and delicate from the balance of its bones. A face that was expertly scrubbed and moisturised every morning. The bloodshot eyes made the colour of the face seem much darker than it was.

'You must be going on a far journey for that kind of money,' the controller replied, sharing the gap in his front teeth with Benji. His eyes looked at the twenty-pound notes in Benji's hand.

Attention fully his, Benji started fishing for info.

'I don't need a cab. Just wondered if any locals have been in trying to sell a phone . . .?'

'A phone? What type of phone?' The controller's head twitched sideways as if the old blackened patches from mosquito bites on his arms were being sucked again. But his face remained set cool.

Thinking they were now a friendly item, Benji moved closer, the edge of the white counter catching his thigh.

'Nokia. Old as the last millennium. Looking for a hooded guy, a bit shorter than me . . .'

'I think much of the world would be shorter than you, brother,' observed the controller, letting his body relax back, as if this allowed him to truly measure Benji.

The fruit machine started fussing loudly, which gave the controller the upper hand to carry on.

'My fellow brother, this is a respectable establishment. I do not deal in impropriety.' The reply was stern, making his face look thinner as his L-shaped sideburns retracted beneath his cheekbones.

'Let's cut the . . .' Benji tried to think of a clever remark to roll off his tongue, but it didn't come. 'I was told this is the place to get the word on what's going down.'

The controller stared at him. Interest? Thought? Curiosity? Benji couldn't tell.

'Going down?' the controller answered, screwing his face. Confusion. 'I do not understand this phrase.'

Benji noticed the accent had become thicker. His dad used to do that deliberately to make people think he was stupid. Quickest way to get someone out of your face besides killing them. Benji shuffled his body closer to explain, but the ring of the cab office telephone got there before him.

'Excuse me, brother.' As the controller spoke, his body language became more lively as if he'd been to cab school. The controller's nail-bitten fingers gripped the receiver. Benji could faintly hear an angry voice on the other end. He knew how they felt. He was starting to feel cranky himself.

'I am so sorry, Madam. Let me see if I can find out where your cab is.'

The controller placed the receiver downwards on the desk and turned his attention back to Benji. Now his whole body was poised.

'I cannot help you. I have only recently arrived to these fair shores and am paying for my studies.' The veins of his eyes were digging into Benji's face. 'So I do not yet know the ways of this country . . .'

'Whatever, let me leave this with you,' Benji's voice broke in, impatient, a touch insulted. He didn't have the time to listen to any life stories and his feet felt wet as if his victim's blood was massaging his toes. He discarded the twenty-pound notes on the counter.

'My number's on the back of one of these. You ring me, and only me, if you hear anything.'

He switched the conversation off and left, the voice of the controller fading as he apologised again to the customer and assured her that her cab would be there in two minutes.

When Benji had gone, the controller swiftly got out of the chair and followed him into the cold of outside. He rubbed his middle finger against the dryness of his bottom lip as he watched Benji's figure getting smaller. He didn't move when Benji turned the corner. His tongue slipped out to wipe his lips. He pulled his tongue back in, creased his lips and started moving his mouth as if he'd been forced to chew something he didn't want to eat.

3

Ashara, more commonly known in Dalston as Number 10, punched back into the cab office and headed towards the money Benji had left on the counter. The angry clip of his strides flicked up dust from the carpet.

'Milo, take over the controls,' he yelled, his accent less pronounced, with the tone of someone who'd picked up English from US daytime soaps and chat shows.

He searched through the notes. Tension stiffened his slim shoulders when he found the note with the mobile number written in black ink. He placed it into his turn-up jeans pocket. The rest of the money he kept in his hand. He returned to the main body of the cab office.

'Milo, take this for your son's trip to Italy.' Milo looked up and took the offered money with gladness plastered across his face.

Ashara picked up the paper he'd been writing on, left Milo and increased his pace to a back office. Sparse, clean, neat, with pictures of his family and friends on the wall. He looked at the one of all his family, with him and his sister as the youngest positioned at the front. They were all modelled in traditional Nigerian dress, gathered together to celebrate his elder brother's business degree. He sat at the Formica desk, not sure what to do first. He decided to finish his letter and then deal with business. No point contacting older brother just yet. He had the thug's mobile number, which was a start. He'd learned long ago that you should never deal with a snake when its mouth was open. Only deal with it when it was wallowing, defenceless on its belly in the dirt. He stared at the letter and re-read what he'd written.

Dear Mother and Father,
I hope that life is treating you well. Myself and Ojo are still
studying very hard at the college. We have been told that we

will get extra funding for another year of study, so I enclose a money order for both of you. We are still hoping to continue our studies in America.

He pulled open the top left drawer and rummaged until he found a small bookie's pen. He bowed his head and continued to write his lies in Yoruba. When he was satisfied with the finished product he folded the paper and placed it to the side. He stood up and travelled towards his jacket, which hung from a peg on the door. He pulled his mobile free and started to dial.

'Wahid, it's me again. A stranger has been in trying to buy info on our missing phone . . .'

'I'm on my way . . .'

'No, dear brother . . .'

'I'm coming over. Don't forget who's Number 1 . . .'

Ashara tugged the phone away from his ear, irritated with the sound of his brother's usual impatient puffing and loudness. He drew the phone back to his ear when he realised that Wahid had stopped talking.

'Wahid, stay put. Let me get a few of the men to sniff around and see what they can find out. Come over about five and we should have much more to discuss by then.'

'Someone's lips have been bellowing our business, but only me and you knew about this, Ashara.'

'Are you accusing me of something?' Ashara's voice was tooled up with outrage.

'No. I'm just worried that America may fall from our grip.'

'Don't worry, brother dearest, we will get it back.'

'OK. But you make sure you contact me as soon as you know anything.'

Ashara hurriedly finished the conversation, needing to sit down and chew his nails. As his front teeth tried to grip a nail he prayed that his brother would never find out that he had told someone. Someone he knew would never dare to whisper their secrets. Someone Wahid thought they'd left back in Nigeria.

Victoria Park was beautiful in the way that Hackney was never said to be. Maybe that's why some claimed that it wanted to deliberately detach itself from its E9 postcode and align itself to the Bow Conservation Area in Tower Hamlets. Others said that could never be because Hackney just wouldn't be Hackney without Vicky Park. The Regent's Canal grazed its west side and the Hertford Union Canal skimmed its south side. Its Victorian terraces stood proud and elusive, bordering the black gloss rails of the park. It pulled the community together. Made them play, laugh and chat together in the light of summer weekends. It made children scream and yell as they splashed in its paddling pool, ploughed down its wonky slides without fearing someone would tell them to 'shut up'. But everyone was also aware that the flecks of the evening light made it just like any other urban area, full of shadows, jostling and reacting to the pressures of city life.

'So what kind of deal you striking?' Schoolboy asked Robbie as they sat on a bench on one of the park's shaded and narrow paths.

Schoolboy cut his eyes at Robbie and stared at his long, thin white face. Despite the raw rash that chaffed at the corner of Robbie's pink nose, his skin was smooth and youthful, just as it had been the day Schoolboy had first met him on remand five years ago. A green baseball cap was pushed low on his head, as if he'd also learned that eyes just gave away too much.

'Let's say £20 a piece, so there are five pieces which makes a total of £120, but since it's you we'll downgrade that by £60 and call it a flat £100.' Robbie stopped, his lips still doing a see-sawing motion as if he was continually chewing.

Schoolboy cut his eyes deeper into Robbie.

'I hear they're teaching basic maths at the community college, so I'll get you an application form. Let's say three pieces at £40. No discounts, no bargains, let's just keep this clean and simple because I don't need to be owing anyone any more favours.'

'You got yourself a deal, mate.'

Schoolboy slid his body closer just as a squirrel scampered by, and whispered,

'Any chance of inspecting one?'

'Sure.'

Robbie shoved a white canvas bag Schoolboy's way and started doing his sales pitch at the same time.

'The best quality Japanese, I've been told. None of that factory-produced shit. These are hand-crafted in the tradition of samurai swordsmen . . .'

As Robbie spoke, Schoolboy unzipped the bag, opened it wide and peered inside.

'Robbie, cut out the Antiques Roadshow spiel so I can look at this gem in peace.'

Robbie closed his mouth as Schoolboy looked at the knife nestled at the bottom of the bag. It had a standard brown handle, with a slight curve for a more comfortable grip. The blade was flat and wide, seven inches of steel that was shaped into an efficient point at the top. The type of graceful slicing knife he'd always wanted.

'What do you want with a bunch of cooking knives?' Robbie asked, his breath heating the side of Schoolboy's face.

Before he could answer, they were interrupted by the ringtone of Robbie's phone. A disco classic that had been remixed and renovated for the energy of today's ecstasy-fused dance floor.

'Give me a minute while I take this.' Robbie groped for his MB in his jeans pocket.

Schoolboy thought about Robbie's question as he gazed at the knife. He thought of the days where he'd learned the art of cooking with Mum. He thought about the time Mum had let him hold his first knife as they made coconut tarts. Then he thought about Mr Prakash, the man who had reawakened his urge to cook. His mind skidded back to that intense August afternoon in '99. He'd been standing on the communal balcony feeling depressed and down, listening to the rupture of traffic and watching the lonely yard where the tired cars came to rest their engines. First day out of prison and he'd known he had a touch of gate fever. That brutal dread that boils inside a prisoner as he steps over the gate into freedom wondering if the world's still interested in what he has to give. The problem with being incarcerated in The Big House was that you and your cellies started to think that you were the world. That is until the world wanted you back. Then you leave with your baggage and gate cash and find that the world has carried on without you. Law-abiders thought it was prison that made you flip. But it wasn't. Being stuck back into a world that couldn't decide what it wanted to do with you, that's what made you turn inside-out, outside-in, with madness. Some of his cellies had feared facing family, others the jump that came every time society stabbed them with its accusing finger. His fear had been going from HMP to HMG – from Her Majesty's Pleasure to Her Majesty's Ghetto. Swapping one lock-down for another wasn't how rehabilitation was meant to be. He'd known a few men who got so fevered up that the only peace they found was in death. Big fat cliché, but as he'd stared at the grain of the ground below it felt like the only respectable thing to do. At least someone might notice him if they had to read about him in the *Hackney Gazette*.

His hands had been tense as they bonded with the balcony's brick, wondering what it would be like to leap up and over. Up and over, it would've been that simple. That's when the fragrance had taken him down. Garlic, onion, a nab of coconut cream, caramelised cane sugar and stewing beef had all marinated in the air towards him.

Around him.

Inside him.

Caribbean curry. The strain in his hands started twitching, distracted by the flavours feasting in his nose. As the zest became stronger his hands had loosened until they flopped at his side. He left his gate fever hanging over the balcony and quietly followed the scent until he stood by his neighbour's kitchen window, letting his nose soak up the air. He was so lushed on the sensation of the food that he didn't hear his neighbour open his door. When he saw his neighbour, Schoolboy had hot-footed it to leave, but Mr Prakash's high Trinidadian voice stopped him.

'So you like the smell, boy. Come on in and taste some. My children them always telling me I can't cook but what you young people know about food, eh? Every two seconds all you eating is a burger and chips. What kind of food is that? Always telling me I need to watch my cholesterol. Cholesterol, my back foot! You think an able-bodied man like me needs to study cholesterol?'

Mr Prakash stood there, peering at him, small in his Indian heritage, but large in the Caribbean cultural mix of his tongue. In the following years, Schoolboy got to know that Mr P might chat a lot of foolishness, but his eyes and head had the lick of a teenager looking for the party.

Grumbling, Mr Prakash turned and went back inside. Schoolboy hesitated for a few seconds, suspicious of anyone new coming into his life, then the smell had cuddled his lips and nostrils. He turned back and stepped inside, letting the essence of Mr Prakash's life come into his own. That's how cooking had re-entered his mainstream. Mr Prakash's advice was simple.

'It's all about how you make your fingers dance. All about how your fingers turn the ingredients on the dance floor.'

Schoolboy had never seen hands move so quickly, except when his mum would give him one when he was young. Mr Prakash's fingers had flexed, stretched, bent, using the tips and the joints in one free-flowing motion. He'd taught Schoolboy how to season, how to let ingredients mate with each other for hours until their juices ran into each other. How a master cook needs to be patient. Above all, Mr P had taught him about knives, showing him a set of sparkling knives, descending in order, lying on faded mauve velvet inside a silver case.

'There are all kinds of knives. Bread knives, cheese knives, meat knives, fish knives. Each has a place. Each has a time. Just like a man loving more than one woman. Never misuse them and they will love you for life.'

His first lesson with Mr Prakash had been to learn how to make roti, a light bread used to wrap around curry. Flour, baking powder, ghee, water, jeera, split peas and a pinch of pepper designed to make the eater remember the taste hours later. Every two weeks he'd have a roti lesson, learning how to glide fingers and thumbs together. After that Mr Prakash introduced him to other partners on the dance floor – split-pea soup, oil down, peanut punch. But Mr P wouldn't let Schoolboy have his rum punch recipe.

'All great cooks have one secret,' he said.

In return, Schoolboy had taught Mr P how to make coconut tarts.

They had kept up their lessons until the night he'd heard Mr P wheezing and groaning through the walls and he'd known that things would change. Mr P had tried to keep up their lessons, but his fingers just wouldn't move the way they used to.

Two weeks ago Mr P had stopped living the life of a sweet boy and died, taking his rum punch recipe with him. Schoolboy hadn't gone to the funeral, but instead had cooked a chicken curry for two, with two rotis, and eaten them in honour of the supreme kitchen-master who understood that a knife was a wonderful thing. Schoolboy had also missed Mr Prakash's family when they had come to clear out his home. As Jackie put it, 'The Council already have another family waiting. As soon as one's out, another's one's in.'

Now Michael had given him the chance to work in his restaurant in Devon, but the condition was he must bring his own cooking knives. Knives that were moulded with the same weight and perfection as the blade now in his hand.

'Hey Schoolboy, man,' Robbie's voice pulled Schoolboy back to the park. 'Do you want to deal or not? You're bloody shaking. You high or something?'

Schoolboy shook his head, not able to control the trembling that sometimes accompanies memories. He grudgingly gave the knife back.

'Give me a day or two to get the cash and we'll meet again.'

He was still thinking of the knives as he made his way to the bus to see Window at the −1 Club.

Schoolboy stepped off the bus and stepped into the style and flash restaurants of Stoke Newington. Current estate agent hype claimed that Stoke Newington had it all. Basement conversions with sufficient space and speculation to make occupants forget they were living below the kerb line. A spring festival that jangled with diversity, but not

enough to bring the Bluebottles out in force. A park that had regeneration planted all over it. But Schoolboy couldn't forget the days it was
strictly known as Stokey. The days Stokey was pronounced hard, with
the last syllable riding and chilling through the teeth. Simply told,
Stokey had a history of violence and death.

His business MB started ringing. Three rapid, high-pitched rings
that sounded as if he'd won the bonus prize on a quiz show. He didn't
want to answer because he knew it would be a former client hunting
something sweet. He hauled out his phone as he halted outside a
window display of gold crosses and chains in a jewellery shop.

'SB on the line.'

'Hey, it's Carlton, man.'

Schoolboy recognised the voice instantly as one of his whiter-than-
white clients who was always trying to be blacker-than-black.

'I'm looking for a Henry, say around 9 tonight.'

'You haven't heard – SB Services has ceased trading.'

'Thought you were having a laugh, bro.'

'Sorry. But if you're still hungry, check out the type of spices
Timmy's using to make his doughnuts in the café on Lime Street.' He
clicked off and kicked on up the street.

Schoolboy's business had been buying and selling. Buying the
sweetest potions of grass and then selling them to his strong base of
clients. Thanks to his last two package trips to HMP, he learned that
the drugs industry threw up more pounds than doing burglaries.
Observing other inmates waiting for their parcel or doing the
nutcracker suite routine, where screws were unwilling to search under
prisoners' balls, Schoolboy realised that he could tap into an open
world of narcotics. His profits were made by buying cheaply in bulk
and then marking costs up on to the customer. Society marked him as
a Dealer. The street called him a Shotter, someone who shot drugs to
anyone with their mouth open. He preferred to think of himself as a
broker. A connecter. Just passing out a bit of love and peace to those
who wanted to escape from the realities of everyday stress. He only
dealt in the good old herb itself – marijuana. But sometimes grass

didn't always smell sweet. He tasted the stench of rottenness that had entered his home four weeks ago. He pasted his tongue around the inside of his mouth, absorbing the taste away.

He left Cumin Road and turned into Juniper Street. As he drew closer to the –1 Club he caught sight of three well-drilled elderly black women, standing in line, catching passers-by with leaflets and spiel. He recognised the format straightaway. They'd obviously role-played their method in lessons. He should know because their manner was the same one he'd played out when turning down drugs on the 'just say no' module of his last probation course. The sun coating the skin of his jacket made him too easy a mark for them not to stop him. When he got closer, the middle one in pleated skirt and pleated wig shoved a leaflet out at him.

'Come and join with us praising the Lord this Friday in our sister church in New Cross.'

He smiled and out of respect for his mum took the leaflet and pushed it into his pocket. He understood why some chose to find religion, but if being saved meant crossing the river they could forget it.

'Don't leave it too long, son, before you come to the Lord,' one of the women called to his back.

He hitched his eyebrow up, pulled it back down, keeping his gaze fixed on to the –1 Club. It was two storeys of beige brick, flat-roofed, and went much further back than it looked like it did from the outside. At night its name radiated in mauve neon light. In the daytime the light was switched off. The building had always been an entertainment spot but hadn't always been a club. It had started life as a community centre, which had cemented itself in the psyche of the community in '91 during the Gregory Marsh case. The brother had walked into Unity Road Police Station and had left a stiff on a slab, minus half his chest. The centre had mobilised all forces under the slogan 'The death penalty is alive and kicking in Babylon's protective custody'. The building's ownership had changed many times along with the interests of the community. But now much of the community was a bit too wholesome. A bit too into their coconut rice and lemon grass to salute the many services the club could bring.

That awesome feeling of nostalgia pressed him as he came through the doors. He walked through the metal detector. Club policy was strict – no hard metal, no hard drugs. Shaka, the bouncer and some-times barman, patted Schoolboy down and then lifted his goatee beard in a greeting. Schoolboy strolled into the lobby, consumed by the blanched red walls. Being consumed was deliberate. Clients needed to realise that by the time they got this far there was only one way to go – forward. He edged through the double doors at the end, entering the heart of the club, which was like sweeping into an art gallery that had decided it had more to preach about than oils, canvases and colour. Not that Schoolboy had been into many art galleries lately, but this is what he imagined them to be like. Full of cleansed whiteness, like the huge wall tiles in the club, with mirrors that acted like paintings reminding the clientele that their reflections were art as well. The platform for the DJ and his decks rose up with the militancy of an urban sculpture that knew how to grind the devil's music into willing souls. Scattered uplighters filtered a haze of turquoise light in the backdrop of the DJ's stage that relaxed and renewed. The first time Schoolboy had frequented the joint he'd thought it was a load of trendy rubbish. But as his visits had grown he realised that the club was as important in his daily refreshing routine as getting eight hours of shut-eye. And that's what Window wanted to create, a place that was different from all the other watering holes in Stokey. A place where people came to shrug off the grubbiness of life and got prepared to be purified. Well, at least for one night.

He smiled forward into the club's company and the percussion section of the music that whispered with his movements as he walked across the room. During the daytime the club was used as a general rave haunt. Near the Ladies and Gents slammed the dominoes tables. Hunched over these were usually the Tourists, those who were newly arrived to England's shores. The way the dominoes banged and bounced on the tables added a triumphant off beat to the music already milling around. Give them a few months and Schoolboy knew that some of the Tourists wouldn't be playing dominoes any more. They soon learned that if you wanted to be recognised, banging and bouncing needed to be done on the streets and not across a table.

The remaining tables were harder to define. They were usually ruled by people deciding fates, exchanging merchandise and creating new designer crimes that had yet to be printed under an outraged headline in the newspaper.

Schoolboy spotted Window sitting high at his usual spot at the Perspex bar. Being high meant Window could see most exits and entrances. Knowing what was coming before it hit was an essential in this life. Although Window had left his old life behind three years ago and settled in Stokey, it was hard for him to give up the body language he had cultivated on the street.

Most believed that Schoolboy had met Window through the usual rounds of being linked up by a friend of a friend of a friend. Truth was they had met during the lazy beginning of '93 in Aldgate Police Station. Schoolboy had been pulled in for non-payment of a nifty fine. Better to spend a couple of nights in fashionable Aldgate than to have his trouser pocket sinking flat with no change. The three-cell block had been full that night. Schoolboy in the far right, unknown in the far left and a troubled soul in the middle. The troubled soul had been ranting, begging and moaning out for mercy. He was going to get no joy here. Aldgate was preoccupied with money not mercy. Back in those days Schoolboy had been a lot less tolerant of others prowling in his space, even if that space was a police cell. His irritation had grown with each curse, with each scream. He'd yelled out with the usual, 'Keep it down.' The voice from the far left cell had taken up his mantra and called out, 'Put a plug in it.' Schoolboy had shouted out another command and the third cell had called another one back. Before long they'd become involved in a who-can-say-the-wildest-shut-it-line slam. One cracking, one calling.

'Other people trying to die in here.'

'Give the world's ears a break.'

'What, Mommy forget to tuck you up for the night?'

'Auditions for Eastenders are next door mate.'

They had carried on until their laughter had become the loudest lyric shifting from right to left, left to right. Eventually the Blues had come when the character in the centre cell had threatened to start eating his own crap. The Blues had got flushed scared. They decided they didn't need any witnesses to their next move, so Schoolboy and the third cell voice had been released. When Schoolboy had clocked the owner of the voice as they stood at the Sergeant's desk, he became as frightened as the Blues left in the back.

The man from the third cell was a living street legend, easily identified by a tattoo that trailed from under his jawbone to his collar line like a kiss diffusing into his skin. The letters of the tattoo were in a foreign script so no one really knew what the tattoo meant. Some said it meant justice, others claimed it meant death. But no one was in any doubt about this man's name. Window. Re-christened such because he had been the eyes for a few of London's major operators. Window had used his quick flashing eyes to dust Schoolboy down. Schoolboy had just stood there with reverence and respect. Laughter wasn't what you heard often in a Blue Boys house but they had both howled when their eyes met. The Sergeant had tutted at them as if he had three nutters on his hands. They had gone straight for a drink and clicked. Maybe it was the way they never asked what both had been doing there. Maybe Schoolboy had needed someone with ten years' more experience than him on the street to show him the way. Or maybe they recognised the loner in each other. Either way they had become close spars like two limes hanging on a tree.

Window's light grin jolted Schoolboy back to the club. Window stood up, revealing his imposing height, and Schoolboy could well understand the myth of muscle this man had created around himself. The skin of his burnished copper face was smoothly framed back by the corn rows meandering from his hairline. His rich mouth had a slight upward pull as if happy memories were nearby.

'How's tricks, G?' Window asked.

Everything about Window was like his voice: solid, big, coming straight from the gut with a gentle puff leaving his lips. A puff that sometimes had the ability to knock someone flat.

Window leaned over the bar so that they could do their usual pal – peace and love – routine. They tapped the pads of their index fingers together, wrapped them at the knuckle joint, shook them, unhooked and beat their fingers to their hearts twice. Greeting over, Schoolboy took his time flowing on to a 70s-style stool that swivelled so that punters could still get into the vibe of the music. The squeeze of lemon detergent danced from the freshly washed bar.

'The usual. You know, getting by with life.' He gulped.

'So you all booked to leave the big L next Sunday?'

Schoolboy didn't answer, knowing that Window already knew the answer. His friend was the only person who knew about Devon.

'So Mikey definitely off the scene?'

Window nodded as he leaned his elbows on the bar. His eyes moved like shadows under the veils of his long eyelashes, so that even after all these years Schoolboy didn't feel that he could fully get into them. But they were shadows that followed and got into everyone else.

'So what you peddling?'

'An MB. Nokia. Retro. The word tells me they're really state of the art now, literally.'

Schoolboy shoved his fingers through his locks as his head tipped into his hand.

'So I hear. How quickly you need the dough?'

'Like now.'

They had agreed early on in their relationship never to go begging the other for cash. The pursuit of dosharama was one of the quickest ways to waste a friendship. Besides, Schoolboy had Evie for that.

'I might be able to help you,' Window said, gliding his elbows further apart on the bar. 'I had a Dread in here earlier, a new face. Originally hails from the Elephant but claims he likes these parts. He's trying to set up his own operation.'

'Any particular brand of phone he's after?'

'I think he'll be interested in the one you're hawking because he don't want a mouth box that's too blatant. Something more subtle, old time, so it adds an air of culture, but doesn't bring too much interest to him.'

'Sounds like the geezer is more interested in setting up a gentlemen's club.'

Window smiled, the shadows dampening in his eyes.

'He left his gate's details so if you want I can contact him.'

'Sounds good. Text me with more details and we'll take it from there.'

He swung his leg to get off the stool, but was stopped by his friend's question.

'Staying for some liquid? My tickle.'

As Window turned around to get a drink, Schoolboy started to talk.

'Let me tell you about Michael . . .'

Window's voice cut over his, in a tone stamped in the beat of the old Window reporting back to a known Face.

'Michael Regis. Thirty, no kids, a mum and dad still breathing. He started life across the water and ended up on the Brookham Estate in Homerton aged nine. Did so-so at school, but wanted to be a chef. So here he is now, with his sister Maria, in their own restaurant in Devon.'

Window twisted round and placed a bottle of Supermalt in front of Schoolboy, whose mouth was braced open.

'You know I make it my business to get to know everyone. Just checking you weren't hooking up with no low life. What I don't know is how you met him.'

Schoolboy eased back into the stool.

'Michael's from this world, but ain't from this world, you get me. He could have been, but Michael was too smart for that. Too focused . . .'

Window leaned back on his stool to listen to his friend.

'I met him just after my second stint behind locked doors, back in '95. I got sent on one of those job-seeker adventures. Sent me to a café to cook . . .'

'Why did they do that?'

'Cos that's what I put on my form when I first signed on. That I wanted to be a chef. And I did and always have. I use to cook like a dream, that was until fucking St Iggy's School came along.'

He stopped, picked up the bottle of drink and tilted it to his mouth, remembering life at St Ignatius School. He sucked and gulped quickly, as if the malt was mouthwash, needing to get the filthy flavour of schooling out of his mouth. He replaced the bottle on the bar, letting his thumb and finger rub against the rim.

'Bebe's kitchen, that's where they sent me. Some café in London Fields. On the first day this geez called Michael strolls up to me and whispers, "Watch me take over this kitchen." I thought yeah, right. But, you know, he did. Just like that. He walks up to Bebe on the second day and asks if he can make a macaroni pie, St Lucian style, for the punters. He goes right up to her and says . . .' Schoolboy got his voice ready to do a Caribbean accent with a hint of a French lilt.

'Madam Bebe, you need to add variety and style if you want all the customers who go across the road to come into here.' I couldn't believe it, because Bebe wasn't someone you fuck with, you get my drift. So she agrees and before you know it that kitchen is swinging with a whole lot of new dishes. My cooking just started coming back to me. Rice and peas, coconut tarts, you name it, we were blasting it. At the end of the four weeks she asked me and Michael to stay . . .'

'So how come you never?'

'The street called me back. Michael pleaded with me to stay. Said that by the age of thirty he was going to have his own place and when that happened he was going to look me up and make me work with him. Didn't hear from him for years and then last year, out of the blue, he calls me up. Tells me him and his sister have just opened their own place in Devon and would I be interested in coming to work for them? I just laughed, saying that my idea of lifestyle didn't include Devon. And do you know what he says to me, he says, "Schoolie, don't resist, man, because I'm gonna get ya." He kept phoning up solid every month, every week sometimes. Then when I got jacked . . .'

'You got what?' Window straightened up as if he was back to protecting a main playa.

Schoolboy waved his hand. He'd never told Window about that incident and never would. It would only provoke a ruckus on the street and Schoolboy was interested in leaving London as quietly as possible.

'That's another story for another time, but you know all of a sudden I saw myself in prison for the next fifteen years. Gone down for drugs distribution. Gone down for possession of a shooter. Gone down for the biggest crime of all, wasting my fucking life.'

Schoolboy stopped when he realised that his voice had risen so that the patrons at the dominoes table were drilling him with their stares. He coughed, bringing his voice way low as he resumed speaking.

'I ain't doing it any more. I ain't going down for nobody. I'm on my way up, Window, on my way up.'

Schoolboy bored straight into Window's eyes and for the first time he could read what was inside them. Sadness. He looked away.

'I'm on my way up and nothing or no one is gonna stand in my way.'

4

'Why did I listen to you? Why didn't I do what I first wanted to do? Why, Why, Why?'

Ashara, Number 10, stretched his eyes, yawned behind the gap in his front teeth, and watched the evening-kissed windscreen with boredom as his brother's words piled high like dung beside the road. When Wahid had got to the cab office at five, he'd been so drenched in rage that Ashara had taken him to sit in one of the cars under the railway arch. Nothing like a small space to remind a man about the bigger and better things in life. Wahid had started to calm down, that is until he decided he needed someone to blame.

Wahid didn't wait for his response but carried on, his words falling into an undefined pattern of Yoruba and English.

'I said that we should have got our own people to get the phone, so why did I let you convince me that we should let an air steward leave it in the pocket of the plane seat and then get a cleaner to pick it up and deliver it? A cleaner who made his first priority getting sassed up at the nearest bar instead of coming directly to us. Now his death may bring a whole heap of heat to our door.'

The news of their courier's body at the Junction had reached Ashara just after three that afternoon. 'I was not to know that, brother, but my way was the best thing to do. Neither man had any connection to us. No one is going to trouble a plane flying in from Addis Ababa . . .'

'So if your plan was so bollocks beautiful, where is the phone?'

Ashara sucked in his lower lip when he heard Wahid use the word bollocks. Since they had arrived in Hackney his brother had adopted the manners of the locals like a fool looking for wisdom in a recycling dump. Adopted their untidy way of dragging clothes on to a body. Even his brother's gang tattoo, which peeped through his partially opened tracksuit top, blended in with the graffiti on the Victorian-bricked bridge walls. Ashara chose to have his gang tattoo embroidered on the label of his jackets. His mark was exactly the same as Wahid's, long like a snake, but with a tiny diamond next to it. The Arabic numeral for number 10. When they had become the Numbers Crew they had decided to adopt Arabic names, which gave them a whole new identity as neither of them had ever been in a mosque. Wahid for Number 1 and Ashara for Number 10. Two side teeth pinched the corner of Ashara's lip. He didn't want to remember that there had been another number. Another member of their crew. A person who had launched back into his life two months ago. His eyes cruised over the revealed part of his brother's tattoo as he wondered if Number 8 was still using inventive ways of recording their number. Number 8 had hated permanency, so their mark was always in a place it could be easily removed. What a team they had been. Family as well as business partners. That was until Morocco. The blood rose to Ashara's face and burned it the way only guilt can.

'Hey, are you listening to me?' his brother's voice boomed. 'If we don't get it back we can kiss Mommy America goodbye.'

Ashara rolled the end of his tongue behind his bottom lip, looking for suitable words to spring back. He found them.

'What is the point of blaming me when you insisted that the only way to get to the States was to live in the mouth of a dog?'

Wahid knew he was referring to Hackney. Wahid kissed his teeth. They could have chosen Paris, Amsterdam, Rome. But no, Wahid had decided it had to be London, which would have been fine if London hadn't translated into Hackney. Hadn't all their acquaintances warned them that they had better be ready to make the lens of one eye become a telescope at night while they slept because the wicked didn't let the dark stand in their way in Dalston?

'But how did anyone else know about the phone? Someone must have been speaking.' Ashara felt the intensity of his brother's beefy eyes bore into him. 'It wasn't you?'

Ashara was glad that his face was cast in the shadows because the sting of guilt deepened on his face. He raised a finger to start chewing a nail. It tasted bad, so he dragged his hand back to his lap and turned to his brother.

'Who would I know to say anything to? It's more likely to have been you. You're the one who has been desperate to get DWI, as you would say, since we got here.'

'Of course I have needed to get *down with it*, so that we can make contacts . . .'

'So how are we going to get it back?' Ashara interrupted, pulling the conversation forward, wanting to move it swiftly on.

Before his brother could answer, a voice rattled at them through the window.

'Got money for a fag, mate?'

Ashara and Wahid twisted across at the face poised at the window. Hooded, swaying, with a need for more than tobacco. Ashara strained to the side of his seat as if his skin was burning for a third time. He was frightened by these nameless street creatures. Sure, Lagos had its problems, but this constant please-empty-your-pockets motif in London was unsavoury. Wahid started shouting at the window.

'Hey, my fellow human being, you should be seeking work with the rest of the community.'

One line, that's all he ever gave them. The body stamped back, moved on, as Wahid turned his face back inside the cab, waiting for Ashara's answer.

'I suggest that we . . .'

Hip-hop mixed with a traditional Nigerian rhythm started blaring from the mobile in Ashara's top pocket. He pulled it free and nearly fell forward on to the windscreen when he realised who the caller was. He gripped it tight because his hand was shaking. His middle finger chopped the power button dead.

'Who was that?'

'No one.' Ashara stuffed the phone back into his pocket, fixed his face, then leaned his head back towards his brother. 'Just some woman who can't take no for an answer, as the English would say.'

Ashara expected his brother's head to be nodding in approval, but it wasn't. Ashara knew that there was nothing his brother liked more than letting some girl know who was in control. Ashara crammed back into the car seat, frightened by the casual expression riding Wahid's face. Wahid never did casual, so Ashara knew there was a problem. Wahid jerked his large head into Ashara's space.

'Didn't I tell you to change that blasted arse ringtone?'

'But I like . . .'

Ashara's words ended in a squeak when Wahid's middle finger stabbed into his forehead.

'How many times do I need to tell you,' the finger poked with each word, 'that doing business in London is all about image, image and image.' The finger suddenly stopped and pressed into Ashara's skin, making him whine. 'What are our business contacts going to think if they hear a ringtone from a band that keep rapping about 419 money fraudsters and people like us giving Nigerians a bad name?'

The finger did a final twist, then fell away.

'But they won't know what it means . . .'

'I know what it means, so get rid of it. Just keep concentrating on finding out who sent the last person to be reflected in our deceased airplane cleaner's eyes.'

The police helicopter lazily circled above the area near Eric and Ernie with the energy of a lawnmower cutting into the night sky. The Blue movie feature, that's what the locals called it – the time when the Blues hovered above using their light and cameras to remind the community that they did still nick bad boys and girls.

Schoolboy couldn't capture sleep and he knew this had nothing to do with the helicopter. Monday night was always Blue movie matinee, which he'd grown accustomed to like everyone else. Tiredness should have been ruling his body after returning from the –1 Club, but his mind was in overdrive remembering. Remembering how the gun had felt in his face.

Lately the memory had been coming to lie with him every night. That's why he'd gone to the Junction this morning. To drive it out. To walk it out. But when he had returned home its image had been on his pillow, as snug as always, as if it knew who the mug was. It was one of the main reasons he was saying see-ya to London and clutching Michael's offer. He twisted to his back, closed his eyes, hunting calm, but the illusion of the gun floated back. Just as it had done a month ago, one Tuesday night, an hour before he was taking one of his thrice-weekly trips to the club.

He'd been glamming himself up, legs bare, chest swimming under Vietnamese silk, when the door had banged. Not expecting any customers or late night deliveries, he had approached the door and asked who it was. A voice answered back saying it needed fixing up and he heard that Schoolboy was the person to see. He considered the voice for a while. Muffled, unfamiliar, male. He doubted it was the Blues because they wouldn't waste their energy on a small-time home-based weed Shotter like himself. He still held back, suspicion scattering its seeds before him.

'I don't know ya,' he shouted.

'But one of my cuz them say that you is the man,' the voice coaxed, along with the sound of pumping feet on concrete.

So he pulled his shirt together with one hand and opened the door with the other, wanting to get business out of the way so that he could be on his way. As the door cranked back a great pressure from outside took over and flung him and the door backwards. He landed, one shoulder cocked up to the wall, legs twisted apart. Two males came blowing inside, kicking the door closed. One rushed into him, slamming him into the wall. A small gun, held sideways, started levitating in his face. A double deuce juice, the street jingle for a Colt 45. Back in fashion, back on the streets, aimed into his life. The barrel bored into his skin, on his cheek, under his right eye. The reflection of terror in his pupil winked back at him, carved in the metal of the piece. Cold, hyped up, ready to do what it might have to do.

'Don't think about knuckling up 'cos we'll mash you. Just chill while we do our collection and everything will be dandy.'

Schoolboy sensed that they were a pair of JVs – juveniles. There was something about the way the boy held the gun a degree or two out from a steady ninety-degree angle. Something about the way his balaclava kept sucking in and out at the mouth as if was biting his lip. Something about the way he still wanted the world to know about his fashion choices by wearing the latest baseball cap over his mask. The second boy leapt into the kitchen looking for Schoolboy's stash and cash. He realised that the prick knew exactly where to look. This boy must have been in his yard before. A customer who had decided to help himself. The JV holding the gun pulled it back so it flicked against Schoolboy's nose.

'On your knees.' Three simple words he didn't want to hear.

So he fell, all the weight of his body sinking into his knees, grinding him into the floorboards. The gun was no longer touching, but he felt the imprint it had left on his flesh pressing on his pores, his nerves, his right to live. That's when the sweat had foamed on his upper face, rolled to the centre of his forehead and leapt one drop at a time into the same space on the floorboards, making the wood so dark and dense that Schoolboy thought it would cave in. Wasn't that the part where he was meant to beg? Meant to wail? But he wasn't able to lift his lips. Wouldn't give them the satisfaction of lifting his lips. That's when the image of Mum came to him, as quiet as the click he hoped never to hear. *Give Caesar what belongs to Caesar; give the street back what belongs to the street.* After that he became numb, detached, tuning into them rather that letting them tune into him. The one above him was shuffling, shifting from toe to heel, from side to side, like a dog with too much spit in its mouth.

'I got it,' the one in the kitchen barked out as he sprang back into the passage.

'Let's have a look.'

The gunman inspected the bag.

'But this is just a load of leaf. Where's the real gear?'

Schoolboy knew that the question was directed at him.

'I don't do other stuff,' Schoolboy replied, his words hitting the floor directly where his sweat pooled.

The gun was back, this time dead centre in the middle of his head.

'I said where's the gear, fucker?'

Schoolboy repeated his answer. Time slimmed down to just him and the chrome fretting in his head. His liquid offering to the floor increased. He gulped, squeezed his eyes. Just one flinch of a finger, just one intake of breath, just one purse of his lips as he pleaded for his life, that's all it would take to puff him away.

'Come on, let's flee, man,' the voice of one tugged the other.

The gun didn't budge. For a second. Two seconds. Three seconds. Then it was gone. A few curse words and the babbling of feet were shoved his way. Then he felt the wind from outside as they left him. On his knees, locks pitching low, with the why-me curse of a victim moaning in his mind for revenge.

Schoolboy had stomped up, madder than he had been in a long time. Despite all his dealings he had never had a buckie stuck in him before. He took the offer of his first instinct and pelted after them. As he hit the ground floor he skidded into Lord Tribulation, the man who kept music humming away at all hours in Ernie and spinning in the −1 club on Tuesday and Saturday nights. Lord Tribulation and his partner MC. Insanity were one of the hottest duos on the Hackney music circuit. That night Schoolboy had become Lord Tribulation's music deck as his hands had spun out to grip Schoolboy's arms.

'Schoolie, what's the big h, man?'

'No disrespect T, but let me by. I'm gonna get them fuckers and I'm gonna get them good.'

'Looking like that? In what looks like your nightshirt and socks?'

Schoolboy checked his socks and no-shoes feet.

'No one comes to my gates and jacks me. No one. Especially two puppies who still need their mummies to wet-wipe their arses.'

Lord Tribulation's fingers became heavier, knowing immediately what Schoolboy was talking about. Why go to a bank for a loan when you could just rob from your neighbours? Schoolboy should know, that had once been his speciality.

'Look, man, if you don't get out of my way I ain't gonna fight ya. There are other ways of making those running so hard realise that the tread of their trainers only last so long. I've never had a piece, but if

50

the only way to get my stuff back is to get it, then so be it, boy, so be it.'

'So you can confirm their theory of black on black?' Lord Tribulation had asked, his tone pasted with anger.

That got Schoolboy's attention. It was part of Lord Tribulation's act to whirl out words and phrases to get you to think. To get you to confront yourself.

Lord Tribulation dropped his hands and started to swing his head. Schoolboy knew that he was going into one of his truth rhymes. When Lord Tribulation had something important to say the only way to do it was through words that comforted each other in final shape and sound.

Black on black
Ain't that a fact?
It's always black on black.
When they find a cell small enough to fit ya,
You think they wanna hear about the bigger picture?
You think they're gonna ask for the name of the white face
Who gave you the gun in the first place?
Or the white faces living it high and hard
Who keep pushing the drugs into our yard?
No they're looking for a frame
And they only want a black face to blame.
You gonna add yours to their list?
Give their conspiracy theory a new twist?
They keep chanting to the world it's black on black
Ain't that a fact?
It's always black on black
So go ahead, Schoolie,
Why don't you add your name to that?

Their heavy breathing filled the night air.

'Society hasn't stolen my gear, those two JVs have. I'll theorise about it when I get my stock back.'

'Stock!' Lord Tribulation scoffed. 'Listen to you, like you is a businessman or something. What did you expect? That they were coming to buy shares?'

He was fucked with Lord Tribulation, but the words stopped him. Anger polluted him up as he darted back to his home. He roamed his flat, taking over the two boys' roles as hunters, looking for his business phone. When he found it he sat on the bed punching in the numbers of a well-known armourer. Then he rammed the phone to his ear, waiting. Waiting for the voice to start talking so he could purchase a gun. When the voice came, middle England, white, with the grapes of wine still attached to each word, Schoolboy couldn't lift his lips again. He saw himself kneeling on the floor. Saw his own hand holding the gun perched over his head. He'd always kept himself on the margins, doing his ting, using his contacts, but he had never had a gun. Sworn not to have one. Being a wannabe gunman was not one of the stories he was going to play on this earth. The problem with wannabe was one day he was acting it big, stoking everyone up so that people learned his name. The next day wannabe was gone, as quick as the click of two fingers, claimed by prison, death or forced to run on. The day after, no one remembered his name. Schoolboy punched the phone off and realised that the only way to remain in his line of business was to get a gun. Times had moved on and were going to carry on moving whether he could keep up or not. He pushed more numbers into the phone, raised it to his ear, waiting for the voice to appear and said:

'Michael, is your offer still open?'

They had agreed a day and a time when he would come to Devon. He hadn't told Michael that all his dosh had disappeared so he might not be able to get any knives. But there'd be a way. He always found a way.

The helicopter chanted into the distance, spinning Schoolboy back to the warmth of the duvet. He rolled over and picked up the brick still lying on the bedside table. The screen flashed on, exactly as it had done earlier. It whined back off. He jabbed the red power button at the top of the phone, but the power wouldn't come on. He wanted to lay it on his pillow, like his newest girl. But he didn't. He didn't like the way it kept blinking on and off any time it chose. As if it was the one really in control of the situation. Schoolboy threw it back on the table where it could learn some manners from his other phones.

'We're in a jam, man. A big jam.' Benji shook his head as he spoke to Josh, his Brummie accent thick with stress. The strain on his face pulled his corn rows, which were thin, front to back, with no fancy slalom work.

Benji and Josh thought through their situation just as the first wave of commuters hit the Tuesday morning rush. Since the upset at the Junction they had been travelling from club to bar, from bars to hush-hush establishments, dropping the word. They had ended up in one of Dalston's all-night facilities and had been too tired to move on. They were in the back room of Marcey's Boutique shop, where the air was tight and old. The drugs that passed around the room from finger tips to palms lifted the spirits, but not much. The owners were more interested in keeping up appearances in the front. Why bother with the back when doped-up minds painted their own colours?

They sat at their own table, detached from the other four bodies in the room. Josh didn't add to Benji's remark; instead he inhaled from the sprong stick hanging from his mouth. A mixture of weed and C should have mellowed him, but it scurried too quickly in his head. Nothing worse than bad buzzing to remind you no one gets a second chance at living.

'Forget your troubles and have a puff.' Josh held out the joint, displaying gold iced around each finger.

Benji turned his head and realised that mistake el primerino had been hooking up with Josh in the first place. It was only when they fast-tracked it to the M1 he'd realised that Josh had a serious love affair going on with the pharmaceutical community. They were friends – well, as friendly as you got on the street, with your eyes still checking your back. But they had both got caught up in some interplay with a rival crew and the stench of blood on the pavement had meant they'd needed to skip out of Birmingham very quickly. The boss had offered them a way out. So they had taken it. A London name needed a couple of unknowns to do a requisition order for his boss. Hijack another operator's delivery and wait for further details. Simple.

'Josh, pull your head out of the bog. We've got work to do.'

Josh's only answer was to munch even harder on his sprong. Jackass, Benji thought. But then his whole life had been flirting with people playing the fool.

'Come on. Stop soaking. We've got business to look after.'

'What for?' Josh challenged, his neck dipping lower. 'No one's talking to me or you.'

Benji pressed his lips. Josh was right, but Benji knew they had a job to do. Since they'd spread the word about the Nokia and unknown face, no one wanted to use their vocal chords. It had nothing to do with the cream on offer not being attractive – locals just didn't want to open their mouths to a pair of outsiders. Hackney didn't take well to outsiders. Your threads, the pattern of the syllables that hatched from your mouth, the way your hair was trimmed and styled set you apart. So they were no closer to finding the yard of their suspect. They were no closer to finding out if he did the deed. They were no closer to the Nokia.

Benji abruptly stood, scraping the legs of the chair, adding another scar to the bare floor, the stress from his mouth travelling way up through his body. A few of the other occupants shifted their gazes to him, judged that he wasn't going to add value to their highs, so shifted their gazes back.

'We're gone.' Benji didn't look around to his partner, but began walking towards the door. Just as he reached for the handle, the mobile in his inside jacket pocket began to ring with his latest favourite track about how a brother should keep his bitch down. His hand hustled to find it. He pressed green. There was no voice at the other end. There didn't need to be.

'We're sorting it . . .' he explained, voice trembling, to the silent caller.

Silence was his answer. After a few seconds the caller finally spoke.

'Sorting it! So sorted I-man have to dig in the street myself to look for it. You better get that phone's arse up to mine quicktime.'

'Yeah . . . I mean . . . Well . . .'

'You and your pussy-faced friend ain't gonna make I-man look stupid, you understand. I've given you a job to do and you better do it. I'll keep my eyes spread as well. But if I don't find it you'd better make sure you have it before the Nod gets back into town tomorrow.'

The caller disconnected the line. Benji knew the Nod was code for the Don. They were in a chain, but the links had been broken by the movement of events. The caller was a middleman acting on the Nod's behalf and they were the soldiers acting on the middleman's behalf. Except they hadn't played it so well.

Benji kept moving forward while his voice moved back. 'Josh, come on, man, let's go.'

5

Put your sweet lips a little closer to the phone
Let's pretend that we're together all alone

Schoolboy was woken on Tuesday afternoon by the sound of Jim Reeves in his ear.

His mind evoked the words that fitted with the music coming from his personal mobile. 'He'll Have To Go' was his mum's favourite Jim Reeves track. That's why he'd asked a friend to compose it into his personal MB. He squeezed his eyes, drawing the music in. Its soothing tone made it so easy to slip back into the Sundays of his childhood, with Mum humming into the fragrance of black-eyed peas, stewed chicken and brown sugar sauce.

The music stopped. Shit, jerking backwards into the past wasn't going to help him get out of London. He rolled over in the peace of the duvet, stretched his hand to find the phone lying on the bedside table. He clutched it, picked it up, letting its trim smallness fit into his hand. The intimate coolness of the afternoon had already eased into its back and now invaded the dryness of his palm. He held the phone high above the bed, opened one eye and checked the name on the screen.

Window.

His other eye hustled open as he lugged his body into a sitting position. He held the phone to his ear and pressed.

'Hey, Schoolie, what's wrong with your phone? I've been trying to reach you since this morning.'

They had a rule that business should always be done on a business line and personals on a personal line.

'I just weren't doing people last night so I turned it off. I clean forgot about your call.'

'You sound like you're still napping, boy. You want me to ring back so you can put your teeth in?'

'Very funny,' Schoolboy answered as his finger rounded the rim of the camera lens on the back of the phone. He took the conversation back to the business they had discussed yesterday.

'You found me a buyer?'

'The Dread I told you about has the cash, so tell me the time for the meet and I'll pass it on.'

'Let me think . . . I've got to be at my sister's later so say seven to eight in your yard.'

'No problemo, I'll let him know.'

Schoolboy twisted his front teeth into his bottom lip. He didn't like getting involved with anyone he didn't have a story on. He had learned that one the hard way, back in '98, when he'd let an unknown come take a cup of grass tea in his home. Before the tea was drawn the Blues were in with Rover shaking him down. He'd gone down for eighteen months, seven months after parole.

'You sure the brother's on a level? Can't afford for no shit or the Blues to be stinking up my door, you check me.'

'Stop troubling yourself, the bredda was blowing sweeter than Chanel.'

'Good, because I can't afford no fuck-ups now.'

'Check you later, G.'

Schoolboy disconnected, and stared at the screensaver: a photo of his sister and her friend Tammy taken at one of those 'blood is thicker than water' happy times. Times that were getting less and less lately, but he needed to revive them if he was going to get those knives. He'd be lucky if the deal over the phone yielded half of the forty he needed. That's where Evie's put-your-head-down-and-go-for-it lifestyle came into play. He was tempted to give her a call, but he knew a face-to-face would be better.

The photograph disappeared, leaving his own face reflecting back at him. Fuck, he looked tired. The bleached brown of his skin had the textured tone of being dipped into finely ground corn. He dragged the still air of the room inside himself. He pressed the MB, bringing the colour of the screensaver back up. He checked the time.

13.45.

Plenty of time for more sleep. He placed the phone back on to the table, pulled up the duvet and entered the peace of the bed again.

Schoolboy flowed into the −1 Club. Tuesday's evening light had long passed on by, setting up the mood for a sky that mellowed somewhere between eight and nine at night. His eyelids sliced down and up, adjusting to the club's lighting. Lighting that was dim and trim. High enough to search expressions marked on faces, low enough for hips to coil and recoil without observed intrusion. As he strolled towards the dance floor he nodded his head to brothers and sisters he knew.

'Hey, Schoolie, how's tricks?' a voice yelled from the edge of the dance floor.

Schoolboy searched through the light, hunting the speaker. When he spotted it he grinned and shouted back, 'Tings is chillin', Jay Jay.'

'Any time you need that favour, Schoolie, just give me a buzz.'

Schoolboy nodded as his grin disappeared, knowing it was going to be hard to leave this place behind. He loved this club. The faces, the puffed-out clothes, the music. Lord Tribulation and MC Insanity were on high manning their decks, while their followers were poised, limbs crooked, juiced, waiting for the music to flip.

'Wheel and pull back,' Lord Tribulation yelled, his accent tripping back to the Caribbean.

As the music rewound to the beginning, Schoolboy knew that the closest he'd come to life-rumbling music in Devon was summer breeze pop reggae. He shook his head. How was he going to give up living in a sizzling social drum like Hackney with its blasting rebel sounds? Freaked-out freedom fanned itself from the dance floor, reminding Schoolboy why the −1 was the PTB − the place to be. Monday to Wednesday, Thursday through to Saturday, the −1 demonstrated how to spell club frontways, backways, upside down. Rammed jammed packed on most nights, unlike its neighbours. How did it get that extra riff on its rivals?

Simple.

Its devotion to pure unstrained music.

If you weren't ready for your clothes to crease up, don't come to the –1.

If your music quest came second best to your need for female company, don't come to the –1.

If you weren't prepared for the tips of your skin to chill the vibe in, don't come to the –1.

But if you weren't afraid to shudder into the music, number 33 Juniper Street, Stokey, could become the newest riddim riding your system.

The mirrors on the side walls doubled the crunch of colours defining the crowd, with sparks of jewellery and energy quivering in between, pulling the ignition on the collective tremor that took each body. Schoolboy wanted to be taken. His interior rhythm started to slacken, lift, slacken, lift. The music shivered down his ears, reverberating through him, mixing his hips as he jangled forward. The music seeped from his toes, connecting him to the dance floor. He spotted a dancer he'd seen around. Small, cocoa-butter soft, with a rump that rippled the way he liked. His eyes froze into hers. Hers checked into his. She twisted her body so that he could see every angle, every slip, every breath. She exalted in the main beat. He wanted to let his pelvis lean into the drop beat. But he didn't. He didn't have time to feel himself go from dry to wet, wet to dry.

If your mouth's already stuffed with coconut tart, no point taking another bite in case you bite your tongue off.

Mum was right. He had too much business to do and didn't need any diversions. He let his eyes drink the dancer for the last time.

Shame. He wouldn't have minded letting his taste buds suckle the sweat from the side of her neck.

Schoolboy caught Window's eye as his friend sat at the bar, so he pushed over to him.

'His name's Sensi. At the last table. Dread with yellow skin,' Window whispered.

Schoolboy nodded, turning, but Window caught his arm.

'But he's got a leech attached to him. There's nothing I could do about it.'

Schoolboy glanced towards the table Window had signalled and drew back, kissing his teeth when he identified the leech. His gaze had hit a face he didn't want to see, much less be seen with. His vision was presented with the image of Dexter B waving his arm at him, indicating that he should come towards the table. Dexter was easily marked out, not because of any accomplishments, but because of his two-year-old afro. The afro was high enough to get him noticed, patted carefully enough to remain in the fashion stream. Sticking heavenwards from the centre was an afro comb, with a Lion of Judah moulded at the top as if someone had put their hand in his head to mix in some sense. They went a long way back, but he wished that he could leave Dexter exactly there – that far back. But more pressing was the fact that the involvement of another person just incurred more costs. Costs he couldn't afford. He carefully set his face as he moved towards the table.

'Hey, Schoolboy, nice. Been a long time, bredda, a long time. Give me a touch.' Dexter hitched out his clenched fists to the height of his chest. Schoolboy lifted his own fists and lightly tapped Dexter's.

Dexter threw his suede-jacketed arms around Schoolboy's shoulders chanting, 'Nice, nice,' like a bulldog blubbering with no front teeth. The cream fur on the collar of his jacket tickled Schoolboy under the chin. Although they had been at school together and had ended up more or less in the same line of work, Schoolboy considered that they were gates apart. Even back at St Iggy's School, Dexter had always chosen to sit in the front, with his nose rolling in the action, while Schoolboy had lounged in the back row, studying the world from a wider perspective. The one word Schoolboy had picked up from the Cockney crowd at school had been wanker and Dexter fit the word as if it was shaved in his afro.

Shit, his mind was skipping along memory lane again. Schoolboy mentally roughed himself up, re-establishing his focus.

'Roll up, Schoolie, and meet my man Sensi. Nice,' Dexter continued, saying Sensi's name as if he was singing the last word of a call and response song. He swivelled on the backstep of his tan Clarks and swept his right hand towards the seated Sensi. His left hand remained spread out in the air, keeping the space around him alive.

'Wh'appen?' was the greeting that came from lips attached to a face that had long ago decided that it had little left to laugh about.

Schoolboy took in Sensi's tied locks and pony-tail beard. His voice marked him as a foreigner, someone from the other side of the river. Heavily vocalised in downtown Kingston, Jamaica, but with the lisp of South London in the background. Definitely old Skool, Schoolboy decided.

'Safe, tings are safe,' Schoolboy replied, letting Sensi know that he could speak his language.

He eased himself into a seat, which enabled him to conduct business comfortably with Sensi, but still gave him the best vantage point on Dexter.

'What's your juice?' Dexter asked, rubbing his palms together as he drooped down into his chair.

Schoolboy's nostrils flared. With irritation. Dexter was using the same tone he used to ask one of his laydeez whether she wanted a three-minute grind on the dance floor.

'Tanks, but no tanks. I'm not into no long ting, so let's freeze-frame the trailers and go straight to the main feature,' Schoolboy replied, shifting his whole self towards Sensi, cutting Dexter out of the scene.

'You have the phone?' Sensi asked, raising his round chin and fixing Schoolboy with red eyes. Red eyes that held not a single whiff of blow or alcohol.

'It's just one.'

'So you have it?'

'I wouldn't be sitting here if I didn't.'

Sensi shuffled forward as if he was shedding old skin. His hands came up and curved on the table, each pinkie iced with glass.

'It would be better if my eye could dwell on it, understand?'

Schoolboy frowned. Only amateurs put their goods on full display at the beginning of a new deal. He hated situations where there were too many why questions aimed at him. Caution made his shoulders tighten while his two fingers and thumb started to rub and ride against each other with the savageness of a razor looking for blood. The base line of the music, nourishing the hecticness of the room, pushed against his chest, deepening his need for air. Maybe his need to get out of London was making him too careful, too paranoid. Still, he needed to know whether they were both dealing with the same purchase order.

'I don't know how they do things across the water, but in our endz we don't concern ourselves with the origins, but just concentrate on the here and now, you catch me?'

He knew he was a bit vex, because he was using the term 'you catch me' as if he had someone slammed up against the wall. He continued, just to make sure Sensi understood:

'Let's discuss what I need to see because other offers are jamming my headset and they're only interested in re-chargeability status not its DNA. And I need to emphasise that the ringtone of the offers coming my way have gone beyond the fifty marker. So if the notes you're offering turn out to be of the red crisp variety, we can arrange for you certainly to see the phone from any angle you like.'

The blood invaded Sensi's face as if the red from his eyes were seeping across his skin. The frown left Schoolboy's features. His fingers and thumb stopped moving. Gaining the upper hand was such a beautiful thing.

'Brothers,' Dexter's voice jump-started them both back to the salty taste of humanity in the club. 'You might as well start kissing 'cos you both seem to want to be in a long ting. We are still doing business? Nice. Sensi, spar, let me tell you how Schoolboy got his name . . .'

Dexter was becoming like a tick in Schoolboy's side.

'Look, I thought I was involved in a one-to-one,' Schoolboy's head moved, swinging the sentence between both men. 'So I need to know who I'm connecting with here?'

Dexter shuffled his neck forward, his hands open and level with his chest, his lips primed and ready to state his position. 'Let's just say we're working as a partnership today. Sensi needed a guided tour and I was happy to be the tour operator. But we are kind of still in the middle of the excursion, so if you want to do business, you get me as well.'

Schoolboy twisted the left corner of his mouth. Same old Dexter. Had to be in control. Just couldn't let it go.

'I don't care if it's you, him, Hailie Selassie, you catch me. I just need to know the price tag so I can see if it's competitive.' He just hoped they hadn't got him here on some fuck-me pretence because the one thing he hated was the feeling of time whizzing by without him.

'Youth,' Sensi addressed Dexter in the rawest Jamaican. His fingers, moulded to their slim shape by the exercise of rolling joints, dug into his pocket, feeling. He threw some coins across the table at Dexter. 'Go and buy yourself some sweets.'

Dexter's cheeks drained back like those of a crack pipe devotee. His neck and teeth retreated back. But his eyes didn't, as if there was a prize in front of him he couldn't quite let go.

'Nice,' Schoolboy mocked, throwing Dexter's own word back at him to rest with the change lying on the table.

Without question Dexter scooped up the money and headed for the bar.

Sensi was the first to try starting over.

'Let's ease it up and settle. We both want to do business. So no disrespect, you understand.'

'None taken. I need to do some quick business and my biorhythms tell me you're my man.'

Sensi nodded his head, his beard sprinkling in the air, so Schoolboy carried on.

'It's a regular mobile, vintage model and features . . .'

'Where it hail from?'

'Here and there.'

'Around these parts or some other spot?' Sensi relaxed his long frame into the back of his chair as if signalling that life could be so easy sometimes.

'What's with the questionnaire?' said Schoolboy. 'If you want a breakdown of its history you need to be tuned into the biography channel.'

Schoolboy felt as if his breath was shaking from the turntable and filling the room. That he was providing the rhythm for couples to whine their bodies to. His fingers and thumb took up their old beat again.

'Just trying to get a feel for the merchandise so I can pitch it to the right customer.'

Sensi started to stroke his beard and Schoolboy was reminded of Mizz Philips, his last parole officer who had a thing about men – she didn't like them.

'Look, is there some kind of remix going on here I need to know about?' Schoolboy asked.

'Blood, it sounds like you're not feeling too sociable tonight, so let me find someone else who feels more easy with I-man's soul.'

Sensi unhooked his hands from the table, starting to rise. Schoolboy knew he didn't have time to find another purchaser. Besides, Window wasn't in the habit of letting bad business enter his house.

'Did I say I had a problem with your soul? I'm just a bit antsi, my gal done left me for some Caucasian geezer.'

Sensi stopped, started laughing, placed his hands flat on the table and resumed his seat. Lies always seemed to make people feel more comfortable than telling the truth.

'You want me to sort his ras out?'

'Nah, no need for that, she was getting a bit too slack in bed anyway.'

Schoolboy started the laughter, drawing Sensi in. Reeling the money in for the knives.

'Schoolboy, I like your tongue, man, I like it. Why don't I drive you home and pick up the phone?'

'No can do. Tonight is booked, but what say we meet back here tomorrow at around four?' This time he wasn't lying, because he needed to get the cash rolling in from Evie's angle as well. 'But it has to be just me and you.' Schoolboy lifted his head in Dexter's direction.

'Don't worry about idiot-bwoy Dexter, I'll make sure that he and his afro comb find a new hairstyle. It will be just you, me and the phone.'

6

The rain and his thoughts followed Schoolboy as he hurried along the stretch of Wapping nicknamed The Island. Wapping New Quay had the quiet isolation of a traffic island. The jostling sand brick of Wapping Housing Estate flowed on one side while the river drifted on the other. He passed this wharf and that wharf, which housed wharfers safe in their Victorian-bricked blocks. A bit like The Scrubs, but with better views. He regretted his earlier decision of not taking Sensi back to his and completing the deal. He just wanted out of here. Wanted out of London with its stand-in-your-face reminders of a life that should have been better lived. He slowly released a gush of built-up air from inside himself as he stopped in front of Nutmeg Wharf. He stood where he knew the concierge could set him apart from the dark. When the man inside spotted him, Schoolboy moved his head in that brother-to-brother lift of the chin, but the concierge just shook his head and Schoolboy knew what kind of brother he was dealing with. He pressed the intercom and spoke into it, slow enough to give the concierge enough time to remember what the Stop 'n' Search law had felt like.

'Number 32. Yvette Campbell – she's my sister.'

The man inside stared back, and Schoolboy felt as if he was being grilled through the eye slits of a white hood. If the brother wanted to think he was a coconut that was his business but as long as he didn't stand in the way of Schoolboy everything should be fine. The man sluggishly stretched across his desk to press the buzzer for Evie's apartment. The rain started to fall harder, jabbing Schoolboy in the neck and the scalp between his loose locks. A movement distracted him from the rain. He hitched his gaze sideways to see a female wharfer standing beside him. She moved in curves carved in Bond

Street, with the air of someone who did not pick up her own dry cleaning. She looked at him and he would've had to be tripping not to see the fear slashing her lines into a new shape. He could have reassured her by smiling. By stepping back. By joining his ancestors cutting sugar cane all over again. But he didn't. And he wouldn't. He watched back with 'I don't do dry cleaning' eyes. She moved sharply away from him and he knew that she had already decided what he did do. She flapped her hands at the concierge who rushed to access the entrance button to let her in. She rushed inside, holding on to the automatic door to make sure it was secure behind her. He was starting to feel proper pissed. He knew he shouldn't. He'd been in this situation before, but having to outrun the double dare of some misguided minstrel and wannabe plantation mistress just to see his sister reminded him of how he hated this part of town. Of how he didn't fit. Of how Evie had deliberately hooked up somewhere she knew would set her apart from him. He sucked and jack-knifed the bitter night air into his lungs. Suddenly he was conscious of the light slicing in from Canary Wharf, which fell into a shuffle searching him, backing off, and searching him again. He hunched nervously. He didn't like being in anyone else's spotlight.

The door buzzed, signalling for him to push into the dryness of the complex. The porter remained seated, so Schoolboy just couldn't resist letting him know that Dalston Lane was a lot closer than he thought. He switched his hip motion into the high-stepping walk that the younger members of Hackney's streets used to show everyone they had arrived. His arms and legs started swinging, criss-crossing, dragging in the menacing tempo of slowness. He kept his face straight, focused on the lift, and took his time. Each step was done deliberately.

Disrespectfully.

Delightfully.

Once he was inside the lift, he forgot everything else but what he was here for. He could already feel the slice of the knives he would soon be united with thanks to Evie's salary.

He knew she would be annoyed. But her feelings didn't even touch the bottom of his priorities. As he advanced towards her door, he got his dimples ready for the onslaught against his brain. She was already waiting for him, defending her patch.

'And what do you want?' she asked, standing fit, firm, three inches taller than him and four years older than him. Her sternness was further stretched by the pull of her extensions, which leapt from the middle of her head like the avenging terracotta leaves of a pineapple.

In response he moved quickly, shoulders swaggering, head wagging, with his lips ready to brush her face. Her perfume hit his nostrils. Expensive and sharp. She didn't budge, but her eyes did. Her stare pulled his attention like plastic melting on his face. His upper body retreated from her heat to his original position.

'What, no hugs and kisses for your younger bruv? I take it your policy of "all the world needs now is love, sweet love" has closed down for the night?'

She continued to batter him with her eyes the same way Mum used to when she received yet another truancy letter from St Iggy's. His right dimple faltered. He didn't need Evie and tough memories bad-mouthing him at the same time.

'What I don't need is you and yours trying to get comfy at my place at ten in the night. I've got company and they don't want some loose-lipped man crimping their thinking.'

He realised that it must be one of her no-man talking sessions, when her closest friends gathered to discuss everything but men. Well, that was the brief at least.

'Look, I'll be in and out quicker than your last boyfriend.'

She kissed her teeth, in one of those long liberal ways that told him once he was inside her space he'd better watch his step. She turned her back on him, so he followed her into the type of passage you could only get in a council flat if you rebuilt the block brick by brick. She stopped and turned under a framed picture of a black version of the cartoon character Top Cat who glared above the question 'Street hustler or urban freedom fighter? Discuss.' Schoolboy's dimples disappeared. That was Evie. Never knowing quite how to get down with the brethren and sistren on the street. To allow some 60s cartoon to rap their militant message to the world. He shouldn't be surprised. She hadn't felt the pain he'd been feeling for such a long time.

He hardened himself. His thoughts were trailing backwards again. He needed to concentrate on the here and now. He looked at Evie's defiant stance before him and he knew it wasn't going to be easy to get her to pass on any money. Wasn't going to be easy to break her, bend her, bamboozle her. He just needed to keep tapping her in the right way and in the right places. Suddenly he noticed the smell. The air turned like a freshly forked allotment with a compelling tinge of ginger.

'You been making those mouth-watering juices?' he asked, finding the first compliment to lay at her feet.

As soon as he had said the J word he knew he'd made a mistake. He'd tapped her in the wrong place. He wasn't surprised to see the thump of righteousness strike her in the face and knew she was remembering that time in '94 when Juice had entered the cuss word dictionary. During his cat-nap in one of HMP's pleasure camps just outside of Ipswich, he'd written to Evie three weeks before Christmas. His pen had crafted a long letter, humming the usual rehabilitation medley of regret, remorse and renewal. He had pictured her reading and smiling with the relief of someone who knew the Lord was finally coming their way. Of course by the time she'd read his PS she was meant to be so grateful that she would have done anything to help him on his new journey.

> p.s. Use the attached V.O. to come up on Christmas Eve. Just to keep my spirit alive in these times of darkness please fill an empty bottle of orange juice with whisky (part Glen, part Johnnie). Then add a nip of orange juice. Don't forget to write my name on the front in large black letters. Two minutes before you reach the prison gates, lob the bottle of juice over the wall. Don't worry, there'll be no trouble. Even screws have a heart at Christmas.

Looking back, maybe he shouldn't have used the word screws. Or maybe it was the word spirit. But deep down he knew it was the way the word juice had seemed to tap-dance around every full stop. Either way, she had come visiting bringing a book as a gift – the prison diary of some Black Power 70s mover and shaker. She had explained that although the author had been shot to death, it wasn't the ending but the process of liberation that mattered. He had felt true freedom when each page had been used as a blowstick to dispense eye-rolling bliss. She just didn't get it. And still didn't get it. Christmas was the least reflective time of the year.

He bounced his mind back to the present.

'Sometimes . . .' Evie started, her lips stretched thin, flapping like paper in the wind, 'I really wish I bought you that drink. Just so you could shut up and leave me alone. You keep coming around here, with your two long arms, as if I never give you anything . . .'

'So one more thing won't matter.'

'I ain't got nothing to give you, you check me.'

He knew she was rattled because her accent had slipped from middle London to rude gal.

The apple-white walls hemmed them in with the discipline of ropes around a wrestling ring. He knew this round was over but that didn't mean he had to wait for the bell for the start of the next one. He moved his hand with the sureness of someone well practised in opening other people's windows and turned the handle of the sitting-room door. He quickly side-stepped into a room which should have been a post-modern celebration of yellow – Zimbabwean sculptures, questing candlelight and the saccharine strumming of the latest acoustic diva. But one look at the gathered sisters and all he could see were selfish and shoving reds walking hand-in-hand with uptight oranges.

His entrance stopped the heated discussion. Ten eyes pricked into him, trying to pin him down with their wall-to-wall misery. Evie was muttering behind him.

'Don't mind me, ladies, just carry on,' he said, sitting on the arm of the single beige sofa occupied by a thin woman with short, spiky dreads.

'You all know, I think, my brother Eli. Don't mind him. He might learn a thing or two.' Evie remained standing in the open doorway, a reminder that he wouldn't be staying.

Eagerness glided into the room, drifting between the voice whining from the CD. One of the group picked up the oration, weaving each word with thought-of-the-day hand gestures. 'It's like what Mother Dorinda says . . .'

Oh, puhleeze! Not that Mother Dorinda 'there's no one who can hold a solid sista back' motivational crap again, Schoolboy thought. Evie had given him one of Mother Dorinda's books of sayings for his last birthday. He had tried to read a few, but each seemed to refer to women being tied down, imprisoned, chained. It all sounded a bit S&M to him. He'd started to read them out just before him and Terri-baby were getting ready for some action. Those sayings had really got Terri-baby stoked up.

The conversation resumed, with their words swinging from 'Don't let some brother run all over you' to 'I'm holding out for a man who treats me like a queen.' When one of the women passionately declared, 'Mother Dorinda says that our lives are like the levels of a castle . . .', Schoolboy knew it was time to make his sister see life from his point of view. Besides, Mother Dorinda wasn't motivating him. She wouldn't be able to motivate herself after getting to level 4 of a tower block.

'I'd like to help here, ladies,' he interrupted, his dimple winking under his left eye. Each eye bore into him. 'But me and the brothers are all around the white girls' castles because it's a lot more comfy around there, you get me.'

'Excuse us.' Evie dived in before the collective sucking of teeth aimed at him could reach its target. She grabbed Schoolboy's arm and dragged him out of the room, through the passage and into the kitchen. A kitchen he always found disappointing. White walls, white units, chrome accessories. A kitchen that just didn't want to get too dirty. Evie faced him while she leaned on the oven hood and he sank into the rim of the sink.

'So what are you after this time?' One of her shorter extensions moved furiously as if doing her talking for her.

'Just forty quid, girl.'

'I told you the last time that I'm not prepared to keep shelling out money to you.'

'Just this once . . .'

'That's what you chanted the last time . . .'

'But I really mean it this time.'

'Like you swore you would give me back the money you borrowed the last time? And the time before that? What do I look like to you, a donkey that ain't working hard enough? Besides, that bulge in your pocket looks like a wad of cash to me.'

Schoolboy's eyes skimmed down to his pocket where the brick lay. He ignored her remark, bringing his eyes back straight into Evie's.

'Charity begins at home, Evie.'

'You're right, so why don't you get your begging bowl and bash on the doors of your neighbours in your block?'

'Because I need it quick. I need to buy some . . .'

'Evie, you all right?' a new voice asked behind him. A voice that was husky, calm, with a slight air of exotic fusion.

He didn't need to look around to know it was the bitch from downstairs.

Tammy.

Since she'd moved into the complex and Evie's life two years ago they had established this one-up one-down relationship. One day it had been just him and Evie. The next, Tammy had appeared making his neck hurt from swinging and switching his perspective from one to the other. He pushed up his hands to massage his neck. He kept his stare on his sister as he spoke, but his words were directed behind him.

'I'm having a private and confidential with my flesh, so why don't you go back to fixing your mashed-up castle.'

'Evie?' Tammy's question and confidence cooled his skin as she pushed past him with the grace of a woman who never ran for a train. A woman who took her time to follow everything through. The same wishbone shape of her nose-stud graced the white varnish of her thumbnail. She couldn't have the nose art without the nail art.

Couldn't have the bronze eye-shadow without the four gold hair-cuffs. Couldn't have piously upturned lips without the matching attitude. Had to have eyes that he wouldn't mind staring into after he'd screwed her for the third time in a night. His lips rubbed together, making his dimples disappear. Just because he wanted to play the hare finding the hole didn't mean he liked her.

Tammy took her place beside his sister. Schoolboy's neck started hurting as he let his gaze take in both women. Both similar in height, hairstyle and high-handedness.

'It's all right, Tammy, because he will be going soon,' Evie fluttered into the room.

Tammy turned to him. Stood three inches taller than him. Had two years on him. She placed one hand on his sister's shoulder, while the other clutched her usual cup of camomile tea. Evie never drank herbal tea, but always kept a box of camomile for her friend. Evie never kept anything for him. His finger and thumb started rubbing together.

'I didn't come up here to chat with you, understand,' he warned.

'Evie, are you sure everything is OK?' Tammy ignored him, like she did most of the time.

Evie nodded, her extensions relaxing. He hated this girl-to-girl thing they had where they talked as if he wasn't there. His backside tightened into the sink.

'OK. I'll see you back inside. But don't forget what I said about brothers being a lethal thing sometimes,' Tammy warned with that smile of peace she always had attached to her face.

She detached her hand from Evie and swirled towards him, heating his skin as she passed him and left the room.

'I wish you'd treat her with respect,' Evie whispered, extensions back on the alert.

'What for? I don't see respect dripping my way from her tongue. Come on, Evie girl, I need that money.'

'Well, that's too bad because I haven't got it.'

'So when will you have?'

'Don't you give up?'

'No. I learnt that one from you.'

The music stirring in the living room joined them as their eyes circled each other.

'I'm not saying I will give it to you, but I'll text you tomorrow and we'll discuss it again. What did you say you needed it for again?'

Suddenly he felt fear. The fear of leaving. Of knowing future tumbles would be hard without her abrasive gentleness to catch him. He wished someone would turn off that flippin' music because its riff was beginning to ride low inside his soul.

He leaned over and kissed her sleek cheek.

'Don't worry about that. I'll tell you when you give me the money tomorrow.'

He turned to go, but was stopped by her voice.

'Don't play smart with me, Eli. I never said I was giving you anything.'

Schoolboy didn't reply but kept walking with his dimples dancing on his face. She'd give it to him, like she always did.

As he stepped into the centrally heated air of the corridor his business MB started ringing with its usual bonus prize ping. It did it once so he knew it was a text. He pulled it out of his fleece pocket, flipped the lid back and checked the screen. He pressed inbox and read the text.

    m8k sure u have dosh by Thursda sum1else wants blades
    L8rs Robbie

Attached was a small photo of the knives lying side by side on a table, like a happy family unit.

Fuckrees.

He hadn't expected anyone else to declare an interest in them. He'd marked them as his own. Schoolboy turned back to look at his sister's front door, as the thumb and middle finger of his left hand started rubbing together. She had better give him the money because by Thursday he knew that those knives would be loving the cooking of someone else.

7

While Schoolboy made his way home from Evie's on the S22, Dexter and his ever-decreasing afro began moving away from Speedball Central towards the underpass as if they were dancing. Speedball Central was a name you wouldn't find in the A to Z. It lay at the intersection of Grove Lane Station and Pitta Road, with Mare Street cruising in the distance. It repelled people. It drew people. It was one of the most dangerous hangouts in Hackney, but if you wanted to sample the newest mixes and speedballs rolling on the street there was no other place to be. Chocolate honey, which was a dab of C and H baked in a block of Moroccan, was what clients were now after to melt their souls.

Some would say that Dexter was jigging from the effects of the chocolate honey that had just entered his body stream. He would say that it was because for the first time in a long time life was moving up. He had successfully made links with another operator on the other side of the water, which was unheard of in these parts. Hackney's operators tended to believe that in-house operations were the best. Dexter slithered down the stairs and into the shade of the underpass. Abruptly his afro sharp-turned backwards as he heard footsteps tripping behind him. He smiled. Speedball Central sure knew how to make people walk good. His afro sharp-turned forwards, to his future and his thoughts. Being hedged in by Hackney's rules wasn't good enough for him, he needed to bust loose, get an international perspective. Meeting Sensi cemented the promising outlook for the future. Even a crap-digger like Schoolboy wasn't going to stand in his way. People like Schoolboy were thrown on this earth for one reason – to add to Dexter's portfolio of accomplishments.

The footsteps behind him began to trip faster, louder. But Dexter didn't have time to study that, he only had time to consider himself.

Sensi would contact him tomorrow to continue the next phase of their acquaintance. Just as he passed a mural of Marcus, Malcolm and Martin, the bone and muscle of an arm locked around his windpipe. Dexter wasn't dancing any more. Surprise made his body relax. He was tugged back, legs shooting, straining, afro quivering. His head shot upwards. He'd lived a life looking down and forward, but never up. Now here he was, eyes bulging up, with death dripping in the stench of designer aftershave. His reflexes kicked in but he knew it was too late. The blood vessels of his eyes popped. He started to grunt and groan as if he was fucking. The owner of the arm choked into his ear, 'If you can't hear you must feel.' The arm tightened, twisted, ending Dexter's last grind on the dance floor. His body fell near the discarded duvet of another forgotten person.

Schoolboy rose convinced that this particular Wednesday was going to be one of the most rewarding days of his life. He felt the mellow temperature of the rain gathering in the sky. He stood in front of the full-length mirror propped against the wall in his bedroom and admired his threads. The way they hung, the colours he had chosen, the silver belt that puffed out his chest like a male peacock ready to prance. And he was ready because life was suddenly kicking. Kicking his future in the right direction. He just knew that today wouldn't be a day for nostalgia, wouldn't be a day for dreaming, wouldn't be a day for feeling that he wasn't finally in control. He'd risen early, around 12 midday, because his to-do list was full. He had to part company with the brick, buy the knives and check that his sister had the money waiting for him so that by nightfall he'd be swinging from the rooftop with the gusts of marijuana blowing in and out.

His personal and business mobiles were lying on the bed. In between them lay the brick. He strolled over to the bed. He used both hands to pluck up his business and personal MBs at the same time. He shoved one into his left-hand jacket pocket and the other in his right-hand pocket. Evenly balanced, he now had to decide where to carry the brick. He plucked it up, loving the feel of its weight, loving the imagined feel of the money that would soon come his way. He pulled open his jacket and placed the brick in the inside pocket. He rustled his jacket back into place and smoothed it with his hand. He moved towards the front door, opened it and stepped on to the balcony, treading on a cheese-and-onion crisp packet. Shit, he still hadn't kept his last promise to Mr Prakash and cleaned the balcony. But that would have to wait. There was a time and place for everything and the time was taking him straight to Sensi and that money.

Start line: *what's the best thing about Hackney?*
Response: *I don't know, what's the best thing about Hackney?*
Gag line: *the bus outta here.*

Schoolboy shook his head as he paid the bus driver and the door hissed shut behind him. He grinned as he remembered one of the most tired jokes about Hackney. But the punchline was right. That's if you wanted quick access to a chemical rush.

Top deck.

Back row.

Monday through to Saturday.

Any of the bus routes provided by the MacDonald and MacArthur bus line, known to all as the MDMA line – the Ecstasy Highway. Take your pick and choose your substance, supplied by a gallery of drug dealers. If you wanted to go up, go down, start speeding or enter a world where time didn't move in seconds and minutes, all you had to do was stand on a street corner, stick out your hand and hop right on. The 21X was the last remaining route that dabbled in offering the public a bit of leaf. Offering short-term relaxation meant it knew how to meander through the back streets and slow everything down. Which was what Schoolboy needed. He needed to slow it down. Way down so that he could appreciate what he was leaving behind. The knife he had handled yesterday came back to him. Poised, proud, propped back. One of the most beautiful knives he had ever seen. Its sharp memory climbed with him as he made his way up the stairs of the half-filled bus. He stepped into the overheated air of the top deck and was immediately drawn into the world of the two dealers who sat talking at the back. Their chat ceased. They lifted their heads. They used their faces and high-street platinum to check his potential as a buyer. He checked them back, running his eyes over their market-stall designer tracksuits and youth. He wasn't interested in the kids' stuff they peddled or the juvenile menace set in their eyes. He'd seen JVs like them hit prison on their first day bouncing with bluster and badness. By the second week they were weeping for either mummy or some foster-parent. The dealers dismissed him, tugged their heads down low, drew closer and resumed their chat. He sighed as he realised that this was another Hackney tradition he would miss. With hand-to-hand drug distributions came the mouth-to-mouth exchange of news. If you wanted to know what the underground world was up to, you just had to swing on the Ecstasy Highway and be transported to the Hackney rolling news channel, where bulletins checked in and out, thick and fast.

This might be one of Schoolboy's final chances to catch the Hackney news wheel, so he sat third row from the dealers, far enough back to catch any interesting reports, far enough forward to dip out when he was ready. The brick thumped against his breast as he sat down. The dealers' tones clocked them for what they were, a pair of Poplar or Bow boys bringing their Cockney Caribbean to E9 and North London. Their tones were hushed, but laced with the type of passion that could never be quiet.

'You can't come into H-Town without a shooter. And I mean a fully automatic, none of that semi-shit. This part of town is ruffer than ruff,' one dealer relayed with a style of excitement lighting his breath that only ever sounded authentic coming from the young.

These two were too young to know you always referred to firearms in code. Too young to know you never talked about banging in front of customers. Just too young to know. The wrong turnings of Schoolboy's own youth stared back at him. He shifted as if the seat's filling was made of boiling ash. He could understand how one minute you could be in school and the next having life press so hard you eased the pressure by forcing a gun into someone's face. He wasn't saying it was right but that's just how it was sometimes. He crammed his eyes shut and shook the memories off. He didn't need to play the rewind and feel like a shit game on such a fine day. His eyes flicked as he continued to listen to the adolescent musings heating up at the back.

'You've got to get married up with an auto,' the dealer continued, his voice muffled by chewing gum. 'No one takes you seriously unless you're tanked to the brim.'

'I'd rather do without. You can do your ting without a gun,' his friend interrupted, voice penetrating and trembling with the shaking of the bus.

'Yeah, nuff man whistling that tune until some gun-toting bod wipes out their stock. Then you see them a while later with empty pockets asking for some armourer's MB number. You need to get ahead of the game.'

Schoolboy saw himself the night he'd been robbed, sweating, poking numbers into his phone. He was thankful he was getting out of a city that resembled a department store called Shooters 'R' Us. A community where piping had nothing to do with cake baking techniques.

'Take that geez . . . what's his name?. . . Dexter . . .'

The name Dexter rang out the same time as a passenger pressed the bell. Schoolboy pursed his lips and just resisted the temptation to look over his shoulder to see who the talking gun-boys were. He jammed his ears straight into the continuing conversation.

'Got mashed near Speedball Central last night. If he'd had a Mac-10 in his coat it might have been a different story . . .'

Maybe it wasn't that Dexter. Maybe it wasn't the same Dexter who had no respect for a classroom or anyone else. Schoolboy couldn't afford for any blood to come dripping his way. Not with his belongings packed, ready, behind his front door. He didn't need any excess now. His mind swung backwards and forwards, forwards and backwards trying to locate any other Dexters he knew.

Dexter from Crisp Street Market.

Dexter from Amhurst Road.

Flash Dexter from any address he happened to be shacked up with at the time.

There were plenty of Dexters out there dabbling in illegals just waiting to be pumped down. His muscles relaxed. He leaned back, reassured with his reasoning. But still only a fool would not take a bird's eye view of a possible situation so he allowed his eyes and ears to slip backwards, tuning into the bustling words firing from the back row.

'Fucking Dexter man, he could have hid an AK-47 in that afro of his. I'd have whacked him for the hair-do alone . . .'

Laughter bubbled on the bus as if the youths were watching the latest buddy movie at the pictures. Schoolboy wasn't laughing. The word whacked started to hold him back. Started to make him think. Started to make him realise there was only one Dexter who had worn his hair as if he was the tallest dude in town. The bus engine blistered, growled as it picked up speed. The intensity of his unease took the empty seat next to him.

'Don't worry about idiot-bwoy.'

His eyes started quick-step blinking, as he remembered the scent and words of Sensi last night. His fingers and thumb on both hands started their circling, pulling into their old riff. He was worried that Sensi had implicated him in something he didn't need to be implicated in right now. He didn't need death blazing a trail around after him, dousing stickiness into his future path, making it too slippery to tread. He didn't need the Blues turning up asking him to participate in a helping enquiries workshop or providing him with rent-free accommodation for the night. He didn't need to be identified on their list of Dexter's last known associates.

'So why did he get hit?'

The question scalded Schoolboy, bringing him back to the broadcast. His ears slipped further back.

'Could have been anything . . .'

'Like?'

The dealer coughed, wheezed, took the phlegm and chewing gum down, ready to start.

'Well, they say he got chicken-squeezed. Can't imagine that. If someone's going to take me down it had better be in a blaze of slugs . . .'

Schoolboy knew that if Dexter had been strangled someone had wanted him to die very slowly. He rewound to the irritation that had heated Sensi's face last night. Whether it was the kind of irritation that wanted to do something to someone bad and slow he just didn't know. The bus increased its pace. The dealer's story seared up into a world Schoolboy hoped wouldn't stain him again. He felt as if the bus was turning inside out, its thick colour leaking towards his feet. Bloody detail after bloody detail flamed from the boy's mouth. But still his tongue wouldn't give up the whole story.

'But who did the squeezing?' the second dealer punched in, his voice loaded with the impatience Schoolboy was feeling.

'Well . . .'

Schoolboy sensed the coming revelation on the dealer's tongue. His breathing pumped low and quick. After waiting for too many seconds he realised the narration had stopped. He felt the ease of someone pass by him and he knew the dealers were back to their main business. He turned his eye to the right and back, capturing the back of a young woman. A back that held loosely permed chestnut hair, side-pocketed combat trousers and a hand that squeezed the arm of a five-year-old. A five-year-old who made no noise, just did what he was told to do. Schoolboy compressed his lips. Drugs and kids did not go. The one time a bod had turned up with a child in tow looking for a handful he had informed them that this was a business not a day-care service. Soon the rustle of voices and plastic bags caressed time, slowing it way down, making Schoolboy feel as if he'd been tied to the seat all his life.

His street instincts told him to get off the bus and delay the meeting with Sensi, but the future was pulling him so tight, telling him this was his last chance. The knife came to him, beautiful in its shape and style, skilled in the art of doing its work. He couldn't give it up, not so easily. Besides, he couldn't risk leaving if both he and Sensi were in today's top ten news items. They'd be at the top of the Blues' questioning list. His shoulders bolted towards his ears, because having decided to stay didn't stop the worry. It didn't stop the panic. It didn't stop the waiting. The heaviness of the woman and child blasted past him towards the stairs. Schoolboy's breathing slowed. Almost stopped. His shoulders unfolded. Dropped.

'Come on, so who topped afro man?' the second dealer asked the question bouncing in Schoolboy's mind.

'I tell you what . . .'

Schoolboy leaned back waiting for the words to hit.

'Arsenal could do with whacking a few guys at Highbury, get the team motivated, you know what I mean?'

More freakish laughter took the bus. Was that it? Was that all he was going to get for them nearly fucking over half his brain? Anger joined Schoolboy as he realised he had waited with the patience of a fool for only dick to come his way. These two knew as much about Dexter's final call as his mum knew about dealing crack on a street corner.

He felt some relief. The relief of knowing that his name wasn't being passed around like some sensimillia smooth stick. But he still didn't know if he had a role in this story. A row of maybe questions began jumping him, searching for that ending. He pulled saliva into his dry mouth.

'Stoke Newington Church Street,' the faint voice of the bus driver travelled up the stairs.

Surprise threw him, as he hadn't realised they were deep into Stokey soil. Strolling into the −1 to find the Blues licking their pencils and flapping their notebooks was not on his timetable today. He knew it was decision time.

He saw the Blues waiting for him.

He saw the knives longing for him.

He saw Devon welcoming him.

The images swapped around, each taking their turn in his head again. They swapped again. And again. Abruptly the whining of a police car jumped past the bus. Only the Blues lodged in his mind this time. Schoolboy pushed up, clinging to one of the poles that felt and looked like jaundiced bamboo. The weight of the brick slammed into him. He took the stairs as if they were moving and didn't stop until he stood heaving in front of the door. He shoved his neck at the door, his nostrils fanning as the bus stop came into view. He plucked the rest of his body into line with his neck, eager to get off, but the bus motored past the stop as if its engine had digested the latest happy pills. Idiot, he'd forgotten to press the bell. The bus stopped at the traffic lights.

'Driver, let me off.'

No answer. He flicked his locks to the front of the bus.

'I said, let me fucking well off.'

'Sorry, against regulations.'

Rules and regulations thrust him back to his last stretch. To being hemmed into 5.5 square metres. Now here he stood stuck behind another door controlled by someone else. He planted his fingers against the dusty rubber of the split door and pressed into it and pushed as if he was straining to come into the world for the first time. His biceps bulged, his eyes closed as he pulled the door's resisting jaws apart and in. The gasps from the passengers fuelled his determination as the door did what it was meant to – it began to open. He twisted his body to the left and plunged against the opening. His ribs screamed with an internal ache, but he only had time to react to the rubber edges of the door as they widened his access to the world outside. The temperature changed and cooled against his face, telling him he was more out than in. He was on the verge of shaking loose. He was on the verge of finding out what quaintness tasted like. One last big one, that's all he needed. He took in a breath, letting it widen, stir, circulate inside him. He let it out, using its oxygen to propel his body one last time. The plastic edges of the door scraped his face, dragged his jacket, but couldn't hold him back. His feet twitched, ready to jump, only for their movement to be taken over by the rhythm of the bus's engine as it revved up, re-igniting the wheels. He yanked one last time and fell free and landed with the posture of someone crippled by too much pain in their life.

The Nokia in his pocket slammed into his belly. Shit. He remembered the knives, the dosh, Devon. His body flicked up, making him dizzy. The blur of the rushing cars, the people, his own thoughts tumbled about him making it hard for him to think.

He tipped his head down and forward. Didn't look back. Didn't look to the side. Just let his feet pick up speed as he steamrolled out of Stokey, with the Nokia shifting with his body, tapping a jarring beat into his side.

8

*If you snuggle down with Satan, don't be surprised if you wake
up with your backside on fire.*

Those had been the first words Schoolboy's mum had uttered to him
after he'd been released from his first vacation inside. And now, here
he was, grinding a path through Liverpool Street's nine-to-fivers as if
he could already smell his arse burning. After jumping the bus, he'd
gone overground and underground. Overground on the mainline train
and underground to the Central Line. He'd flowed from Liverpool
Street to Holland Park, from Holland Park to Liverpool Street. He let
the red line take him down and up four times just so he could distance
himself from the bloody mess Dexter had left behind. A point's failure
on journey two had calmed him down. A defective train on journey
three had cooled him down. Gave him enough time to get his story
crease-free if the Blues came gate-crashing to his door. Experience told
him that the likelihood of their enquiries getting anywhere near his
home were nil. The chances of the −1 patrons opening their mouths
were as likely as Prince Harry cribbing up with a sista from Stamford
Hill. Doing a piece of performance poetry for the police and being a
regular in Window's house didn't mix. If customers had something
they needed to get off their tongues they talked first and foremost to
Window.

During journey three, Schoolboy had considered going back to his
flat in Ernie with the speed of a joyrider creating new turf on the road.
The trouble with hiding was you stayed rooted, and he needed to keep
moving to find if the street was connecting him to Dexter.

Now he stood overground again, hood snug around his locks, in
the semi-bonkers bustle of the concourse at Liverpool Street. He didn't
have time to admire its wide whiteness or its upper-level Perspex-
domed shopping centre. He only had time to move his life forward

while scrapping the past as far back as his mind could butt it. The best way to move forward was to ensure that he was going in the right direction. He grasped his personal MB from his jacket pocket. His fingers did their pressing routine while he waited for Window's number to come on the screen. He pressed it against his ear.

Voicemail.

Fuckrees.

He didn't want to be talking to a personless machine when he needed to find out if life had become a little too personal. He left a message using a tone that was husky, low and quick.

'It's me. Sorry for the p.m. delay. Tell Sensi I'll rearrange. Call me asap. I need some advice on a few tales being told.'

He thrust the phone back into his pocket. His left hand dipped unconsciously into his other pocket, caressing the brick as he cursed with speed and annoyance. His breathing started picking up again. It came shallow, rising and quenching with his chest, stinging the roof of his mouth. His vision roamed over the commuters, who were all done up in respectable threads but behaving as if an annual bull-run festival was a daily occurrence.

His mind leapt to his next option. If you wanted serious information you needed a Class A bus. The best operating out of Liverpool Street was the S53 bus route. Some said it was the originator of all the narcotics bus routes. It was certainly the most profitable. Having a gateway to the city and Hackney gave it a wide clientele, with an even wider price list. As the most lucrative part of the journey were the four bus stops between Liverpool Street and Shoreditch, the S53 route had acquired the nickname The Ditch. Some gave a different interpretation to the nickname story. They claimed that although the chemical concoctions took you high they could also take you way low. Take you to a ditch you never even knew was part of your anatomy. Along with the selling of gear came the telling of stories. The S53 had some of the most comprehensive news reports you could hear outside of the World Service. And the most renowned and detached orator of all was Frankie.

Decision made Schoolboy keep his pace lively. He searched the digits of the station's clock. The most popular S53 buses at Liverpool Street were the 8.16 a.m., to give that high enough space to enter punters' bloodstreams before they said good morning to the boss, and the 17.43, ready for whatever the evening had to offer. 17.41 was tapping into its last ten seconds. Shit, he'd been underground too long. His heart banged as if it were in the wrong body. He swung forward, head leading the way, trying to mould through the wall of people. But the stubbornness of their bodies held him back.

The clock looked at him again. 17.42.

Politeness was forgotten as his elbows jabbed flesh and bones out of his way. A briefcase smacked his calf muscle. Accidental? Deliberate? He didn't care because he was already falling. His feet flopped and tripped. He wobbled, shook just like St Hilda's tower block seconds before its demolition last week. Trousers, ankle bracelets, shoe all rose up in an embrace, but he swept the palms of his hands out to break any intimacy with the tiled concrete. He grazed the ground like a prisoner who just hadn't realised he shouldn't have picked up the soap in the shower block. He popped himself upright as 17.43 openly laughed from the clock. He steadied himself, checked for the brick in his pocket and began to steamroll. Through the spiced scent of doughnuts. Up the escalator. Through the hurried spitting of the rain outside. He didn't need the know-it-all ticking of a clock to tell him that he just needed to keep going. He cast his eyes into the distance and saw the bus at its usual spot, the second-last passenger already fading into its entrance. Fuck London Transport's efficiency targets. He sprinted, legs churning, skin burning, heart yearning, as if seeing his dreams driving away. He closed his eyes briefly, the lids squeezing more energy throughout his being. He tipped his head back and pushed his chest out. He didn't have time to study the sweat peeling down the groove of his back. He didn't have time to study the tickle of cramps dancing in his thighs. He didn't have time.

The last passenger vanished from view. He was close enough to hear the wheels wake up, re-starting their circuit. The doors puffed back ready to close. He vaulted forward, gravity pushing his hood and locks back and pulling his legs forward. He landed, hardness making his skin tremble. The brick inside his jacket slapped with the lightning strike of a new disease against his side. One foot skidded along the wetness of the pavement. The other shoved between the spaces between the closing doors. The doors jammed against his trainers. He began rocking with the unsteady motion of someone whose life just wasn't right any more.

Ashara sat waiting in the back room of the cab office, crunching the nail of his middle finger. His eyes were pinned to the mobile in front of him on the desk, waiting. Waiting for it to ring. For the last two months the call had always come on a Wednesday, between five and six. As his teeth ripped a large piece of nail off, the afrobeat of the MB's ringtone vibrated in the room. He spat the nail out of his mouth as he snatched for the phone. As soon as it touched his ear he began speaking.

'You shouldn't have phoned me yesterday. We agreed a set time, a set day. Wahid was there. I almost . . .'

'Slow down. Forget Wahid . . .'

'Number 8 . . .'

'No names, little brother, remember.' The voice had a vicious layer that Ashara rarely heard. The viciousness disappeared as Number 8 continued, 'So what happened?'

'About what?'

'Don't play stupid-stupid with me. You know what I'm talking about. The phone, O!'

Number 8's use of the letter name O at the end of the word pitched Ashara back to Lagos. Back to a place where people used this sound to give emphasis to what they were saying, to give meaning. He knew exactly what Number 8 meant by using the sound. Number 8 was annoyed.

'Wahid wouldn't approve. I should never have told you about this in the first place because someone has opened their mouth to the wrong people. It wasn't you?'

'Me? We know that it isn't me who has a mouth as big as a bush-cat.'

Ashara's hand tightened around the phone with guilt and sadness. Morocco was always going to be between them until he had a face-to-face with Number 8. His eyes lifted to gaze at the family photograph taken at Wahid's graduation ten years ago.

'I wish we could all be a family again,' Ashara let out. 'I've got a present for you . . .'

'That can keep. Tell me about the phone.'

'You know I can't. I beg! Wahid would string me from the nearest street lamp . . .'

'That's OK – you're not really important enough to know, are you? You're right, I shouldn't have asked – you're not really in the loop anyway, O! It's up to you if you want to behave like a Johnny Just Come.'

'A Johnny Just Come!' Ashara squealed as his body sprung tight in the chair as he reacted to the Nigerian phrase for newly arrived brothers in England. 'Of course I am in the loop, as you put it, but I can't tell you. If Wahid knew I was even talking to you I'd be manure before nightfall and he'd hunt you down . . .'

Ashara felt the vibrations of Number 8 kissing his teeth, long and quick.

'Two can play at being hunted.'

'What do you mean?' Ashara coiled harder into the chair.

'Don't worry about that, just tell me about the delivery.'

Number 8 coaxed in a tone so gentle that Ashara felt they were children again, planning a new game.

Silence gripped him for a time, then he made his decision.

'OK. But this doesn't go any further.'

'I'm listening.'

'Our courier was jacked as they would say . . .' Ashara explained tentatively.

'Jacked? By who, O?'

'We're not sure. At least we're not yet. We've heard things. We think it might have been organised.'

'They knew what they were looking for?'

'It seems so.'

'Was it some of your own people?'

'No, of course not – it was those stupid West Indians . . .' he said bitterly. 'Them people always want what doesn't belong to them.'

'So no more America now. What ill-luck. After all that planning. What will you and Wahid do? Imagine the shame of having to face our parents back home with no money? Imagine the taunts from people who Wahid kept telling he was going to come back to Nigeria richer that the last oil strike? Imagine . . .'

'No, you don't understand. We might still make it.'

'What do you mean? You just said that . . .' Number 8's voice choked.

'You didn't let me finish. Whoever jacked us, things went wrong for them too . . .'

'But they couldn't have. I . . .' Number 8's voice abruptly chewed back any remaining words and became silent.

Ashara straightened up. 'You did what?'

'I never said I did anything.'

'Please, I beg, you didn't tell anyone?' Ashara cried, imagining Wahid slapping his head.

'Of course not. I'm going to meet you in America, remember. Just tell me what happened.'

'They were scared off while they were beating our man. Someone else appeared and picked the phone up. Some street boy.'

'Know who any of these people are?' Number 8 puffed.

'We're finding out. We know our man was jumped by two men hired by a local outfit. We don't know which one. We're not sure about the area boy – but the name Schoolboy keeps cropping up.'

Ashara heard Number 8 let out another puff, suck in a breath and then slowly release it.

'Are you sure of that name?'

'Of course I am. These people have such stupid names. School-boy . . .'

'Fine, O! I may be able to help you locate him.'

'How?'

'That isn't your problem. Just leave it with me.'

Schoolboy pushed past the pushchairs, a walking-stick attached to a stooping man and the plain I-ain't-getting-out-of-your-way ignorant to rush up the stairs of The Ditch. His chest muscles were hurting. He was getting too old for this type of runaround. Or maybe he was more scared than he thought. He swept those thoughts aside as his head rose up into the upper deck, a world where everyone looked as if they were stuck in some kind of emotional hinterland. Some tired, some excited, some looking as if they were ready to throw up on the world. No one looked behind them. What happened at the back was none of their business. If the Blues couldn't be bothered to sort it out, why should they? But this didn't interest him because for the second time in hours he entered the world of the travelling drug dealer. His vision followed the strip of fluorescent lighting on the ceiling to the back where the chairs were arranged differently from the rest of the upper floor. Five facing forward, four facing back, like a mini conference centre. The four-seaters were really two pairs stuck together with a space in the middle to continue the flow of the deck's pathway to the back. An ideal set-up for the dealers who could pretend that the rest of the world did not exist. An ideal arrangement for the city money-dealers who didn't want the world to see them as they exchanged notes for narcs. Schoolboy caught the eye of a man, flash jacket and expensive tie from neck to waist, who sat outside the dealers' domain in the next row. The man looked nervous, watchful, needy, as if he knew that stepping into the back would be like seeing the inside of a police van – but what alternative did he have when he needed that chemical jerk? Schoolboy blinked and left the man behind as he settled on to the four men in the back. The back of a designer-dressed customer, two dealers in the centre and the main dealer, Frankie, in the far right-hand corner seat.

He caught Frankie's caramel face and green eyes, the same green eyes that had got him the job as the main dealer on The Ditch. Frankie's boss thought that city folk would find green eyes less threatening to look into than eyes that had their heritage in Africa. The type of Africa that had nothing to do with cosy package holidays to Gambia and more to do with life that started on the Kingsland Road. Frankie acknowledged Schoolboy with a smile and punched his goatee-covered chin downwards. Schoolboy knew this was Frankie's signal for him to turn around and go back downstairs. They had done this many times and had long ago established the pattern of communicating through their mobiles. One up, one down, just in case the discussion was too hot for other ears to know.

The seat in the left-hand corner of the lower deck was free – well, almost free as a lady in turquoise cotton and a head-wrap had half the seat covered in her don't-mess-with-me backside. Schoolboy wasn't about to create any unnecessary cabaret so he squeezed in as best he could. Once The Ditch hit the Hawksmoor church that marked the end of the City and the opening of Hackney, the suited passengers began to get off to make their return journey to Liverpool Street. Schoolboy pulled out his business line, scrolled to phonebook and pressed Frankie's number.

'Hear about Dexter?'

'Which Dexter?' Frankie answered with the kind of voice that would ring perfectly in the alto section of a choir.

'The one that I hear got done over at Speedball and is now brown bread.'

'Oh, that Dexter. Yeah, it's just surfing the news wave. The police have Speedball all taped up. No one's going in, no one's going out.'

'What I need to know is what's doing the rounds about it?'

Another passenger started to talk loudly on his mobile phone, distracting Schoolboy, making him miss Frankie's words. Schoolboy shifted closer to the emergency door.

'Frankie, I couldn't hear a ting. Some geezer doesn't realise that he don't need no mobile 'cos his family can already hear him all the way back in Kurdistan.'

Frankie's voice rose a touch.

'I said the facts are that his back and neck were found all floppy and there was no way he was going to be straightened out. The rest of the grapevine is a maze of fact and fiction. Some saying this, some saying that.'

'So run me through a few of the stories.'

'You know the usual – it's a drugs ting; owing someone too much dosh ting; running his mouth a bit too much ting. The unusual lines are that he was dabbling in someone else's honeyz pot. Another one is that he had a new acquaintance from across the river who was taking him to places he wasn't meant to be . . .'

'What acquaintance?' As he spoke, Schoolboy felt the warmth from the woman's bum push him further into the corner.

'Don't know, mate. I would tell you if I heard. I don't usually ask the questions, but why the intense interest? You and Dexter weren't exactly Batman and Robin.'

Schoolboy could have told him the truth, but he'd already decided that this would be a need-to-know conversation. And what Frankie needed to know was that he lamented the death of an old school-friend.

'Although Dexter was never part of my inner crew, we did go to school together. I always take an interest in the death of former class-mates.'

Schoolboy let Frankie take control of the rest of the conversation, which veered from how well Frankie's kids were doing in school to how the new East London Line tube connection was going to open a new vein of possibilities for the trading of drugs. The right side of his brain was listening but the left side was trying to decide whether he still had anything to worry about. The woman's body squeezed him harder, pushing the brick close against his chest as if it wanted some company. But the only company Schoolboy wanted and needed were the knives.

9

Evie swallowed the evening air with frustration as she tucked her car into the small space under the red and blue markings of a street scribe, which graced the large peeling canvas of the anonymous building like multicoloured damp. This was a moment for cursing, but she wasn't going to do it. Chucking out bad energy meant a bad evening. Parking at one of these Hackney school-based meetings was always such a mess. There was never any room left in the playground with its territorial parking games. You either parked in the light so that the thieves could see what they were doing, or in the dark so that no one could see them. Either way it didn't matter. Like the rest of Hackney's population she had no alternative but to let her car take its chances.

Hackney.

She tasted the word inside her mouth as she cut the car engine. It had once been her home, but not any more. She ran her tongue around the topside of her gums as if she was getting rid of something sour coming from the root of her throat. She knew she was late. The meeting started at 7 p.m. and she was at least ten minutes after that. She couldn't stand unpunctuality. Couldn't stand the fact that she might be perpetuating the myth of BPT – black people's time. She'd grown up in a family where if you were meeting at eight everyone knew you meant nine; meeting for nine everyone knew it meant ten. She couldn't stand the fact that she was like what *they* accused *us* of being. Hadn't Schoolboy confronted her with that once? Whether he was right or wrong was for her to know and for him never to find out.

Cold air and an interest-free credit leaflet licked the turn-ups of her black trousers as she briskly took the pavement towards St Dunstan's Primary School's Victorian building. The black gloss gate was already opened so she continued across through the peace of the playground, thinking she didn't really want to be there. Meetings, meetings, meetings, governors' meetings, committee meetings, bored-out-of-your-box meetings. But the worst, the absolute worst were these community meetings. 'Parents against violence,' 'Mothers against violence,' 'Kids against violence.' They were running out of names – what about 'Violence against violence'? The inside of her single-ringed hand pushed against the swing doors. She knew she shouldn't mock because that's how she'd got where she was going. What got her one step ahead was that she was a local girl. Born, bred and schooled. None of this scholarship stuff. What better way than to get the community to reform its slack ways than to park one of its own in front of them. She was one of the most sought-after consultants in this field. Not many of her colleagues were willing to come into urban melt-down. Writing articles from a safe distance was more their style. But not her, she was known for getting her hands dirty. She'd rejuvenated project after project, had the ear of some people in local government, and was considered good for getting results. She soon realised that people were willing to pay a bundle to someone who was willing to roll around in the filth, so she'd gone freelance three years ago and never looked back. The only problem was lately she'd started to think that her job was a lot of doo-doo in the sky. Things had got worse not better and she was tired of telling herself anything else. But still here she was at the first Rainsbridge group for 'Safe schools, safe kids.'

She entered a long corridor with its eye-piercing yellow walls and standard brown tiles that reminded her of the time she'd been summoned to the headmaster's office when she was twelve years old. Assault and battery Mr Wicks had called it, she'd called it defending her own patch. She stretched her lips, letting her school memories dissolve in her mind as she soaked up the warmth from the display of children's work on the panels on the wall. She briskly strode on, with the hurried hum of a Hoover in the background accompanying her to the double blue doors at the end. Evie stopped, settled her shoulders, breathed in and out, then pushed forward. She entered a hall where the smell of spaghetti hoops was overpowered by the scent of emotions emitting from the sparse group in attendance. Evie walked quietly between the rows of orange seats towards the long table at the front. Mr Prince already stood in front of the twenty-strong audience warming the agenda. His habit of putting an 'h' sound in front of every word marked him out as a Jamaican. She knew he meant well but the times were striking for younger men to get on the platform and let it all out.

What, like Schoolboy?

She did not need him jeering at her hypocrisy throughout the meeting. She shoved him out of her mind. Mr Prince needed to take his pork-pie hat and thirty-year-old suit back home where he could relax and reflect on a life well lived. Smile fixed, she scanned the audience, the smile drooping inside as she saw most of the usual suspects. Mr 'something must be done', Ms 'things can only get worse' and Mr and Ms 'everyting will be cool come the revolution'. Not many dads present, which didn't surprise her. There were a few faces she hadn't seen on the circuit which made her hopeful that some decent dialogue would be forthcoming.

'Now, ladies and gentlemen, I would like to introduce Yvette Campbell, one of our most prominent community workers, who will talk to you about some of the work she has done with schools to make them safe and secure for our young people.'

There was a hard bash of applause. Evie stepped forward and let her mouth and hands do the talking. A talk she knew was full of this project, that project, this conclusion, that conclusion, this statistic, that statistic. And of course there had to be targets. Targets to show how many children would be involved. Targets to measure success. Targets for the sake of bloody targets. She gave them what they wanted to hear. But she wasn't happy hearing it. Back in the day she'd been in the right place at the right time. Teaching and social work had been in much demand. Now she felt that the time was still right but the place so wrong. Evie stopped after twenty minutes, standing drained in the energy of the crowd's applause.

The next stage was the bit she hated. Question time. Time for members of the community who came to these meetings because they didn't have anyone else to talk to, to throw out their deranged enquiries.

Without being invited, a woman in the back row stood up. Small, suited, with straightened hair pulled back into a ponytail as if she wanted her black and blatant face to be remembered. Evie didn't let herself be fooled by the appearance, she'd met enough so-called professional black women who might no longer have the purple-and-gold weave-on but still couldn't get the ragga gal out of their system. The woman started speaking in a voice that had grown rich somewhere in East London.

'I have two children at this school. See that picture over there?' She used her well-shaped nails to point at a child's picture mounted in a large clip-frame outside the door of Emerald class, Year 2. The picture was thick blue, black and orange brush-strokes of a house with the obligatory tree and flowers. The woman quick-stepped over to the picture and stood in front of it.

'One of my girls did that. I'm really proud of her and I'm going to make sure I remain proud of her when she leaves school. Proud when she goes to university. Proud when she gets her first job. Proud when she becomes a mother.'

She stepped away from the picture but did not approach her seat.

'Since I was their age I've been hearing the so-called community round here weeping and wailing about violence, guns, drugs, underachievement, racism and the rest of it. Why don't the government or the council or the police or the schools or the teachers or the man in the moon do something about it? Well, let me tell you people, if you want to wait for the government or the council or the police or the schools or the teachers to do something about it you'll be waiting till kingdom come . . .'

'We're here, ain't we, so we must be interested,' challenged a woman from the middle row who wore a striped bobble hat.

'So you think coming to meetings and sitting on your broad backside is going to get the job done?'

People at the front swivelled their necks to bend into the face with the words. Evie wriggled to the front of her chair. The woman didn't look so small to her any more.

'Let me tell you that life don't go so. If you want something done about it – do it yourselves. You want dealers to stop juggling near our schools – go and confront them. You're fed up with what your children are taught in schools – teach them yourselves. You're tired of the streets being dirty and covered in graffiti – go and clean them up. You understand? The people who run this country don't give a damn about places like this – they want us to live in squalor, they want our children to grow up and be thick, they want us to have a brain but not use it – that way we're no threat. But if people stand up for themselves and take control – that's when they start worrying. So get off your knees and start acting like men and women for a change. And if you're not going to do that then shut up and keep beating your tambourine on the street corner and stop telling yourself you don't like the music you're hearing because you're the one spinning the turntable, darling.'

Chairs began to squeak as the audience moved around in unease, but Evie tingled in excitement. It had been a long time since she'd met another sista who thought like her. The woman finished, neck strapped back as she walked back to her chair, leaving a fire smouldering in the room. Another person took the floor but Evie's mind was ticking away at possibilities.

When she saw the woman from the back leaving early, she handed over to Mr Prince and rushed to follow her out into the corridor.

'Excuse me – I'd just like to say I was very impressed by what you said.'

'Thank you, darling.' The woman turned to face her.

Her neck was pumped well back, stretching the troubled skin on her face. A face that Evie suspected was only a few years older than hers. The woman's eyelashes fluttered rapidly as if she was trying to get away from the glare of cameras at the wrong press conference.

'I was just wondering if you were active in the community or the school? We could use someone who's passionate and committed and believes in action . . .'

The woman smiled, her eyelashes slowing down. Evie stared into eyes that were such a light brown she suspected that if this woman had stayed in the womb one more day they would have had a touch of green.

'I'm very active in the community, sweetheart – but I'm afraid my professional commitments mean I don't have any time to sit on any of your "committees".'

She turned to go. Evie dug into her pocket before the woman could disappear from her life.

'Please take my card in case you change your mind.'

The woman took it and then strode off.

'I'm sorry, I didn't catch your name.' Evie called after her.

The woman turned back and smiled her smile.

'People just call me Queen.'

Queen turned sharply, pushed through the doors and strutted across the playground. When she got to the school gates Evie saw her pull out a mobile and make a call. Evie sighed. Another one had got away. Then she went back to her meeting. When she returned, a man was on his feet explaining that the education department must be run by aliens because he'd written a hundred letters to the Director of Education and not received one reply.

The silver Jeep waited for Queen across the road from the Little Monkey pub, a few minutes' walk from the school she had just left. She admired their choice of vehicle. Nothing like sitting on twenty-two wheels with a .22 calibre in your pocket. As she approached she knew that the three men inside could see her getting bigger in the rear-view window. The two men in the back sat with the expectation of having enough puff to go round a prison yard one more time. The man in the front had the same air but was leaner, the bones of his fingers grasping the steering wheel. Queen opened the front door and climbed inside. Usual practice was for her driver to get out and open the door, but they knew better than to make a fuss today.

'Is this car clean?' she asked Cuttie, the driver, verifying its stolen status.

The warmth from the car began to moist over the foundation on her forehead and nose.

'Yeah, Queen, some consultants got it from Essex way this afternoon.'

'Did they avoid the main roads and go down the side streets like I've told you to tell them?'

There was a slight pause. She hated pauses. They always stank of trouble.

'Yes . . .'

'Are you sure?' she cut in quick, voice compact, each word uttered as if it was stuck in the back of her throat.

No answer came because he knew she already knew the answer.

'I've told you before about main roads and cameras – it's sloppy, Cuttie, don't do it again.'

'I'm sorry, Queen.'

'Sorry? Do I look like the parole board?' she continued, her voice slipping further back into her voicebox. Sorry was her most hated word in the world and he'd been working for her from the beginning and should know that. Sorry was for pussies who had too much time on their hands. The whimsical tune of Three Blind Mice floated from the mobile in her pocket. As she pulled it out she smiled, remembering that the nursery rhyme was her youngest's favourite. She stared hard at the text message:

the MB has gone in2 fin air 8

Queen's lips turned around each other. The signature of 8 was all she knew about the contact who had given her the information about the phone a week ago. Her source wouldn't take money, didn't want a cut of the deal, just claimed to be doing the world a favour. The heat renewed its attack on Queen's face. Favours always came at a price. Eyelashes rapidly sweeping, she pressed the button underneath the window.

The wind rushed her face, but the most powerful feeling blowing in the car was her annoyance that other people still had the power to fuck with her life. Well, her next visitor would soon learn that he had chosen the wrong person. She'd relied on him to get things sorted. Allowed him to choose two idiots to do the job and what did she have to show for it, zero merchandise. Some men just wanted to dribble over her hips, her heels, her hair-do. The smart ones saw her for what she was, someone already reclining in a first-class seat on the ride to success. Her hand cupped her neck, then one finger began to move across and back, back and across, as if she was trying to create a chain. Yes, she was looking forward to meeting her next visitor.

'This isn't the bumper cars, Cuttie, so put your foot down because we've got a lot of calls to make before the school run starts tomorrow morning.'

The comfort and seclusion of Ernie had never looked so good, Schoolboy told himself, as he forced the key into his front door. Schoolboy pushed in, turned back to the door and clipped it shut. Neck bent, he gazed at the bare floor below the door. No calling cards greeted him from the Blues. He knew the police were not in the habit of leaving *we missed you* cards, but you never could tell what new strategy they would use to try and get in tune with the community. For the first time in hours the pulse of his eyes beat to a regular rhythm.

He stepped forward the same time that Jim Reeves started jangling in his clothing. He didn't need to be talking to anyone before he had time to sort out his own thoughts. But that was people for you, always demanding he give them priority over his own progress. He pulled out the first MB his hand fell on. Once in his hand he realised that it wasn't ringing. He dropped it back into his pocket and tugged out his personal mobile. Only three people had his personal details. Window, Evie and Tammy. He'd only given Tammy his details in case anything should ever happen to Evie. His ladyeez were kept strictly to his other mobile like the rest of his business. The ringing stopped just as his finger touched green. Window's name came on the screen. Shit – he'd forgotten all about him since heading home. Boy, his mind was feeling too messed up. He pressed redial.

'Window. So glad . . .'

'You've made me and my house look foolish.' Window's words came deep, clenched and booming.

Schoolboy remembered the fear he had felt the first time he'd met Window.

'Look, I called . . .'

'You know the rules. If you can't make the meet you let me know. Before not after.'

He knew that if there was one thing his friend hated it was lecturing so-called professionals on the rules of the game. Besides, he could understand Window's anger. Protocol demanded that you let the householder know of any change in arrangements. But to leave the householder and guest in a position of no-show left the householder having to make your apologies. Having to feel the anger of the guest. Having to feel fucking stupid. By the sound of Window's voice Schoolboy could tell Window felt more than stupid.

From the hitch in Window's voice he knew he wasn't finished.

'I was worried about you, G.' The soothing quality was back in his friend's tone.

Window's enquiry knocked the breath back out of Schoolboy. The last time someone had worried about him had been when Mum tidied his shirt collar as they stood in front of passport control at Gatwick. Waiting three long years for someone else to touch their warmth to him made him understand the loneliness of his life.

'Sorry.' His breath parted with the word because he really meant it.

'So why you didn't come?'

'Cos I heard that Dexter has finally met the woman of his dreams. The only problem is it's Lady Death.'

'Dexter B?'

'One and the same. I take it you haven't heard?'

'Nah, my nose has been rooting in too many other things today to take notice of punters' tales at the bar. So what took place?'

'Details are a bit fluffy at the mo. What I need to know now is whether I feature on the Blue boys' list of potential helpees and if they've been around roaming in your yard.'

'The colour of my house remained strictly Blue-free today. You're worrying too much. Getting too para. No one is going to help the Blues find directions to my door.'

'Hope not 'cos I can't afford for the Blues to hold me back now.'

'I was just calling you to say you need to keep your vision projected over your shoulder because Sensi was making some kind of noise when you didn't show . . .'

'About what? Anything specific?' Suspicion was back as his best friend.

'The usual – pride puked over in public; who did you think you were. I even offered to put him in touch with other wholesalers if he wanted a phone but he wasn't interested. He was one vex brother when he left, so watch out. Business is calling me out of town until Saturday, so we'll see when I get back.'

They swapped words for a while longer and then closed the conversation down. Schoolboy tapped the mobile twice against his heart, knowing there would never be anyone like Window again in his life. He tucked the phone back into his pocket. He drifted towards the bedroom and wondered how he was going to live in a place where he just knew people wouldn't understand him the way Window did. The way Evie did. The way London did. As he shrugged his jacket off, he reminded himself that today's events meant he might never leave so this whole nostalgia trip might be for nothing. He tipped his timepiece into the light. Minutes were speeding to eight, while days were spinning closer to Sunday. And still no money. Still no knives.

Schoolboy slipped into the kitchen and flicked the light on. Stupid move, he realised. He flexed back his finger against the light switch, but the sound of the front door banging with the hardness of someone looking for trouble got there first. He didn't move. His finger didn't move.

Fuckrees.

The Blues had finally found him on their radar. The last time they'd picked him up had been to try and get info on another dealer. They'd kept him in a holding cell for a day and night, but his lips had remained stuck tight. He didn't have another day in his life to give them because he knew then he'd never get out of London. The door lifted again with the determination of someone who was going to get their way. No way was that the Blues. They didn't do second knocks, just burst into your life. The only alternative was this Sensi character blowing steam outside his door.

He knew Window wouldn't have given his personals to Sensi, but somebody else sure would have. That was the trouble with modern Hackney, it was too full of people grinning in your face one day and running you down with their mouth the next. His finger curled off the switch. He crept, on the pads of his toes, to shove himself against the wall between the bathroom and the kitchen. His breath came in shallow, soundless spurts. If there was a third knock he knew he would have to answer it. His mind began to run through a library of stories to flip out to Sensi when he opened the door. He waited, sending out the strongest prayer for the knock not to come.

But it came rebounding throughout the whole flat, swinging the bedroom door shut against its frame. The only way to deal with Sensi was to have one of those man-to-man discussions which made Sensi feel as if God had created him on the eighth day and Schoolboy was the most innocent person on earth. Once the ground between them was smooth the deal could once again take place. His dimples started to appear because the day could once again be his. But if Sensi was packing a piece he might not have time for any story. He shook his locks back and eased towards the door. No point asking who it was because he knew who stood in front of his life. He opened the door with fingers firmly in control.

'Hey, bredda . . .' he started as the door opened, keen to get his version of events in first. His words were cut off when he realised that it wasn't Sensi who stood before him.

10

The jeep and Queen's enforced silence bent towards Clapton's high street. Two minutes later they turned into Castle Lane and into Castle Terrace, its slim iron balconies and Victorian Gothic style still trying to seduce people as they passed by the Upper Side. It sat on the edge of what outsiders called Murder Mile. Media hype claimed that it had become one of the most dangerous places in London for multiple gun play, but locals said the real murder was that the authorities had let its ninctccnth-century splendour dissolve into decay. Queen knew that her next action wasn't going to help its image with the outside world, but everyone has to take care of their own business in their own way.

'Cuttie and Glass-Eye, you come with me. Thimble, keep an eye on the wheels,' Queen ordered as she eased out of the vehicle. She swung the door behind her, breathed in the cooling air and let her head and chin retract. The two men bundled around their leader as their heated steps burned towards the block. The air was diluted with particles of dust coming from the men working on scaffolds on the neighbouring block. Castle Terrace had an intercom service, but the door was partially opened. The inside of the building was cream white, narrow, anonymous. Queen hiked up the concrete steps shielded between the bulk of her two men until they found the flat they were looking for. Flat 9A.

One of Queen's henchmen fiddled with the lock of the sturdy door until it clicked open. The single-bedroom flat was typical passing-through territory. Short-term lease, limited furnishings, mash-down kitchen slumped in the living room corner. Enough to get by, but not enough to relax. Which was just as well because what she had planned would fit exactly into that ethos. They marched further into the living room, where the only sign of occupancy was the mound of clothing littering the tobacco-infested carpet. The groans from the closed adjoining room added to the cheapness, like a man trying to expel phlegm. Queen nodded to her men. They knew the routine. She held back as they bowled across the space and watched as they kicked the door of the room containing the noises. The human noises were still grunting, but with the pitch of surprise taking control. She followed at her own pace, her expression primed back with the look of someone who had just had dirt flushed into her face. The smell of sex and its by-products of sweat and smoke were the fixed fragrance of the room. In the room were a woman and a man. Queen ignored the woman. Her prey was twisted up on the mattress, his body tensed as if nailed against the disillusioned green-papered walls. His frantic breathing propelled his collar bones up and out, stretching the skin around his neck veins a lighter brown than the darkening colour of his face.

'Jackie.'

The name groaned from Schoolboy's throat as his eyes ripped into Jackie Jarvis. The breath that left his mouth swelled more with relief than with the syllables that made up her name. His instincts had been wrong. Now, with the darkness bedding down for the night before him, he realised that his instincts had been going wrong since the brick had caught his hand on fire at the Junction. Jackie's orange ripe hair and searching freckles added to the blush of the balcony light. She didn't have on any make-up. But she didn't need it with all the different emotions colouring her face.

'Jackie, I could squeeze you with love,' he exalted, but he wouldn't because she was such a downright pain.

He couldn't afford to get carried away with the rush of relief because he still feared that Sensi or the Blues were going to hitch themselves over the balcony. He grabbed Jackie's bony wrist, pulled her inside his home and kicked the door shut. Her presence made the passage splash from brown and pink to red. As he opened his mouth to speak, Jackie thrust her pelvis forward, forcing him against the wall. She tipped up on her toes, as if she'd been waiting in a queue for too long, and imposed her lips over his. Her soaked mouth started sliding, slipping, slipping, sliding. Finally it found and fixed to a position it liked. The sensation was like having his bum groped – nice, but unnecessary. The feeling moved upwards and he noticed the smell of nicotine-blown apples in her hair. Red apples. Their combined feeling travelled downwards to his fingers stapled to her wrist. He felt her pulse moving as if she knew she'd better make the most of the moment because she didn't know when it would happen again. The feelings joined with his brain and he finally registered what she was sending into the world – loneliness. Funny, all that noise coming from her kids and video and he'd never figured her for the lonely type. He eased his head forward and let her take from him, not sure what he was giving. Satisfied, she unglued their lips and boxed him in with her gaze.

'Don't get any ideas. Just me and your lips had some unfinished business.'

He was grateful that it hadn't been undesirables brooding at the door, but that didn't mean he had time to play Kiss Chase with Jackie.

'Look, Jackie . . .' he began easing his body and fingers away.

'You ever tried cocoa-butter lip balm?'

'Jackie . . .'

'My ex Paul used it all the time.'

'From what I hear your Paul wasn't only smearing cocoa butter on his own lips.'

He stopped when he noticed her hurt push her back on to the balls of her feet.

'Jackie,' he started to apologise, his hands fluttering at his side with indecision whether to touch her with regret or to stand there like the plank he was.

'Don't worry about it,' she interrupted, but the shadow dusting the outline of her face gave him another answer. 'I just came up to give you this. I signed for it when you were out.'

She dug into her back trouser pocket and pulled out an envelope. Registered delivery, with a Grenada stamp at the top. He took it, but didn't really see it, still preoccupied with more pressing thoughts.

'I've still got that parcel downstairs for you. It was too bloody heavy to lug up the stairs again. If you don't come and get it soon I'm taking it down to the Oxfam shop. I'm off.'

She had already opened the door and banged it behind her before he could say thanks. Before he could say that she wasn't the only one feeling lonely.

He remembered the letter in his hands, already knowing it was from Mum. She always knew when he needed someone to blow words of confidence his way. He moved into the kitchen. A kitchen that was the most important room in the flat. The kitchen wasn't fitted by House Beautiful standards but it was the most fitted part of his life, with its beige aged units, hand-me-down cooker and fridge and work surfaces that he cleansed daily with vinegar and lemon. No curtains or blinds covered the windows because he loved the feeling of light flooding him as he stood and cooked. It was his real home, the other rooms were mere outbuildings. He leaned against a work surface, even forgetting the possibility of trouble peering through the window. It was hard for him to break the lifelong habit of bowing down before his mum. Everything and everyone else just had to wait in line. He held the envelope with both hands, feeling its calm, its blessings, its spirit. There was no point going into all the patterns in his mum's life because there were only three things you needed to understand about her.

She worked hard for her children, her man and for the first twenty years in England, to send money down every month to her parents and grandmother back home.

She didn't give out any nonsense, so she didn't expect to take it.

She'd lived for the day when she would build her house and settle on her share of family land in Grenada's idle sun.

Simple life with simple rules and she had stuck to each one. There had been a few loops along the way, but she'd stayed centred, fixed, kept her head forward, eyes blazing straight. He'd never expected her to leave even though he knew it was what kept her going after Dad's death. So she had left on a drizzling day in March. Schoolboy cut his finger under the envelope flap, shook out the paper and began to read, knowing the pattern of the letter would be the same as usual. How's life treating you? A description of the daily death announcements on

Grenadian TV. A more in-depth description of some everyday life occurrence – this time it focused on Mrs Williams swearing that she knew when her Ted would be dead because spirits were pulling her big toe while she slept for a week before he keeled over in the rum shop. The final section always came back to him. Had he stopped all that rude behaviour? Had he found a sweet girl to help him smooth the bedclothes? Had he gone back to the kitchen to take up the knives again? He laughed out loud as he opened a drawer and took out paper and pen. He scanned his cookery book collection on the windowsill and pulled off his *Italian Meals for Crowds*. He ran to his bedroom and sat cross-legged on the bed and started to write. He needed his mum to know that he had made a change. That he was back doing what she had always wanted him to do. That he was back in the kitchen using his knives the best way that he could. He bowed his head and started to write furiously. He told her all about Michael's offer for him to come and join his restaurant in Devon. He lifted his head and smiled because he could hear her asking, 'Are there any black people there?' His head tipped forward again as he resumed writing. When he finished he swung his eyes over his written words. He pushed his own letter aside as he picked up Mum's letter, which lay on the bed beside him. He read her last words.

May the spirit of God be working in you. Remember, son, if you want something out of life, you got to keep running like a goat looking for a pea tree.

The woman next to Sensi crushed her eyelids together as another squirt of his blood hit her below the ear. It didn't drip but leeched on to her skin, thick, like dull brown gum absorbing into her pores. Her head bowed low towards the filled ashtray marooned on the floor. Her rambling breathing spread ash like flecks of white and grey paint against her shocked brown skin.

Queen balanced her stance at the foot of the bed, while one of her men stood at her side, the other delivering a few slaps to announce her presence.

'I'm so pleased, Sensi, that you're managing to enjoy my hospitality, but I have to say that isn't the level of femalehood I would have provided for you.' Queen raised her voice to compete with the noise from the building works outside.

She heard his bubbling breathing, watched his squirming, smelt his metallic salty blood. The best way to get a man's attention was to get right inside his face. She let her gaze terrorise Sensi's bedmate. The woman lifted her head towards Queen. Although her cheeks were wet from the fear battering her face, the backdrop of emerging creases across her face told another story. She was a classic one-credit twenty-pound girl. Give her enough to pump her mobile with a minimum of £20 worth of credit and she was yours for the night. This type of woman had appeared on the scene the same time that phone texts had started to do the public's talking. Buying them a drink wasn't good enough, they needed to leave with some evidence of progress.

Queen felt for the bundle of fifties in her jacket pocket and pulled out a ton. She used her forefinger and thumb to wave the two notes in the air as if moving dirt away from her face. Sensi's new friend was lost to him as her eyes remained transfixed by the money. Queen didn't judge her. The business now ruffling the bed no longer had anything to do with Sensi's ex-lady. The woman leapt up, took the money, careful not to snatch it, and rushed from the room to pick up her clothes and say see-ya to the flat that had offered clitorious sex, but now was simply no longer a turn-on.

Queen turned her head and lifted her right eyebrow to Cuttie, who stood next to the bed. Sensi needed to feel what could be coming his way. Cuttie hesitated for a second, then galvanised his frame with ease and landed a knuckle-based punch straight across Sensi's belly button. Sensi bawled in pain, his body kicking upwards. Queen was pleased with his response because she wanted him to remember what his own pain felt like scraping the walls of this room.

'So where is the phone you were meant to jack?'

Although he was still obviously in discomfort, she knew he would answer immediately because fear was the rawest emotion kicking in the room.

'Someone, them have it.'

'And that someone is?'

This time his words never came. She wasn't surprised. She wasn't surprised that in her absence he had devised his own plans. Plans that involved him and the mobile phone. Plans that didn't include her. People like him always had their own plans. Queen's fingers stretched and danced because his greed became the strongest emotion in the room.

She lifted her left eyebrow to her other man, who took out a roll of silver tape. He unwound it and cut off a strip with his side teeth. He passed the tape over to Queen who took the ends between the forefinger and thumb of both hands. While she strolled around the side of the bed, Cuttie grasped Sensi's pony-tailed beard and snapped his head back. Queen bent close over him and saw the fear in his face.

She placed her mouth next to his ear and whispered, 'I hope you didn't let on why I want that phone.'

Sensi quickly shook his head. She raised her mouth away from him, satisfied. Her men only knew that she was expecting a delivery and nothing more. She pulled the tape taut and laid it across his mouth. She used the pads of her thumbs to smooth it across, giving it the finishing touches of a masterpiece.

She straightened and spoke.

'I don't like to ask questions more than once.'

She turned her back, letting her boys do their job. The pounding and screeching of the building works became louder as she moved to stand near the beaten bedside cabinet. She opened its single drawer. Two books stared back. She lifted one out to check out its title. Hickson's *Commentary on the Gospel of St Mark*. All the noise around her sliced away from her ears and vanished as she began to remember the choking coldness of the Stepney nights of her childhood as she read the Bible in preparation for her Holy Communion. The sacrament of salvation. She flicked through the pages of the commentary and stopped at a passage describing the relationship of a vine to its branches being like a believer who needed to be constantly cleansed in order to enter into eternal glory with the Lord.

She turned back towards the bed, just as a rush of rain began to fight with the window. Book still in hand, she stared at Sensi, not interested in the blood. Not interested in the contorted pain surging in his body. She was only interested in his fright. She locked straight with his liquid-filled eyes.

'Do you feel cleansed, because I feel you're starting to understand my question?'

Cuttie whipped the tape from Sensi's mouth. Sensi's sour breath punctured the air, revealing the flattened clots of blood that moistened the inside of his mouth. If she hadn't been wearing nail polish she would have done it herself, but plum and red just didn't mix.

'Him name's Schoolboy,' Sensi pushed out, hurting.

'And where can he be found?'

'I don't have him details.'

She believed him. The name was enough. The rest would be easy.

'Now I want you to get your mobile and give them out-of-towners you hired a ring.'

Queen saw Sensi unfold and lengthen his hand towards the floor where his phone lay. Looking at his face, she knew that if that were one of her daughters she would have felt their pain.

'Now tell them that you want them to meet you later at the Junction at 2 a.m.'

His pain held him back, but she only had time to keep moving forward.

'Unless you're looking for another slap or two you'll hurry it along,' she said, allowing Sensi for the first time to hear the Stepney Green roots plugged in her voice.

The phone slipped at his ears from the fresh blood. He pulled it back into place, punched the buttons and waited for the voice to appear.

'Listen, be at the Junction tonight at two. The Nod wants to meet . . . Just listen me say.'

He paused as a trickle of blood renewed the colour of his top lip.

'Nothing will happen to you . . . Me say use your ears to listen, right. The Nod just wants to talk and find a new strategy, understand.

Don't even think about using your roller skates up the M1 or me will find both of you and mash you up so your legs won't be any use again, check me.'

He kept the phone gripped in his fist when he finished. She turned her back and her men got ready to follow her. Just as she got to the edge of the room she slowly turned back. Her men had already anticipated her move and stepped to the side. She faced Sensi, who had sunk back to roll with his pain on the bed. She took her time flexing her legs his way again, enjoying the unknown look of panic she saw floating across the skin of his face. Once she stood over him she took out five notes from her pocket and threw them across the bed sheet, which was twisted into his bare toes.

'I think that my association with you this time, Sensi, has been a great disappointment, so the best thing you can do is to get back across that river. I hear that The Elephant and Castle is on the up and up these days.'

She slid the warmth of her palm across the cover of the book and held her eyes shut for a few seconds. She was oblivious to the eye contact that passed between Cuttie and Sensi. She reopened them and carefully placed the book and her memories back into the drawer. This time when she dismissed Sensi with her back she was already twisting through the new information. Her mouth screwed into a smile. Thinking of the phone. Thinking of the idiot bwoys who were next on her calling card list.

11

12.30 a.m. Thursday was usually prime time for Schoolboy to select his most classic garms and breeze-step it to an all-nighter. But this Thursday he knew there was going to be no party time. He was still worried about the Blues. Still worried that he wouldn't be able to purchase the knives on their last day up for sale. He sat in the front room, the TV his only companion, with hardness eating into him from the settee's texture and his feelings inside. Worry had become a stimulant, stirring him up, keeping him awake. No way was he going back to a cell for a day, a night, an hour. That was the problem with trying to let your life glide forward, there was always the possibility you could step into a pile of cack. Hadn't he learned that one with Susie-honey? She had moved in bringing sanity, security, stability. Well, that's what she'd told him. Life would be so good, she'd gushed. Life had been total good for all of one day. Then she wanted some ice around her fingers, not one but two. Engagement and wedding. He'd done the first, not the second. Then she wanted to give birth to his Isaac, wanted to be a unit. Kids spelled responsibility, a responsibility he hadn't been ready for. So two months after she had moved in he had provoked a fight and Susie-honey had thrown her ring at him. Susie-honey had left and he'd pawned the ring. That was the first and last time someone had got deep inside his space. Better to stay in the same place where at least the ground around remained clean most of the time. Who was he mugging? Not much purity left in his life.

Thursday started taking hold, bringing with it a sense of safety. The Blues were unlikely to come calling now. He imagined Dexter's name being written under the file headed Black on Black. No point spending too much time investigating that. If the community didn't want to speak up let them shoot each other to death. Less work for the

Blues to clean up. The settee fluffed back into its usual snugness, with Lord Tribulation's music floating warm and giddy from two floors up. He wasn't much of a drinker but always kept a bottle of brandy in the place for emergencies, colds and relaxation. He stood up, heading for the kitchen and bottle to drink in some calmness. He turned and stepped towards the door as a news update flashed on the TV screen and sparked inside his home.

> *The police in East London have insisted they're keeping an open mind after the discovery of yet another murder victim in the Cinnamon Junction area. It is believed that the victim, thought to be Turkish or Kurdish, was found by two boys while they were walking to school on Monday morning.*

Schoolboy swung back into the room, shoulders stiff, as his every sense tuned into the voice of the newscaster.

> *The police have refused to comment on speculation that the victim may have had connections with organised crime in the area. Now to a story about the increasingly disturbing world of what is commonly called car-jacking.*

Schoolboy flew to the television and banged the off button as the newscaster started reporting about an Essex girl-about-town whose silver Jeep had been stolen. His hand came up and cupped the hot breath pouring out of his mouth.

Fuckrees.

Fuckress.

Fuckrees.

It had to be his guy at the Junction. His hand fell from his mouth as he began stalking and pacing the room. Now he had two dead men trying to suck his future life from him. If the Blues were still after him he couldn't be lifted with the brick. What if they took fingerprints? What if they found Mr Istanbul's life all over it? What if they decided to hold him because he was their only connection, not just to Dexter, but the dead bod at the Junction? The room started to close in, the dampness of a cell sniffing about him, over him. *Mingling in the breath of a dead man can only bring bad luck.* Why did his mum have to be so right all the time?

He belted into the bedroom, finding the dead man's phone lying alone on the wooden side table Evie had bought him for his twenty-fifth birthday. He couldn't even call it the brick any more. Nicknames were for things and people you liked. Now the Nokia was just another obstacle adding to the wall he had to climb over to get to his future. Yesterday the Nokia's buttons had laid back with the frivolity of good-luck chips. Now they reared up with the reality of polished tomb-stones. The mini-button at the top stared back at him with the fixation of an eye up to no good. He snatched his gaze away, not wanting to give it a chance to start winking with the seduction of a pro knowing she was going to rip him off as soon as she got him round the corner.

He made a decision. The brick had to go.

He rummaged in his wardrobe and hacked out the first coat his hands fell on. It was his best coat. Bruised beige, Thai cotton and moving like a dance partner who loved the feel of him. He couldn't believe that yesterday he had stepped out of his flat into a world that was wrapped over all neat, straight-lined, defined, and now he prepared to go out again with the start of a new day with all kinds of shit stinking up his life. As he rapidly fastened the buttons over his boxer shorts and bare chest he legged it back into the main room to put on his Tims. He dived into the kitchen, pulling out a drawer to find some newspaper. He pulled out a sheet, letting the rest of the paper glide to the floor. He returned to the bedroom and stared at the Nokia. He knew it was leaving, but how the fuck was he going to get money now? He hated to rely on Evie because she might enjoy just keeping him dancing, and the knives would be lost. He was tempted to hide the phone, but it was too much of a risk. He leaned over, tucked his fingers into the Nokia's side, and shoved it in the news-paper, on top of a headline about stolen African art treasures. As he wrapped the paper over, the screen blinked on. The surprise made the phone fall from his hand as he jumped away. It bounced on the floor

116

like the bad little omen it was. Schoolboy scrambled to his knees and folded the newspaper over the phone like a shroud. He didn't want to see that screen blinking because it made him feel as if the phone was pleading. The type of on-your-knees pleading you got to practise before Top Face in some penal rehabilitation facility. He walked over to his puff jacket and pulled his personal MB out of a pocket and placed it in his coat. He never left the flat without one of his phones. He stepped into the passage and moulded his hand around the latch of the main door. He opened it, stuck his head out, checked sideways left, checked sideways right and then shuffled outside. He grasped and pulled the door knocker without looking back and squeezed the door shut. He hurried along the balcony, thankful that only the wind and moonlight were interested in messing with him. The stairs took him to where he wanted to go.

As he moved he could hear the friction of the newspaper he had wrapped the phone in scraping against the lining of the coat.

His stride shortened, quickened, reaching the first landing and the panic of a woman's tears. He hoped that wasn't Jackie. He heard a bleep in his pocket and knew the phone's screen had switched itself off. His emotions weakened. Maybe he shouldn't be throwing it away. He told himself to forget that type of foolishness. Hadn't he had enough of people slinking into his life one day and then tearing it up the next?

Someone's mucus-induced smoker's cough joined his interior conversation. A nasty sound, just what he needed to remind himself what he had to do. He climbed off the final stair, rounding into the bareness of the courtyard. Without the combustion of human relief, this was a dreary, sorry place to be so early in the morning. Even the pigeons had the sense to put their heads down somewhere else that night. The cars were parked on the rectangular border, not remotely interested in playing defiance under the No Parking sign. This was the place where residents entered the block, left the block and dumped their rubbish. He'd come to dump his. He moved further left to the single mini-block which housed the rubbish bins. He pulled the unwilling and rusty door, knowing that adios moment had arrived, which was no bad thing, as he'd need the practice for the coming days of helping him to let people go. Once it was open he was propelled back by the smell of the residents' lives clambering from the three large steel pan-like bins. He didn't really need to go any further. He just needed to stand there, lob it in, turn and shut the door. If only the rest of his life could be so easy. Find a bin and simply empty the debris from his life.

Terri-baby.

The guilt that stretched with him every morning he woke up for doing a residential in that 75-year-old woman's home when he was sixteen.

His slackness for ignoring that youth doing his first bird who'd only wanted to talk, whose neck had been broken the next morning by the bedsheets attached to the window bars.

He shook himself up. He hadn't come down here to poke his own eyes out. Leave that to people like Evie. His hand slid into his pocket and grasped the newspaper parcel, bringing it out into the light. He tensed his hand around the object as if it was the knives resting in his palm. Indecision came, making the grip of his hand grow stronger.

Maybe the Blues just had nothing to go on?

His hand grew tighter around the phone.

Maybe the phone was his only way to finance his way into Michael's beloved kitchen?

The newspaper started to cut into his fingers.

Maybe he was the ultimate fool for having taken a step back and ended up getting stuck in his own waste?

He lobbed the parcel into the nearest bin, feeling pain as if the knives had sliced through his skin. He closed the door. He just hoped that Evie wasn't going to slam her door in his face when he upped his money request. He knew she wouldn't give enough for the knives, some Amsterdam and some spending money. The Amsterdam came off his list. She still hadn't contacted him, so he decided to give her a bit of prompting. Nothing she hated more than him being in her face all the time. He pulled out his personal MB and punched the address book. He activated her number.

Voicemail.

He listened to the 'please leave a message' crap. His mouth opened to speak, but the words tumbling on his tongue were too angry. He snapped his mouth shut, rolling his tongue behind his lips seeking the right words and tone. When he found them he began to speak.

'Hey, big sis, still waiting for that call. Looking forward to that cash. Why don't I drop by tomorrow and collect? Less hassle for you.'

He punched off, knowing the knives were only going to be around for the rest of the day. He started towards the stairs, with the sound of a rogue bird whistling what felt like the bars of a dirty tune in the air.

Josh and Benji didn't want to be at the Junction. Not at two soddin' o'clock in the morning anyway. But orders were orders. They huddled two doors down from Milo's Kebab House and three doors up from Cass & Co's Legal Services. They knew the reputation of the Junction was for destruction and dying. A reputation they had added to a few days ago. They remained silent as the Raven Club cast its arc over them from across the road. They had twisted their mouths at the low-level media response to Mehmet's death, although they knew Sensi said that the Don wanted to keep it as quiet as possible. Not even a yellow police board to testify to their contribution to local history. Inhabitants said Bluebottles only put out mustard Valentine cards in honour of multiple murders or the discovery of a body that obviously linked a chain they knew about. Mehmet's didn't link to anything or anyone. An illegal in the wrong place at the wrong time. Anyway, word was the Bluebottles were too preoccupied with upcoming anarchist demonstrations in the City. Civil disobedience near wads of cash took precedence over lives snuffed out on the East London mainland.

A single ceiling light at the tip of the club flicked on, glazing a window with a blast of red light that looked like a random red eye watching them. Benji's skin started to dust dry as it used to when his father would line all five of them up ready for the belt. The worst part had been his father's lecture that went on for half an hour. He'd swing the belt as he talked, him sitting, them standing. When the licks came they hurt, but not like that voice talking, not like that belt swinging.

'Fuck, I'd wish she'd hurry up,' Benji complained, allowing the stale stench of kebabs to cement on his lips.

Josh didn't bother to answer, preoccupied with where his next chemical hit was coming from. Benji knew they had ballsed up. No mobile. No answers. Even after three full days the locals had been reluctant to open their mouths wide for a pair of outsiders from Birmingham. As one punter put it, 'When you learn to speak the Queen's English and not like some dumb yokel, then apply and we might swap clogs.' Benji had nearly back-handed him one when he thought he was taking the piss using the word Queen.

'We could still leave . . .' Josh theorised in a voice dowsed high in the passages of his nose.

'What and have her find us? From what I hear this woman has got longer arms than, than . . . than.' He gave up trying to find a comparison, his mind had never been able to stretch that far.

'Than the longest joint in the world,' Josh filled in, laughing and coughing at the same time. 'It'll be all right, Benji boy.'

Benji cut his partner's jokes and comfort from his head as he swallowed the thick spit resting in the base of his tongue. Hackney hadn't been the easy option the boys back home had said. After this job he was going to find a part of London that didn't think peace and harmony was a riff on an old reggae track. But for now they just had to wait and freeze. Freeze because the early morning air was taking no prisoners. Freeze because anticipation can be the coldest emotion of all when you're not sure what is waiting for you. Benji's eyes were high white, testifying that no chemicals were in his bloodstream. They had never met Queen, but the stories circulating were enough for him to know this was a woman who you needed to meet with all the still-functioning parts of your brain moving.

'I fucking told you to remain sober that night,' Benji blamed, anger suddenly sitting on his overcoat shoulder.

'Don't blow up at me,' Josh sniffed the way a man did after a day spent in the gift of other people's white powder.

'But I told you to keep the old head clear and what did you do? Stamp around like you just discovered you have a cock.'

Benji smiled, a little. That was the most clever remark he had made since sailing into London's shores.

Josh kissed his teeth just as the red square eye in the club flicked off.

'Don't forget that our line is that a gang jumped us and roughed us . . .'

'This is her country remember. She ain't going to believe that. She ain't stupid.'

'Yeah, but you are, so just stick to our story. We take our money and then we go . . .'

'Go where?'

'I go one way and you go the other. Because let me tell you . . .'

The blast of a car's front lights blinded them and their spray of words came to a halt. They hadn't heard the engine creep up. They looked at each other, both feeling the temperature dip. They heard a door slam but still couldn't see anything. The lights blew off and both Benji and Josh were startled by the nearness of a man's face, which hung in the air, almost devoid of a body, with its nostrils sneering to the beat of something it knew and they didn't.

'Benji and Josh?' the face asked in a tone so light Benji began to feel as if the man was only asking for directions.

Both men nodded in unison.

'Follow me,' the man turned away.

They both stumbled forward. Benji puffed out his chest to expand with courage, but his chest remained flat. He could hear his father talking.

They followed, wanting to get this over with, so they hurried through the spit-lacquered pavement. The three men stopped once they reached the rear of the Jeep whose metallic reflection absorbed the grimness around them. Benji hovered one step back as if that one step forward was a make-or-break moment.

'Get in then.'

They both looked at the man, noticing he stood a good five inches taller than Josh. They weren't sure what to do until the man put them in the picture.

'Get in,' he said. 'It'll be better in the long run.'

As Benji and Josh took that step forward, the back doors flew open and Uzi submachine gunfire began to ride the upbeat pulse of the street. Their bodies started flailing as if they were practising one of those grassroots dances that came out of the Kingston dance hall scene. The guns stopped. Benji and Josh fell backwards until they lay ejecting a new layer of liquid lacquer on the pavement. The only sound was the diving and scattering of patrons and drivers in Rosaman's Cabs. One of the gunmen stepped forward and inspected the bodies.

'OK,' he confirmed to the other. 'We're cool. Them gone.'

They both stepped back, knowing no one was going to come screaming for the police. Keeping your nose primed in your own business was the best thing you could do. One passed his gun to the other, who clutched them close to him like children who needed soothing after some mishap. They climbed back in.

'Are they dead?' Queen asked from the passenger seat, her plum-covered lips stretching wide, her eyes not bothering to look at Cuttie as he sat next to her.

He looked baffled, wanting to reply that they weren't sunbathing on the beach, but he knew better than that. He raised his hand slightly and gestured towards the two bodies on the street.

'Are they dead?' Queen repeated, this time her eyes rocking sideways. 'Only I was reading about some rapper in New York who took ten bullets and then appeared at a Peace for the Ghetto rally a couple of months later.'

Cuttie's bracelet flashed as he signalled to one of the men in the back. The man picked up his baby, snapped on a new magazine and got out of the vehicle. A few seconds later the pulse of the street rippled again.

'Yes, they're dead.'

'Always make sure,' Queen told Cuttie, squeezing his arm. 'Let's get out of here. Tomorrow's going to be a bitch of a day. I have to take the girls swimming and you lot need to find out where this Schoolboy lives and then make sure you get my ting, you understand?'

The engine of the Jeep pumped the road and swung into a U-turn. Queen tapped the man next to her so that it screeched to a halt by the bodies. The automatic window fell and several hundred quid in used tenners was thrown at the bodies. The Jeep sped away, moving the notes up and around the bodies like the hum of a flirtatious secret never to be told.

12

Schoolboy knew the rain was coming because the moisture was digging the heat out of the sky. That wasn't going to help his headache and red flush eyes. Schoolboy's tracksuit bottoms brushed a 'Join Jesus on the frontline' poster taped to the railings, as he waited for the S13 bus to come along to take him to Evie's. After dumping the Nokia this morning, his eyes had finally closed up at four and took in the world again at eight, nine-to-fivers' time. As soon as he'd seen the light another way out came to him. Why not change his ticket time and leave London early? Goodbyes would have to hold on for another time. He'd make his excuses to Michael about the knives and show his commitment another way. Michael would be disappointed, but disappointments only made the good times feel much better. The worst that could happen was that Michael would give him the finger and he'd be stuck in a town that was suspicious of him.

So, first stop that morning had been the travel agents. 'Hi, my name's Brenda. How can I help you?' had informed him that he would have to purchase a last-deal platinum saver ticket. He had begun to grin, but he should have known that you didn't get anything for nothing in this life. Well, not legally anyway. She'd wanted the type of bread and honey that wasn't sticking in his pocket. Another option dried up so he was back where he started. With Evie.

Two teenagers stood ahead of him, exhaling and playing with the smoke from a spliff as if they knew it was the only high they were getting that day. They wore grey school uniform with the lazy style that showed their regard for education. A subdued Schoolboy waited behind them, with anxiety trying to muscle into his life much more than the smoke entering his face. He was anxious over the knives, anxious over tight-fisted Evie. She hadn't even bothered to reply to his message. Robbie wasn't going to hold on to the knives for ever.

Schoolboy couldn't blame him. Bizzness was bizzness. The fingers of both his hands curled into his palms and began rubbing the skin as if they were they trying to keep warm, but he knew he was remembering the imprint of the knife in his hands. Those knives were his and he wasn't about to let them go. He unfolded his hands and searched in his pocket for his personal MB. He pulled it out and started to text Robbie.

```
don't sell the tings 2 no1 else dosh will b with u
soon
```

Schoolboy didn't sign his name. Robbie would know who it was.

He glanced at the sky. The sun had long quit work for the day. The intimidating bleakness above sent his head back towards the road and the dragging lives of motorists as they went by. The S13 was the last great bus route in Hackney. If you wanted a chemical high the S13 was not the place to be. It was the original sightseeing tour, linking the different histories of the East End. From Hackney it swung into Bethnal Green, looped into Whitechapel and then into the sleepy watchfulness of Wapping. He'd heard that June would see the last days of its tour. Hadn't reached its cost targets – whatever they might be – that was the explanation given. For him it was efficiency supreme because it was his direct route to Evie. Which was the source of his unsettled mood. She had the power to send him forward or back. He needed to keep her sweet. To make her feel that she was in control. Whatever she wanted him to do, whatever she wanted to hear, he was prepared to give it up.

He had begun the process by carefully choosing his clothes. Yardified clothing was out. She scorned baggy riders, string vests and Timberlands. Pure street slackness, that's what she said – the clothes symbolised the community behaving in a way *they* wanted us to be. He'd never asked her who *they* were, but today wasn't the day to start. So he'd dressed in that stiff respectable way he knew would please her. Jeans, loafers, open unzipped hooded top and a 'Black 'N' Strong' logo sweat shirt. Nothing tickled Evie more than having the fist of black consciousness bobbing in the face of the world. He'd taken half an hour to get his garms on. The seams were smooth and in place so that she saw the lines of his life in a new way.

The voices of the boys in front began to rise, bringing him back to the bus stop. One boy started blowing up, upset about something his companion had said.

'I'm telling you it can be done,' the one with the red gelled hair and squinting eyes insisted, in a tone riddled with a rhythmic pattern, which told Schoolboy that most of his friends were of Caribbean descent. Times had moved on. Back in the day, only black kids chatted that way.

'And I'm saying you can't do that,' was the reply.

'You can't do that.'

Four words that made Schoolboy forget the youths. He began to rub his lips close together as if scrubbing sourness from them. The type of sourness that hurt. This pain was mean and lasting much more than any prison time he'd done. He wrestled with the words for a while, but they shoved him back to a place he didn't want to be. Where was the bus when he needed it? But the words had taken root and began a journey in his head that he couldn't stop. He relaxed, knowing he had to deal with this. He let it come. The tale of how he'd turned from Eli into Schoolboy. It had been suffocating him for so long that he needed to get it off his face. Better to deal with it on home ground than for it to become a blight in his new life in Devon.

It had been 1987.

He was fourteen years old.

A ridiculously humid March day.

'You can't do that,' Mizz Havers had told him firmly, her dangling fish earrings circling below her cropped silver hair. Her cheeks had been drawn so high back that it had looked like she was sucking a lemon, with the fruit's colour dying the second layer of her facial skin.

It had been the start of his work placement interview. St Iggy's had been involved in one of those inner city 80s experiments. It had been called Putting Vocations First. Her office walls had been mounted with posters advertising black this and black that, with plenty of pictures of

Marcus, Nelson and Norman. He wanted this chance so he had taken it seriously and tried to set something up. He knew what he wanted to be.

'But Miss, my Auntie Cee works at the hotel – it's in Mayfair – and they are looking for youngsters to work in the kitchen so they can show them what being a chef is all about.'

'If you want to go into catering we can get you a place at Marty's Burgers . . .'

'But Miss I don't want to go into catering – I want to be a chef.' As he'd answered he shifted closer, so that he'd been close enough to his teacher to smell regret. Not hers but his.

He couldn't believe she was asking him to flip slabs of greasy meat with Garvey, Mandela and Beaton encouraging him from the wall.

'What you want to do, young man, is to listen to me because I have spent a great deal of my time setting up these links with local businesses.'

'But Miss this is a wicked opportunity for me . . .'

'You never listen Elijah Campbell. Always stuck in your own world. Why don't you do one of our black history lunch-time classes and raise your self-esteem.'

He hadn't quite known what self-esteem was but it sounded like some academic insult against him and his bredren. Besides, just because she had obviously had a bit of black between her Moroccan blankets on a few occasions didn't mean she could tell him about being a brother.

He remembered how hurt he had felt at this point. His hands had started waving, Grenadian style, to give an extra dimension to his words.

'Miss, I don't know nuthin' about going up and down on any self-esteem but I know what I want and I know how to get it.'

'Elijah you are becoming offensive . . .'

'But Miss . . .' his arms had taking up the beat of his hands at this stage.

She had rushed out, bringing back the Head of Year and before he'd known it he'd been given a five-day suspension.

For 'using threatening gestures'.

For being 'aggressive'.

For being 'disruptive'.

When his suspension was over his mum had told him to go back and keep his mouth still. He had returned, mouth closed but with a fresh take on school. He'd felt as if school had hyped him up and then blown him out. Schooling was the ultimate con. That's where he'd learned the tricks of his trade. Soon bunking off had become as natural as wiping the sleep from his eyes in the morning. Get his attendance mark at registration in the morning, bunk off, registration mark in the afternoon, bunk off. Three months after ditching the life of a conventional pupil, one of his mum's friends from church had seen him at the shopping centre with a group of his similar-minded friends.

'Eli, aren't you meant to be in school?' Mrs Green had asked.

'No, it's one of those teacher training days.'

Mrs Green had shaken her headscarf at him and lamented, 'You use to be such a good schoolboy.'

After she had departed his friends had teased him by calling him Schoolboy again and again. The name had stuck. He was pleased with his new name because it reminded him that nothing or no one was going to string him along again. Only in the last couple of years had he realised that this didn't mean he couldn't strive to be what he wanted to be.

A lone tear began to swell but refused to fall as he remembered that the worst thing was that his cooking had suffered. The spit foamed in his mouth. The bus came around the corner and he was relieved. Relieved because he had to stop looking back.

He breathed easier and got on the bus, but those memories had allowed anxiety to get the foothold it needed in his thoughts. As he paid the bus driver, Jim Reeves floated from his pocket. Just once so he knew it was a text. As soon as he had dished the coins out to the driver he took the phone out and read the text.

Watch your . . .

The phone cut out before Schoolboy could read the rest of the message and find out who it was sent by. No credit. He kissed his teeth. Twenty quid, that's all he had left grazing in his pocket. Now he'd have to use half of that to grease his phone up. He'd never been without a personal line and he wasn't about to start now. Besides, it was his hotline to Evie's bank account.

He climbed the stairs to the upper deck, still fiddling with his mobile.

'Schoolie,' a voice called, resonating from the back of the bus, making him look up.

He grinned, dimples blazing, when he saw the face of Lord Tribulation. Lord Tribulation's face was small, oak-brown deep with the roundness of a CD. His head was covered in his customary do-rag, which was always purple. The colour of justice, Lord Tribulation told everyone. He had a do-rag for each day of the week so that he could write, in red lipstick, a headline from one of the day's newspapers with a large question mark. Today's headline was 'Workers' stress the biggest factor in cutting company profits?' He never asked anyone to discuss the headline with him, he just wanted to get people to think. His head moved with a slight zigzagging motion as if still trying to fix itself to its neck.

'Hey T, good to see you. Sorry about that bizzo on the stairs the other week,' Schoolboy apologised, strolling over and clasping the rough hand of the man in the back row.

'No problemo.'

Lord Tribulation made no reference to whether Schoolboy had taken his advice about going after the men who had robbed his flat. What you did after someone tried to put you straight was your business.

'I hope that ain't the phone,' Lord Tribulation said with a tickle of laughter in his throat as he looked at Schoolboy's other hand.

'What?' Schoolboy answered, his dimples falling and his eyebrows creasing in confusion.

Schoolboy dropped into the seat in front of Lord Tribulation and twisted to face him.

'The phone that was kidnapped at the Junction. It's causing a whole heap of noize on the street. All man, them after it 'cos the reward sounds so sweet.'

Schoolboy froze with the look of a mugger who had heard that the death penalty was being touted for street robbers.

Cuttie drove the BMW with Queen's instructions speeding through his mind. Hackney's clogged streets hustled by, which he sometimes thought was the best way to see Hackney. It going one way while you went the other. The back seats were packed with the muscle and meanness of three other men. They had left the Pond, the name the locals used for Clapton Pond, and were moving to the South side of the borough. Their instructions were to find Ernest Bevin House and wait until their target came home. Finding Schoolboy's details had been easy. Flash a wad in someone's face and they'd sell their heart and worry about blood circulation later. If they didn't find the phone they were to wait for him outside. No extreme violence was to be used. They knew that extreme meant death. That wasn't necessary. What was necessary was to get the phone. If that meant a couple of slaps, a few mangled bones, then so be it. Queen was already annoyed with the exposure the Nokia was getting on the street. So they needed to cool it down, but still attain their goal. Funny woman, Cuttie thought. Any other gang leader would have wanted to be there. But she said that she had to take her kids swimming. Thursday was swimming day and they were expecting it.

Queensbridge Road came into sight and they knew they were almost there.

'Schoolboy, you all right? You look like you're in the twilight zone,' Lord Tribulation asked, wiggling his neck towards his neighbour.

Schoolboy opened his mouth, but no words came out. He tried again, but the same thing happened. His friend moved in closer.

'What's up Schoolboy, you got superglue on your tongue?'

Schoolboy swallowed the spit foaming in his mouth. He reopened his lips and this time the words came shooting out.

'Are you saying that a phone that's running hot was stolen from the Junction?' Schoolboy's voice was slurring with the first drink of information.

'I was only joking, G. No way you would be tangled in that type of mess,' Lord Tribulation reassured him in a voice so contented that you wouldn't believe he was the same person who could fire a dance floor apart and then unite the crowd.

'I know that, but just tell me about the phone.'

Lord Tribulation eased back into his seat. Schoolboy knew what was coming next. Presented with a story to tell, Lord Tribulation would go into rhyme time.

His head started swaying, his fingertips started knee-tapping and then his voice joined the background track of the jolting bus engine.

The tale goes that some Turkish brother
Gets hijacked at the Junction
Transporting a phone
I hear in his shoe
But who knows its function?
He's doing his ting,
But gets held up
And smashed up very sadly
But the way the streets are mumbling
Two crews want that Nokia badly
But the story's not over
Because them say some other G snatch it
And both crews are blowing heat
Cos they're severely out of pocket
Who's mugging who?
Can't tell you that
But I know there's gonna be 'nuff ruction
But you know what they say,
Don't find yourself after 12 a.m. at the Junction.

Schoolboy knew the G was him.

Fuckrees.

First the dead bloke was mentioned on the local news headlines and now his name might be the next to be written in bold black ink. He couldn't stop the spit leaking from the back of his throat and flooding behind the barrier of his dry lips. He gulped a second time.

His instincts had been right all along. He cursed Sensi and Dexter. He cursed himself.

'You're saying some bloke got done over at the Junction for a phone?' Schoolboy bumped closer to his friend, keeping his voice low so that the other three passengers on the top deck couldn't hear.

'That's what my lips said.'

'What kind of mobile?'

'Old style. Like what that Shoreditch artist used to educate people like me and you about the civil war in Congo because we Westerners want to have mobile phones . . .'

'T,' Schoolboy started gripping his friend's arm, 'the only civil war I'm interested in is the one happening at the Junction. Tell me exactly what kind of phone was it?'

'Like I said, old style, you know, the kind that's workable but not desirable, despite costing the lives of innocent . . .'

'Thanks for the memorial service. And that's all the streets are broadcasting about it?'

'Don't quite know. It ain't where I'm concentrating my headlines today.'

Schoolboy touched his hood, flipped it up and shuffled it around his locks. He bent his head slightly and turned his face away from the window.

'What's with the look on the face?' Lord Tribulation asked, settling himself close again to Schoolboy.

'What look?'

'The one you're wearing that makes you look like you just caught TB in Belmarsh.'

Schoolboy ignored Lord Tribulation's enquiry and asked, 'Any idea who the mysterious Lone Ranger they're scouting for might be?'

Lord Tribulation head began snaking again and Schoolboy knew it was time for another rhyme. The DJ started with a new beat.

For now lips aren't moving and the word is silent
But when them buck up with him
you know its gonna be bitch-packing violent.

'You sure there are no names?'

'Not that I've heard.'

Schoolboy leaned back. So he was safe for now. Possibly.

'Who are the two crews?'

Just as Lord Tribulation opened his mouth, Schoolboy continued, 'No disrespect, I know it's your trade but can we ditch the rhyming ache and just tell it as it is.'

'Just chill,' Lord Tribulation put out his palms like a peacemaker. 'Just telling a story the way it should be told. Reward money's coming in from two sources – the Numbers Crew and her Royal Highness The Queen.'

Schoolboy jammed forward again. The Numbers Crew were a Nigerian gang whose higher members only used numbers for names. Myths about their use of numbers ranged from them representing the first digit of their passports to the number of people each member had killed. On a street grading from pussycat to scary, they were scary. Their MO was easy to follow – drugs, financial scams and opportunity. Queen had her own street scale, with the lowest side starting in scary. A woman with a reputation for redirecting lives in a very unique way. Queen was what the street called fearless. Someone who kept advancing forward because they didn't care what might be in their way. The tips of Schoolboy's locks began to shake.

'You're wearing the mask of a man who would like to be disconnected,' Lord Tribulation stated.

That was the problem with street poets, MCs and DJs, they were always catching you off-guard to add to their lyric bank. Schoolboy knew that he had to bluff it.

'If there are any notes being passed out for info I'd like some to fall across my palm,' he said, reverting back to the old Schoolboy, which Lord Tribulation would understand and it might take him off the scent.

'You don't want to be dealing with any handouts from Queen. You stretch your hand out and your arm will come back with your five fingers hacked off.'

Schoolboy bounced his head so that his hood shrouded more of his face.

'Look Schoolie boy, I'm off at the next stop. If you are really interested in that reward let me give you another verse or two on some new headlines that came through this morning.'

Lord Tribulation ignored Schoolboy's request to stop rhyming. Lord Tribulation had started in the raw beat of 90s dancehall, before it became Pop commercial. His face had become more serious, taking the edge off its complete roundness.

I wish you luck
If you get your dosh
But remember Schoolboy bredda
You need to be tough
Last night at the Junction
Two out of town boys forget to check them back
Them find their bodies a.m.
It was no euthanasia pack.

'Wo!' he wailed, long and hard, at the end, in that dancehall tradition.

The last foreigners Schoolboy had seen had been at the Junction.

Fuckrees.

Ends began to tie themselves up and he started feeling tight because he was in the middle.

Lord Tribulation swung up and bored his eyes hard into Schoolboy. 'My advice is to forget the money on offer and heed the words on your sweatshirt.' Schoolboy followed Lord Tribulation's eyes to the Black 'N' Strong motif on his clothing. Lord Tribulation lifted his eyes and carried on. 'Because the word is convinced that the two latest bods at the Junction just didn't understand how Queen likes the leaves picked up in her back yard.'

When Lord Tribulation was gone, Schoolboy sensed that the leaves in Queen's yard were now storming in his direction.

13

Schoolboy was biting his bottom lip because the words coming from his sister weren't very pretty. He sat facing her, the shine on the bruised brown laminate floor making her seem further away than the next sofa. She sat in front of the wall that was bare brick. Red-brown with spots of white. The wall looked exactly like the walls of Martha Gardens where they had grown up. The same Martha Gardens they had both vowed as children to get away from as soon as possible. She had made it. So why would she want the same walls staring at her each day?

'You need to tell me if you see Evie's Loans for Loafers Bank written anywhere?' she answered, standing, and he knew she had really slipped into Grenadian mode, hand gestures wide, fingers slanted, pointed at her forehead. If you ever see a Grenadian with hands flapping you know they aren't finished with you. He didn't bother to open his mouth.

'Why don't you put your card here,' her mouth swung open and she pointed at it. 'Because I'm a walking cash till.'

Don't tempt me, Schoolboy thought. Anything to gag her self-righteous mouth. But he didn't because Sunday was screeching towards him like a Victoria Line train arriving bang on time. And his name might soon be on the announcement board.

He knew he had to sit there and take it. Her lips continued to scrape all over him like sandpaper on brick. He knew which surface would win. But he needed to make sure. He stared at the far wall, which had four white shelves running across its full length. He stared at her collection of books – *Black On Black*, *Gangsta Rap Can't Hold The Pussy Back*, *The Bill Omnibus Collection*, among the titles – and slightly pushed out his sweatshirt, so that his Black 'N' Strong logo read like her newest title. She lived her life through slogans and he knew that his slogan would cool down the patter hightailing it from her mouth. Get her to thinking in a way no words coming from his mouth would. As her mouth eased down he noticed her face looked strained with the colour of the inside of a nutmeg shell and equally as dry.

'Are you all right?'

'Just a bit tired.'

He knew that type of tiredness that had nothing to do with not having a good night's kip. Fuck, hadn't he felt like that since finishing his last stretch in '99.

'Tell me about it,' he coaxed.

It had been a long time since they had had any kind of talk. When they were young, especially if Mum and Dad had one of those arguments, they used to talk. Although she was four years older than him he had never been born with the immaturity of boys. They'd talked about anything. School, music, the day they'd both be living as far away from the estate as possible.

'It's just that . . .' she paused, then he saw the fire reignite in her eyes and knew that the patter was coming back, 'So why do you need two hundred all of a sudden? What, your latest woman into the high life?'

She had long ago stopped asking any of his girlfriends' names. There was no point getting attached when they came and went so quickly. He felt the same way. He decided the time had come to answer her with truth.

'No, nothing like that. I'm going to be . . .' He was stopped by the sound of her doorbell. He kissed his teeth. He couldn't believe that Evie was saved by the bell; saved by a bloody cliché.

She turned her back on him, preparing to leave the room.

'Don't answer it,' he called.

He could hear the tremble in his voice and it wasn't because he was afraid it was someone come looking for him. He just wanted to savour and soak up the sound of her voice. A voice that could yell, shout, scream, demand, patronise, soothe, cry. And a laugh that had taught him how to smile. He didn't know when he would hear it again. Fuck, was the whole day going to be filled with touching moments and a bagful of disturbing memories? Not if he could help it.

He hardened his heart. He didn't call her again and she left the room, leaving him in one of the coldest rooms he could remember. Even the small photo of them, taken in her last year at primary school, couldn't warm him up.

Evie re-entered with the bitch from downstairs.

'Fuckrees,' Schoolboy let out under his breath when he saw Tammy.

He knew there was no way that he was getting access to his sister's bank balance today. She'd never choke it up in front of matey from downstairs. That would be selling her sistahood principles in public. He might as well be asking her to become a lap dancer and shake-her-ting.

As soon as Tammy entered she gazed at him and he was surprised. Her eyes weren't filled with her usual superiority, but with alert warmth. The type of warmth that would soothe him for all of one minute and then chill his bullocks for the rest of his days. He stared hard at her. She smiled back at him, with that pious glow that she carried from morning to midnight. Her wishbone-shaped nose-stud twinkled at him. She swept in, drenched from head to purple-painted toes in the type of white linen suit that made most women hang loose in all the wrong places, but made her look fit and trim. Maybe that Caribbean saying that claimed a woman with a gap in her front teeth possessed a bag of sugar that only a man could find was right.

'Eli, got to rush you, me and Tammy are on our way out to celebrate . . .'

'What, she finally hooked a man on the internet?' He knew his voice was laced with jealousy, but so what. Evie was his sister and they had business to attend to. The steel of the knives cut into his mind.

'So, sister dearest, you got my bread?'

'Eli, I wish you'd stop talking like some street bandit. If you mean the forty pounds you originally asked for, I'll let you know later.'

'We'll make it a standard one hundred nicker . . .'

'Stop riding my back . . .'

'Come on, I really need it.' He stood up, forgetting he had to butter her very gently. 'You're going to mess me up . . .'

'Me, mess you up?' Evie's eyes popped wide as if someone had accused her of lying in court. 'You must be getting me confused with one of your dippy-dippy girlfriends.'

'I'm sure that if both of you fantastic ladies opened your fat purses you could whip up one hundred in half a minute.'

Both women sniffed at him as if he didn't have enough money even to rent the space on the sofa for a night's sleep. He knew he was dismissed.

'So I'll hear from you later, Evie?'

She ignored him, her raised eyebrow pulling her extensions tight on her head.

He wasn't disappointed. Disappointments were for people who weren't prepared to go after what they wanted. But he was desperate. He'd be back and keep bugging her until she gave it up. He knew he only had today to grind her down because the knives might not be chopping around tomorrow. He smiled at Evie, then turned to leave. It was time to hit the streets and discover if he needed to take care of his back.

Schoolboy approached Ernie knowing he had to get in and out with the speed of a cat spraying in the wrong garden. No greetings. No goodbyes. Just him, his possessions and time to think of his next move. It was just a matter of time before his name was connected to the phone. But if someone had got there before him he knew he'd have to play a different game. As Schoolboy got closer the unnatural hush told him the rules had changed. Four to five was the kids' hour. That time of the day, between the end of school and before dinner, when the kids from the block had exclusive run of the place. He saw no children's heads bobbing like architectural features along the balcony ledges. No catching. No throwing. No cussing. Something or someone had cut their playtime short and left behind stillness. A stillness he sensed had something to do with him.

Fear, like his hood, hung over his face. He inhaled and swallowed in one fluid movement. He continued walking at an even pace, with his eyes searching. The building. The yard. The car park. He found what he was looking for. Parked under the Keep Clear sign, near the main entrance, was a BMW. It waited, primed and black, with four men filling it like silhouettes ready to spring into real bodies. They were either there to stop him making a break for it or as a back-up to their posse trashing his flat. Either way it didn't matter. He didn't have the choice of turning back. Not with their rearview mirror open in its pursuit of him. He needed to keep going straight and that meant passing them.

He didn't kid himself. He knew this wasn't going to be easy. As he drew near the car he began to sniff repeatedly and rub a finger under his nose, deliberately taking on the characteristics of a crack addict lamenting the good old days of his last wheeze. He could feel eyes measuring him. Assessing him. Phlegm started sticking in his throat, but he kept moving forward. His body was in line with the car, but he kept slipping forward. His nerves waited for the slam of the car door. For the pulse of feet. But they never came. His body passed out of the shadow of the car. His eyebrows lifted in a superior smile as his old self slipped back into place. Wankers. Didn't they know that sentry duty was now done in Morris Minors or Minis? Beamers were just too flash. Just too overstated.

'Hey Mister Schoolboy when are you going to come up and read with me?' a child's soft voice challenged him from the first-floor balcony. Schoolboy's body reverberated as if he had slammed it against the wall of the building. The kids around here just couldn't keep their friggin' mouths shut. He knew he shouldn't look around to see if any of the men parked in the car had heard. But he was like a tongue on a bad tooth, he just couldn't stop himself. Although the occupants hadn't moved, he knew he had to get out of here. He started power-walking towards the courtyard that connected Ernie to Eric, ignoring Ryan, Jackie's nine-year-old son.

'Hey, Mister Schoolboy, you gone deaf . . .'

He started running because he knew Jackie had trained her kids to be heard. He began to run fast, his feet setting the pace while the rest of his body followed their direction. He ground his teeth together, needing to drive his pace even higher. He heard the reverberation of a slammed car door, the awful tremble of a car engine and the slapping of heels and rubber soles pounding into the concrete he had just left behind him.

'We're gonna get you, fucker,' a voice screamed, bouncing off his back.

He powered to Eric's staircase, skidded, turned left sharp into the adjacent block. He reached the wall of the kids' playground, which was sealed from the rest of the estate, and launched himself, with the know-how of a mountain goat, against the brickwork. He began to slide as the anti-climb paint tried to bring him down. He wasn't letting go, not when he could feel the heat of his assailants getting hotter against his arse. Dread and anxiety pushed his legs over. Too much adrenaline made him dizzy, loosened his focus so that he toppled over the other side. Suddenly he squeezed his face as if electricity was jolting through him as his arm became tangled in a trap of stinging nettles and broken branches. Bloody greenery always growing in the wrong place in Hackney. He didn't need to look to know his arm was bleeding. How badly he'd have to find out later.

He kicked up, eyes rushing, circling wildly. Although the playground had long since been trashed and chained up by the management, he spotted a climbing frame still propped up against the wall opposite. He used his good arm and leg muscles to shoot up it. He sat on top of the wall and booted the frame away then dropped, with the blessed energy of someone flopping into bed, down the other side.

'Take a breath,' Evie always said, and for once he followed her instructions. But it was easier said than done when his breathing was only trickling from his windpipe. Then he picked up the pace again and began to really motor. Past stairs, along corridors, underground and overground, until he realised that he'd doubled back on to himself and was back at Ernie. This time at its back entrance. He staggered to the first floor and lay bent below the height of the balcony beside the rubbish chute. He panted from the pain in his arm and the realisation that he'd fucked up again. Evie was so right, he'd been losing his life since the age of fourteen. He wanted to cry. But what was the point of that when it only gave you temporary relief, soon replaced by the same problem flaunting itself in your face.

'Mister Schoolboy.'

The young voice jerked him. He lunged forward to fight for his freedom at least. His head swung forward just as his arms were ready to make contact. He saw that it was Ryan and quickly moved his arms to the side to avoid hitting him. He moved his arms up again and placed them on the boy's shoulders. He pulled Ryan down with him below the balcony line.

'Is your mum in?'

'What are we doing down here? I'm meant to be finding the others.'

'Just a game . . .'

'Can I join in?'

Schoolboy needed to hurry, he could hear his chasers' impatient voices. The acoustics of the block made it hard to tell whether they were above or below him.

He kept his voice soft. 'Another time. But is your mum in?'

'Yeah. Watching Corric on the video. She don't like to be disturbed.'

'Don't tell anyone you saw me. Don't forget about those spellings I gave you. I'll be testing you next time.'

He patted Ryan's shoulders and crammed himself along the balcony towards the boy's home. As he moved he could hear doors being banged on the balcony above. He could hear the swing and then the voices.

'Excuse me, we're the police. We're looking for a street hustler' – fucking cheek, he thought – 'by the name of Schoolboy.'

'Police. Yeah right and I'm Marilyn Monroe. Wanna see a twirl?' Schoolboy snickered and felt relieved, hearing the liquored-up voice of Len. Good old Len.

He reached Jackie's, knowing the door was always open at this time so that her children could get in and out without disturbing her. He crept in, his blood weeping slowly on to the laminate floor of the passage. He felt her shadow before he heard her.

'What are you doing? You're making a total mess of my Bermuda beech floor.'

'Jackie, please just hide me.'

'I'm glad you're here though. I've got that package for you. It's on top of my Corrie video on the telly . . .'

'Jackie, stuff the package, just help me.'

She gestured with her head at her front room. As he eased towards the room, she gently shut the door. The room had been put together using two styles – stall propping and catalogue chic. The pictures, centre glass table, ashtrays, curtains, were the staple of market stalls. The white leather three-seater, wide-screen TV and matching DVD were from the pages of the latest catalogue that came through the door. Schoolboy ran towards the catalogue chic and threw himself behind the settee. Not much of a hiding place, but he couldn't see what else she had in mind.

The tap of someone's feet brushed into the room. He cringed behind the settee.

'Schoolboy,' – his body relaxed, realising it was Jackie – 'not being funny, but they only do that in the movies. Very bad movies. Sit on the bloody thing. They won't come in here.'

He peeped over the top, picked himself up, stiffening in pain, and slumped across the settee. Jackie had sorted out the problems in the block so there was no reason to think she wouldn't see him right.

The hammer at the door came, making them both tense. They stared at each other then looked away. Jackie leaned over and pulled the cigarette packet from a side table. She withdrew one.

The door banged again.

She placed it against her moist lips. She stretched into the pocket of her stone-washed jeans and pulled out a green lighter. She lit up.

The door banged one more time.

She inhaled and exhaled with the words:

'I just wanted to see how much they wanted you.'

She left him and shut the door behind her. For the first time Schoolboy felt the clinging sweat across his clothes as he heard her open the front door.

Wahid looked at Ashara as they sat waiting for their buyer in the basement of 24/7 cabs. They always agreed that when they did business they should be in a calm, jovial mood. Just like a snake ready to bite if things went wrong. Wahid knew Ashara was anything but calm.

'Come on, you need to be ready for the man. We must make sure he believes us.'

Ashara didn't answer. Wahid wasn't surprised. He'd be surprised if he had even heard a word he had said. He knew his brother was eaten up with thoughts of Number 8. Why he was still letting that little shit into his thoughts after this time was anyone's guess. So it was Number 8's birthday. As far as he was concerned he hoped that Number 8 was long dead, with no more years to celebrate.

'What do you think Number 8 is doing?' Ashara asked as he bit hard into a nail.

'Rotting in a hole somewhere, I hope.'

Ashara winced and shut his eyes. Wahid hated sentimentality. Number 8 had been blood, so he could understand how Ashara was feeling, but that didn't mean it was acceptable for the room to be filled with the self-pity of what-ifs.

'We need to get our act together. The man's expecting the goods and we haven't got it.'

No response. Idiot, Wahid thought. Acting like a stupid woman who can't remember which bed she left her panties in the night before.

'Let me do all the talking.'

Ashara nodded.

The door swung open and they saw the face of the buyer for the first time. They had been ear-to-ear with his voice many times, but never his face. The man was white, which they didn't like too much. The last time they had worked with someone white, a European, they had nearly ended up in a Moroccan prison. But the difference this time was he was an American. Wahid, broad smile extended, rose to meet the newcomer with the same pleasure he knew he would feel flying first class to New York.

'Well, finally good to meet y'all,' the newcomer announced.

'Come my fellow brother and sit down.' Wahid knew exactly how to get this white American to feel at ease. Get him to think you're some native in a Tarzan film and feel that he was in control. That's as long as he didn't expect cowrie shells for the goods.

The buyer eased his stumpy bulk and tailored suit into the chair on offer. He looked at them with caramel eyes that were slanted from the frost of dipping over a bottle of malt whisky every night.

'What can I get you to drink?' Wahid enquired

'Not when I'm doing business, fellas,' the American answered, but his flabby tongue licked his lips as if he really wanted one.

'Let's just get this over with. Let me have a look at the little beauty.'

Wahid knew this was where his Tarzan act started.

'Brother we are sorry to say that the little beauty, as you call her, is not with us at the moment . . .'

The American shifted, annoyed in his chair.

'Come on, fellas. I've busted a gut to get here, so stop jerking me around.'

Both brothers knew that this man had spent most of his own life jerking himself around, which made their game much easier.

'Our leader felt that it would be better for us to organise the details of the deal . . .'

The man jostled his flesh out of the chair, breathing hard as he stood up.

'Your leader? So who the fuck are you guys? Don't tell me I have to negotiate with the yard boys . . .'

He stopped, seeing the looks in their eyes. A look that reminded him he was on their soil, so he needed to stop beating his chest. He plonked his body back down. Wahid's voice was soft and easy as he spoke.

'We are all leaders here. But in London, our organisation prefers to work in a precise processed way. We organise the details and then our

Director will bring the goods himself. So don't worry.'

'Still, expected to see it before final delivery on Monday . . .'

'Well, as you say, it is a little beauty and our Director has got somewhat attached.' A harder edge changed Wahid's tone as he continued. 'So let us go through the details. Number 5 bring in some drinks,' Wahid ordered, looking at one of the men who stood near the door.

The man looked surprised because there was no Number 5, but the damn fool American didn't know that. They started negotiating about the details, waiting for the drinks to arrive. When they came the buyer fell on the bottle of whisky like a priest drinking in private. These Americans were so predictable. Whoever he was representing needed to find a new buyer for the future. As the juice flowed, the buyer forgot about the little beauty and started talking about his love of beautiful black pussy. Could they fix him up? Of course they could.

When he had gone they knew they needed to act quickly.

'So what are we going to do?' Ashara asked, back to his usual self.

'Now we know that it was Queen who tampered with our plans we can keep an eye on her and follow her every move,' said Wahid. 'There is no need to find this Schoolboy. Queen will take us right to him.'

14

'Are you the blokes from the washing machine company?' Schoolboy heard Jackie speaking with a voice high enough for him to hear. He could imagine her posture. Legs held wide apart by her Roman Road slippers. Hands rolled into fists and attached to her hips. Neck thrust forward as if she was the most menacing species on earth. Her voice rose another notch as she continued. 'Because if you are I've been bleedin' waiting so long . . .'

'I think . . .' the man at the door began.

For the first time, Schoolboy heard the voice of one of his assailants. London-Jamaican, deep with the texture of someone rolling cough sweets around their mouth. Definitely one of Queen's men.

'You think?' Jackie's voice blasted out. 'Let me tell you I wish I had time to think. Two little 'uns to look after and a thirteen-year-old with not one bit of respect left in his bones. Time to think, I wish. What do I look like, I'm on Mastermind or The Weakest Link? So I ain't got time to waste waiting for you lot to turn up to fix the machine. So what are you waiting for? Come in and get it started . . .'

Schoolboy started to rise because he knew Jackie was playing a dangerous game. The settee squeaked, freezing him in the air. He eased gently back down, knowing he had to trust her instincts. He heard the scuff of trainers enter the passage. Schoolboy leapt up again.

Fuckrees.

He tiptoed, dripping blood on to the carpet, to stand behind the door.

'Where the hell do you think you're going, mate?' Jackie yelled, her voice much closer to Schoolboy this time.

Schoolboy battled with his breathing as it became harsher. As it became louder. He felt the heat of someone outside the door.

'The washing machine ain't in there. It's in the friggin' kitchen.'

The handle of the room door began to turn. Schoolboy wanted to move but he couldn't. His brain was no longer connecting to his legs. The handle turned again like a demon creeping in a nightmare. The lock clicked back as the door burst half open. Schoolboy stretched himself against the wall, held his breath and slammed closed his eyes.

'Does it look like I keep my washing machine in the front room? Look.' Jackie roared, her voice clear in the doorway.

The door pulled back in and snapped back into place with its frame.

'The washing machine's this way.'

'We're not . . .' a male voice started to answer, but Jackie came right back at him pulling him into her net.

'If you tell me you can't fix it today I'm phoning your company straight up. Or maybe what I should do is do what that woman did, you know the one who took that repair man hostage until he'd done the job . . .'

'We're not here to fix your fool-arse machine!'

Schoolboy imagined the man hyped up, a foot taller than Jackie. Intimidating. Getting frustrated because the woman before him just wasn't taking any notice.

'We are . . .' the man's voice stopped with exasperation, anger fuelling his breath as his feet banged away from the sitting-room door. 'I don't think you can help us.'

Schoolboy heard the grind of shoe-heels on concrete and their hard click as they moved along the balcony.

Jackie yelled after them so that even the junkies sleeping it off in Eric could hear.

'I'm telling you if you're from that soddin' company I'll be straight down to your office tonight. I'll bloody well camp there until it's done. I don't care that it's in flippin' Glasgow or is it Delhi?'

Schoolboy opened his eyes, bent over and gulped in air. He heard the soft rubber of Jackie's slippers quickly flip against the concrete of the balcony floor.

'Going already?' Her voice was so high he knew she was shouting over the balcony.

People in the block knew better than to come out when Jackie was shouting.

'What about my machine? Don't think driving off is gonna save you. I'm getting on the blower right now to sort all your arses out . . .' abruptly her voice halted. Stilled.

The repeated breathing of a large car engine took over, made its last angry salute in the yard, and then blended into the distance.

Jackie's edged-out breathing entered the passage as she shut the door. Her feet retraced their earlier steps back to the living room, and before he'd wrenched himself from the wall she stood in the doorway. Imp smile dancing, fag lighting, pleased. She entered as she had left, with a cigarette and confidence in her hand. She didn't say a word to him, but placed the tip of the fag against her mouth. She dragged the smoke in. He could hear the jerked rumbling in the pull of her breath. She puffed out and then spoke.

'Told you that they wouldn't get in. Nothing like a ranting woman to keep a man out of the house,' she said with first-hand experience. 'They've gone. Their car couldn't leave quick enough.'

'Jackie, you shouldn't have done that. Please don't ever do that again,' Schoolboy pleaded as he moved from the shadow of the door towards the settee. He flopped down, shaking his head. She stepped closer to him, ground out the butt in the ashtray, and eased down beside him. Her hands fluttered out, like the calmest wave on the nearby canal, and took his arm.

'You're bleeding. Let me fix that for you.'

Schoolboy pulled his arm back.

'No. I can sort myself out.'

'What, like you did today? Besides, I can't afford for any blood to get on the settee because I haven't finished paying for it yet.'

She got up and was soon back with a small bowl and cotton wool. She placed the bowl on to her lap and dipped the cotton into the water. He pulled up the sleeve of his torn sweatshirt and stretched his arm out. She took it and started dabbing and sponging the blood, dirt and pain away. The weight of his troubles hustled his eyes together, making them close. He couldn't remember the last time anyone had taken the time to cleanse him. Even Evie hadn't kissed him in such a long time. As for his ladyeez, well they only did it when they were in pretty-please begging mode. The texture of the touch on his arm changed. Warm, soothing, human. His eyes flicked back into the room to catch Jackie with her head bowed, circling and pressing her fingers around his wrist and pulse.

'Jackie . . .'

'We could be good together because we know how to have fun.'

Her head came up. She rested the live green of her eyes straight into his.

What he loved about Jackie was she didn't ask any questions. She didn't expect any explanations. Both her hands softened and skated up his arm as she moved closer to him. Her hand stroked him in a different shape to the way she held her fags. She let her palms shift across his Black 'N' Strong sweatshirt. He looked down and stared at her. He didn't believe in that type of love. Fancying. Getting his leg over. Allowing the heat from someone's body to rejuvenate him. Yes, he believed in all that. But that wasn't love. And that's what Jackie needed. Some open and pure love in her life.

'Jackie . . .'

'Sh. Just let me and your lips finish what we started.'

He leaned over and pressed his lips across hers. She felt so clean. Their mouths opened and tongues took on the journey she had been looking for. Her tongue started running along his teeth and he felt good. She was good at this. He wasn't surprised. Jackie was good at most things. He could feel his dick getting hard. But he wasn't going to disrespect Jackie. He pulled his lips back.

'Jackie, I need to keep moving.'

'Sure. No problem.' She eased back and he couldn't help but see she wanted more.

He stood up.

'Thanks. I'm going to pack some things and then I'm out of here. I may not be back . . .'

'Story of my life,' Jackie breathed. 'Remember, you might be gone, but me and your lips have still got some unfinished business.'

She climbed up and squeezed him.

'You take care of yourself.'

He left while he still could. He moved quickly along the balcony. So quickly that he didn't hear her call his name. Didn't hear her calling him about forgetting the package again. Didn't hear her decide not to follow him because the tears were flowing, stinging and strong.

If your head gets bust wide open from the beatings of life remember that sometimes it's your own hand holding the stick. That's what Mum had written to Schoolboy during his second sentence, when she refused to come and see him. He'd been pissed with her at the time but now as he stared at the screwdriver-jammed front door of his flat he knew exactly what she meant. He had bought all this badness to his own yard. All because he couldn't think of getting that extra forty quid another way. All because the crooked road seemed so much easier to travel than the narrow one ahead. His eyes openly skated with fear.

He cautiously moved forward. The sense of destruction was powerful long before it came into his vision. He knew it would look like the devastation him and Manny had left at that 75-year-old's home, back in '87 While in police custody they had found out she'd been forced to enter a residential home all because they had decided to do their own residential.

He stepped inside, leaving one storyline behind and entering another one. He didn't need the *what goes around, comes around* narrative digging doubt in his head. The doors of the bedroom and sitting-room were flung wide, like the envelopes of his letters the screws would read before he got them. The sunlight ripped across the floorboards. It ripped across his possessions scattered on the ground. His life had been thrown up and slashed to pieces as it came down. He was glad he hadn't been around. The knife marks he saw might have ended up in him. Queen's people meant business. Queen always meant business. Ditching the Nokia was not going to stop her from seeking him out. He left the haven of the front door and slowly slid forward. As he got closer, the inside of his nose and the tips of his lips began to eat up the taste and sting of garlic. Liquid garlic.

The smell froze him. His bottom lip widened the gap with its upper twin, from shock. Shit, his recipe book. His feet did an unco-ordinated fast shuffle as he rushed towards the kitchen. The scene there was picture-postcard the same as the other rooms. Wilful destruction the only theme tune being synthesised. Drawers, cutlery, his spices and herbs all smashed and trashed. His beloved cookery books lay in the middle as if their descent to the floor had been an afterthought. He kissed his teeth. A short, abrupt kiss that spoke of his disbelief. The intensity of his breathing raged through his open mouth. He realised the shake-down that was rippling through his body was the slamming of his heart. He could hear the squealing of Flat 7's baby, two floors down. He leaned over, like a man genuflecting for the first time. His overheated palms pushed the books aside until he found what he was looking for. He rescued the recipe book and held it up to inspect it for damage. It had the smallness of a child's blue wordbook, the thickness of the only pride he still felt in his life. He had been compiling his own recipes since the age of ten. The book was everything to him. More than Evie. More even than Mum. More than this crappy wreck of a phone the whole world was tracking. He thrust the book into his pocket. The pain from his arm returned. Sharp and throbbing. He scrunched up his eyes and groaned deep from his chest. Nurse Jackie obviously needed more training.

The bonus-prize ring of his business line vibrated in his trouser pocket. Text. He pulled it from his pocket with his good arm.

Call me. Michael.

He scrunched his eyes for a second time. This time in annoyance. He'd forgotten all about contacting Michael with details of his arrival in Devon. Michael would have to wait till later. Anyway, this wasn't the right time to return the call. The opportunities of his new life touching the mess of his old were not how he wanted to play it. Priority one was to collect what he needed. He realised that walking with a large rucksack or Dad's old suitcase would make anyone he ran into ask questions. His eyes flicked the kitchen, thoughts roaming for an answer. His eye fell across a large carrier bag discarded in a corner of the floor. It was decorated with summer fruits and the promise of a good life still left to live. A bag for life, the supermarkets were calling them. Nothing was for life. Maybe supermarkets were giving reward points for lifestyle choices now. The word 'reward' brought him back to his situation. He needed to move fast. He knew he was now running hot. He began a swift tour of his home, concentrating on what he needed to collect, not on the devastation. His hand snatched only essentials.

A photo of him, Evie, Mum and Dad at Clacton in 1985.

A few garms to get through to Friday.

Bandanna.

His most expensive trainers.

MB chargers.

Toiletries.

Address book.

Train tickets.

Mum's First Salvation hymn book.

By the time he'd finished, sweat was oiling his clothes. He couldn't take any more stuff. Everything else would have to stay until tomorrow morning. He'd make the contact later and get it sorted. That was priority number two. Priority one was finding a crib for the rest of his time in Hackney. Somewhere safe for his running to cool down.

He pulled out his personal mobile, found Window in the address book and called him.

Voicemail.

Fuckrees. He remembered that Window said he'd be unavailable until Saturday. He clicked off, leaving no message. No point ringing Terri-baby and trying to muscle in on her Victoria Park liberal luxury. He'd finished with her last time he'd phoned her. She had cried, he had severed the phone connection. He could call up a few spars, but that reward for the phone might compromise one or two allegiances. Nothing like the sight of brass cooing in the distance to make someone forget they ever had a conscience.

The only person left was Evie. He shivered thinking of himself in that cold duplex. He shivered even more when he thought of himself laid flat in a coffin, just as it was lowered into a hole. Evie's it would have to be. He tugged his hood back over his head and pulled the front door open. He turned back and the only thing he could feel was spiteful regret at having to say goodbye in this way. He'd lived here for twelve years. Some good, some wasted. He'd planned his goodbye. Saturday night–Sunday morning, whizzing with some Amsterdam and spinning his favourite Ragga collection. Barrington, Yellowman and Shaggy all toasting him as he packed and made ready to go. He stared back at the mess and wished he could say something off-hand like that's life. But he couldn't because this wasn't life at all. He turned back to the open door and pulled the bag closer to himself. He moved over the threshold, closed the door gently for the final time and shuffled under his hood as he headed for his sister's.

Queen's fingers bent like repressed wire around the mobile pressed into her ear. One leg folded on top of the other, with the tip of her lower shoe the only part of her grounded with the floor. The force of the swing she initiated with the swivel chair made her foot roll from little toe to big toe, big toe to little toe. The glossed stillness coating her mouth told of someone thinking nasty thoughts.

'Queen . . .' the voice on the other end called.

'Fucking shut up. Just fucking well shut your mouth, Cuttie,' she yelled loudly, her voice vibrating and bouncing against the front of her windpipe.

She thrust upwards on the second fuck, her lashes blinking furiously. She hated swearing. Told both her girls that she better not ever hear them do it. Her spiked heels trod the varnished floorboards as if she was already feeling the pain she was going to have to mete out. She weaved back and forth, an athlete with no more laps to do, but with adrenaline still coursing thought her body. This was her favourite room in the house. It could have been a fourth bedroom or another reception, but she had decked it out as her office. When she had visited the house, despite its position with the garden this room had been the darkest. She had kept it that way. Its brooding edge helped her deal with her work more efficiently.

Her mouth was so strung up with anger that she couldn't talk. Not yet anyway. She moved towards the french doors. They were closed but that didn't stop her admiring the peace of the landscaped garden. The heat left by the long-gone sun lay on the grass and began to grace the surface of her face. More warmth gathered as she stared at her daughters' area of the garden. She smiled, creasing the corner of her eyes. Both of her daughters kept their own patch. They needed to understand responsibility if anything ever happened to her. Her temper rolled back, started to cool. She was ready to deal with Cuttie.

'So, let me see if I can still do arithmetic. There are four of you and one of him. He slips through your fingers like Jack Iron rum down a throat.'

She hated sarcasm, not because some claimed it as the lowest way to get a laugh, but because it was just a waste of time. Who had the time to try and be clever when you could be getting on with the next scene in your life?

'It's his estate, people must have been helping him . . .'

'Don't play the violin with me.' She swung away from the garden and back into the heat of her anger and the scent of the pineapple from the Hawaiian pizza her girls had gobbled up earlier.

'I think you need to be asking yourself whether you're in the right job, Cuttie. Plenty of other dumb boys looking for a job opportunity. And the graveyard is always hiring.'

She didn't have to see Cuttie's features to know his six-pack was twitching as intensely as if he had been hit with an electric prod.

'He must have been warned – he just disappeared . . .'

'So, what, now he's David Blaine?'

'No disrespect, Queen, but someone on the estate must have been hiding him . . .'

'And you missed him and my stock.' She gulped and switched the phone to the other hand in one motion.

'I need to get this sorted,' she added. ' In the meantime you and two of the others can spend the whole night until tomorrow at noon sitting outside that block. And if he turns up, don't do anything. Just ring me.'

She snapped the phone and closed down their dialogue.

Now she decided she could play this three ways. Be nice and accommodating. She dismissed that. What did she look like, the Pope doling out canonisations to suspect saints? She could contact her source to see if they had any info on the whereabouts of this Schoolboy. That was certainly an option. If the Numbers Crew had already negotiated with Schoolboy she'd have to find a way of making him come over to her side. The best way to do that was to take a family member and listen to him agree as he heard screams bellowing on the phone. But she didn't want to do that unless she had to. That might bring too much attention and the dead fools Sensi had employed had already sent up too many smoke signals. Her thoughts flexed and flowed as she sifted through her next move. She stabbed her fingers into the buttons on the phone to contact her source.

'What do you know about someone called Schoolboy?' she cracked, hearing the sound of loud voices and music on the line. People having a good time really pissed her off.

'Queen, my friend, the arrangement is that I do the contacting.'

'Too busy strutting your stuff at a party?'

'Even in a sinful bush like Hackney, people need to relax every now and again. I would have sent you an invitation but I thought you would be busy.'

Queen started pacing. She knew that she was being mocked, but she had to swallow it.

'Just answer the question.'

'Wish I could, but I can't.'

'You put me in touch with this delivery, so whether you like it or not you're with me to the end.'

'Every end has a beginning.'

'I don't need any more sewer-backed defiance today, just tell me if you can help me.'

There was a pause.

'I'll keep my ear in the bush. I may have heard that the leaves are rustling a few phone numbers. If it comes my way I'll text it on to you.'

'You sound like you know where Schoolboy's hiding out?'

'Maybe, maybe not.'

There was hitched hack of laughter in the voice which made Queen feel worse. But she kept it cool. She couldn't afford to alienate her only contact.

'I like the way you do business. Maybe you could join my team? I'll need a name though.'

'A name one day may not be the same name you find tomorrow. But just for you Queen, my unique friend, you can call me Eight.'

'Eight?' Queen shot out, but the line had already gone dead.

Her mouth twitched as she stared at the phone. She threw the phone on to the desk. That was the problem with go-get-'em Hackney, too many people who thought their gun was the most devastating on the block.

'Mum?' a high voice faltered from the doorway.

She turned to see her youngest standing there. She was the image of her worthless father. God rest his soul because Queen only had time to spit on it.

She rushed forward and hugged Jasmine.

'Mum, can't sleep. Please read me the end of Goldilocks.'

'Of course Jassy, honey. Anything for you. Let Mummy finish what's she's doing and I'll be right up.'

As Jasmine skipped out of the door, Queen compressed her mouth, deciding that after she read her daughter a bedtime story she'd see about tucking Schoolboy in.

15

'What are you doing? Stalking me? We just got back from a wonderful evening out.' Schoolboy's sister spoke, her extensions moving lazily as she left the door open for him to enter her home for the second time that day.

'You've even got the heavy breathing right,' she continued as she turned her back.

He hadn't realised how hard his chest was rising, falling and rising again. He turned his head to the left side, the right side, checking the cold blue corridor. He knew no one could get in here but he felt as if the whole world was on his tail. He skipped inside the passage and shut the door. He placed the bag for life on the wooden floor. He slid the double bolt across and if he'd had the key he'd have done the mortice lock as well.

'Evie,' he called as he turned back, but she had already gone into the main room.

He scooped up his bag with his stride and followed her. He stepped into a room that he found alarmingly soft. Peach lamplight dampening the walls, the tickle of white port scenting the air, and the melodic four-beat riff of a guitar rose, fell, and then rose again. Even Tammy melted, with her feet tucked under, into the armchair. Her bag of sugar had improved since he saw her earlier. Now she was complete bronze. Hair twists, the flush of her nose-stud, two new gold cuffs in her hair. The bronze from her lipstick had escaped her mouth and was doing the rounds against the rim of her glass. His eyes started blinking, adjusting to the room. He wasn't use to this type of tenderness. He moved further inside, bringing his own brand of hardness and his bag for life.

'Let me get you a drink.' Evie began pouring before he answered. 'Here you go. What's that, about a quarter?' She shook the glass in front of her, looking at the volume of liquid. 'I should be asking you for, what is it, twenty pounds?'

He'd forgotten how downright rude her tongue got when she'd had a couple of jars. If she had a beef with you, don't let her catch you when her liver was full. Definitely not a good night to be asking favours from her.

'I'm not dealing any more,' he continued, answering Evie's question.

'It that a fact?' Evie wriggled her hips as she asked the question. 'Tammy, did I tell you that they've asked me to be the new Bond girlie?'

He flicked his eyes at Tammy, who had shoved her legs down to watch the cabaret before her.

'Tammy, I need to talk to my sister.'

'Tammy, stay where you are. This is your day. If anyone's moving it's him.'

He wasn't going anywhere.

'You got the dosh you promised me?' He stared straight into Evie's alcohol-hazed eyes.

'I thought banking hours were from 9 to 5.30.'

'I thought I was dealing with 24-hour banking. Even you will have heard of that. So why don't you deal with the customer's request?'

'What, you need to do more shopping?' Her gaze touched his bag.

'I'm leaving.'

'Nice seeing you. You know where the door is.'

'I'm off to Devon.'

He felt Tammy shift. Evie twisted her lips smugly at him.

'Good luck and don't forget to transfer your bank account. I hear they only open till lunchtime.'

Her extensions had woken up and were swaying in irritation at a narration they didn't want to be part of.

The track on the CD changed to something harder, a story of my-man-done-fucked-me-over-for-the-tenth-time-but-I-can't-live-without-him.

'So that's all I am to you? Someone who knocks on your door and asks you for money? But then that's you all over, Evie, someone who's too busy *helping* the community, but pretending she can't remember what the dirt in the street feels like.'

The CD track changed to a furious two-beat.

'I could tell you things about community life . . .'

He didn't let her finish, ripping and erupting into her words.

'Like what? Like how it feels to live somewhere where you've got your own porterage service? Like how it feels to have your car safely tucked up behind bars for the night? Like how it feels to have the best view over the river? The problem with you so-called community leaders is that you don't even know where the "community" is any more. People like you, sister dear, refuse to smell the filth. Refuse to smell the rottenness of disaffection. Refuse to listen. All you lot do is tell the rest of us how deprived we are. Deprived of fucking this, deprived of fucking that. And when we feel so low because deprivation has been beating about our balls for so long you lot want to empower us . . .'

'At least I managed to finish my schooling and make something of myself. Make Mum and Dad proud.'

Only the music could be heard as they both fell into a crushing silence. His skin colour drained to funeral brown. The same colour his face had been the day they and two hundred people had buried Dad. She knew that the one area they never discussed was his experiences at school. Just because she had made it through she couldn't understand how other people didn't. How some black males didn't. How he didn't.

Tammy sprang up, like a white sail blowing with the sea after the storm.

'I've got to make a phone call, then I'll make us all a cup of camomile tea.'

She was gone when Evie finally spoke.

'Eli, I'm sorry, I didn't mean . . .'

'Why feel sorry?' His arms flung wide, the bag banging into his side. 'That's me. Schoolboy the shitbag, Schoolboy the scum of the earth, Schoolboy the fucking idiot who thought his sister was going to

159

help him. You know what the scariest thing is? Mum asked you to look out for me, so I came up here to ask you to share your home with me, just for a few days so that whoever mashed my flat . . .'

'What? Your flat's been . . .'

'Why so surprised? I thought you knew all about the *community*. Let's face it, Evie, the community isn't even worthy enough to wipe their feet on your doormat much less get anywhere near your balcony to peek at the river.'

His fingers pulled at the bag as he turned to go, but his shaking bones couldn't hold it and the bag fell, spilling its contents in front of him, in front of her, as if marking out a dividing line between them. His recipe book, the photo of him and her, Mum and Dad, his trainers, all fell. The shaking of his bones swirled up to his skin. To his head. Stuck in his throat. His cracked lips wouldn't move but he had to make them. He had to make her understand.

'This is all of my life.' His fingers stabbed at his belongings on the floor like a man croaking at the unfairness of having to stand at his own graveside. 'Ain't much, is it? Not quite up to your standards of books, records, this statue, that statue. You've even got the doll from downstairs practically living here adding to your still-life collection. But the street don't give you much time to add to your collection, only time to live.'

He scrunched to his haunches and started to pick up his belongings and replace them in the bag. The pressure rose in his face. The tears which he knew he'd been holding back since he decided to leave London were now puffing the bottom of his eyelids, ready to fall. But he wasn't going to cry in front of her. No fucking way. As he picked items up he let one hand wipe his eyes. He felt and heard Evie next to him. The shadow of her hand and the alcohol on her breath reached out to touch him.

'Don't.' His command was hot and hurt. 'Anyway, there's only enough for one person to put away.'

She picked up the same speed she had used to move towards him to ease her shadow away. He carried on picking and filling, mouth closed, over a decade's worth of words churning against his teeth. But he didn't say any more. The time spent trying to convince other people was over. He stood up and started heading out of the room, almost knocking over Tammy who perched in the doorway.

'Eli!' Evie yelled.

He closed the door and just kept walking.

'I thought I'd find you here.' Evie's voice was quiet like the ripples on the river they both looked at.

Well, I wasn't going to go back to fun-filled Hackney, he wanted to say back, but he didn't. He'd had enough of firing verbal bullets for the night. Besides, his temples were sore in their need for food. They both stood at the rail in Wapping New Stairs, a few minutes' walk from her place. He remembered the first time she had shown him this spot, soon after she had moved into the wharf. It had been snowing and she had insisted on dragging him from the warmth to see the river from a new angle. Beauty had long ago left his life, but he'd had to admit that the river had revealed itself with a serene elegance that none of his girlfriends had ever shown.

Evie moved to stand next to him and lean on the black railings.

'We as a race have come a long way since the Middle Passage . . .' Evie began.

He let his sister continue, knowing she was going into one of her 'Do you remember the days of slavery?' speeches. He'd never had the guts to say what he really thought. Since he was moving on maybe he should.

He interrupted her. 'Not being funny or nothing, Evie girl, but we grew up opposite a railway arch off Mare Street. Not exactly Africa or the Caribbean.'

She looked startled. Startled that he had the nerve to challenge her, with her African History degree, with a minor in Arabic? Startled that he knew what the Middle Passage was? He wasn't sure, but she needed to know he wasn't some passive observer watching his life cruise by. At least not any more. Her next words challenged him back.

'Don't you feel sometimes like you're in the Middle Passage? People still crapping on you from a great height? People still keeping you in the depths of the ship denying you access to all those other options in life . . .'

'If you asked me this five years ago, a year ago, six months ago, I would have agreed. But you know what, I started to realise, so I went to a shithouse of a school, so some of my teachers were full of out-and-out fuckrees, so the screws in prison weren't looking for me to enlighten them about the events of Black History Month. The one thing I learnt on the street was that there's just you, your intentions and a world out there. And you have to decide, where do I fit in? Do I want to spend the rest of my days eating peri-peri chicken from Nando's? No fucking way. This is my life, this is my time, this is my . . .' He stopped, looking for a word to complete what he wanted to say.

'Pilgrimage.' He found his word and stopped. Fucking hell, he sounded like Mother Dorinda.

'I don't want any more excuses . . .' he began.

'Yeah, but . . .'

'I know what you're going to say. Ain't it tough for our black men? Ain't that another boulder someone has put in our way? And it's true, but the power I'm feeling inside of me, right here – '

He grabbed her wind-warped wrist and placed her hand over the pulse in the groove of his breastbone. They felt it belting, beating, alive, awake, joining them for the first time in years. He forced her hand deeper.

'This keeps telling me that I am the most powerful thing in my life and no wall, no teachers, no . . . nothing is going to stand in my way. The only thing holding me back is myself.'

He stopped, his breath coming hard and confident. He released her wrist, but her hand stayed there, and he hoped it was feeling the truth of what he was saying. He turned to the side, making her hand fall, and shoved his fingers through his locks. He felt a bit foolish because he wasn't one for speeches. Wasn't one to start letting other people off the hook. Her hand started rubbing his back the same way it use to when he'd had a rough time at school. He hadn't felt her warmth for such a long time. His back melted into her rhythm. He felt her rhythm change as she started speaking.

'I came to say that I think I might have found somewhere for you to stay. It can't be mine because I don't need any trouble in my home, but a friend of mine, a good friend, can help. He won't ask any questions and I will be doing the same. I don't want to know the whole story. Just make me a promise, Eli.'

He fixed his eyes on her. So she wanted a favour for a favour. She wasn't so different from other people.

'Just promise me that when you're nice and settled in Devon me and Tammy can come and visit.'

They both grinned at each other, looking more alike than they had in a long time. He picked up his bag and they trod the path back to her home.

16

The south side of Hackney was on the way up. It had been for the last
few years. Some said the renaissance first started grooving in Hoxton.
Others claimed it happened in the Shoreditch end of Kingsland Road.
Hoxton was all funked-out people, watering dens spilling on to the
street and nosh shops aplenty. There were still buildings that had a
long way to go, but that just added to the atmos. The other contender,
the nearest piece of Kingsland Road, was still cutting its umbilical
cord with Dalston. Now it was name-dropping itself as Kingsland
Village. The Vietnamese community used it as a chance to extend its
trade from nail bars to eateries. Plain cafés that were sparse to aid a
quick bite and the more luxurious types that gave punters enough
time to use the tooth-picks on offer. The only ache in the village ideal
was Parkview Heights. The tenant population had been decamped to
other buildings while the council tried to fresh-start the block with a
refurbishment programme. The building's east side, west side, front
and back all had views of the planned park below. Someone should
have suspected there was a trick in here somewhere because there
were no trees. Who ever heard of a park without a tree?

Parkview was a tower block whose top floor was cursed locally as
Death Row. In the last two years it had become the most popular spot
to dish out retribution and warnings to those who had forgotten the
rules of the underworld by tossing them from the top floor. The first
one had been at Number 90. Teenage girl, no shoes, no identity, with
the earphones from her Walkman cut into her neck. The Blues found
her Walkman still playing the riff of some rapper who insisted he
needed to take five caps before he could check out what life was really
about. The second one had been at number 93. Smooth-boy type, too
much gold jewellery and pulped face. The last one had been on

Christmas Eve last year. An arm, a leg and a bagful of money. By the time the Blues had arrived the bag had gone.

When the number of incidents passed into double figures most locals thought that would be the end of the revival. But death pushed property prices sky high. It wasn't just anywhere in London you could get a memorable meal, a trendy bed for the night and the local crims providing the cabaret. That was art, dahling.

Schoolboy sat, with Evie and Lloyd, in the car on the street next to Parkview and art wasn't what was brushing through his mind. Weariness was burning a fever through his skin, but time was scratching him like jaundice, reminding him that his time was here and he couldn't afford to let it get away.

Lloyd had arrived at Evie's looking noble, but overburdened in the shoulders, as if he wouldn't mind living his life all over again. Schoolboy had warmed to the way he wore his garms. Patted down, but with enough flare and spill for the world to take him seriously. And he was a serious brother who didn't let the strain of smiling get in his way. Evie had called him up because he ran the housing section of one of Hackney's divisions, which meant he held the keys to a variety of unoccupied properties. Lloyd had started bleating about it being highly improper, a professor doing his inaugural speech. But Schoolboy could tell him bits about Evie's early life that showed she was no stranger to the street. But those tales were for another time, another place, not tonight. So all three of them had sat there while Evie went through her idea. Hide him in a block where no one would think to look for him. The way she'd spun her idea, walking back and forth barrister-style, he was surprised that Lloyd couldn't tell she had cultivated her mind interacting with the street. Lloyd had taken Evie aside and started whispering in her ear. The whispering had gone on a long time, until they had both reached some type of agreement. An agreement they hadn't shared with him. Now as they sat near Parkview he understood why.

The car was warm and smelt sweet with the purchased fragrance of something no doubt called Citrus Simmer or Calm Breeze. Lloyd parked up and shut off the engine, eliminating the glare from the headlights, one of the only sources of light on Peppercorn Avenue. Those operating in the dark needed exactly that – the dark. So most of the street lights had been destroyed. After a while the council had simply stopped fixing them.

'Doesn't look as frightening as you would think in real life,' Evie jumped in. Her voice sounded bold. Schoolboy turned his head to look at her in the back. He saw how she clutched her shoulder bag and knew she had fear panting through her body.

What, was she having second thoughts about coming along? Visiting the wilder side of the urban landscape a bit too real? She was on his turf now and he wanted her to know it.

'This isn't a day trip to Alton Towers,' Schoolboy said, slipping his head back towards the front.

'Make sure you have this on at all times when you are around the block,' Lloyd's quiet tones stepped in.

He handed Schoolboy a black baseball cap with 'Hackney Council' written in fluorescent script on the peak.

'None of the workmen will challenge you with this,' Lloyd continued.

Although his tongue was talking to Schoolboy, his eyes were checking Evie in his rear mirror. The surface of blood filling his lips told Schoolboy that Lloyd liked what he saw.

'Right, no time to fool around. Let's go,' Evie said. But she didn't lean over to open the door.

'Before we go I should say,' Lloyd paused and let his tongue wet his lips, using the same lift a hand uses to pass someone a tissue after they have received bad news, 'All the flats are being done, so the only ones that are still untouched are on the top floor . . .'

'No way, no way,' Schoolboy hammered in before Lloyd could finish, letting his body fall back and take root in the seat.

He'd already let the decay of two dead men blow into his face and he wasn't about to let any more of the restless dead force him to smell their breath. Even the street couldn't give you that type of courage.

'But that's exactly the point,' Evie explained.

Suddenly Schoolboy knew what she and Lloyd had been whispering about before they left.

She continued to outline her idea: 'No one is going to think you'd be bonkers enough to stay here.'

'You're right, they won't because I-man am not booking in.'

'But this is such a brilliant idea.' She pressed forward and folded her arms and elbows over the back of his seat. 'It may not sound safe but it's the safest place we could think of.'

Looking at her poise he could smell satisfaction all over her. Then it hit him and he knew why she had come along for the ride. She wanted him to suffer. She wanted to see him suffer. To suffer for all the grief he had given to her. To suffer for all the people he had done over in his time. She had him well and truly kippered, as they used to say back in school. But her reasoning made sense.

'But can't you find one of the other flats, like on the ground floor?' he asked Lloyd, but he knew he was going to be defeated, because Lloyd was too captivated by Evie tempting him with a piece of her fanny in the back.

'Not really, because the only keys on site will be the flats not already done.' Lloyd's voice drifted into the one he used for presentations. Flat, monotone and boring. No wonder he was looking for a pleasing bit of muff to make life worthwhile.

They sat there in silence, with the seen-it-all-before grandeur of the local museum in the far shadow across the road. He had no choice. He grasped his bag for life and opened the door, signalling his decision. The wind was cold, not bitter, but with enough bite to make him think of being somewhere else. As Lloyd fiddled with the keys and he heard his sister giggling her thanks, he let his eyes roam up the block. To describe Parkview in relation to its bricks and mortar was missing the point. Everyone was only interested in what happened at the top, so its height was what took over. It wasn't tall by high-rise standards but it was far enough away from the ground to end a dream. He wondered if you could smell the young daffodils from the top. He turned back to Evie and Lloyd and saw that they too were wrapped up in assessing the block's height. For Evie he knew what it would look like. The first time everyone saw it they thought of all its stories and instantly saw a free-standing coffin. He began chilling and it wasn't the cool street variety.

'Let's get this over and done with,' he said, moving forward.

Lloyd quickly overtook him and led the way. All three went past the black railings and stopped at the entrance. Life had long ago rubbed off the main doors' simulated walnut glaze. The slats of glass that ran halfway up were so smeared with hand-prints that Schoolboy knew that the entrance system hadn't worked for most of the time and the residents had used their palms impatiently to bang their way out. Lloyd unlocked the padlock and opened the way. They all began coughing from the dust that shook in their faces. Lloyd switched a light on and Schoolboy wasn't surprised to see the reception filled with heavy-duty builders' bags. The walls surprised him. Sparkling white tiles set out just like those makeover programmes told you to do in the bathroom. Schoolboy wondered if they were going to follow through with a laminated look to the floor. While he and Evie checked out their surroundings, Lloyd disappeared into an adjoining room. He was soon back with a new bundle of keys.

'Number 95 I think will suit your purposes,' Lloyd remarked, grinning with his top teeth for the first time that night.

Schoolboy nearly asked him what he thought his purpose was on earth, but one look at Evie's stern look told him to keep his mouth firmly shut. Lloyd called up the lift for the even-numbered floors. When it came each got inside with their own brand of hushed composure. Although the lift had been cleaned up there was still an aroma of ingrained urine washing in it. Schoolboy stared hard at Evie and Lloyd. He didn't know why they looked so uptight. It wasn't them who would have to bed down here. The red light of the floor buttons blinked 2, 4, 6 until it reached 14. The doors peeled back. Schoolboy and his bag for life took the first steps into Death Row.

He'd heard so much about this place that he had his own fixed image of what it would be like. Dark hall, graffiti, and the noise of bad people doing bad things. What welcomed him was worse. This looked like the part of a psychiatric unit where the sectioned patients were kept. Dull cream walls so quiet that the mind started to conjure up its own noise of voices demanding, pleading, screaming. The stale air was hard for them to move through not because of its stench but because it was thick with the unfulfilled lives of human beings. Given a blank canvas, the mind can make up its own dreadful stories. Schoolboy still took the lead and wondered which cell was his. He passed number 93, number 94 and then stood stiff outside number 95.

Number 95's door had a flimsy and shrunken relationship with its frame. Schoolboy blanked his thoughts. He didn't want to think about what had happened beyond the door.

Lloyd came forward, still doing his caretaker bit, and started opening the newest chapter to Schoolboy's life. Once having done his part, Lloyd hustled back. He wasn't interested in carrying Schoolboy over the threshold. Schoolboy suddenly wanted his sister to come forward to hold his hand.

'Come on,' her voice was beside him. She looped her arm into his, making the bag for life feel much heavier than it was. She pushed the door open, and he made the first step over the entrance. He felt against the wall and flicked the light-switch on and his mouth drooped down, wide enough for any passing spirit to float into.

Schoolboy knew that behind every door on every estate there was a story. You never knew what to expect. That's what you expected. Behind some doors were sumptuous and palatial furnishings. Behind others were crates for chairs and cardboard for carpets. There were as many types of flats as there were tenants. So he shouldn't have been surprised by the flat at Parkview – but he couldn't help himself. He stood revolving his eyes around the main room after completing his tour.

'I thought you would like this,' Lloyd started, professor back in his shoes as he perched with Evie on the chaise longue. 'We couldn't believe someone was living like this. Most probably one of those Yardie types, who really didn't need all of this when he was moving on. As long as they have got their gold chains, their women and fast cars . . .' Lloyd lectured on with the authority of someone who got all their information from the broadsheets.

'Lloyd, are you sure this is appropriate?' Schoolboy didn't even need to look across the room to see the outraged fix of Evie's face as she asked the question.

Lloyd was staring at her and her tone, knowing he had made the wrong move.

'But I thought . . .' He stopped because her expression didn't obviously change.

She was pissed because he wasn't going to suffer. This flat was all about pleasure. The type of home that kept bags of weed hidden all over. The hall was colour-washed blanched lilac walls and ivory sanded floorboards that trickled into the bedroom and bathroom. The scents that fought for supremacy in the hall told Schoolboy that the bathroom would be accommodating a range of oriental scents and massage oils bought from Woolworth's. The bedroom ceiling was covered with a full-sized mirror – although what the point of that was with a four-poster, Schoolboy couldn't say. Perhaps the roof came off. The main room was pure brothel chic. Rag-rolled gold walls that twisted into flame-blown red walls. Two high-backed armchairs that sank into the cushion of the gilt-coloured carpet. The hot pink chaise longue lay back ready for action, although it was clear from Evie's body language Lloyd was out of luck tonight. Along one side of the room was a narrow ersatz bar with half-empty bottles of supermarket cocktails propping it up. Heavy cherry curtains framed by a plush pelmet made sure that the world kept its nose out.

Schoolboy dropped his bag and sat, king of the castle style, on an armchair. He gazed thoughtfully round the room before saying,

'I don't want to be picky – but I wasn't expecting Del Trotter meets Cynthia Payne . . .'

Abruptly, Evie pushed up and began stomping towards the door. Her extensions double-flicked against her shoulder as if they were muttering to themselves.

'Come on, Lloyd. I'm sure Eli can take of himself in his new-found luxury.' Her voice bounced off the walls as she kept up her manic pace towards the front door.

As Lloyd picked himself up, Schoolboy knew he had to get to Evie before him. They had unfinished business. Schoolboy rushed to his sister, catching her back as she entered the passage.

'You forgot to give me the money, right?' he whispered.

She spun around, her face blowing with acrid annoyance.

'Wrong,' her answer rippled like a bell, reminding him of wake-up time in prison.

She started swinging back to her original direction, but the quick tap of his fingers against her arm stopped her.

'What's forty small ones to you? I ain't even got enough dosh to put credit in my phone,' he wheedled, even though he had topped up his personal MB earlier on in the day.

'Are you freebasing or something? I haven't got it in my pocket.'

Evie stuffed her hands into her coat pocket and pulled the lining out. She was pissed, big time, but he noticed that her voice hadn't slipped into rude gal styleee as it usually did when they argued. He realised that she was conscious of Lloyd and couldn't afford for him to see her slip into the street. Everyone has a weakness. Sometimes more than one. A different weakness for a different situation. And his sister's weakness at that moment was Lloyd.

Schoolboy twisted around to Lloyd, stepped towards him as a surprised Lloyd took a pace back.

'Lloyd, what about a brother-to-brother loan? I only need forty . . .'

'You are unbelievable,' Evie yelled as she stormed towards him. She turned her eyes to Lloyd. 'Come on, Lloyd, we'd better get out of here before he tries to rip off our political consciousness from our backs.'

Lloyd stood there and looked at both of them. His delicate eyebrows moved together, wriggled and then slipped apart. Schoolboy knew he was weighing up jeopardising having fun with fanny tonight or bonding with the brotherhood. Lloyd's hand began to creep into his pocket.

'Lloyd, don't do it,' Evie demanded.

But Lloyd ignored her and started to take something out of his pocket. Schoolboy grinned, dimples jubilant as Evie flounced towards the door. Lloyd took a step towards Schoolboy. Schoolboy stretched his hand out. As Lloyd dropped the item into his hand, Schoolboy was already thanking him.

'Thanks, bro'. This means so much . . .' His words dried up as he looked at the small card in his hand.

'A phone card?'

'Fully charged. I believe you said that you needed some credit.'

Both Schoolboy and Evie gazed at Lloyd with the same look – pissed-off unbelievability.

'I would say thanks, Lloyd, but I can't use it without your SIM card,' Schoolboy said, breaking the silence, but he didn't pass the card back.

'Only trying to help.'

Schoolboy wanted to tell him he could help by emptying his pockets, but he didn't.

Evie ripped at the door handle and briskly left the flat. Lloyd followed after her. As he reached the door, he turned back to Schoolboy and groaned:

'Sorry, man.'

The doors closed, leaving Schoolboy with the sound of their footsteps fading along the outside corridor. His thumb and forefinger started to rub together as he wondered if any of Parkview's victims had plunged, head first, from Flat 95.

17

After Evie and Lloyd were gone, Schoolboy paced from room to room. From the kitchen to the bathroom. From the bathroom to the bedroom. Then back to the kitchen again. The type of kitchen he'd always wanted. Long, not too big. It knew how to use its space. Chrome work surfaces, hood and handles. Beige leather floor tiles that gave the duel-fuel cooker the elevation it needed to strut its stuff. His mind was ticking, but it wasn't thinking about decor.

Arms braced, gripping the edge of the sink, with the energy of a sleepwalker he let the questions come. Some had answers, some didn't. He thought about hitching to Devon. He shook his locks, dismissing it. A black man standing on the side of the road was likely to make the speeding fines look like peanuts as cars whizzed past him. Just because Queen hadn't found the Nokia wide awake at his gates didn't mean she was going to slow the hunt for him. Just because he'd severed his line with the phone didn't mean she was going to stop trying to connect with him. He knew the rules of the streets too well. Once you were in the portrait it was hard to be removed from the shot. He could hawk all the gear in this flat and Queen would still hunt him in Devon. Look what happened to Boxer. Knuckles like stones, rolled fingers that had the gift to knock someone flat. But he never did. He'd used his quickness another way. But quickness hadn't helped him when that counterfeit plate passed his way. He'd only embraced it once, then moved it on. They still found him dead, on the borders of Stokey and Dalston, minus his memorable hands. Schoolboy allowed his to tighten into the bareness of the sink. No way was that occurring to him. His mouth felt nasty. He spat heavily into the sink, turned the tap on and washed it away.

He groaned as he began moving out of the room. That's why he never let himself stand still. Too many memories ganging up behind him just to bring him down. And the biggest memory of all was how much death had become a part of his life. He knew he had to keep it together, so he distracted himself by looking for that leaf he suspected was hidden in the flat. He dislodged drawers, searched under the bed, shook down the bathroom as thoroughly as he could. Nothing. He wound up in the kitchen again. His drugs hiding place had been inside the loose top of the kitchen cupboards. No chance of sniffer dogs going that high. He leapt up on to the work surface near the cooker and stood up. He looked down. The kitchen was even more beautiful from that angle. He hoped Michael had one just like this. He opened the door facing him. The cupboard was full. Surprisingly. Canned this and canned that, along with the odd packet of white flour and refined sugar. People really needed to start getting into wholemeal. He bent his knees low so that he could hook his hand inside. He pressed his palm hard against the top. It came loose. He shifted it to the side and let his hand roam, like a blind man checking the outside world for the first time. Nothing. He checked the next one. Nothing. And the next. Nothing. He jumped down and checked the cupboard next to the sink.

The bag of leaf wasn't even hidden. It lay between a box of non-biological soap powder and packet of big-and-strong condoms. He lifted the small bag out and kicked the door shut with his foot. He opened the bag and inhaled. Mellow, mature, with seeds that were already giving him a lift. Life was on its way up.

Ten minutes later found him inhaling on the kinky purple-covered bed. He had no intention of slipping beneath its covers. He knew what type of sex games had been played there. The only item he put under the spread was his train ticket which he hid under the pillow. The contents of his jacket were lying beside him as a result of his search for his papers. King-size, none of that small stuff. His eyes began to smudge, blur, close as the leaf took his mind to another zone. He drifted, relaxed, falling into the state of inactivity that he so longed for. He had started to drift when he heard the sound of his bonus-prize ringtone join him in the room. Evie. He shot straight up. It must really be bonus-prize time because she finally had the money for him.

He groped for one of the two phones that lay between his keys and the 'God's gonna save you' leaflet the church sisters had given him near the –1 Club. As he relaxed back on the bed he pressed green and held it to his face. The line was dead. He pulled the phone away from his ear and inspected it. He realised he'd picked up the wrong phone. This grass was really fucking and floating his mind. He dropped his personal MB and lunged for his business line. He leaned back again as his voice soothed into the phone. 'Evie, I knew you'd come through for me, girl.'

'Sorry to disappoint you, Mister Schoolbwoy, but this isn't Evie,' came the voice. Female, angry, tone clipped out of tune.

His eyes and body popped open and up. The fever was back with him, this time scalding his tongue, making it impossible for him to speak. He'd never heard that voice before, but he knew who it was. The Queen herself. He took one last drag of smoke, let the smoke add a new colour to the room and answered.

'Wrong number, luv.' Better to play dumb then to enter the truth.

'I never get anything wrong, Mister Schoolbwoy.' Only his mum had called him Mister when he had done something wrong.

'OK – so what do you want?' he asked, wondering who had given out his number. But since he had so many contacts that was like trying to count how many people wore red-and-white at Highbury.

'I don't want to fall out with you, bwoy, but you've got something that belongs to me and I want it back.'

'So I hear, but what would be in it for me?'

'I don't do deals with people who have taken my property, especially when they're two-dollar street bwoys,' she continued, her voice becoming hard. 'Either way you've got two paths in front of you. One will take you to a great light. The other to the terrors of the shadows of death.' She stopped after finishing her Bible class.

'And why should I trust anyone who thinks they are Mother Teresa with a Kalashnikov?' That one came out of his mouth on its own. The spirit of the weed was taking over.

'Think about what would be in it for you if you don't hand it over,' Queen hummed.

'And would it be over?'

'You'll be over if I don't get it back. Ask around,' she proclaimed proudly, 'I think you'll soon get a picture of what happens to those who upset me.'

Schoolboy was silent.

'Look, kiddie, just give it up. I'm not patient,' she growled.

'That phone must be very special if a lady like you is willing to stoop to chat to a bod like me. So what's going on with the phone, Queen?'

'You're already up to your balls, bwoy, I wouldn't want to have to squeeze them as well.'

Schoolboy retreated back to silence.

'I'm not vindictive. If I've got my ting back why would I want to do you a badness? We could say it was all a misunderstanding.'

Her tone was soft, melting, a bit like Terri-baby's when he'd given her the old heave-ho. He couldn't think. His forehead was pressing towards his nose. Everything felt heavy. He stood up to take charge. It was either him swaying or the wallpaper on the walls was peeling off.

'If I did, how do I know you won't close me down for good?'

She started laughing. Deep, long, unhealthy.

'What would I gain from that? There's already too many bodies piling up on the pavement because of this business.'

'OK. I would shake your hand but the phone's in the way.' That was the smoke talking again. He shook his locks. He couldn't have her thinking he was taking the big P out of her.

'Good. So we will meet . . .'

He cut across her confidence.

'But since we're becoming such good soul-mates, why don't I choose the ground to do business on.'

Silence. It stretched and he realised that his heart was shaking. A loud, powerful voice started wailing from the loudspeakers of the nearby mosque. Then it stopped, obviously not a call to prayer, although Schoolboy knew he could do with someone lamenting on his behalf.

'What's that noise?'

Schoolboy could feel the sensation of Queen's ears open up.

'The only sound I need to hear, Queen, is you agreeing to meet me on neutral ground.'

'Not my usual style but I'll do it for you. Just this once,' Queen grudgingly accepted.

Shit, now she'd chucked the card back at him he couldn't think of anywhere. His new plush pad was out big time. As he rummaged in his brain his eyes dipped around the room. They stopped when they caught sight of the church leaflet praying on the purple spread.

'Come on, man, stop playing me for a fool.'

He quickly picked up the crumpled leaflet on the bed and read out loud, 'The Church of Celestial Peace. Expect a miracle! Tomorrow at 5 at 10 Lime Lane, off New Cross Road.'

'That's not really within the boundaries of my yard, bwoy.'

'Then consider this an opportunity to go global.'

He pressed red. The line went dead. He slumped down. He couldn't remember what day it was. Monday? Wednesday? Friday? He pulled the phone low to check the date. Thursday 25th. Thursday, Thursday, Thursday. Which meant Friday, Saturday, Sunday. Three days left. Three days to hide himself away from the world. But time had found him and he didn't have the phone.

Bandanna on, hood up, puff jacket zipped to his mouth, Schoolboy and the first flecks of Friday were driving the streets again. The imposing dark added to his cover. He didn't want to be here but what option did he have? Being backed into a wait-and-see wasn't his style. He heard his mum's warning – *Cockroach have no right in fowl party*. Do not put yourself where you shouldn't be. But what could he do when he suspected he'd created the barriers himself? A car horn blasted as his thoughts led him aimlessly into the road. He lunged back but still got a mouthful and a few gestures. He didn't have time for small people, only the big ones snapping at his backside.

He smiled to himself. A crooked smile that was half pleasure, half sad. All those people looking for him and they didn't realise that Parkview was a ten-minute walk away from his old flat in Ernie. That's where he was headed. To Ernie. To the bins. He had to get the phone back. His feet picked up speed as he prayed that the bins hadn't been emptied. Usual day was Friday, but knowing the council's drive for efficiency the day would have changed just to spite him. His smile became straight as the chances of the council becoming efficient were about the same odds as Devon hosting the annual Reggae Sunsplash.

'Mate, you got any spare change?' a voice suddenly choked beside him.

He looked up to see a teenager, sick from too much H and loneliness. Couldn't tell if he was black or white from the dark and the dirt creamed across the face.

'Do I look like the dole office?' he handed back, pissed that anyone was getting in the way of his rhythm.

He swept past knowing he should be feeling bad and all that, but at the end of the day he hadn't force-fed him drugs. That was someone else's problem. He had his own problems, or issues as Evie liked to call them, in his way. Ernie came into view. He stopped to shuffle his head deeper under the hood and to check the scene. He wouldn't be surprised if Queen had sentry duty posted again. He crept forward and checked out the courtyard. No Beamers, only the cars in their usual rectangular pitches. He noticed a new one. Sports car, laid-back red, with wheels that were an accessory not an addition. Someone in the block had struck lucky. The beat of the latest hip-hop star rippled across the block and jiggled in the yard. That wasn't good. He didn't need any night-dwellers recognising him.

He approached the bin lock-up with feet as soft as the piano G note being repeated throughout the music drifting from Ernie. He took off his bandanna and wrapped it around his mouth. This was going to be hard. He forced the door open and the bandanna could not freeze the smell of waste. He closed his mouth tight but the abrasive flavour of the stench had already settled on the back of his throat. Piles of tied carrier bags were littered around the three large rubbish containers. It had definitely been the middle one. He used his gloved hands to grip the edge and tip it forward. He hunched down and let his hands pull rubbish forward and searched. Anything with newspaper was what he was after. He felt paper, soaked with he knew not what. He began tearing the paper. He jumped back, his mouth flapping open when the ugly body of a dead pigeon and live maggots were exposed.

His feet crunched into carrier bags as he threw himself out of the lock-up, coughing and spitting. Fuck, he couldn't do this. He gulped the air, not clean but not fetid. He blew three breaths as if he was getting ready for a fight and dived back in. The second unveiling was even more obscene. The nappy of a baby that just hadn't got on with its food. An untied blue carrier bag of torn letters came next. Rotten chicken skin and bone wrapped in soaking newspaper came after that. The fifth offering made him hesitate. Hesitate because a small transparent bag of meth crystals lay in the palm of his hand.

Street value was twelve to twenty quid a wrap.

Jail value for supplying could be fourteen years.

His value was zilch.

Selling them for money wasn't going to get him to Devon. Queen didn't want cash, she wanted the Nokia. Besides, he didn't need the heat of whoever they belonged to added to the list of people already licking at his tail. He threw the bag with the rest of the exposed rubbish. By the tenth package the sweat was dripping like juice from his forehead. He threw packets out of the bin like a kid at a lucky dip. He kicked the bin when he realised the Nokia was not there. He stared at the other two bins and knew what he had to do.

The second bin was tipped down. More mess, junk and the plain curious fell out. Why would someone want to throw out this beautiful photo he was holding? Then he remembered where he had seen those faces before – Kiley, who lived on the first floor, and her new baby. The baby had died one month after getting its first tooth. He placed it gently to the side. He supposed some memories are just too painful to look at each day. He carried on. The second bin yielded nothing. His frustration pumped sweat and despair on to his skin.

As he pulled the third bin, the sound of voices caught his ear. He steadied the bin with his hands, stopping its fall. He swung around, reached for the rusty door handle and pulled it shut. He stood in the darkness with fear freezing next to him. He pegged two fingers over the bandanna at his nose. The darkness smelt bad.

'Bloody kids.' The female voice was so close Schoolboy was sure it was in the lock-up with him.

'Ruby, what are you doing?' The second voice was male, more distant, as if the smell of human waste was too strong for him.

'Someone has to clean this up.' The voice drew closer. It was nasal, impatient and fed up as if it had spent too much time in its life looking downwards.

'Ruby, you can't do that now. You'll stink by the time we get back to mine. Come on, Ruby, I thought you wanted to play with my trembling torpedo.'

Masses of giggles and laughter licked up against the door. Schoolboy was glad that someone was having a good time tonight. He didn't smile. The click of thin heels and rubber began to move away, until he couldn't hear them any more. He unpegged his nose but held his breath as he started to push the door open. The approach of more footsteps stopped him. He reared back and jammed into the second bin. He scratched his leg, as if the pigeon's maggots had got to him. The steps got closer, jangling the ground like tap shoes. They stopped outside the door. The sound of a zipper being pulled filled the air. Then the sound of liquid being poured took over. The steam of urine wafted under the steel door and vaporised on Schoolboy's face. He quickly pegged his nose again.

'*Moon river*,' a rough, liquored-up voice began to sing. Out of tune, not a care in the world.

Schoolboy identified the voice of Luther, who lived on the first floor, near the lift, number seven. Dirty old boy. So it was Luther who had been desecrating the block. Jackie had been after the culprit for ages. Leaving his mark in the lift, on the stairs, in the kids' playground.

'Ah,' Luther let out, happy and high. The zipper went back up and the merry feet went on their way.

Schoolboy's body was hot, his own salt liquid streaming down his back. He gently pushed the door. Satisfied no one else was coming, he thrust forward into the yard and started breathing. Breathing as if he was taking his first-ever breath. He knew that the third bin still had to be done. He mumbled an offhand prayer and drove back into the lock-up. He dug, scattered, opened. Nothing. He stood upright and took a step back. He stank and the biggest stinker of all was this idea.

As his eyes fell about the mess, he tried to think of more options. His eyes moved around as his brain tried to bring together thoughts that created ideas. Nothing. Shaking, he stumbled forward, avoiding Luther's visiting card, and leaned his hand flat against the door. He started swinging his foot in frustration, kicking the rubbish further into the yard. He kicked and kicked until his leg hit something thin and long that sprayed liquid all over his trousers and against the door. The object hit one object and hit another that lay peeping from newspaper so wet it appeared grey. The last object tumbled out and over, revealing itself. A phone. Schoolboy forget his wet trousers and sprinted forward. He leaned down and laughed.

There was his beloved brick. He picked it up and cleaned it against his jacket. He stared at it, his nostrils flaring in relief. The white buttons looked like teeth smiling back at him. He shoved it in his pocket. He knew he'd made a mess but that was someone else's problem. He could hear Jackie's voice in his head, scolding him. His smile disappeared. A dozen memories started hassling him. All funny. All mournful. He stared at Ernie, capturing it for what he knew was probably the last time.

He still had three more jobs to do. He took his business mobile out of his jeans pocket, removed the SIM card and tossed it in with the rubbish. A phone for a phone. Sounded like a fair swap. It was hard to let his business line go, but the priority was to cut Queen's direct line with him. Now he was back with two mobiles, his personal line and an old-fashioned brick he just wanted out of his life. Now he was only available to Window, Evie, Tammy and Robbie, the four people with his personal MB number. He looked at the bins. He picked up Kiley's photo. His second job. He didn't know if this was right but he couldn't leave that baby in the bin. He hurried forward up the stairs so that he could leave it outside Kiley's door on the first floor. After he'd placed the photo outside the blue door, he pulled out his personal MB and tapped in a number from his address book. Last job. He knew this meant that one other person would now have his personal number but he needed to do this.

'Hey, G, it's SB. Good to see you at the club on Tuesday. I think it's time for that favour . . .'

Schoolboy paced around the main room in cell 95, Death Row, with his curiosity churning up the floor. Curiosity about the phone. After returning from the bins, face blazing, sweat leaking from his back, he'd dropped the phone on to the chaise longue as if he'd been carrying a hand grenade in his pocket. Except it hadn't exploded but lay there like an old woman on a park bench too frail even to feed the birds.

Now, with a smooth stick drooping from his lips, he strode towards the phone and stared at it. He bent down, inhaled and blew smoke over it like an open challenge for it to come clean about its secrets. This phone had been around a long time and obviously had a few stories to tell. Schoolboy knew he shouldn't be doing this, but when you'd lived a life where coincidences and opportunities rarely rubbed rhythms, it wasn't that easy to walk on by. Maybe if he knew what its secret was he could set up his own deal. Win himself a packet of bread. A ton would get him rigged up again to the knives and the Amsterdam. A pony would get him the knives, enough puff for a month and a few new garms. A grand, now that sounded so sweet. His tongue flexed inside his mouth. He'd be able to strut into Michael's restaurant, tanned fur collar turned up, tickling his neck as he breezed out, 'Hey man, Schoolboy is in the house.' He knew he was dreaming, but it was better than thinking of himself mashed to death like the geez at the Junction.

He shoved his face closer. Peered harder. Abruptly the screen blinked on, manic deep green, making him tumble back. His Tims tangled and he fell, arse first, on to the floor.

As his body folded together, the scent of the bins rolled towards his nose from his clothes. But he didn't have time to clean himself. He only had time to make that phone talk. He pushed himself up, stretching towards the phone. The screen was back to being blank.

There was only one way to get this phone talking. He rushed to the bedroom. He grabbed his bag for life and rummaged inside. He dragged out both of his phone chargers and took them into the main room. He scanned the room for an electric socket, finding one near the goatskin red lamp beside the door. He dragged a last hit from his spliff and squashed it into the ashtray on the table. He moved steadily towards the phone and plucked it up. He took his new companions in his hands to the socket. He fell to his knees and plugged in his personal mobile phone charger. He lifted the phone, angling its base towards him and then tried to fit the end of the charger's lead into it. It wouldn't fit. His personal charger had three pins and the phone had one hole. Idiot, Schoolboy cursed. He ripped the charger from the socket and chucked it to the side. He picked up the next charger and inspected it, finding that it had one pin. He smiled. He tried once again to connect the phone to electricity, but the charger's pin was too small. He huffed as he heaved the charger to the side without unplugging it.

Fuckrees.

So the phone didn't want to jump up at the carnival tonight. If he couldn't get it working he knew there was no way he could discover why the street was hot on the phone's tail. He bowed his head, feeling the edge of the floorboard cut into his leg. Seeing his sweat drip on to the floor, he travelled back to the night the gun was aching above his head. He sprang up. He refused to go back there. Maybe he should heed Mum's words and stop behaving like a cockroach with a can of insect-repellent ready to be sprayed in his bug eyes. He just hoped that tomorrow Queen didn't have plans to have another gun hanging over his life, because he knew this time the trigger wouldn't hesitate to blast him and Devon away.

18

Cuthbert, known to his crew family as Cuttie, was on the phone as he sat in the Beamer watching Schoolboy's flat in Ernest Bevin House.

'Dread, stop calling me so often. If Queen find out, who will pay for me pickney them private school fees? When me have news me will call you.'

He rang off, focusing on the flat. The morning was loafing with the promise of rain and wind to come. He settled further back into the leather seat because the cold was starting to carve its way through the window screen. Queen had told him to do this job on his own. Less obvious she had said. But as the BMW was the only large engine on site it couldn't have been more obvious. He checked his timepiece. 11 a.m. He'd already been here for four hours and still no sign of his prey. Queen had told him to come straight here yesterday evening, but when his woman had offered him some homemade lovin' there had been no contest.

Two more hours to go and then he had to get ready for the next job. Some low-life thinking he could hide away from Queen in Vicky Park. He was distracted by the arrival of a white van. Large, with 'J-J's Collection' written on its side. Cuttie's lips primed down on his B and H, sucked in and watched as three men jumped out of the van. Two white, one black. Maybe all their job applications had said only apply if you have a 50-inch chest because all had fronts that put Cuttie's to shame. They left the courtyard and Cuttie's eyes let them go. He looked the block up and down. He saw the head of the mad red-haired woman from the first landing. He shook his head. Too many off-the-wall people stomping around Hackney these days. His eyes trailed upwards and saw the heads of three men bobbing along the second floor. He yanked up, shifted his head low and forward and peered through the windscreen. The three men stopped at the flat he had helped turn over the other day.

The heads disappeared. He jostled the door open, stood heavy with his converted buckie in his pocket and ran for the stairs. He took the stairs two at a time. He swung into the second-floor landing, then his strong strides were stilled by what he saw. The smaller furnishings they had ripped through yesterday were now being loaded into black bags waiting on the balcony. He had no idea what was going on but he was going to find out. He kicked up the motion of his body and went forward. One hand lay across his gun in his pocket, the other swung at his side. As he raised his leg to step over a bag, one of the men came outside. Cuttie's hand firmed around the metal in his pocket. The man looked at him and dropped a black bag.

'Looking for someone?' was the question thrown at him. The voice was tough like the acne-marked pink face. The man's body was rigid as if he wasn't going anywhere.

'I could ask you the same thing,' Cuttie replied, shoving his neck up to look taller.

'You what? If you're looking for the tenant, a . . .' the man pulled a piece of paper out of his overall pocket, 'Mr E. Campbell' – his eyes returned to Cuttie – 'he ain't here.'

'A problem, Gerry?' a voice called from the doorway.

Cuttie swung around to see the black one's muscle-wrapped frame standing in the doorway.

'Geezer wants to know about the tenant.'

Cuttie felt more comfortable with a bredda, so he slipped into a language they both understood. A language that would keep the one called Gerry in the cold.

'So where him there?'

'You mean the householder?' the man in the doorway asked.

Cuttie nodded.

'Me nah know. I just come to do my work. All me can say is that the man never bother to pay them people their council tax and rent. So me and the boy them collecting him stuff as payment.'

Cuttie clicked. His hand came out of his pocket. A debt collection agency. Schoolboy had been a bad bwoy. He turned to leave them and slammed straight into the mad redhead.

'Don't I know you? Weren't you meant to fix my washing machine?' She was pointing her finger right in his face. He'd mashed people up for much less.

He shoved past her, forcing her against the wall. Too many freaks out on the street. Even as he drove off he could hear her giving J-J's Collection a hard time.

The flat at Parkview lingered with the smack of yesterday's grass. Schoolboy checked himself in the heart-shaped mirror. Back to front, front to back and then side shots of his reflection. He sniffed himself for the millionth time. He could still feel the rubbish, Luther's calling card and the pigeon's maggots crawling up his leg as the shimmering light came through the gap in the curtains. He knew he was taking it one sniff too far but he couldn't help it. He gazed back at the mirror, tilted back to give the watcher a deceptively slim view of themselves. He moved forward and pulled the mirror straight. Illusions were no longer his style. His front teeth pinched his bottom lip. He wasn't sure that his garms were polite enough to see the Lord. For a start he was dressed totally in black. Straight down trousers, polo neck, Tims and sombre face. He knew that his mum would not approve of his trip to church. But he wasn't sure that he did either.

He stripped off his polo neck, looking for a more humble colour. Purple shirt, Mum said that was for mourning. Yellow summer shirt, Mum said that was for carnival. Red sweatshirt, red was downright rude. Green or blue. He opted for the blue. Frosted with darker buttons down the middle and a lone pocket at the top. As he wrestled with the shirt his phone started ringing. Jim Reeves as mellow as ever. He stopped, heart going at it. It could only be one of four people. He hoped that it was the newest person he'd added to his personal number list.

He moved towards the bed where the phone was resting up and answered it. He remained standing.

'Schoolie, it's me.'

He sat down with relief.

'Jay-Jay. Good to hear your vibes man. So how tings go?'

'Good, good.'

Jay-Jay and Schoolboy went back a long way. Back to the days when Jay-Jay's brother André had killed himself. André had been one of Schoolboy's classmates, the one who kept his head down and slaved hard. Straight As in his GCSEs, straight As and Bs in his 'A' levels. But that hadn't helped him find work. Finally pleading with companies to recognise his talents had become too much. He'd taken to hitting the sauce and roaming the streets. One sleeveless day in July '01 his girl-friend had found him hanging from the banisters in his flat. Schoolboy had helped carry his coffin and shovel soil into his grave. Jay-Jay had never forgotten this and said that any time Schoolboy needed a favour he should give him a buzz. Now Schoolboy had called that promise in and wouldn't ask him for another.

'Any interruptions?' Schoolboy asked.

'One or two. Some bad ass making a fuss but he quickly moved on and some little red-haired gal, all over me like a plague.'

Schoolboy started laughing. Jackie. What was life going to be like without her?

'In the believability stakes how far do you think we got?'

'Total, man, total. All your stuff's back in my space. Didn't think that red-head was your type.'

Schoolboy was going to answer that she wasn't, but he felt his anger rising. Jackie had been there for him. Had always been there for him and he wasn't going to let anyone put her down.

'Totally my type, in fact we have been in a ting for years.'

'Well, good luck, because the woman looks like she's got too much pepper for me. It was good to see you at the club on Tuesday.'

They ended their conversation soon after because they were both remembering André. Schoolboy didn't get off the bed, but thought about what Jay-Jay had said about Jackie having too much pepper for him. Maybe that's what he needed, a woman with so much heat he'd feel like he had permanent security, but challenged. He stood up.

Anyway it was too late. Jackie was going one way and he was going another. But still he couldn't forgot those ripe green eyes and sharp red hair.

He checked himself in the mirror as the sound of a traffic altercation below the block drifted his way. Satisfied with his look, he headed for the kitchen to make a mug of tea, to relax him but not enough to slow him down. As he passed over the kitchen's threshold a thump at the main door stopped him. He should have jumped but it made him freeze. The type of motion that only allows your eyes to react to the moment. His eyes moved up and down, side to side, stretching, the colours of the room becoming elongated and distorted, trying to find a solution. Pressure and internal sweat began building in his head. His heart began to beat in the well of his stomach. It could be Evie, it could be Lloyd. But say it wasn't? The knock came again, making him flinch because he felt as if the knock was against his forehead. He told himself to move and he did. He wasn't going to be Parkview's latest nose-dive statistic.

Primed on the heels of his toes, he moved quickly until he stood where he wanted to be. Near the doors that led to the balcony. Just as he decided to step out, a thought stopped him. Maybe they had managed to get up there and were waiting for him. A headline dived into his mind: *Notorious building claims another victim.* His leg swung back in. There was only one alternative. He skated back into the room and plucked up the 1970s ashtray that sat by the foot of the bar. The type of ashtray Camden Market was flogging for fifty quid a time. Black base, black top, with a long silver neck where the ash slivered down. Not much against a gun, but it had enough weight to damage a few bodies. He shifted the weight in his hands as he stalked towards the door. He side-stepped to the right side of the door frame and leaned his back against the wall. His hand slid, hot and wet, to the handle. The handle turned with the expectation of a B-movie moment. He eased it open. Then he let it go, so that it could free fall with gravity itself. He raised the ashtray high, his full power ingrained in it. The tinge of fragrance more expensive than his fortnightly giro came slinking through the door. The Bitch. He'd heard that Queen loved to dress up when she ended someone's life. He saw the top of the head and let the ashtray fall.

Schoolboy peered at the woman standing over him, looking down at him as if he were part of the care-in-the-community drive.

'What the hell are you doing here?' He struggled up as he threw out the words.

'Just wanted to talk to you, so I dropped by,' Tammy babbled nervously as she held out a hand to help him up.

He ignored it and just heaved himself until he was in a standing position opposite her.

He had lunged hard with the ashtray, intending to make a point straight into a head or two, only to fall on his face when instinctive danger told the newcomer to move back. There had been a high squeal, making him crawl forward on to his hands and feet to push himself up. The varnished floorboards just wouldn't play along and he'd slipped back painfully on to his face. He'd finally rolled on to his back to view his terroriser.

He stepped once towards her, making her eyebrows rise in alarm, but she didn't move forward or back. He shoved out his hand, letting it fly over her shoulder, to bang the door shut.

He didn't need to ask how she knew he was here, that was obvious from his sister's big mouth.

'So now you've had a good look at the peep show, what can I do for you?'

'Evie was right. I like your hide-out. Maybe a bit too much gold, but I'm sure you can live with that.' Her eyes roamed around the room, almost sighing in pleasure.

'How can I enrich your life?' he repeated, slowly stressing each word.

'Something wicked and loose from the bar.' She swayed and giggled forward and took the high ground to the chaise longue and fell into it. She rubbed her back against the softness.

He didn't have time for Little-Miss-Duplex-Diva and her fashion tips.

'The only liquid I'm providing today comes pleasure of Thames Water.' But he didn't move to the kitchen or sit down.

He checked his timepiece. He should be making tracks.

'Going somewhere?'

'Maybe I'm off to church to think about higher things.'

'If you don't want me to know just say. There's no need to get all rude.'

The colour in his face sucked away when he realised why she might be here.

'Has something happened to Evie?'

'No. Not really except she's very upset. Feels she doesn't understand you and was unfair.'

His body stood easy again.

'So the point of this visit is?'

'I went out last night with one of my many friends and let's just say your name came up . . .'

'What do you mean my name came up?' He stepped closer.

'Did you really take a phone from a dead man?' Her neck thrust out quick as the words rushed from her mouth.

'Where did you hear that from?'

She didn't answer him but carried on with her own tale.

'I started thinking that maybe your flat got done over because you had something someone wants. And my friend said that you have.'

He rushed towards her and she pushed herself back, fear playing a nasty game of dot-to-dot on her face.

'I only came to offer my help,' she squealed, which stopped his movement. 'I'm only doing this for Evie. I've got a . . . let's just call him a friend. He specialises in doing deals. A sort of negotiator. A middleman.'

'You have been rubbing your face in the dirt?' His voice tumbled with curiosity as he continued to lean into her.

'We all have our moments of madness.'

'Yeah, the need for a good old poke can take us to all type of places.'

'I didn't come here for you to mock me. I just want to help my friend.'

Poor old Tammy. Just because she'd met a leaf-peddler or car-jacker, she thought she was mucking around with the big swing boys now.

'Friend? I don't like you and you don't like me, so cosy companionship has never been part of the package.'

'You're right, but I like Evie. Love Evie. What are you going to do if anything happens to her?'

He stepped back, giving her some space. He hadn't really thought of anyone being interested in Evie, but when the street wants something it will drag in anyone who could help it get it.

'So what kind of business is your *friend* in?'

'Let's just say that he does a bit of door-to-door that has nothing to do with supermarket internet delivery services. He can make a few contacts and sees if he can shift the product back to someone who will appreciate it.'

'How can I trust this friend?'

'He's good for his word. Let's just say that we both have fond memories of each other.'

'So how will we play this?'

'If you stay here – don't bother with church – ' they both laughed, his weaker than hers, 'I'll get the ball rolling. He'll cast the word around and then I'll get back to you.'

'Sounds good. So why don't you, my new-found friend, go and get that ball whizzing.'

She pushed up, swirled into his space and hugged him. Her orange-blossom perfume peeled over his face. Her heat was too intense for him to remain still. His fingers fluttered against her back, moved lower finding the fire of her bum. He'd always had a thing about her high-handed arse. Cuppable, round, bad. She eased her chin from his shoulder and peered into his face. She placed her thumb on his bottom lip, massaging it as if she was pressing sweet promises from the wish-bone-shaped art on her nail. Her lips wavered over his. They touched. Then meshed. He forced his tongue around her mouth, through the gap in her teeth, while his lower body sought that bag of sugar. He broke the kiss when he realised that her toothpaste was the same as the one he'd used in prison. He pulled back, saying nothing. She grinned up at him and squeezed his arm.

'You won't regret this. We'll get this sorted and then Evie will be all smiles again. I'll give you a ring. Don't go anywhere. Remember it's one big dangerous bush outside. Just stay put and wait for my call.'

She was gone and he still felt her lip-colour on his. He stared at the closed door. Let Little-Miss-Duplex-Interference do her contacting. He just wouldn't be there at the end of the line.

He pulled his jacket on, turned his phone off and wiped the lipstick from his mouth. He couldn't go to church with Jezebel smeared across his face. He moved towards the chaise longue and pushed aside a cushion to reveal the brick. He picked it up and started to remove one of his Tims.

19

The only beauty attached to the East London Line, locally baptised the East Looney Line or 'ell, depending on how bad commuters were feeling, was that it could take you from the East End to South-East London in minutes. Schoolboy stepped into New Cross High Street, stretching the clothes he was wearing, trying to find a comfort zone. He wasn't comfortable about being on the other side of the river either. The last time he'd been anywhere near this part of the capital was at a wall-to-wall party in Peckham in '99. New Cross hadn't changed much. It still looked like one weary chain of mini-supermarkets, barbers and pizza joints.

He started walking, with a slight limp in his right leg because of the Nokia placed inside his shoe. Every tenth stride he checked over his right shoulder, his left shoulder, just in case Queen had devised a new plan. He was an hour early to keep one step ahead of anyone else's plans.

The last time he'd been to church was the day Dad was buried. Back in '97. Heart attack. Just like that. Slumped over the domino table as he made double blanks. That day had been a contrast to the days when Mum would take him and Evie to church on a Saturday. Mum had wanted them to find piety but hc had been fixated by the energy, colour, the voices. Voices that made him believe that angels walked this world and not just the next. But his energy had gone elsewhere when he realised that he wasn't allowed to touch women, drugs, alcohol or dirty money – that was too high a price to pay for saving his soul. But he'd seen how that potent belief could recapture hearts most thought were lost. Some bad-ass rude boy would be turning tricks on the street one week and then you'd see him prophesying, testifying, believing, the next. Hadn't that happened to Manny during his last stretch inside? You could go four ways in prison. Either pick up with Jesus C, pray multiple times a day with Mohammed, concoct your own home-brewed belief or get back into the tread and slabs of the cracks in the street. Schoolboy was embarrassed to admit that the last time he'd seen his former spar he'd crossed the road to avoid him but Manny had checked him hurrying along.

'Hey Elijah,' he'd shouted across the road, his words whistling through the gaps in his side teeth, 'You may be cloaked in the name of a prophet but you're still doing Satan's work.'

Schoolboy had kept on grooving with the pavement, but Manny had continued to spread the Word.

'Hold your finger in the flame of a match, Elijah, imagine that pain all over your body, then imagine that through all eternity – that's where Satan's work leads . . .'

'I'm doing all right,' Schoolboy had shouted over his shoulder.

'All right?' Manny had repeated, horrified. 'All right? Rebelling against the Lord God Almighty? Wake up, Elijah. Repent your sins and throw yourself on the mercy of the Lord – before it's too late. For time is short, brother,' he'd warned him, ' – time might be very short indeed.'

Supposing Manny was right, Schoolboy questioned himself as he hit the end of another tenth stride and forgot to check over his shoulder. Supposing it was tonight and he got caught up in a fight and stabbed to death? Then descended into hell for eternity? Sometimes he would go home and get his mum's hymn book out and start singing. But thoughts of salvation were always pushed aside when a customer rang.

He willed Manny and eternal damnation from his mind as he reached the Church of Celestial Peace: the Ministry of Joy, Love and Splendour. It was a plain white flat-roofed building, nestled between Marcia's World of Nails and Ibrahim's Communication Centre, with a wooden door widened with enough curiosity to beckon passers-by inside. He checked both shoulders again before he went in, into a world dominated by the collective rush of people singing. The voices were back in his life. As he followed the angels to a non-gloss green door, the words of the chorus became clearer:

Sweet Lord, redeem me.
Sweet Lord Jesus, save me.

The see-sawing voices took his head forward but his feet held back. Held him back. But he knew that he wouldn't find his own brand of calm and peace until he got the phone out of his life. His feet rejoined his head and entered a world so full of bright sound that the Lord could not fail to see this congregation. The church was an array of worshippers, all praising in shades of black, yellow or blue. The colour was finished by the white hats and scarves worn by women and the bare heads of men. White and black swayed to the motion of affirmation. Affirming in the key of faith. Affirming in the key of hope. Some affirming in the radiance of having already found the Lord. The communion was complete by the cream-shrouded choir and the preacher on the stage. The preacher was big, brown-suited and prowling the stage with a fire in his step as if he had unfinished business to attend to. Schoolboy remembered his own business and checked the rows for Queen's crew. Satisfied they weren't present, he nestled in a seat near the back next to an old woman who was so aged and frail she looked as if she'd come to book her own funeral. Dressed in a coat and one of those hats that reminded Schoolboy of a meringue, she was hunched over her Bible paying homage to the scriptures.

On stage the preacher was waving his Bible and blazing into his mike:

'. . . You know, people, we have many young men in our community, they call themselves rude boys or playas or dons or G-boys – and you know why they call themselves that? Because they're afraid of their real names – the doers of evil and the agents of Satan . . .'

Shouts of 'That's right!' and 'Tell them brother!' from the congregation torched the heat in the preacher's feet.

'. . . You know these young people are dealing in narcotics, they're trading in women's bodies, they're extorting money from God-fearing people – and are these men ashamed of what they do? No, brothers and sisters, they are proud! They have murder and hatred in their hearts – and they are arrogant and proud! Can you believe it . . .?'

Worshippers opened their mouth scattering gasps, boos and hisses, but the preacher waved his hands.

'No, brother and sisters, these men are no worse than we are, they are wretched sinners just like us and they need forgiveness and salvation just like us – and you know where they're going to find forgiveness and salvation, don't you . . .?'

Shouts of 'Jesus!' and 'the Lord!' lit up the church. The preacher put his hands to his ears and feigned deafness.

'I'm sorry people, I can't hear you. The Lord can't hear you. The wasted on the street can't hear you . . .'

The shouting and crying redoubled before the preacher tossed his head, burst into laughter and cried:

'Oh – you mean the Name above all Names? You mean the King of Kings? You mean the Prince of Peace? You mean the only One with the authority to forgive sins and save souls? Yes, I'm talking about Jesus – it's Jesus I'm talking about . . .!'

The amplification of his convictions was drowned as the congregation leapt to their feet, spinning, some on both legs, others on one, dancing, holding hands high, allowing their belief and colours to flash in the way of the truth. The old woman next to Schoolboy stood on her chair, stamping her feet, punching the air with one hand and waving her Bible with the other, shouting, in a strong Bajan accent:

'Tell them, preacher! – Tell the evil-doers to seek salvation while it may be found . . .'

The wave of committed belief swept Schoolboy half out of his seat. Then he remembered why he was there and dropped himself down. He gripped his fingers around the edge of his seat because there was something powerful trying to pull him towards a different plan. The preacher threw up the hand with the Bible, making the congregation retake their seats. The rejoicing simmered low, but still hummed in every corner. The preacher paced up and down, down and up, from left to right, right to left until he was sure every ear was with him. He faced them and yelled:

'And you know, brothers and sisters, I'm sensing that we have some troubled souls with us here tonight, sinners in word and deed who are groaning for salvation – I want to see those who are breaking under the burden of sin and evil – I want them to come up and join me here on the stage and confess the name of Jesus – feel the power of the Lord to save your soul from death and perdition . . .'

Schoolboy's fingers began shifting, loosening, rocking to the preacher's words.

'Don't be afraid of salvation! Be afraid of the flames of hell! For there is no hiding place in eternity from the avenging arm of Almighty God! Don't leave it till tomorrow – there may be no tomorrow for you! Do it tonight! Do it now!'

The preacher went for it, taking up the old woman's mantra, stamping his heel:

'So I am calling on you – brother or sister, black or white, old or young, rich or poor – if you are crying after salvation – then come forward and tell the world, "I believe in my heart and confess with my lips that Jesus Christ is Lord!" Feel the joy of forgiveness and look forward to eternal life with Almighty God and the saints of Heaven! And do it now!'

He came to rest on his lectern exhausted, sweating, but already in the congregation there were shouts and movement as a young man supported by two women walked, baffled and bewildered with tears running down his face, on to the stage. The preacher approached and put his arm round the man and sat down and talked to him. Their heads were bowed in prayer. Schoolboy saw himself kneeling on the floor, sweat heaving, the gun shining in its power over his life. Schoolboy's breathing started to rise and fall with the mumbled prayer of the preacher and man. Both men rose again to their feet. The convert was presented, like the newest dawn, to the congregation:

'What's your name, brother?'

The young man shook and sobbed so hard that the words were not yet ready to leave with his redemption. The minister soothed him with his own words.

'We know how you feel, brother, salvation is a powerful thing and does powerful things to a man's soul – there's only one thing we want to know, brother – whose name are you confessing before these people?

In whose name are you asking for salvation and forgiveness? Who are you confessing with your lips and on whom are you believing in your heart?'

The man managed to say 'Jesus!' before he held his head in his hands. Once again the people erupted in joy while Schoolboy shifted uneasily in his seat because he knew there was more to come. The convert sat on the stage while the two women put their arms around him and whispered words of comfort. The preacher was stalking and yelling again, the search for sin never-ending.

'You see, people! You have seen the power of the Lord! And we're going to see it again because there are others here tonight groaning under the weight of sin and searching for deliverance . . .' His eyes scanned the congregation and drummed to a halt when they finally gripped Schoolboy. Schoolboy's eyes bulged back. The preacher pointed straight at him and shouted:

'You, brother! Do you know Jesus Christ as your Lord and Saviour? If you do, jump up and shout his name, if you don't – confess, repent and come into the Kingdom, for the Lord Jesus is knocking at your door . . .'

The white and black heads turned back to look at Schoolboy. The old woman next to him whispered, 'Confess his name, brother!'

Sweat re-baptised Schoolboy's face with a new feeling. His fingers dropped from the chair. Spit began rising in his tongue. He was tempted, so tempted to push forward and confess. To let God take the burden of his troubles. To let the whole congregation carry his cross. His gaze darted over the faces looking at him, their eyes telling him that they were ready whenever he was. He rushed up, bolted out of his chair and headed for the exit. He'd completely forgotten about Queen and even if he hadn't, even if she'd been standing in front of him with a piece in her hand, he'd have still gone. The preacher cried out as he left with his back to the stage, ' No, brother! No! There's no salvation out there! Please, brother, I'm begging you, don't leave us tonight! There may be no tomorrow . . .'

The believers held out their hands towards him as he walked by.

Old, young, broad, small voices all urging him to stay, but Schoolboy kept walking. His feet faltered when he heard a child's voice call out:

Sweet Lord, redeem me.
Sweet Lord Jesus, save me.

He pulled his feet back into line and plummeted out of the double doors into the beginnings of the sunset. He stopped, gasping on the street, bending low, and spat out what tasted like the badness in his life. His breathing started to slow, came back to him when he heard a voice say,

'Schoolboy?'

He looked up, screwing his eyes in the gathering darkness, to see a professionally dressed woman standing over him. She pursed her lips with disapproval.

'I'm Queen, otherwise known as your maker.'

'I thought we had a deal, man. We're supposed to be meeting inside the church. You've got our relationship off on the wrong foot and we've only just met. Now, let's get inside before I get angry.'

Schoolboy shook his locks vigorously as he sank back downwards.

'I ain't going back in there. No way. Shoot me dead – but I ain't going back in there. And you won't be getting no phone either . . .'

Queen sighed heavily, then she drifted downwards herself and put a motherly arm around his shoulder. She whispered tenderly,

'What's the matter, boy? Some raving reverend been getting to you? You know it's all fairy stories, don't you? That's how they keep us people down . . .' She broke into a stage black accent, '. . . if you's not being an obedient little negro down on the plantation, the white bogie man in the sky will come and whip your black ass . . .' She squeezed his arm. 'It's all lies, boy. Now get up and start acting like a man . . .'

Schoolboy shook his head.

'I ain't going back in there.'

Queen blinked furiously. She got back up, sucking her teeth. She walked a few yards down the road and began whispering into a mobile.

Schoolboy, still badly spooked, only caught a few words.

'No, outside not inside . . . I don't care what I said . . . outside . . .'

Then she was kneeling by him again, helping him to his feet.

'OK, Schoolboy, no problem, we can talk business out here.'

They were standing looking at each other now. How could such a small woman have so much power? Queen was smiling but it didn't reach her eyes. Schoolboy could see she was uncomfortable. She stole a glance at the doors of the church. Schoolboy followed her gaze.

'Everything's going to be fine, man, just relax. Nothing bad's going to happen here. We're just going to do some business.'

So what were they waiting for then? He turned around again to where Queen's eyes had gone and his eyes froze on the entrance of the church. He swung around so quickly that even his brain didn't have time to catch up with what he was doing and snatched Queen by the collars of her jacket and forced her up against a wall. Then he shook her like he was trying to shake out every piece of filth in his life. Now it was her turn to gasp and clench with shock. He knew it was a long, long, long time since anyone had done that to Queen.

'So you just couldn't play it straight, Queen. You must think I'm some kind of idiot-bwoy . . .' he hissed.

He shook her again, dragging her polished heels off the ground and sending his locks pelting in the sunset. He dropped her hard and ploughed up the street. The phone in his shoe made his run unsteady. He could hear the doors of the church finally burst open and Queen's men piling out but he didn't look back. Twenty yards down the road the doors of a car flew open and a crew emerged, blocking his way.

'Give it up, fool,' a stocky playa told him, 'Give it up . . .'

He spun around and bolted back towards the church but the pavement was busting with a wall of men coming towards him. He twisted into the road only to find another wall of humans waiting for him.

Schoolboy retreated with panic against the shuttered windows of a jeweller's. Both walls stalked him, crowded in on him, reared up in front of him. The soaring harmony from the church also found its place next to him.

Sweet Lord, redeem me.
Sweet Lord Jesus, save me.

The men pinned him with menace but made no move to grab him. The men parted and Queen chopped through to stand in front of him. Her clothes were back in place but she was convulsing with anger. Her lips parted to say something but her tongue was flattened by anger so heavy no words came out. Instead she nodded at two of her crew. Metal-tight fingers grabbed Schoolboy's arms as he was dragged towards a black car. A black car that reminded him of a hearse. The men picked him up and hurled him into the back of the car with such force his head slammed against the far passenger window. His eyes crumpled together with the agony of the blow. He tried to reopen his eyes but couldn't because he felt as if he was sinking. Hadn't the preacher warned him about tumbling into darkness? He felt the heat of a large body jam so close to him in the car that he could inhale the fluids of dry cleaning on a newly pressed suit. He opened his eyes slightly to scan who was next to him. The profile of the man was long, solid, the type of face he knew his sister would go for. All of his senses flooded his ears when he heard car doors slamming and ignitions blasting the air. Abruptly the face next to him turned and lowered towards him. Schoolboy shoved himself further down into the brown leather seat.

'Just keep quiet and everything will be cool.'

Schoolboy nodded briskly back, remembering how he'd heard that same rolling voice outside Jackie's door while he hid in her sitting-room. The man pulled his face away from Schoolboy, tapped the driver on the shoulder and leaned back like a good soldier as the engine of the car drummed on.

The car backed up slightly and then he heard the clicking of an indicator as the driver tried to pull out. The driver was forced to wait as two Jeep-style vehicles came slowly down the road. The driver banged his horn at the Jeeps, but they kept their speed slow.

'What the fuck,' the driver cursed out in time with the rhythm of his horn.

The pace of the Jeeps remained steady. The man in the front seat of Schoolboy's prison turned the ignition off and started opening the door. The man next to Schoolboy furiously leaned forward and demanded, 'What the arse are you doing, man?'

The driver swung his head around and shouted back, 'I'm going to make those fucking idiots get off the road . . .'

'Get back in the car and just keep driving. You know what Queen will do if you don't follow orders.'

The man ignored him and carried on opening the door. The man in the back pushed his body over the front seat and grabbed the other man's jacket collar. The driver fell back into the seat. Schoolboy eased his hand from under his side and reached up to the window lock. His hand froze, knowing if he was caught he'd be brown bread. But it looked as if Queen was planning to toast him anyway, so his fingers gripped the lock and pulled it up.

'What was that?' The man next to him twisted around.

Schoolboy's hand fell like lead smacking into a body. The man shafted his eyes into Schoolboy's face. Schoolboy shook his head and stared limply back. The man squinted at him and then moved his gaze above Schoolboy's head.

'How did the window lock get up?'

Schoolboy sunk lower and shook his head again. The man thrust his hand into his pocket and Schoolboy knew the preacher had been so right. As the man lifted his hand out of his pocket the car was violently struck from behind. The man tipped to the side and the driver's head hit the steering wheel. Abruptly the motion changed and Schoolboy was pelted forward then jarred back as one of the Jeeps in front rammed the car full on. The glass from the passenger windows sprinkled on his head and crashed to the car floor. The mania of running feet outside joined the sound of the broken glass. Before Schoolboy could react, one of the back doors was ripped wide and the man next to him was tugged and tossed outside. Schoolboy pushed his body up and grasped for the door handle as blows and groans came from nearby. His hand started turning the handle the same time as a face breathed hotly into Schoolboy. Schoolboy gradually turned his head to look, frightened of what he'd find. He found a new face next to him. Broad, stained with sweat and what girls on the dance floor called plain nasty. The man rubbed a Tech-9 against Schoolboy's temple.

'Forget the door. You're still in trouble, man, but it's a different kind of trouble. So ease yourself back into your seat.'

Fuckrees.

Schoolboy did as he was told. Suddenly, the whole road was filled with a raucous melting-pot of noise. Screaming, shouting and engine play. Then one sound became supreme – the ripple of gunplay. Instinct made Schoolboy drop down to the floor and cover his head like a naughty kid told to repent in the corner. He kicked his body back when he felt the cloying residue of blood running down his hands.

Sweet Lord, redeem me.
Sweet Lord Jesus, save me.

Winding around with fear he felt his body, looking for the wounds and trying to avoid the sight of his blood-splattered clothes. The man next to him slumped down, clinging to him so tightly that Schoolboy could smell the almond and jojoba oil in his hair. The man moaned, clutching his side. Schoolboy whipped his eyes to the man's hand and saw a gaping hole in his side. The air drained from Schoolboy when he realised that it wasn't his blood. He used his feet to kick the man's body away from himself. He struggled over the injured man and clambered out of the open door until he was on the road. He didn't look up or to the side. He kept his gaze down as he dashed towards the nearest Jeep.

Gunfire was riding the road from all directions. Schoolboy rolled himself under the Jeep. The heat of the vehicle's exhaust and the stench of the gutter entombed him as he lay flat. He felt something soft grind into the back of his jacket.

He lay trembling with the fumes of petrol pumping into his nose. With the ugly metal bottom of the Jeep oppressing him. With the pressure of the phone in his shoe reminding him of the agony the man at

Cinnamon Junction must have felt before he died. Mournful sirens in the distance made the guns fall silent. Soft and hard heels mixed with shouts blended into the distance. He saw other feet drawing closer. Schoolboy shut his eyes and started to chant softly:

Sweet Lord, redeem me.
Sweet Lord Jesus, save me.
Sweet Lord, redeem me.
Sweet Lord Jesus, save me.
Sweet Lord, redeem me.
Sweet Lord Jesus, save me.

Schoolboy's sense of reality came and went as if he was travelling in a trance. Flashing blue lights soon became the dominant colour of his mind. When he heard the voices he realised that the flashing lights meant the police had arrived. His mumbling stopped as he saw the green trousers of paramedics whizzing by the Jeep. Then the voices returned.

'I'm sorry, Reverend, we have a crime scene here, I'm going to have to ask your people to withdraw . . . yes of course, you may pray and hold a vigil but you'll have to do it further down the street as this area will be sealed off while the dead and injured are recovered and a search begins for evidence . . .'

Schoolboy knew it was time to check back into reality and quick-step out of the situation. He slid the top half of his body from under the Jeep and peered down the street. The Blues were busy shooing everyone back. He jerked the rest of his body out and struggled to his feet. In the chaos no one noticed him join the congregation as they hustled behind the yellow tape the police were putting up. He moulded his eyes down, avoiding contact with the slumped bodies hanging from cars and lying on the road. He shook his eyes to stop them twitching. He rushed off leaving it all behind, but the smell of the street wouldn't leave him.

As his steps picked up speed he realised that something soft and wet was clinging to the back of his jacket. Maybe a bullet had found him after all. He kept moving forward as he tore his jacket off. He swore when he came face to face with the mess that only bad dogs dump in the street. Relief started warming in him, even with a smashed turd now part of his life. He kept walking into the last threads of the sunset. Kept hearing that child calling him:

Sweet Lord, redeem me.
Sweet Lord Jesus, save me.

20

Schoolboy was jammed back against the train seat, muffled by an emotion he had only dealt with twice in his life. The first time had been seeing a dead body thanks to Her Majesty's pleasure. The second time had been when Mum had up and left England. And now shock found him again. He hadn't moved since rushing on to the train at New Cross station. He sat third seat from the window and second row from the back. The train had already swung from New Cross to Whitechapel and was rewinding its wheels from Whitechapel to New Cross Gate. But wasn't that the sum total of his life? Going up and down the same track. He'd tried to change the journey and look where it had got him. Not one grim reaper but a full posse of them on his shoulder. When you only have Whitechapel at one end and New Cross at the other to look forward to, you know you're stuffed.

The East London Line only had seven stations, one of which had previously been a dock but was now a quay and another that was called Shoreditch but was actually in Brick Lane. Typical of him to end up on a line that masqueraded as something that it wasn't. He shifted his trembling body as the woman sitting opposite him started to slide towards the corner seat. He knew she could smell the high dried sweat creased all over him. Terror can produce the most nose-pinching ranges of smells. Before boarding the train he'd wiped the back and front of his jacket on a patch of grass to get rid of the dog droppings and as much blood as possible. He cast his eyes around the carriage but all he could see were flashes. Flashes of the stench of blood mixed with almond oil draining over him. The preacher's mouth big and wide, steeped in saliva. The congregation at peace, looking down at him as he was lowered in a glass-topped coffin into the worm-infested soil.

He tried to think of his next move, but his mind wouldn't connect. The train hit Canada Water and the lady got off and he remained alone with up-front fear next to him. He should have got off at Wapping to get to Evie's but he couldn't move. Couldn't confront the unknown that might be waiting for him above ground. Better to stay underground until the way ahead was clear enough to see.

No one was talking. Well, at least not the type of story the Law wanted to hear.

'I've told you, Officer, that I was on my way to a christening,' Queen answered as she sat with her brief next to her.

The room was small, bare, with only a bright light, tape recorder, cheap tables and chairs. All that was needed for a good old fashioned Metropolitan Police interrogation. The officers were young and shone with the type of idealism that would scoff at a few fifties offered under the table. Shame, because she had quite a few in her purse.

'You've already verified my client's story, so unless you've got anything else you wish to discuss I suggest you release her immediately,' her solicitor admonished them, as if addressing a jury.

Queen saw the indecision in both officers' eyes. Superiors most probably told them either to charge her quickly or let her go. They needed to concentrate all their resources on the up-coming anarchist march through the City next week. If gangs wanted to kill each other on the street, then let them. Less work for them to do.

The door opened and a large burly detective stood in the doorway. He beckoned to the other two policemen and they stepped outside. Queen's mind rolled back over the evening and she wasn't what her daughters called a happy bunny. She was one fucked-off bunny. Two of her best men were in hospital and one was dead. Now not only did she have the street thief with her goods to deal with but the Numbers crew as well. Her mouth screwed tight because she knew she hadn't been paying attention. She'd walked straight into their trap.

The door reopened and the two officers returned. The youngest one's face puffed pink as if someone had been slapping him around the chops. They took their seats.

'We're releasing you. But if you hear of any information regarding this incident please contact me.' He passed her his card. The other officer switched off the tape.

She looked at the card. Detective Paul Bernice. She kept it in her hand.

'Detective, I'm only too willing to assist the police with their enquiries. Maybe we can help each other. A sort of reciprocal relationship. I help you, you help me.' She spoke as she stood and moved towards the door.

The officer's face now moved from pink to red. Too incorruptible for her proposition. She wondered if she met him in five years' time whether he'd feel the same.

The uncompromisingly cold night air surrounded her as she got outside. For the first time she allowed herself to remember the feel of Schoolboy's hands on her clothes, pulsing near her throat. She smiled. When she caught up with him the first thing she was going to deal with were his hands.

By the time the train struck Brunel's tunnel for the fifth time, between Wapping and Rotherhithe, Schoolboy had cooled down, started to think. He just had to stay one step ahead of everyone else. It was that simple. As his thoughts began to make sense, the rasping voice of the woman next to him butted in.

'What you looking at me for?' her voice accused.

This was a woman whose only friend in life was the freebie blue carrier bag she kept scrunched with her at all times. Both seams were split, showing the dozens of used tissues it contained.

Schoolboy folded his arms across his chest and kept his head bowed low. The woman tucked her body closer to his. No wonder everyone called this the East Looney Line.

'I know you're all after me,' she whispered, her scent of urine and desperation swarming all over him. He shouldn't have answered but he did. Just wanted the hag to sod off.

'Look, I haven't been looking at you.' His head remained low.

'Course you have. They all have. Do you want me to flash my

knickers? So why weren't you looking? Not good enough for you am I? You think you're too fancy for me, Mr Fancy Pants, because you've got some other floozy's lipstick on your sleeve.'

His head shot up, caught her eyes and followed their direction. The inside of his sleeve was turned outwards and he could see the stain of black red as clearly as the green and silver eye shadow spread across the top of her eyelid and below her eyes. He hadn't noticed that blood. Nor had anyone else. Commuters using the 'ell route had seen too much blood and shock through the years even to notice it now. He sprang up and moved away as the train began its journey towards Shadwell. He still couldn't leave. The time wasn't right.

24/7 cabs was closed. The sign on the door stated that this was due to refurbishments. Those looking for a hit would have to take a trip to Speedball Central. Wahid and Ashara were in the back room arguing.

'I told you we should have waited for them to get the phone and then strike.' Wahid's voice was filled with anger as he paced the room.

Ashara remained a fraction calmer as he sat in the chair.

'And what would that have accomplished?'

'We could . . .'

'I'll tell you what. It would have given Queen an opportunity to get back to her own ground and play us like the idiots she thinks we are.'

Wahid stopped. Frustration made the line of his mouth an ugly sight. If there was one thing he hated it was being outwitted by a female. That had only happened once before and it wasn't going to happen again. Wahid stopped his pacing, but inside his body remained a mass of movements.

'The buyer's back on Monday and so far we only have our empty hands to show him.'

'Don't worry. The buyer will be too preoccupied with licking pussy.'

'So what do you suggest?' Wahid asked, not liking it when he had to defer to his brother.

'Obviously we will have to deal with Madam Queen and this Schoolboy. Tell our people to start asking questions about him. If we can get to him first then our future will be fine.'

'And how do we plan to do this?'

'Don't worry, dear brother. Remember you don't always have to eat chicken with your fingers.'

This time Schoolboy was sitting in the seat one from the window and four rows from the front. Over him was a cartoon-style poster issued by London Underground, which read '78 injuries, 2 deaths,' and someone had scrawled in furious black pen, 'One million delays.' He'd lost count of how many times the train had moved from south to east, from east to south. The geezer opposite released a long puff of smoke from his cigarette. Schoolboy inhaled. He was no nicotine freak but when you're in a jam you have to take what drugs are on offer.

'Excuse me, it says no smoking,' a small woman challenged in an Antipodean accent. Australian or New Zealander, Schoolboy wasn't sure, but her vowels were doing an odd sticking motion in her nose.

'And what business is it of yours?' The challenge was flung back by an olive face that was young and smooth, but the eyes were full of scars.

'It's all our business. It's all our health.'

The woman cast her eyes to Schoolboy for support, but the man was providing him with a much-needed service. His eyes perched downwards.

'If you're so interested in your health you'll fuck off and leave me alone.'

'How dare you? I'll pull the red wire if you don't stop.'

'Pull the switch, darling, and it'll be your last tug.'

The train hit the open-air track of Surrey Quays and the woman took her appalled righteousness to the platform.

'Need a one-day travel card?' The man directed the question at Schoolboy, his words punctured with fag smoke.

Schoolboy opened his mouth to say, 'Sod off,' but the bleep of one of his phones got there first. Personal MB or the brick, he wasn't sure. A bleep always replaced Jim Reeves when his personal was low on juice. His eyes widened, watered, filling up with panic. Abruptly he pushed up, needing privacy. Needing to think. He staggered to the end of the carriage where he pulled out a fold-out chair. As he heaved down into the seat, he rationalised that it must be the brick in his shoe, finally coming to life just as he had tried to move it on.

The phone bleeped again.

Fuckrees!

He tucked his head down towards his Tims. He swung his eyeballs to the left, then to the right, checking that no one was watching him. His eyes tightened to their usual size, realising that his fellow passengers were too tangled in their own thoughts and troubles to have time to sneak into his. He concentrated back on the brick. He spread his right toes, rocked them, letting the pressure lift his back heel. He rocked and squeezed his toes against the bottom of his shoes, rolling his back heel further up. Easing it out.

The phone bleeped again.

Fuckrees.

He realised that the noise was coming from his personal in his pocket. That was the problem with life at the moment, every rogue sound seemed to be connected to the friggin' brick. He jammed his foot back at the same time as his hand dived into his pocket for the phone. He pulled it out and squinted at the screen. The video icon was showing. His thumb hovered over the button as his tongue slid up and down, down and up across his lips. Maybe Evie had come through with the bread and honey? Maybe Tammy had news of her contact? Maybe the knives were still in circulation? His tongue swept up and down once more then his thumb pressed.

He waited for the video recording to activate itself. When the recording started, his spit gushed to one side of his mouth. He gasped at Queen's face on the screen, feeling as if he was crammed into a cell, with the world able to scrutinise him, but with no window for him to peer back. Queen contorted her mouth. His world shrunk to just him, her and the accompanying sky that surrounded her which was the same mournful colour as the sky that had lain outside his dad's hospital window the night he had died.

Queen's lips rolled to the centre and strained open.

'Mister Schoolboy, your day will come. Your day will come.'

Her mouth twisted, then froze as the recording came to an end. He clipped her face off, leaving him to stare at his reflection in the finger-print-smeared screen of the phone. His mind began to rock to how she'd got his personal number. He'd been so careful with who he gave it to in the past. He'd never given it to one of his ladyeez. Not even to Jackie. The only business bredren who had it were Jay-Jay and Robbie and that had been through necessity. No way would it be Jay-Jay; Robbie maybe. But that was the street for you, it always knew more about you than you thought. He desperately needed to spit, but he couldn't get off the train now that he realised maybe the street had more connections to him than just his personal line.

Queen had two lock-ups. One was in her home ground of Dalston and the other was in Clapton near the Pond. The late night sky was packed with a damp bleakness as she walked towards the lock-up. She'd instructed all her men to meet her there. Tiredness accompanied her as she shifted the doors open. After leaving the police station, she had made calls to her men in hospital, contacted the family of the man who was dead to assure them of her financial support. She had also contacted Rufus's girl with the same information. The difference was that Rufus wasn't dead.

As she moved towards her men, she could see their eyes widening as they looked at her coat. The same coat she always wore when she was getting ready to dirty her hands. Those who were seated abruptly stood up. Queen clipped her heels on the concrete as she circled the small space in front of her men. She began turning, twisting, shooting her head and neck back and out. She stopped. She kept her back turned to them as she started ripping the space with the snarl in her voice.

'Today was a total let-down. I know that some of you left school at a tender age but even you should have understood that today's plan was simple. Get the idiot and free up the phone. But that obviously wasn't simple enough.' Her heels stamped louder against the concrete as her words rang and raged.

'Now I'm standing here with a pack of losers and you know what the worst thing is?' She shivered. 'Some bit-part player had his hands all over me and around my throat and where were any of you?' She was shouting now.

'If you can't protect me, what am I paying you for?' The Smith and Wesson was in her hand as she swung around.

'Now which one will it be?' She clipped towards the men, who had each taken a step back. 'Who's going to pay the price?'

She stuck the gun in Cuttie's belly. 'Should be you, because your job was to make sure that everyone stayed in line? Or what about you, Thimble?' The gun decked into another man. 'Or what about you, Leroy, for having a fucking stereotype for a name?'

She turned the gun towards the next man, Rufus.

'And you, Rufus, I understand, just wanted to play the big man when you should have kept driving the car.' Each word was accompanied by a prod of the gun's nozzle.

'Queen, I . . .' his voice was small, feeble.

'I've already contacted your woman.'

The other men gasped as if they were inhaling their last breath. They all knew what her statement meant. Rufus started backing away, but Cuttie rushed behind him and held his shoulders. Queen took small steps, walking towards him. She caught up to him. The gun caught up to him. Her finger cocked back the trigger. Rufus's movements became wild as he tried to twitch loose from Cuttie's grip. Cuttie ground his power and held him tight.

'So what's it feel like, Rufus, to have death poking into your life?' she whispered, but every man heard.

Rufus stiffened, then dropped, crying, at Queen's feet. Queen and the gun bent down to him as she asked, 'How many kids you got?'

'Three,' he let out between gulps and sniffles.

'Girls or boys?'

'All boys.'

'I prefer girls myself. They don't argue with you, they just get on with the job.'

Suddenly Queen swung upwards and swept her gaze to stare into each eye at the same time.

'And that's what better happen from now on, you hear. Outsiders taking the piss out of me I can handle, but my own crew, no way. So listen up. I want to know everything about this Schoolboy. I want to know what school he attended, who his family is, which supermarket he shops in, whether he gets reward points. Everything.'

The men nodded. She revolved back down to Rufus and uttered so quietly it was like a goodnight kiss on his cheek: 'What you still doing down there? You've got work to do.'

Thirty minutes until Saturday started. The last leg of the train's Friday run had begun. Just Schoolboy and a few other subdued passengers. The first part of his plan was to stay on the train until the line closed to the public. His head was rocking with having to deal with one too many off-the-wall people. The only looney left was the driver.

'I keep telling everyone to stop touching the doors,' the driver had yelled through the intercom, as the train pulled out of Rotherhithe. 'But you lot are still not listening to me. The next one to do it and this train will be out of service.'

By the time the train reached Wapping he'd flooded the carriages with 'I hope that no one's riding the roof because we are going to be moving like we're going to hell.'

At Whitechapel his words had burst with the type of bitterness that was contagious. 'Hope no one is getting married tomorrow because some friendly advice is just don't do it.'

By the time the train slowed into Shoreditch station, Schoolboy was the only one on the train and the only sound from the intercom was the sound of deep inhalation, as if the driver was enjoying the effects of some type of solace drug.

Schoolboy got off with the start of Saturday five minutes away. He was weary. Been on the line for over four hours. Four hours of pain. The phone in his shoe was still pinching him. The second part of the plan was to walk back to Parkview. He hadn't figured out the third part, but once he was back in the warmth he knew it would come.

21

Schoolboy stood on Parkview's roof with the ghosts of the dead at his side. The warmth hadn't brought anything new. When he'd got back to the flat he'd checked windows, locks, under the bed. His earlier ten-stride motif had shifted into checking windows and locks every ten minutes. He'd swing between the window and the balcony, searching for unexplained cars and figures below. For nine minutes he'd sit, chair rocking, tummy rolling, thoughts jumbled, fingers rubbing and riding. During his last sitting, Saturday had come reminding him of the time. Taunting him that he was never going to leave. Screaming that if they didn't catch him there was plenty of time to fuck with his sister. That had sent him crazy. He'd dug his nails in his head with the need to roar. That's when he'd seen it. The brick lying back on the carpet like a curse that was meant to be. Schoolboy had dived on it and thrown it with the power of the roar inside him. The phone had crashed, then smashed into pieces behind the bar. He'd yelled:

'Don't play your bad-ass juju justice with me!'

Only then had he realised that his whole future was wrapped up in that phone. He'd crumpled to the floor, beating his forehead with the base of his hand. His head had risen when he thought he'd heard a noise outside. He remembered the staircase, so he'd run to it listening anxiously for footsteps. But only the wind had chatted back.

That's when he'd noticed the rusting steel ladder up to the roof. It was surrounded by a metal cage and at the top and bottom of that were manhole cover-type contraptions to stop kids climbing on to the roof. The one at the bottom was hanging loosely where its locks had been knocked off and Schoolboy had seen the one at the top was open.

He'd scrambled up, pulled himself on to the roof, dropped the cover and sat on it. That's when he had remembered to breathe. Remembered what it felt like to be completely safe.

It took him ten minutes to get up and patrol his new kingdom. He'd wandered towards an abandoned shopping trolley shifting in a corner. How that had got up there he would never know. He'd forgotten the trolley as the edge of the building had called him like a child with a secret to show. He'd felt himself pitching so close to gate-fever he doubted he would ever be able to leave Death Row.

Now he stood, eyes closed, convinced he could smell the daffodils fifteen stories below. He opened his eyes when the wind began to rush under his jacket, making it puff up to its name. He saw the top of the disused bakers' almshouses laid out in their incomplete rectangle, with rows of trees making up the unfinished side. Some trendy new museum, that's what the rumour mill said they were going to be. The light of the mosque's minaret caught his eye, looking like the needle of a rocket about to be launched.

He stepped closer to the edge.

He just wanted to see Dalston one more time. From a distance – the best way to see something you love. Get a perspective that you've never had before. See all its faults and all its beauty. He shut his eyes again, swaying, but he still couldn't think of a way out of this mess. A mess he had created. He didn't need any of Mum's reality-licking sayings to tell him that.

His feet moved closer to the edge.

The first time he'd been locked up in a YOI, he'd wanted to die. Sixteen years old, ten months for breaking and entering, seven of which he had to share with someone who moaned himself to sleep every night. Mum wouldn't visit. Dad wouldn't visit. And the type of so-called spars who wanted to visit he didn't want to see. The resident psych had said he was finding it hard to bond with the other inmates. When he'd stood up and yelled it wasn't a fucking school reunion they had dragged him off to solitary. That's when things had got bad. Just the word solitary made him feel alone. Locked up and locked down in a cell so small his chest had found it hard to expand. Now he stood here on the roof, without any walls, and his chest still couldn't expand.

His Tims trembled closer to the edge.

He shivered with the wind. He peered down. It looked inviting. His personal MB began to bleep. His hands jumped over his ears to block the noise out. He shook his head in the cooling air. He didn't want to see that woman's face again. Reminding him of what a complete shit he'd made of his life. Telling him that his day would come. Didn't she realise that his day was already here and falling before his eyes? He eased his hands from his head just as the phone bleeped again. He shoved his hands into his pocket and plucked the phone out. His last phone. What did he care what Queen had to say? He pressed for the text message to come up.

```
u can xxxx the blades goodbye they r in nu hands now
robbie
```

So it was all over. He scraped his feet closer to the edge. Better to throw himself and his dreams over the side than let someone else do it for him. If he was leaving this life he was going his way not theirs.

Schoolboy squeezed the last smoke from the spliff as he half-watched the telly. He blew the smoke out knowing he'd been brushing dangerously close to madness on the roof an hour ago. He'd been wavering, dizzy, hearing the daffodils calling, when the delight of someone's early-morning cooking had taken him. Just like that. The aroma of fried chicken had stirred him, lured him, shoved him away from the edge, reminding him that he had a talent that other people needed. The ability to put food in others' bellies was big business and Michael was giving him a chance to join the movement. As the wind had dragged the shopping trolley closer to him he'd thought of what Michael would say when he heard that he'd become another doomed black statistic.

'Stupid fool, when he could have been cooking something sweet. What wrong with the boy?'

He'd grabbed his personal MB and sent Michael a text.

```
I'll be there c u soon
SB
```

Sending the message was like affirming he was going to be there. Had to be there. He'd climbed down the roof shaft still without a plan.

Now he wheezed on his smooth stick one last time trying to smoke up that focus. With the phone smashed he knew his options were limited.

The telly was on low so it didn't attract any attention from the living or the spirits still dwelling in the block. Some US-imported chat show hosted by a former rapper called Princess Takesha had just started. She had been done up to look palatable for Middle American audiences with straightened weave-on, skin-blending make-up and a high voice that contrasted with her in-your-face life-is-a-daily-roots-feature-in-the-hood sound. But they couldn't quite hold Princess T back because a slice of her belly and accompanying button were peeping through.

'Tonight I am so excited to welcome our guest. This woman is known for turning lives around. She has motivated me to free myself from the urban burdens that have held me down, held me back. I want everyone to put their hands together for Mother Dorinda.'

The audience began clapping while Schoolboy groaned, knowing he didn't need this right now. A tall, imposing woman wrapped in mauve cotton from high forehead to smooth searching shoes drifted out. She took her applause and the fluffed cream seat and placed her hands gently open, pointed towards the audience on her knees as if she was giving an offering.

'Mother Dorinda, we are just so excited to finally get you on the show,' Princess T gushed and wriggled on her seat.

'Why, thank you Sista T. It is a great honour to come and mingle my energy with you.'

'Mother Dorinda, your mouth has so many powerful words. I understand that you have taken your power and energy to Africa.'

'Yes, the power and energy of Africa is with me always. I have just returned from a tour of Ghana, Nigeria and the Côte d'Ivoire . . .'

'The what, Mother Dorinda?'

'The Ivory Coast, child. I feel so blessed that I have been able to spend this time with my brothers and sisters in Africa. I felt such a deep potency and spirit from these people that I knew we have been united since the day I was born. You ever been to Africa, Sista T?'

'I don't think so. I was in Jamaica last year . . .' Princess T offered.

'Jamaica is not in Africa, my child, but you are right, we must not forget the richness coming from our Caribbean bredren and sistren.'

'Mother Dorinda, tell us a little bit about what you were doing in Africa.'

'I went to research my new book, which I'm going to call "The Spirit of Africa Can Smash Those Ghetto Chains". I went to collect sayings from the mother country to bring back to help our tribe overcome their problems.'

'I know that you found some of these sayings to have a certain drive which can help all of us.'

'My favourite one is "Pick up the reins and pull the cow in the direction you want to go". There is no point letting other people take control of your life, pulling you in any direction they want to, leading you to the slaughterhouse when you know you're the one who is going to be butchered.'

He imagined himself tethered with a thick chain around his neck being led by Queen into the darkness of a warehouse. The urgency in Mother Dorinda's voice lured him back to the telly.

'Pick up the reins and pull the cow in the direction you want to go. It doesn't matter what your situation is, you can turn yourself around just like that.' Her two fingers clicked together straight at the camera. Straight at him. His body snapped up and forward.

Suddenly something moved into place.

Suddenly the warmth of the Devon coastline brushed over him.

Suddenly he realised why Evie and her friends soaked up every word this woman had to say.

He smiled. 'Quaintness, coves and cooking,' he mouthed towards the television screen.

Suddenly he knew Mother Dorinda had propelled him back into picking up the reins of his life.

22

'So what have you found out?' Queen asked, as she leaned upright on her heels, draining the smoke from a ciggy. She hadn't felt the harshness of nicotine against the enamel of her teeth in four years. She'd stopped because her eldest said school told it her it was bad. There was no way she'd disappoint her kids, so she'd have to sneak into the garden shed to smoke.

The lock-up in Dalston ached with the raw early morning Saturday wind, but Queen couldn't feel it. Her body ran with a heat generated from anger and anticipation.

'I found a sister,' Cuttie answered, voice peppered with weakness.

'Address.'

Cuttie went through his pocket and took out a yellow notepad. Queen snatched it from his hands and read. Her eyes zoomed across it. They restarted at the top and zoomed across it again. And again.

'Are you sure this is it?' Her tone had a far-away quality as if she was in the room on her own.

Cuttie nodded.

'Be back here at nine. Bring along two others.'

Cuttie knew he was dismissed, so turned and made his way to the door.

As Cuttie left, Queen stared at the notepad, the lifting and draining of her blood changing her complexion from brown to a colour yet to be named. Her heels ground briskly towards her coat, which sprawled on the seat and back of a chair. She bent over and felt in the right pocket. Her nails scraped the metal of her keys and money and finally found what she was after. She pulled out the small violet business card and read:

Yvette Campbell
Social Regeneration Consultant
Unit 24 Nutmeg Wharf
Wapping New Quay
09578 12134
evie.campbell@hipgals.com

The same name, the same address. Queen moved around the square room, her body pumping annoyance. The worst type of annoyance. Annoyance with herself. All this time the answer had been in her grasp. Who would have thought the same blood ran through the veins of some street hustler and the conscience of the community? The last time she'd gone through the extended family route had been last Christmas. She'd yanked a rival's nephew off the street. His sobbing and screaming had thumped against the walls that he didn't know where his uncle was. It took her an hour to be satisfied that he was telling the truth, so his burnt body had been flung outside the nearest hospital. She didn't really want to involve Yvette, but what options did she have? She wanted what the phone had badly. Two of her fingers did a slicing motion across her neck. Her fingers fell. Yes, she wanted what the phone had. But she didn't like the idea of having to trouble someone who was looking after the future of her girls. Not many people around these parts took much interest in the welfare of the coming generation. But it wasn't her business that Yvette Campbell had come out of the same womb as a street worm. Her body rippled. It tensed forward. She felt the prints of Schoolboy's hands again. Maybe she could get rid of this feeling by doing the same to his sister.

The metallic Merc took the A10, took The Highway and took Wapping. Its only business was acceleration. The same intention of Queen and her men inside. A flick of Cuttie's wrist at the ignition key broke its speed. The engine faded to dead outside Nutmeg Wharf. The type of wharf Queen had once been tempted to buy. But she had decided against it. Better to be in the core of the community she did business with. Anyway, once you took your eye off the community you'd better be ready for the chilled touch of someone's piece leaving black residue inside your temple.

Queen could feel the rumbling energy of her men. Nothing like the mingling of a botched job and death to raise testosterone levels. She pulled on the last bite of her tenth cigarette. Men and their pride. Still, she wasn't complaining. She turned to Cuttie and held out the fag-end. He took it, pulled the built-in ashtray and mashed it out.

'I'll be gone twenty minutes. If I'm not back by then come up and get me.'

She didn't look at their faces. She kept hers fixed forward as she opened the door. She breathed in the untroubled village mentality that was Wapping. Definitely not her end of town. She pressed the intercom, with nails that she had varnished between cigarettes.

'Yvette Campbell, Unit 24.'

A brown face peered back. Youthful, bored, with eyes that melted up and down her black skirt-suit through the glass door. Queen wriggled her backside muscles so that the skirt began to ride past her knees. She widened her stance so that he could see thighs that were regular visitors to the gym. She smiled. The long buzz she wanted to hear came. She touched the door and pushed inside. The building's warmth momentarily clouded her face, then cleared. She approached the desk with the male eyes still melting all over her.

'I've got a meeting with Ms Campbell.' She presented the business card and a voice she only ever used in bed.

His eyes never wavered from her suit.

'Third floor,' he grinned back, showing off his short-cut teeth, as if they were his greatest feature.

Queen pulled the card back, returned the smile and within seconds was riding the lift to the third floor. The third floor was what she was expecting. Bland, cheap carpet foxed-up to look expensive and chrome that just reminded her of the gunmetal poised in her pocket. She stood outside number 24, shook her skirt back into place and knocked. Even before the door was opened she knew someone was in. In her game, being sensitive to the spell of human activity before you saw it was just part of day-to-day life. As the door rustled back, an impatient, husky voice started to broadcast.

'I wasn't expecting you back yet. I'm still hunting my stupid purse. That'll teach me to drink so much on my bir . . .'

The woman in front of Queen stopped midway with surprise when she saw her. The woman was bigger than Queen remembered. Queen felt small. Men didn't bother her, but big women did. She hadn't remembered having to lift her eyes this high when she'd met Yvette at the school. The woman in the doorway smiled at Queen. Queen smiled backed with her mouth but not her eyes.

'I was hoping that you would remember me, Yvette. You did say to look you up if I was interested.'

Queen held out her hand. Her gun hand, but her piece remained in her pocket.

'Look, I'm not . . .' came the reply as a cool, dry hand squeezed into Queen's palm.

'I have an educational proposition that I thought we could discuss.' Queen's body breathed closer as she interrupted.

She'd long ago learned that you should never let an opponent play the lead in your show until you had them in a position where you were looking down on them and they were looking up at you.

The cold hand disengaged from Queen's. Queen stared back, lips and right eyebrow tilted up. She noticed that the woman's hair was sprinkled with gold hair-cuffs. Queen took the moment of silence to move closer, sending the woman in front of her breathing back.

'Look, I'm not . . .'

'Ready? Don't worry, you look great. The problem with us women is that we spend too much time glamming ourselves up and not enough time using our ears. And hands.'

Queen stepped closer.

'You don't understand . . .'

'I apologise if I caught you at an awkward moment, but you did say to look you up if I was anywhere near Wapping.'

Queen was so close she could smell the orange-blossom perfume on the other woman's skin.

The door widened to show the occupant's neck-to-toe black clothing. Jeans that were split then rejoined at the seams above the ankle and a baggy hippy top that cost a fiver on a stall and three times as much in a chain store. She raised her arm to peer at her watch. She lightly kissed her teeth, let her arm fall and stared at Queen again. From the shine in her eyes Queen could see that the woman inside the door was so distracted that she no longer saw her. Queen screwed her mouth to the left side. Distractions made fucking up people so much easier.

'I suppose you can come in and wait . . .'

The voice stopped to fill itself up with more oxygen as it turned and went inside. Queen took her cue and followed, using a movement that suggested she was getting ready to slow-dance rather than do business. As she felt for the pistol in her pocket the voice behind continued.

'You shouldn't have to wait too long because . . .' The woman in front of Queen began to swing around to face her.

Queen knew the moment was right. She thrust the gun forward as if she was introducing another person to the conversation. Her elbow locked under her breast. The woman in front of her stood bolt still as if she'd been caught in bed with someone else's man. Then she swerved back as if boiling water was being chucked her way. Her bronze lips buckled open, gasping in breaths that could only be heard because the flat was so quiet.

'There's no need to get your extensions all in a twist. Just shift yourself into the sitting-room and I'm sure we can get this all sorted before your next appointment.'

Quaintness, coves and cooking. Those were the three words joy-riding in Schoolboy's head when he woke up. That's the direction he wanted to go in. He'd woken up same time as the nine-to-fivers. Now as the shower darted and renewed his body he knew that Devon was his again. Today was his, tomorrow was his and the day after that was his.

He was finally running tings.

If Michael really wanted him he'd take him without the knives.

He'd show Michael through his talent that he was the best there could be in a kitchen. But Schoolboy knew that even in Devon his demons could find and hunt him down. So before he went anyway he needed to stop his biggest demon, Queen, riding his back. He sauntered, chin elevated, into the sun-shrouded sitting-room. Earlier he had deliberately tugged open each pair of curtains. There was no point thinking in the light and living in the dark. Shame he wasn't going to church today because he felt like testifying. Testifying with his arms out high, palms flat, drawing energy from on high. Life was finally his for the taking. Yes sir, his.

A powerful, draining sensation gathered within him, stopping his movement towards the settee. It felt painful. The type of pain a patient has to feel before he is cured. He closed his eyes and he knew. He knew that Mizz Havers, his detested careers teacher, had finally left his life. He sat down, mouth ajar, gulping air. Gulping the sweetest goodness he'd felt in a long time. His eyes flicked open, shining with confidence that was more Eli than Schoolboy. All four of his dimples joined his new party. He picked up his mobile, which rested on the settee's arm, and dialled Window's number. If that new life was going to be his he had to deal with those blocking his view.

'Hey G, it's me, how are tings kicking?' Schoolboy asked in an easy tone.

'More jumping than kicking, but all's well. The word in Stokey is that you're running way too hot man.'

'Don't worry about me, I'm not on the barbecue quite yet. I just need you to give me the running scores on a few items.'

'Like?'

Schoolboy shifted forward. The towel pulled tight until his naked thigh thrust through.

'Why this phone's connecting me to too many idiots on the street?'

'Whatever it is hasn't run past my ears, but I can tell you that the idiots are Queen and the Numbers Crew.'

'So what type of belly-cord would be tying both of these players together?'

'The way it's being told is that the Numbers were expecting a delivery and Queen told her posse to liberate it. But that business near the Lord's place is bringing a bit too much heat on the street for other crews' liking. If it doesn't simmer down soon I hear that other crews may be stamping on both Queen's and the Numbers' toes.'

'And you've got no idea what the delivery might be?'

'Speculation is swinging from the phone having a message about the new formula of a drug to some importation from Africa.'

'I take it we're not talking about a Back to Africa movement?'

They both laughed. It felt so good to feel joy again. Schoolboy noticed that Window's laughter ended much sooner than his. It didn't end in the way laughter drifts up, down and away, it just got chopped in mid melody. Schoolboy's free hand started playing with his towel.

'Window, is something up?'

'Schoolie, look G, there is something else. Someone's contacted me and would like to face you across the table to deal with some business.'

'Who that?'

'Can't chat it on this line, bush have ears and all that. No pressure, it's your decision, but remember the type of temperature you're packing could give London a heatwave long before summer reach, so this could be the way out you're looking for.'

One woman sat while the other remained standing.

'I like your style,' Queen admired as her eyes did a tour of duty around the room.

The room had an afterglow of pineapple and coconut. A Malibu home. Queen liked that. But she wasn't there to like or dislike, but to get on with business. She pinned her eyes back to the victim who sat a sofa throw away from her. She steadied her gun, which pointed at the woman before her. She widened her stance as she widened her mouth.

'Do you think blood-caked walls will add or detract from your style? Maybe I should be entering your broken head for an art prize. If they can have a dead cow why not some dead woman? Let's see, what should I call it . . . Yes, what about "Installation of a head that

226

wouldn't open its mouth"?'

'How exactly can I help you?'

The question melted confident and clear across the room. Queen's hand shook, caught off-guard. Most women would be crying, babbling, on their knees praying by this stage. But not this one. Her question had been formed with relaxation and a lucidity that suggested being held in a choke-hold situation was nothing new. Queen chopped over as fast as her snug skirt would allow and reared over her quarry. She didn't like the fact that even though the woman before her was sitting they were almost eye-to-eye. She pressed the gun a bullet's breath away from the face turned up to her.

'Baiting someone who's desperate for a fag is a dangerous business.'

The seated woman opened her mouth and Queen knew she was going to say something clever. Queen's eyebrow lifted, a warning that being clever was her domain. The mouth cracked closed, then reopened.

'So tell me what you want.'

Queen wasn't sure that she'd grabbed back the higher ground but she moved back, re-treading her slow-dance steps.

'I really admire the work you're doing.'

'So we've established I'm a pillar of the community. Now tell me what you want.'

Queen frowned, noticing the gap in the woman's front teeth. She hadn't noticed that before. She must be losing her street touch if she couldn't remember the imprints of a face. Her hand started trembling again, this time for nicotine. She didn't like the way the eyes were assessing the lines of her clothes, the cut of her face. She didn't like the way the chin was set back as if enjoying the sun that had fled across the river into the room.

Queen realised that her feet were nowhere near the upper ground.

'Your brother has something that belongs to me.'

'Schoolboy? I should have known. You're not one of his disillusioned lady friends, are you, because if so my advice is to turn around and find yourself a man that acts his age not his nuts size.'

'I haven't come here to play games,' Queen squeezed out as her finger moulded on the trigger.

'I know that, so why don't you put your metal friend away and let's talk because I'm about sick to death of Eli's crap stinking up my life.'

The seated woman flew out of the chair and Queen mirrored the action and flew back. The room was no longer quiet, but overpowered with busy breathing. One woman inhaled frustration, the other let out domination. Queen watched as the larger woman kept coming her way talking with each step.

'I think that we can get this sorted. We're both businesswomen not bush bandits who don't let anything or anyone block our way. So why don't you take a seat while I get us a drink?'

Queen watched as the woman began walking towards her. Her steps were unhurried and peaceful. Queen remained rooted. Indecision took hold. Just like the first time she'd ordered her boys to blank out a life. She felt the slick warmth of the metal in her hand. Felt the heat of the moving body. Felt the steps lean closer. Queen's finger curled tighter. The sun tripped out of the room. Queen's eyes got harsher, watching the woman getting closer to her. So close that she could smell the scent of calm and reason. Tacky smell that had no business being in her life. Her victim now stood in front of her. Smiled gently down at her. Then shifted to the side of her. Finally falling into the shadow behind her. Queen swivelled on her heels, her gun cutting into the line of the shadow.

'Bitch, you're crossing a line that not many people get the opportunity to tread back over.'

'What about a camomile tea to get us both in the right frame of mind?' The voice called from the threshold of the door.

Queen's neck snapped back as she rushed forward.

'Come on Window, spar, you yourself taught me to never meet anyone without having their birth certificate in front of me,' Schoolboy's bare feet were prowling the room, from gold wall to rose wall back to gold.

'Can't chat it on the phone.'

'As my skin seems to be the most valuable commodity in Hackney at the mo, why should I take a malt with Mr X?' Schoolboy asked, squinting. The light was starting to bother his eyes.

'Let's just say I hear he was on the end of a Jet Lei and is looking to even the score.'

'Against?'

'Come to my house to find out.'

'So what's Houdini saying he can tell me?'

'Let's just say that you won't hear this on the six o'clock news.'

'How are you so sure he won't turn into the devil while in your house?'

'He knows that if he does, his previous beating will feel like he was an extra in *Playschool*. Let my tongue do some more talking so that I can see what else I can find out for you about Queen or the Numbers. Come over in an hour and we can chat before my guest makes an appearance.'

Window's voice held that base quality that the street knew so well.

Schoolboy swung his lips around, not sure what to say. His skin was starting to itch from the chalk in the water. What-ifs started drumming that old beat in his temples. He snapped down his eyes. Quaintness, coves and cooking.

'OK, I'm on my way,' he agreed.

They had nothing else to discuss so he pressed red. Trust was something you felt within not outside and he could trust Window. He had to trust Window.

This time both women were seated. Queen dipped the gun into her jacket pocket. Its talent for tormenting people wasn't working today so it might as well leave the equation. Besides, she still had her knife if things went wrong. The bleakness of the sky had long since pushed the sun aside.

'Isn't this so much more cosy, Queen? I'm sure you can't remember the last time you sat and had an honest-to-God discussion with another woman.'

Queen didn't answer straight away. She plucked up her small cup lying on the table between them. She sucked it up and hastily spat the tea back into the cup. How this stuff ever relaxed anyone was beyond her. She replaced the cup. Now her lips were moist she was ready to talk.

'I can remember all right. Last year, at the beginning of the school summer term. Her name was Tanya. We talked about babies, families, our visions for the future . . .'

'I knew you would be a reasonable woman . . .'

'Of course Tanya couldn't stop crying. Couldn't stop bawling. After I had her in the lock-up for thirty seconds it clicked that she might never see her babies again. That members of her family might end up mashed in intensive care. That there was no point her dreaming about the future because she was going to end up in a coma if I discovered she was the one skimming off the cream of my money. You dig, Yvette?'

'It's Evie. Call me Evie.'

Queen screwed up the lower half of her face and shuffled to the edge of the seat. The word 'Evie' sounded foreign in her opponent's mouth. Sounded like someone's voice she had heard but not at the community meeting at St Dunstan's School. 'Evie' drank her tea, both her hands encased around her mug. As the tea entered her throat the sucking sound it made told Queen this woman was much more nervous than she let on.

'Evie, did I know you before we met at that meeting in the school?'

'Queen, I don't think we travel in the same circles. You're a memorable lady, Queen. You're not someone I would forget meeting.'

Queen nodded, but remained perched on the boundary of the seat.

'Evie, I'm curious as to how you're living with the river lapping your feet and Schoolboy's still in a cesspit.'

'Some of us are on the way up and some of us are on the way down. The problem with people on the downswing is that they want company and I'm tired of holding other people's hands.'

Queen could understand that.

'Let's just say that while you haven't been holding Schoolboy's hands his fingers have been wandering into my life. Now you don't need to know what he's taken – I just need to know where I can find him.'

'My brother being the little reptile that he is could be anywhere. He's been found under many a dank stone. But what I could do is help you if you help me.'

'I'm sure you don't need any more help.' Her eyes cast around, 'You seem to have done all right on your own.'

'Let's just say that there have been one too many complaints about Eli's behaviour from my good neighbours. Now I do not wish to move but if he keeps it up I will have no alternative.'

'So what are you suggesting?'

'That I contact you when I know where he is and when you finally catch up with him just make sure that he doesn't come back around here . . . let's say for a good six months.'

'If I agree, how do I know that you won't contact our friends in blue?'

'What's in that for me? I've got no friends there . . .' The voice stopped, flashed the gap between her front teeth and then rushed on 'with my work in *this* community.'

Queen shifted further off the sofa. She could swear that the woman in front of her was more fretful now than when the gun was in her face. Queen's eyes trod into her face looking for whatever it was she couldn't see. The woman opposite her pulled the cup up, cast her eyes down and started drinking. Queen eased back knowing that there was no point looking if you couldn't twist into someone's eyes.

Queen knew her options were limited. She dug into her pocket, using the edge of her nails so they didn't break and pulled out a card. White, with her name in italics, accompanied by a mobile number. No address, no fax, no e-mail. She placed it on the table, near the cup, like a napkin yet to be used.

'Contact me. I like your style, Evie, but that won't stop me from bustin' up your respectable arse if I don't hear the sound of your voice bleeping on my phone soon. I wouldn't want to make more trouble for you and the neighbours.'

The rain slashed against the balcony's french windows as Queen rose up, shook her skirt back into place and turned to leave. As she reached the door, she slowly pivoted back to face the woman in the room.

'One last thing, I'd get rid of the nose-tinsel if I were you. It doesn't suit you.'

23

The brooding beat of Evie's feet padded along Wapping New Quay. Petals of rain played around her as she worried about her brother, as she envied her brother. There, she had thought it, it was out in the open. Envy. It could be such a nasty business. She envied the constant twists and turns in his life. She envied his ability to serve but one master – himself. She envied the way he said *what's occurring* one day and then *see yah* the next. Evie shoved her hands into her beige bootleg trouser-pocket, letting her bag swing on its own on her shoulder, as her home came into view. Now that last night's alcohol was free from her mind she realised that Eli was leaving and she felt jealousy and loss all at the same time. But jealousy was by far the stronger emotion clawing away at her. That's why she'd been so taut with anger and spite the night before. To see freedom in the distance just waiting for you. Her tongue peeped out, wet her top lip, her bottom lip, then popped back inside. The freedom to pack up and start somewhere else was as strong in her as it was in him. But she couldn't do that. Too many responsibilities. Too much investment. Too much commitment? She questioned herself about that one. Questioned what she was actually committed to.

The rain stopped fooling around and started hitting her face. She lengthened her stride, controlling the movement of her bag with one hand. She noticed the Mercedes outside her building. She let her eyes dip down inside and spotted three healthy brothers. Her eyes left the car and drifted around and stopped when she spotted another brother standing outside the estate agent's, deep into a conversation on his mobile. Her gaze massaged him. Powerful, sure of himself, just the type she was looking for to replace her summer duvet. So it sounded like a stereotype, but so what. Rolling around with a stereotype taking the place of her summer duvet for a few months sounded hot. Her eyes lingered and caught his. They locked. She smiled, he didn't. He snapped his eyes away from her and carried on talking. That's what she wanted to be committed to, but that type of commitment had long ceased coming her way. All she had to look forward to were the Mr Lloyds of this world. Stable, financially sound and boring. She could bring stability and finances to the party. She wanted to be hooked up, arm-in-arm, with someone who bought excitement to the rave.

She sighed as she entered the building. She told herself that would be her last sigh of the day. No point grabbing for things that weren't there. Well, at least not yet. She pushed into the building.

'Hello, Miss Evie. I thought you were in . . .' called Mackintosh, who manned the desk.

'I keep telling you to call me just Evie,' she replied as she moved towards the desk.

But she knew he never would. She'd managed to get him this job at a time when his parents thought that he was taking life as a joke. A word in the ear of the management and the job of day concierge was his. His parents had been grateful. Just another reminder that she was fed up with playing the strong black woman. She felt that second sigh coming on and suppressed it.

She approached Mackintosh and asked, 'Why did you think I was in?'

'Some spanking-looking woman came looking for you. She had your business card. She hasn't come back down yet,' he ended, looking worried.

'Don't worry about it. Whoever she is she won't be roaming around the building because I left Tammy in my place so she must be looking after her. Tammy knows that I only went out to get some bread. I'd better see who it is.'

Evie headed for the lift. Its red numbers were shooting up, so she decided to use the stairs. As she opened the door for her floor, she saw the shadow of a small woman sweep into the lift. Maybe that's who Mackintosh meant. She ran towards the lift. She could hear the doors closing, but she motored on.

'Evie,' a voice ripped from behind her, making her fudge a step and almost trip into the wall. She heard the lift doors close. She steadied herself, puffing, then swung around to see Tammy hovering, in those wonderful split jeans that Evie admired, outside the comfort of her door. Except Tammy didn't seem comfortable. Her eyelids were flashing up and down, the movement of her bottom lip moving her jaw from side to side.

'You all right, Tam?'

'Yeah, yeah, I'm just relieved that I finally found my purse.'

Evie started walking towards her friend, talking at the same time.

'Mackintosh said someone was looking for me. I just thought it might be them in the lift.'

'Some woman came knocking, with the usual Jehovah's Witness patter on her lips.'

'That's strange, Mackintosh said she had one of my business cards.'

'Evie, you give your card to so many people that one was bound to slip into the hands of someone doing something. Wasn't it Jesus himself who said that you must spread the word by any means necessary?'

They both laughed. Evie's high and free, Tammy's low and wobbling.

'Time for a cuppa?' Evie asked.

'Sorry,' Tammy's palm squeezed Evie's forearm once. 'I've got one or two things to do. Maybe later.'

As Tammy rushed off, Evie stepped into her home. She hoped that the fit brother on the phone downstairs wasn't a Jehovah's Witness devotee because if he was she was more confused than she realised.

'What do you look like?' Window's tone tickled with laughter, heightening the sparkling quality of his skin.

Window wasn't the only one looking at Schoolboy. The few patrons at the tables were also gazing as if they had seen something they wish had stayed in the past. Schoolboy knew that the best way to walk the streets was in disguise. He'd considered lopping off his locks, but his hair was sometimes more important than his garms. The best solution had been to search through the wardrobe at the flat. The wardrobe seemed to have been divided into four collections – the soul raver, the raga bwoy, Superfly pimp heaven and late-night loving. He'd reluctantly gone for pimp heaven. Bark-brown pin-striped suit, beige coat with bushy lapels and wide-brimmed hat dropped at an angle so that it was tipping his nose and tipping the world. He'd decided against the silver-topped cane. The only part of him left was his faithful Tims.

'I think what you mean, my man Window, is what's cooking, dawg,' Schoolboy answered in a deep US accent.

He swaggered over to the bar.

'Schoolie, don't let all that heat go to your head, boy.'

His response reminded Schoolboy of how they met. Through laughter.

'Didn't think any street brothers would connect this,' he pulled at the edges of the coat, 'with me.'

'I hear that pimp is on its way out and all man are going for a bowler hat, classic black umbrella, city-man style.'

'You're joking.'

Seeing the I-got-you look on his friend's face they both started to laugh.

'Let's chat in the back.'

He followed Window past the bar and the curried fumes coming from the kitchen. That would be him in Devon soon, spreading joy and curried goat from one end of town to the other. Or was it village? They entered a room that, though Schoolboy had been in it many times, still amazed him with how un-Window it looked. Stark butter-orange, with small and large candles, an array of hubble-bubbles and Islamic prints and pictures. Relics from his days of dealing with his Muslim bredren, as he put it, in North Africa. A late Victorian fire-place, whose black tone was raised by the walnut table and chairs. No sign of family or friends.

Schoolboy sat down as Window also took a seat.

'My nephew, Lynton, sends a big thanks for letting him stay in your pad while he's at university down here.'

'No problem. Just tell him to keep on the right side of Jackie.'

Pleasantries over, Schoolboy took the conversation to the mystery man waiting for him.

'So what's going on?'

'Before we get into the meat of things let me tell you what I've got on the Nigerians. I don't think I ever told you where I first came across Wahid.'

'Wahid?'

'One of their main playas while I was doing some work in Morocco. They were involved in a deal that went wrong.'

'What kind of deal?'

'The way it was told to me it involved the movement of jewellery and art, from all over Africa, especially Egypt. They were working with some Italian that did a double-cross and got one of them slung in prison.'

'This is starting to sound a bit too Danielle Steele for me. So who are *they*?'

'I only ever met Wahid, but there were two others. One of them is his brother, Ashara or Number 10, who is operating with him in Hackney. The other one I never met. Just know his street name was Number 8. But he must be back in Nigeria because he ain't here.'

He shoved his muscles up and walked towards the wall to the left of the door. He reached up and pulled a postcard-sized print with Islamic script off a hook on the wall. He came back and placed the picture flat on the table.

'All their names are Arabic for numbers. "Wahid" is the Arabic for Number 1.' He pointed to the first script on the picture. 'Ashara means Number 10 and Number 8 must be called Tamania.'

'You what?'

Window let his finger jab the picture again. 'Tamania is the Arabic for Number 8. Can't say I've ever heard of anyone with that jingle. Since coming to these shores the Numbers gang are reported to be dealing in some drugs, but they ain't touched the usual 419 money scams you would expect, so the phone must have something to do with drugs. As for Queen, sky's the limit on that one.'

Schoolboy was no longer listening to his friend. His eyes were pinned to the Arabic script for Number 8. It resembled a triangle squeezed at the top, without a line at the bottom to complete it. Schoolboy raised his head and started to look at his friend's neck with heated eyes. Started to check the tattoo living on Window's skin.

'Schoolboy, what you doing?'

Schoolboy dashed his eyes to the side.

'Nothing.'

'What you looking at me like that for?'

'I said nothing. I'm just jumpy, that's all.'

Before they could continue, they were interrupted by a knock at the door. It made Schoolboy's belly roll. Made Schoolboy realise that he couldn't trust anyone any more.

The door opened to admit Shaka, the barman-come-bouncer.

'Him come.'

'Bring him through.'

'I need to know . . .' Schoolboy held back in the room, voice shaking.

'No, because if I do you'd just turn around, leave and go about your business. Just play it easy. Let the man talk and then make your decision.'

The knock came again. Window moved towards the door to open it. Schoolboy twisted his hand behind himself, swiped the Islamic print off the table and shoved it into his pocket. Schoolboy just stared as the door began to open.

Window was right. If he'd known who Houdini was he'd have left, kissing his teeth, long ago.

'Now, gentlemen, I'll leave you to it,' Window started as he stood at the door. 'Remember I have customers out front, so keep it easy. The first sign I hear of any arm-wrestling you can take it to the street.'

Window was gone as soon as the last word was out of his mouth.

Schoolboy stared at a face he didn't want to see. A face that reminded him of toasted Dexter. A face that still bore the marks of a beating.

'So you finally made our appointment,' Sensi said, breaking the silence in the room.

Sensi now occupied the chair that Window had recently vacated. Schoolboy didn't answer but let his eyes bite all over Sensi's skin. The same beige face, with more red than brown. The same rustic locks, with one strand used as a hairband to make a pony-tail. The same closed look, but bruised from a recent pounding. Schoolboy suddenly slammed up, almost overturning the chair. Sensi moved his body protectively back into his seat. He cupped his hands, the air between them, as if he was going to catch a ball.

'Look, I have got no words to say to you.' Schoolboy's words were as short as the breath shooting his chest.

He started marching towards the door. Pimp heaven now seemed the most stupid clothes to wear.

'Well, my mouth have 'nuff to relate to you. Information about Queen and her next move.'

Sensi's throaty voice froze him, his hand already settled on the door handle.

Schoolboy started speaking but didn't turn around.

'So why should I trust a footman of the great Queen, you get me?'

'Let's just say that this footman went to the Tower and wants to make sure you keep your head. Take a seat, man, so that we can settle and cool it down.'

Schoolboy remained focused on the door. Reason told him to go back and listen. But everything in his life had started going bizzo when he'd bucked up with Sensi. He was moving up and he didn't want Sensi to move him down.

'Come on, man. What have you got to lose?'

'My life, like Little-Big-Afroman-Dexter.'

Sensi laughed, long and rounded.

'What make you tink Dexter got anything to do with this? That donkey got done because him keep poking around in the bed of a man who didn't like Dexter's smell on his pillow.'

Schoolboy re-focused, turned around, and sulked back to the chair. He gripped the top with his fingers, his knuckles taut and tight. He scraped the chair away from Sensi, sat down, making his coat flop open to the sides, like a mouth ready to do his talking.

'I like your threads.'

'Stop hawking. Just get on with it.'

As Sensi opened his mouth, Schoolboy's phone started crackling with Jim Reeves. He pulled it out and checked the name of the caller. Tammy. Shit, he should have contacted her this morning. He pressed red and stuffed it back in his pocket. Schoolboy stuck his eyes back up and seized Sensi's face.

'Get talking.'

'People is saying that Queen is going to set you up.'

'Look, I didn't bust a nut to come here to find out something I already know. I've already had the pleasure of your big dog's hospitality, you get me.'

Sensi started opening his mouth, but crammed it shut. Whatever he was going to say he let go. His skin wrinkled across his forehead as he reopened his lips to say something new.

'But the grapevine's whispering that she have a new source. A source close to you.'

Sensi wriggled his backside to the edge of the chair in that shedding-old-skin movement Schoolboy knew he did so well. Schoolboy could feel his heart start to rage.

'I don't have any close sources. I work as a high plains loner. Always have, always will.'

'Are you sure 'bout that? No one you come running to when tings get too mean? No one you come running to when your cheese has long gone? Come on, spar, we've all got a helping hand waiting around the corner.'

'So why would you want to tell me this?'

Sensi pointed to the bruises on his face.

'OK.'

'So who's the source?'

'I don't tink you want to know, understand.'

Schoolboy swallowed the liquid stuck between his tongue and the roof of his mouth. It didn't go down so well. His mind clubbed through a list of names and faces.

Lord Tribulation.

Jay-Jay.

Professor Lloyd.

Even the spar of all spars, Window.

'Stop playing give-us-a-clue and start dropping the name.'

'It's your sister.'

The inside of his mouth restricted, desert-dry. His heart started a double beat, a treble beat, a beat that banged from the soles of his feet to the holes in his ears. Sweat trickled down the sides of his mouth as if it had escaped from his nose. He shook his head once, twice, then reared up. Now standing, he realised that his whole self was shaking.

'I knew I should never have come here.' Despite the tremble in his vocal cords he carried on. 'Pure bollocks and bullshit. My sister and Queen are as far away as Princess Diana and Lil' Kim.'

'I'm telling you . . .'

Schoolboy pounced, without breath or warning. He grabbed the upper half of Sensi's flannel shirt as if he was a bag of sweet potatoes, flung him out of the chair and stuck him on the wall. A large Islamic print picture flipped and dived to the floor.

'Your info is wrong, you get me.' Schoolboy didn't recognise his own voice.

He'd always skirted around violence. Lived on its margins. But his stays in HMP had taught him that sometimes, some days, your hands were all you had. Sensi wasn't even squirming, as if he'd been expecting it. He stood as peaceful in Schoolboy's hands as he had done sitting in the chair.

'This info came from a G so close to Queen it more or less came from inside her own mouth.'

Schoolboy tightened and pressed the man he held into the plaster. He shook his head, locks swaying, brain glowing.

'Your sister lives at Nutmeg Wharf, Wapping.'

Schoolboy increased the pressure and could almost feel Sensi's spine grazing the knots in his fingers. Sensi's face lost its brownness and became blanket red.

'Queen went up there today and your sister said she'd give you up. Said you're a leech . . .'

Schoolboy unlocked one hand, clenched it, but didn't swing. Instead he looked into the depth of Sensi's red-baked eyes. He searched quick and hard. For the lie. But all he found was an unsympathetic truth.

The door suddenly rocked on its hinges, injecting new air that made Schoolboy gasp. Then strong familiar hands were caressing and grabbing his shoulders at the same time. They pulled him off Sensi. The hands dropped away and Schoolboy let his head hang to the floor. He sprang towards the table, picked up his glass and spat inside it. He heard Window's mint tone fill the room.

'You need to go. Maybe you should take your mistress's advice and stay on the other side of the water.'

Schoolboy placed the glass back on the table. He braced both hands against the table's edge, as if he needed support or he would fall down. His nose and eyes were drizzling tears.

'Schoolie, rest yourself.'

Schoolboy swung around and stared at Window as if it was the first time he'd seen him.

'He's lying.'

'What did the pussy say?'

'I'm a fucking all-time failure. All I want to do is to move on. I made one mistake, one poxy mistake, so what, I've got to pay for it with the rest of my days doing time on this earth? If I have to crawl across broken glass to get to Devon I'm going to do it.' His chest puffed forward. 'No one's going to stand in my way. Not Queen, not no fucking Arabic-loving band of no-hopers, not no Ev . . .' he finally stopped, his breathing picking up any rhythm it could find.

Schoolboy looked around the room for his hat. He walked towards it.

'Schoolie, let's talk before you go,' Window coaxed as Schoolboy picked up the hat.

'No need for no long chat, isn't that what you always told me. Keep it brief, simple, to the point. I got one or two things to do. I'll give you a bleep before I go.'

Schoolboy's eyes vaulted to the tattoo on his friend's neck.

'You're one of them, aren't you?' Schoolboy cried, knowing he was on dangerous ground accusing someone as powerful as Window of any crime.

'One of who?' Window shook his head as he stepped closer to his friend.

'One of them Numbers people. You must think me is stupid. I can see that Arabic mark for number 8 on your neck. That's why your bloody club is called the –1, ain't it. What did you plan to do, have me taken down by Sensi?'

He stopped, gushing hot air in each direction. Window just stood there, his whole face taking on the shadows of his eyes. Schoolboy knew he couldn't trust anyone any more. He grabbed up his hat and set the hat on his head. He pulled it down so that it tipped his nose, but the angle made sure it wasn't tipping the world.

24

He rode the bus back to Parkview. The pressure in his head tightened with every choke of the bus engine. Tightened with the knowledge that he didn't know who to trust. The tears had long left his thoughts, but Evie and Window hadn't. His beautiful Evie. The spirit Mum had left behind to take care of him. He thought of that day when she had needed his help.

It was 1985.

One of those same old, same old autumn days when the only thing that changes is the number of leaves gathering on the streets.

Evie had come home from school, blouse torn and madder than the milkman when Schoolboy had tipped water on his head from the second floor. Mum wasn't in because she had just started a part-time job and Dad was at the All Fours Dominion Club planning the club's annual seaside trip. Evie had stalked the sitting-room crying and screaming revenge. When Schoolboy had calmed her down, sat her down, the story had hiccupped from her lips. Shaquille Mason, bully extraordinaire, had roughed her up and stolen her dinner money. The next day, at home time, Schoolboy had made sure that Shaquille wouldn't be waylaying any other girls. He'd never told Evie what he had done, but she had been grateful.

Now someone was telling him that she'd forgotten that the same blood flowed through their veins. He remembered Sensi's eyes, open in their honesty. He still wouldn't believe. Couldn't believe it. But that didn't make the seed stop sprouting.

He squeezed his eyes, seeing the Arabic writing. Knowing he'd seen it before. Window's tattoo reflected back at him. There were so many marks on that tattoo that Schoolboy just wasn't sure. There had been one mark, like the script on the postcard, but it had been lying on its side. It couldn't be his liming partner – no way! But how did sentimentality explain why Sensi had contacted Window? How did it explain why Sensi had sat in that chair with such ease as if he had sat there before?

He shook his eyes open.

Quaintness, coves, and cooking.

He was running tings. He needed to keep chanting that.

First he had to deal with what he knew or thought he knew. He thrust his hand into his inside pocket, pulled free his last remaining MB. He pressed address book, Evie's number came on-screen and he pumped green.

'What a go on, sis?'

'One of these days the English language will come back to you. How are you doing in your new residence?'

'Sorted. Evie, I was thinking that we haven't really had a chance to say goodbye, so why don't I make you one of my new curries tonight.'

'I was going to pop out, but why not? Say around seven.'

When he agreed, both their lines clicked dead. He kept his face straight and his thoughts still. He sucked his lip as a plan began to form. He jumped up and pressed the bell. If his plan was going to work he needed to hit the shops with his last tenner.

When he got back to Parkview he'd had his second shower of the day. There were one too many story-lines singing a tune in his head. Sometimes only water knew how to cleanse the mind. Even Thames water. He'd replaced pimp heaven where he had found it and jumped back into his own garms. He had one last remaining person who he could pump dry for info – Tammy.

'Tammy, my sister, got your messages, so what's occurring?' He made his tone sound light as it blew into the phone.

'Ah!' she exclaimed, showing her irritation in a very foreign way. 'Where have you been? I've been trying to get hold of you since this afternoon, O!'

'Skip the interrogation and cut to the action.'

'Is that any way to talk to your fairy godmother?'

'Let's cut the long chat. Just tell me where we're up to.'

'My friend has been making enquiries and he can help you. All you have to do is to stay as snug as a bug on Death Row until I contact you again.'

'OK, massa boss.'

'Come on, Schoolboy, how are you going to feel if they come looking for Evie?'

The blood pooled in his cheeks and around his nose. Evie, bloody Evie. Maybe he should switch the interrogation patter and put Tammy in the spotlight to find out what she knew.

'Tammy,' his voice was soft as it fluttered in her ear, 'You seen anything of Evie today?'

'Of course I have, she lives upstairs, remember. What do you want to know for?'

'Nuthin', I just want to make sure she's around to say goodbye to her.'

Silence came and he knew Tammy didn't know any more than he did.

'I know what it feels like to want to move on, so I understand where you're coming from. Let me take care of this and you'll be in Cornwall before you know it.'

'Devon.'

'Whatever.' He could hear the laugh in her voice.

She continued, 'I've got to go.'

'I'll be here waiting for your call.'

One story-line was clearly in play, now he had to chip through the other one. He headed for the kitchen and started to cook.

Schoolboy stared at the bread knife, the only knife in the kitchen. Obviously the previous occupants had no class. They just didn't get it. There was no point fitting the perfect kitchen if the knives weren't right. And a bread knife was not what he needed to create a tongue-loving curry. Still, it would have to do for now. He gazed at the vegetable in front of him on the chopping board. Or was it a fruit because it had seeds? Thais called it phru khi nu. He called it Hotter than Krystal. Krystal had been the best legover he'd ever had but this fruit smoked a fire in every pore at the same time, something Krystal hadn't quite achieved. The chilli lay twisted and small in its yellow skin in front of him, ready to be cooked. He clipped two fingers around its stalk to hold it firm and sliced it down the middle. He tossed it into the heated oil-based saucepan and fried. The instant smell smacked up, making his nose and eyes preach water. He stirred, making sure that the seeds and membrane stayed intact. The sting was stashed in the seeds. They were going to be the most important part of his curry. As Evie was going to find out, there were other ways of finding out the truth than dishing up violence.

When the knock came at the door, Schoolboy wasn't ready. Everything else was in place. The curry was cooked, the atmosphere of the main room was deepened by the candlelight brimming in each corner and Hotter than Krystal was ready for action. But Schoolboy wasn't. He hadn't taken any time to prepare himself. No time to balance his mind. No time to consider what he would do if Sensi's tongue was telling the truth. Panic swamped him. No time to consider what to do if Evie had brought unexpected guests to share their table.

'Eli, let me in. It's spooky out here.'

Each of her words hinged on the energy provided by short breaths.

'You on your own?' Stupid question, but he had to ask.

'Of course I'm not. There's Michael, Tito, Randy, Jermaine and the other one. Even Ma and Pa Jackson are here. Of course I'm on my own. Just move this door.'

He cupped his hand and wiped the threadbare sweat sitting above his mouth. He took one breath. Two breaths. His mind became loose and rock steady. Now he was ready. He turned the handle. The lock stuck midway so he added extra pressure to get it to slide all the way into the door. As the opening revealed his sister, he decided it was better to have a smile or a song on his face than a dumb look if she'd brought company. He started to sing, key flat and a couple of notes above toneless.

'Oh, baby, just give me one more chance, to show you that I love ya . . .'

'Very retro Afro 5,' she snapped smoothly as she pushed inside, extensions and bag swaying to the same beat. Irritation.

Evie was decked out in shades that disrupted the balance of the room. The blue of her hair scrunch and the black of her polo neck and turned-up jeans were too harsh in a room that shimmered in gold. Only her bobbing silver earrings tried to keep up the room's theme.

'I don't know how you sleep here at night. It makes me come over all funny.' Her voice was quiet as if she was scared someone outside might hear.

He let his secret eyes jump over her. She was shaking, lashes twitching, one hand stroking her bag as if she was trying to get a baby to burp. He saw her nose flare, as if trying to lead the way, and he knew what drew her. The fragrance of lime, lemon and coconut flirting in the room.

'Is that dinner I can smell?' Her tone and extensions were now more brisk and bright.

'Let's put it this way, it isn't another recipe for Malibu.'

They both smiled at that. Hers comfortable, his remote and relaxed.

'Fling your coat and bag somewhere and come on through to the kitchen.'

'Listen to you, Lord of the Manor.'

They both giggled as she flung the coat and bag on to the single armchair. When they entered the kitchen the way her lips parted and neck perched around he could tell she was impressed. Then she shut her eyes, letting her nose go into overdrive at the scent of curry and rice. He studied her face. He crawled over it trying to find anything that shouted liar. Anything that screamed betrayer. Anything that showed that she had become as bitter as he sometimes felt. Before his judgement came, her eyes unfolded with the gentleness of flower buds in spring. That made his suspicion flex. No one came to Parkview to feel refreshed. He moved to the cooker and started to stir the pan of curry. She followed. She shuffled around as if she had an itch, then found her spot next to his left side.

'Great kitchen. How come you always land on your feet?'

'Better than landing on my nuts.'

'Always got a clever answer . . .'

'I was taught by the best.' He hitched his neck muscles to the side and balled her square in the eye.

She was the first to slick her eyes away. Then she stepped away. He turned back to the pan but focused on her voice.

'So if I'm the best, why are you the one moving on and I'm the one left behind?'

The harshness of the colours she wore were now coating her lips.

'You're not getting all jiggy jealous on me?' His question was deliberate, provocative, nasty.

'Why would I be jealous of you?' Her tone coughed up in the back of her throat like a flamenco guitarist plucking the wrong string. 'It isn't me who's in hiding.'

Isn't it? His question never cracked past his lips.

'While you finish up I'll take myself on a more leisurely tour of your new palatial residence.' Her voice was mournful as she left the room.

He wanted to call her back, to squeeze his arms around her, to hug their warmth together. He gazed inside the pan and saw Sensi's face. He smashed the wooden spoon into it, but he knew what he had to do. He opened the oven and took out the two plates that had been warming inside. He dished out the rice and decorated it with the curry. He reopened the oven and stared at his accomplice, the chilli. It lay with an air of shrivelled harmlessness on the small saucer on the top shelf. He took it out and let it slide on to the front of Evie's curry. He used the wooden spoon to bury it deep. This wasn't a nice thing to do, but when was the last time life had been nice.

He took both plates through to the main room. Evie was slumped back on the chaise longue looking uptight.

'Grab a plate. That'll bring a smile to your face.'

She took the offered plate and placed it on the table. He joined her coat and bag on the armchair opposite. He let the interrogation begin.

'So where have your legs taken you today, sis?'

'Here and there . . .'

'Such as?'

'A bit of business, a bit of soul-searching, a bit of laundry.'

'What business?'

'Am I going to be allowed to eat this?'

He just laughed as he watched her spoon dip into the far side of the plate and go to her lips. Shit, he'd forgotten that she had this far-sided routine of eating. Never started at the front, always at the back. She wasn't the greatest of eaters so she might be too full-up to get to the front.

'Eli, this is so good.'

But it wasn't, not for him.

Deliberately he let his spoon clatter on to the carpet, taking some curry with it. He made the usual fuss about how hard it was to get curry stains out of a carpet.

'Evie, get us another spoon. In the drawer near the sink, while I wipe this up.'

When she left the room, he leaned over the table, twirled her plate around like a magician, shifted the mound of food with her spoon and then re-positioned the single piece of cutlery. As his fingers flew back, he heard her footsteps near the door. He dashed back on to the sofa, crushing her coat. He sat outwardly calm but wet under his arms.

'Here you go.' She passed him the spoon as she sat down.

'Thanks.'

He tucked into his dish and didn't have time to consider that it needed a touch more salt. He ate and watched at the same time. She pulled up her spoon and let it dive into her dish. She mixed it around trying to get every flavour on the one spoonful. She hoisted it up, let her nostrils clench and retract and then started moving it towards her lips. He had stopped chewing. Her lips puckered open, letting the spoon move inside. The spoon retreated, her mouth closed and the chewing began. He started chewing again, waiting. And waiting.

'Eli, whoever you're going to work for, I hope he knows what a good cook he's getting.'

He just smiled, waiting for her next mouthful. The process started again. And again. On her fourth mouthful he knew his accomplice had gained entry. Her mouth flashed open as if she wanted to speak but no words came out. She began to cough and splutter like some wino on the street. Her open hand dived to her neck and started rubbing. Both eyes developed a new skin of water. Her extensions were tangled, partnered together in some wild dance.

'Eli . . .' she croaked.

He pretended not to hear.

'Eli . . .' Her chin almost burst through her skin as she rasped.

He threw his plate down with mock concern. He didn't get up but spoke to her across the table.

'Oh shit, I forgot to take the chilli out. Quick, go and have some of the Coke in the kitchen. It's in the fridge.'

As she leaped up and out of the room, he dived into her bag. His fingers moved fast, feeling for the two shapes he was after – her mobile and address book. The address book came quickly, its leather cover and pages easy to identify. He pulled it out and flicked straight to Q. A single name – Quincy. He flipped through the rest of the pages, checked the inside and back cover, but didn't find any links to Queen. He held the back and front covers high by the tips of his fingers, as if he was checking for lice, and started to shake. A lilac card chopped down on to his knee. He picked it up and read.

Discretion
Sexual Emporium for Women
Everything you ever wanted
Kiss those lonely nights goodbye

He flipped it over, checking the contact details on the back. It could be a front for Queen, but somehow he couldn't see Queen hiding behind a dildo.

'Eli.' His sister's weak voice squealed, getting closer.

Suddenly his fingers felt as if he had done E and speed all at the same time. He shoved the card in the book, crammed the book into the bag and stuffed the bag behind his back. Evie staggered in, still rubbing her throat. Large pearls of sweat were rigid on her forehead, nose and upper lip. He wasn't surprised at how razzled she looked. One of the best ways to stoke up chilli heat was to have a fizzy drink.

'Evie, babe, I'm so sorry. Go and wash your face in the bathroom. That'll cool you down.'

He watched her go with a sympathetic smile attached to his lips. He did feel sorry, but it just had to be done. When the bathroom door closed her image from him, he whipped the bag from behind and pulled it open. He needed to use his eyes as well this time. He couldn't see the phone. A whimper coming from the bathroom made him stop. His breathing was charged. He waited a few seconds and then started looking again. His hand moved inside, feeling.

Lipseal.

Keys.

Black pen.

Address book, again.

MB.

He grabbed out the phone. Unlocked and on. He pressed address book and then began to scroll. Names popped up. Most he didn't know. She knew some weird people. Who the backside were Yellow and Mellow? No entries under Q. The electricity in his breathing let go. Old-fashioned relief took its place. So Mr Sensi had got his messages mixed up. He dumped the mobile back into the bag and placed the bag at the foot of the sofa.

The bad feelings started to come. Assault by a deadly fruit was not the way he should be treating his older sister. But what alternative did he have? He could have come straight out and asked her. He lifted an eyebrow at that one. Definite no-go area. He stood up and wandered to the bathroom. He rapped softly on the door.

'Sis, you all right?'

No answer. He pushed the handle down and pulled. She stood in front of the love-heart-shaped mirror, shoulders shaking. So that had been the sound. He rushed forward, turned her around, didn't utter any words and hugged her.

'Evie, girl, don't cry, it was only a chilli,' he soothed.

Bad feelings didn't come any harsher than the ones now riding through him. She lifted her head up to stare at him. Her skin was criss-crossed with tears and an emotion he couldn't place. Her hand fluttered up to touch his cheek, under the spot where one of his dimples usually appeared. Her palm was warm, cool, reassuring. Finally she spoke, her voice a whisper in a cold room.

'It's not the chilli. We've been a partnership since the word go. I know you've gone your way and I've gone mine, but we always meet up. I wish it were me going . . .'

'But why?' He was surprised by his surprise.

'Because all I really want to do is put my feet up, find some hunk of a man and have two little ones who rush up to me when I get in from work and shout Mummy. But do you know what the worst thing is? I stood here and looked in the mirror and noticed these hairs growing out of my chin. Who's gonna want to hook up with a someone who looks more like a billy-goat than a woman?'

She backed away from him.

'I'm so tired. Evie Campbell, the girl on the way up. The girl who was going places. The girl who has everything and nothing.'

She left the room and he couldn't reach her.

He stood for a moment, watching her back and extensions getting smaller as she strolled into the sitting-room, and realised that he'd been so locked off in his own pain that he'd stopped feeling anyone else's a long time ago. Hadn't he accused her of doing the same?

He left the bathroom behind and joined her in the sitting-room. She was already struggling to hoist on her coat and bag.

'I'm off.'

'But, Evie, you haven't finished your meal.'

'What, and get the rest of my head blown off? Your cooking's more dangerous than Cinnamon Junction at midnight.'

They both smiled. The type of smile that just compresses lips because there's something aching inside.

'I never realised that you felt this way.'

'I took myself for a long walk this morning.'

Schoolboy's eyes opened wide as he reared back.

'You went for a walk this morning?'

'I am allowed to go out, you know.'

'But I tried to call you this morning . . .'

'Tammy didn't say anyone had called.'

'Tammy?'

'Yes. I left her while I went to buy some bread and go for a stroll. She couldn't find her purse and thought it must be at mine. I think she was a bit strung out from all that Malibu last night. The only thing she did say was that some woman came calling.'

'A woman?'

'Don't get your hopes up, Eli, she was definitely not your type. Tammy said she was a Jehovah's Witness.'

The set of his face didn't change. His primary concern was Evie. Other things would have to wait.

'One more drink, Evie, to warm you up before you go?'

She nodded back at him.

'What about one of my special cocktails from the bar, madam?'

She laughed as he pranced over to the bar. He went behind it and dipped low to catch the top of a bottle of Pina Colada. Abruptly he twitched still. Something was watching him. Even Queen couldn't fit behind the bar. He slowly slipped his eyes to the side and moved them downwards to the wreckage that had been the Nokia. His eyes skated further along.

'Fucking hell,' his voice cried out.

He didn't hear Evie rush to stand over him. She followed his gaze and stopped when she saw what he saw.

25

'You stole something from the dead?'

Evie twisted her stare into him with disbelieving eyes.

'What's a dead man want with a MB? Ain't exactly going to help him chat with the devil when the flames are licking his arse.'

'But Eli, a dead body. What has got into you?'

'Look, you kept telling me that you were through giving me cash and I needed some quick cash to buy the knives.'

'Knives! Eli, please tell me you're not involved in something stupid.'

'No, of course not, silly. Michael, that's my mate in Devon, insists that anyone coming to work in the restaurant must bring their own knives. Evie, forget about the fucking knives, what am I going to do about that?'

They both stared at the object that he had picked up and laid on the table.

The cross was half the size of his hand and resonated in its white gold. The gleam that it sparkled into the room made Schoolboy suspect that it had been polished every day until recently. The top and bottom were united by a strip of gold. At the bottom it flared into a square with six tiny circles which made it look like people sitting at a dinner table. The other end frilled out into the shape of a cross that resembled the crochet Auntie Cee used to make. Within the cut latticework were diamonds within diamonds, crosses within crosses. But what grabbed his eye was not the material, not the pattern, not its shape, but the green stones that lay at the far top, the middle and the end. The craftsman had obviously loved his work to be freestyle because the latticework lacked symmetry, but each stone had been placed precisely, carefully, to catch the eye. It caught Schoolboy's but he didn't want it to. Frustration dragged Schoolboy to his feet as he turned his back on the object and Evie.

'Fuckrees. I don't need this one day before I go. It was meant to be mashed for good, but what does it do, give me more shitty trouble.'

'Under each pile of cow's mess is another layer of slime,' Evie chanted, bringing one more of Mum's sayings into his life.

'Thank you for the words of complete nonsensical wisdom, sister dearest.'

She peered at the object.

'It looks like one of those Christian crosses we saw when we studied Ethiopian history at uni.'

'I don't need a history lesson now, I just want to get back on with my life.'

'So what are you going to do?'

Evie dragged her eyes away from the cross to her brother.

'I don't know, I don't know, I don't know,' he repeated as he marched up and down the carpet.

'Take it to the police and tell them the whole story.'

'What, and let them do me for the whole lot? I don't think so.'

'Dump it then and walk away. Give it to a charity shop. I don't know but just get rid of it. I don't like the way those stones are staring at me.'

He shuffled his gaze back to the stones. He had to agree with her, there was something bewitching but beguiling about it.

Evie stood up and hurried to stand in front of him. She placed the comfort of her hands into his.

'Your hands are shaking,' she told him.

'So are yours,' he told her.

'What are you going to do?'

'Dunno. Maybe this is fate. Maybe this is God's parting gift to me. A sliver of gold and a few gems chucked in for good luck . . .'

'You mean good luck like finding a body in the place that even bad boys avoid? Good luck like having your home mashed to pieces and then people them running after your skin? Like . . .'

'I get the picture, Sherlock.'

'So why don't you let me get the picture as well and tell me what's going on?'

Her hands tightened on his. He didn't answer but tipped his stare over her shoulder to the cross.

'Because you wouldn't believe me. I don't want you involved in any of this.'

'I'm already involved, you know that.'

He looked at her, seeing them back when they were young, making plans on the stairs.

'OK sis, but only if you do what I ask you to do and you let me take you somewhere you most probably haven't been for years. If you want to help we have to bring this cross along and we'll talk while we walk.'

Evie arched her head at him. She didn't want to be here and he knew it. But he needed her. He couldn't do this particular goodbye without her.

'You need to have your head examined if you think I'm going any further than this,' she whispered to him as they stood near the railway arch besides Martha's Garden, the council block they had grown up in.

It was the same railway arch that had made the TV picture jump every time a train tore by. Her brother didn't answer as he took in its small structure in a road that was growing tower blocks. It had been such an intimate community, with children, adults and animals cruising in and out of each other's business. Some said that it was part of London Fields, others claimed it belonged to Hackney Central. But its dual identity was the correct story to tell. Its sole purpose during their time there was to educate them in the ways of the world. So it became a place where some of their best memories were set. It became a place where it prepared its young people for some of the unexpected and sometimes choking moments in life. Like Dean. Dean from number 13, fresh, 23, who only ever had the softest words perched on his lips. Dean who had gassed himself after his girlfriend had left. Like Mr Hussein. Mr Hussein, the classic grump who everyone made themselves laugh with because he was the cheapest and best handyman around. Mr Hussein who had slipped off his ladder while cleaning a window and taken his grumbles to the grave as he hit the pavement beneath.

Schoolboy turned to Evie, whose face was hidden by the evening light.

'Come on, Evie, just this one little pinch for me.'

He started walking forward, knowing she would follow. The communal stairs had changed. Back then, every resident ensured that they remained pristine. No one was going to say that their place wasn't fit for children to live in. Now nameless varieties of dirt were engraved in each step, mingling with the fragrance of human waste and desolation. The handrail was the worst. Unfolding petals of black paint lifted by too many tightly held fingers or plain neglect, Schoolboy wasn't sure. He let his hand smooth over it like a brush sent to give it back its old life. Evie wouldn't be doing the same.

'Eli, I don't want to do this.'

He ignored her plea and kept stepping higher, knowing Evie would keep with him but feel as if she was going lower. He stopped when he reached the third landing. Their landing. His sister moved closer to him as if she wanted protection. But that was Evie, someone who refused to root herself in the past.

'Do you remember . . .'

'Yes,' her voice put in quickly.

She didn't want to remember, but he did. He took a breath that came from his throat, clenched his eyes closed and let his vision drift back to a time when the stairs bounced with the naive laughter of youth. They had been Evie's gang. Her hand-picked followers who did what she told them to do. She had assigned each one of the gang a step representing age and status. Schoolboy's had been the third step, somewhere between eight and twelve years old. Evie had been the eldest at twelve so was always presiding at the top. Poor Youssef had to sit at the bottom despite the length of his legs. It became a place to recite stories, cruise through the latest cuss words and melt back into the stone of the steps as the nicotine-fuelled smoke of life misted by. His first and last ciggie had been more a dog-end than a full-grown fag, but it had still made him feel that his head was being pulped at the sides.

'Eli, I still can't believe what you told me earlier. There is no way your version of events can be right.'

'Fine, if I'm wrong then tomorrow will prove that. You'll still do your bit?'

'I promised, didn't I.'

'You got our little friend tucked away safe?'

Evie nodded, stroking her bag.

He knew she hadn't wanted to believe it but for once he'd given her the truth.

'Eli.' Evie rushed into his ear, spinning him back to the present. 'I know for some reason this wreck of a building is important to you, but life has changed, moved on. And so have I.'

She turned to take the stairs back to her world. He breathed deeply, this time the air coming from so deep within that he had to suck it out to free it. His sister was so right. He didn't belong here either.

He followed her, back to the arch, back to the streetlight.

'Evie, one more request.'

'Let me guess, now you want to take me to one of the crack dens on the top floor?'

He wanted to laugh, but he couldn't, not without knowing her answer to his question.

'Promise me you'll come to the station with me tomorrow.'

Her head bowed low like she was praying. He stretched over and cocooned her in his arms for the second time that night. They remained wrapped together while the traffic and a dog's bark blew around them. They fell apart. He stuffed his hands in his pockets and she stepped back.

'I'll be waiting.'

He watched her hunched figure move away and blend into the distance. He could come over all sentimental, but he didn't have time for that. He had people to catch. He gripped his last remaining mobile from his pocket and punched in the number.

'Tammy, my serene soul sista, sorry I was unavailable before, but you know how life stays. So where can I meet your friend tomorrow?'

'At the Liquid Fetish bar, the new one near the canal at Broadway Market. Do you know it?'

'Not my usual hang-out, but I know the spot.'

'Tomorrow at four.'

He paused before saying.

'I need to talk with you, but not on the phone. Come up in say two hours.'

'What for?'

'I just need to chat to you about Evie.'

'Schoolboy, it's late . . .'

'I know, but I'm worried about my sister.'

'OK, but I can't stay long.'

'Cool.' He clipped off, satisfied that he might not be the only one running hot soon.

Tammy, Tammy, Tammy.

Schoolboy chanted her name somewhere in his mind as he plugged at another pull of the last bit of weed in his mouth. His head softened and smoothed further into the purple pillow below him. She was certainly the woman Sensi had thought was his sister. He examined the Islamic print, which he held above his face. The picture was the reason he'd rolled his last spliff. He couldn't believe what the postcard was telling him. He let out a stream of smoke, which drifted up and dusted the print. He knew it was true and there was no point telling himself anything different. Coincidences were for people who chose not to see the truth. He lifted his head and tucked the postcard under the pillow to rest with his train ticket. He pushed his head back down.

The grass started to spin his head, making the walls' high-bred mauve brush all over depressed. He blinked both eyes trying to restore the colour to its rightful calling. Relaxed, massaging, peaceful.

He shut his eyes, concentrating on the music drifting from a neighbouring block. New-wave commercial dance hall that had a four-pulse drumbeat that warmed his soul. He let his thoughts and mind shift along with the drum. One, two, three, four. Hard and carefree. The back of his head pumped gently along against the pillow. The energy reminded him of the parties Mum and Dad and their friends had at Christmas. Back in the days everyone would just get along and enjoy the spell of music as a time to forget any troubles that had been floating in their life.

The drum came stronger, pulling him deeper into the gentleness of the pillow. The rhythmic riff was wild now, making his head rock from side to side, puff the joint from corner to corner. The drum hiked up harder. This time his sweat joined the party, pooling in the grove in his chin.

When a fifth pulse added to the beat, he realised that it wasn't the music but the door. The type of knock that wanted instant access. The type of knock he'd never associated with easy-moving Tammy. He could barely lift his head up. Too heavy from the drum that tapped right on top of it.

He wriggled off the bed, bare-footed with the music, and padded towards the door. The muscles in his left hand started bunching and twitching. He shook his fingers to the side, letting the warm air massage them. He pulled his hand back in, then out again to open the door. Tammy swept inside, bringing the high sweet smell of immorality and orange blossom with her. She wore her saint's smile and a long black coat. A coat that was not too heavy, not too light, just right for what he planned to do.

'What's the problem with Evie?' she asked, remaining in the passage, her head and twists shifting to the side.

Schoolboy gazed at her nose-stud, while his nostrils flared strongly.

'Just wanted to thank you for all your help.'

'You said that there was a problem with Evie, O!'

'I know you wouldn't come over if I told you I wanted to show you how much I appreciate your help.'

Her head reverted to its dead centre position. Her shining eyes swept him from open shirt to eager toes.

'You don't need to show me anything, just as long as Evie's OK, that's all the gratitude I need.'

He made his move, arms and legs wide, and pushed closer to her.

'I think we both know how eager I am to show you my thanks.'

He felt her breath ease past her lips, lick his face and then shy away. She tied him with her eyes. A warning or telling him something else, he wasn't sure. He decided to take it the only way he knew when a fine woman stood aching in front of him with her belly the only part of her rasping and shaking. He took a loose step forward. She remained passive as she stood her ground. He moved again, this time his hips staking their turf as well, flicking and winding in the figure of a handcuff. This time she moved back until her pressure seized the wall. She held herself the way a woman does when she wants something but won't ask for it. Bold, restricted, intent. His next step took him so close that he could feel her hips rotating to his tune. The music from the neighbouring block started to belt in their space, in a tempo so consumed with impatient fire that he knew when he got inside her it would hurt. Her lips parted but no words came through. He took his cue and hooked his head low. He strapped his lips to her mouth. He thought of Jackie's lips and the unconditional feelings she had tried to give him. He shook Jackie from his mind. She was too pure to be anywhere near this situation.

Instinct made his eyes start to close, but he forced them back. He had to stay with Tammy's face every step of the journey. His hands dived under the collar of her coat, glided along the slippery lining and pulled it from her body. It dropped behind her black heels leaving only her clinging T-shirt and jeans in his way. He decided not to remove them. He would do that in the bedroom when he was unknotting all the other revelations. He wasn't sure whether it was the music popping with the wall or the fastened coupling of their breathing but he knew a DJ would kill to sample that on a deck. His teeth threaded against her bottom lip as his chest arched when her nails dipped into the back of his shirt and cuffed into his skin. Shit, this was a woman who would love what he had to give. He roped his hands around her buttocks and knew that he was a man who would usually love what she wanted him to receive. But he knew what he wanted to receive. And what he wanted was sometimes the simplest, sometimes the most difficult thing to utter – the truth.

26

Leave a woman to marinate in the spice of sex and secretions and she would be gagging to tell a bloke anything he wanted to hear. That's what life had taught him. He cooled himself in Tammy's skin and knew that she wouldn't be any different. They lay on the bed. No music, just uneven air blowing from their bodies. Her fingers created their own dance-steps in his locks as his head lay fluffed against her breasts.

'Your mouth's a lot more sophisticated than I thought.'

He was glad that she had started their conversation because he had screwed her body and now the time was ripe to screw her mind.

'You could have found that out a long time ago if you just let me in. So tell me how's a honey-gal like you end up in a wannabe place like Wapping?'

He let his tongue trace a path of drying sweat under her breast.

'It's all about connections and family.'

'So your brothers are connected?'

She stiffened. He moistened his lips, then tasted her again. She softened.

'Who said anything about brothers?'

He started sucking her sensitive spot. Just above her right nipple. Always be prepared to find a woman's sensitive place on the first date. After that women were like Es in your hand, ready to be taken down whole. He didn't need to look lower to know her midriff was moving again.

'I heard you say it to Evie once, honey-gal.'

'I said a lot of things once. But yes, I have some brothers . . .'

'So how do you use their connections?'

He let his hand drift lower to guide her to the right rhythm.

'My family are connected but that doesn't include my brothers . . .'

Her voice cut short as her breasts were finally infected with her lilting motion.

'Do I smell the rust of bad blood?'

'Forget about family, Evie, Ashara . . . I mean my brothers . . .'

Her hands flew above her body as she twisted with him and the sheets. He leaned up, letting one hand continue to rock with her movements, while the other locked with one of her hands above her head. He stretched up, pulling her fingers towards his mouth. He kissed each finger. Middle with its two rings, index, little and then it was time for the thumb. His tongue traced over the wishbone shape of her nail art, starting at the right hand corner, sweeping up to the top, then skating down the line of the left side. Identical to the Arabic numeral for 8 on Window's postcard. He traced the number again, this time deeply. This time with anger.

'Schoolboy, you're hurting me.'

'Sorry, honey-gal.'

He released her hand and let his fingers in her lower flesh continue the melody of his rage.

'I love the way you style yourself. Same beauty mark on your nail as the one on your nose-stud.'

'Schoolboy, this is so good.'

'I thought you would enjoy this ride, Tamania.'

'Oh Schoolboy . . .' Abruptly her swaying stopped. 'What did you call me?'

'Tammy.'

'No, you called me something else.'

'Sugar? Babe? Honey? Choose any name.'

His voice softened, sank with the increased rhythm of his fingers. She started gasping, he knew he was hurting, but it was the type of hurt she expected to get here tonight. His hand felt dirty. He didn't want to be anywhere near her skin any more. His fingers flexed to a furious beat until he felt her strain, stretch and shudder. His hand took up her movement but not through satisfaction. He sprang off the bed and stared at her. All the things he could do to her. Place his hands around her neck and show her a different style of rocking. Make her the latest Death Row feature as her body sought the daffodils below the block. But instead he folded down gently to his knees and blew in her face. She opened an eye and let it rove over him.

'If we don't stop now I'll never make tomorrow's appointment and we don't want that, do we, Tammy-honey?'

He remained on his knees as he spoke.

'You're right, of course,' she agreed and swung off the bed.

He was thankful she didn't want the after-dinner speech as well. She dressed as he fixed her with his dimple-laden smile. Fully clothed, she approached him. Bent down to him. Kissed him. Filling his body with the bitterest taste he had digested in a long time.

'Let me know how it goes tomorrow.'

As coolly as she had breezed into his sister's life, she prepared to leave his. She picked up her coat and bag and made her way to the door. He watched her go, his mouth filling up with spit.

Every pig shall have their Saturday.

He'd never known what Mum had meant by that one, but he suspected Tammy would find out if his plans came right tomorrow, hopefully his last day in London town.

Schoolboy stood with his faithful hood, bandanna and last bit of smoke in East London's favourite open-air spot for lyrical disobedience. Kingsland Road, Dalston, was the place where words flipped and fought like the six-month interest-free credit leaflets that skipped at his feet. This was the place where the community used their tongues to combust, rail, explode. The place where the community was open in its defiance against the world and sometimes against itself.

Schoolboy lounged at the bus stop outside Jamal's Pide Parlour and lamented as Sunday began to pay its respects to the world. The fear of leaving stalked him again. If all went well later that day he wasn't sure he could do it. How could he up and leave a place where the people were so frank and fresh in their openness with the world? Diversity did that. The type of mix he knew that Devon could never offer. The pigeons peeking on the ledge from the opposite building crooked and wriggled their necks as if telling him, 'Brother, you must be even mad to let a tear drip from your eye.' He knew they were right, but what people saw from the inside and what they saw from the outside could be two different things. He was on the inside but making that break would mean becoming an outsider. Becoming a tourist.

He plucked the joint into his mouth and inhaled. Strong. He pulled again, wrapping down his eyes, and waited for the last piece of verbal disorder to come his way. All manner of voices, accents, discussions circulated by him, but he wanted to choose the right one to remember this place by. He recognised it as soon as it came. Classic Dalston stand-off, with the collision of individual pressures head-butting each other.

'Lady, you got any spare change?'

'Are you having a laugh? I've got three kids at home with their mouths open waiting to be fed and you're asking me if I've got any spare change?'

'All right love, I . . .'

'No, it ain't bollocks all right. Why don't you get off your skinny arse and start earning your own spare change?'

The woman's strained tone cut off and rustled by with the plastic sound of carrier bags. Schoolboy let her go. Let Dalston go. He reactivated his vision and began the stroll back to Parkview.

Tammy stared at her youngest brother and thought of all the people she hated in the world. They sat face to face in the yawning Sunday-morning haze of the Liquid Fetish bar. Centre table. She didn't need anyone from the outside looking in or the distraction of Ashara looking out on to the canal. She wanted his attention to be on her. Wanted him to remember. Remember what he had done to her. She cast her look into his watery round eyes and knew that his guilt was still strong. Still burning away. Still waiting for the day she would forgive him.

Not so long ago in her past he had been near the top of her hate list, but not any more. She had long decided he was too weak. Weak people were to be pitied not hated. Never spend too much time on them as they would never change, but never take them for granted because they used their weakness to trip people up. Ashara had used his to trip up the last four years of her life.

'Tamania . . .'

'Don't call me that,' her voice cut through, edged with bruising irritation. 'Everyone calls me Tammy.'

Nigerians always had a name for every story. Tammy and her brothers were no different. Their story was in their lifetime they had each acquired three different names with three different stories. Three story lines that threaded back to one story. The story of their childhood. A childhood where each of them had their place chosen long before their birth. Ojo, Ifetayo and Adebayo. Three siblings, each a year apart, growing up in the eye of Lagos. Ojo had taken the heat of the family's expectation of the first-born, getting to university. But Ifetayo had got there first. She always got there first. Making money the fast way was her suggestion. Getting involved in money scams was her suggestion. Getting those false passports and hitting the global market was her suggestion. The passports had been the narrative for their change of names. New passports needed new identities. It had been her idea to take the first digits of their passports and convert them into Arabic names. So she had become Number 8, Tamania. Christened with new names, they had become the Numbers crew, stepping into the lucrative world of art theft in Africa.

Tammy swallowed, thrust her history aside and stared into the face of her bewildered brother, letting her fingers stray towards her empty glass. She touched it, bent into its shape, finally taking on its coldness.

She had deliberately chosen to meet Ashara at the bar near the canal because that's where she had instructed Schoolboy to come later with the phone. A potentially stupid move, she knew, but she wanted to know what it felt like to sit in a chair one of her brothers might choose to sit in today. To die in today. She knew the chances of choosing the right chair or death were slim but still she got a thrill from just imagining the blood sticking through her back.

'Tamania, sorry, I mean Tammy, I feel so ashamed of what happened. I should have told Wahid the truth . . .'

'But you didn't,' her voice grated with gentleness but the inside of her mouth was parched with harshness.

She shrugged off the harshness and remembered why she was here. Her hands fell on to the table with bent fingers making her gang mark on her nail point straight at him. She pulled in a deep breath, lips tucked apart.

'It doesn't matter, brother. What matters is that we are here together,' – her fingers stretched – 'and from now on we are going to remain together.'

Ashara's hands lunged forward, hesitated, then grabbed the tips of her fingers, spreading his nervous sweat to her body.

'But what about Wahid? He won't be so pleased.'

Everything always came back to bully-bush-boy Wahid. She shoved her feelings aside. Her eldest brother would have his day.

'Come on, think about it,' Tammy answered as she shifted in her chair. 'When have you known him to be pleased? During our whole childhood he was as sour as the smile on Grandmother's face.'

They looked straight into each other's eyes and started laughing. The twin gaps in their front teeth made their joy whistle high in the way that only memories can. She shifted closer.

'Do you remember the time we put pepper in his water that he used to wash his face?' Ashara nodded, the laughter too much for him to speak. 'And he started dancing like he'd heard the latest High Life tune?'

The laughter carried on through the telling of a few more stories, but by the end of the last recitation Tammy's fingers had wrenched free and slipped back on to the glass.

'We were such a great group,' she sighed.

'You were the one always in charge. It was never Ojo. We just let him think that.'

His hands fluttered up and dared to touch her again, brushing the gang mark on her thumb. His imprint was warm and cold. Confused. She began her assault, knowing this was the right time.

'You have been in my thoughts every day, Ashara.'

'I still keep that picture of us at Wahid's graduation. I keep it in the office to remind me of you. You were always the best . . .'

'So if I was the best why did you let me take the rap for you, O!'

'I was stupid. Foolish. I couldn't tell everyone that . . .' His voice stuck well back in his throat.

'After all these years you still can't say it? Still can't face up to the fact that you like shagging blokes?' she smiled. Shagging, that was her best English word.

Ashara's head bowed. She couldn't see his eyes but knew they were closed. That's what weakness did to you, made you look down instead of forward.

'I had no problems with you shagging our Italian contact, but did you have to tell him all our plans?'

Ashara's head flicked up, eyes back with the world.

'But I thought that he loved me. His love felt so sweet . . .'

'Thick enough with honey for you to forget the family? That the family comes first at all times?' Her breathing was harsh, unforgiving.

Her hands jerked off the glass with the quickness of flesh on fire. Her left hand skidded in the air, stretched flat, palm up, then her right hand slapped into it, skin down. Her hands slapped together on every fifth, sixth and seventh word.

'So, when the police chopped us up and told us that the Italian is claiming he found out from one of us in his bed, Wahid naturally assumes it's me, and you were happy to play the man with two heads and let him carry on believing that.

'Do you know what it felt like to have your body and head in prison at the same time? Do you know what it felt like to be left alone in Morocco while you two ran back home? And when I got released, after dishing a few notes into a few palms, I come back home begging to be taken back. And what did you do, my sorry little brother? Stand there and watch as Wahid booted me aside. I never once told him the truth. Never once confessed that the reason we could only smell bush-shit was because you couldn't keep your little man-stick in your trousers.'

The clap of her hands stung every word of her final sentence. Her eyes trod into Ashara's. Tense. Hurting. Wanting to squash him. Wanting to drill retribution into everyone she had learned to despise in the last four years. She remembered why she hated them. She remembered what she was here to do. She relaxed, letting her hands unclasp, move forward, back on to the glass.

'Brother, let's not quarrel. I have news for you to help you get to America. This Schoolboy will be meeting a contact at this bar at four with the phone.'

'Today?'

'Yes, of course, we aren't talking about yesterday's news. Quick, you need to get going to tell Wahid.'

Ashara leapt up.

'Ifetayo, you are brilliant. When I get to America I will send for you. I have bought a present for your birthday. I am sorry I couldn't be with you on your day.'

He reached into the front pocket of his leather jacket, pulled out a small box wrapped in shining gold paper and held it out to her. She took it.

'I'll open it later. You need to hurry. We will speak later.'

As her brother rushed out, Tammy picked herself and her bag up. She wandered into the ladies and pulled her phone out. She could now punch in this number without looking because she had done it so many times. She held it to her ear.

'Queen, my friend, I have news for you. Be at the Liquid Fetish bar near the canal at four. I hear that the bush-snake Schoolboy will be there with your property. Don't wait for his sister to call you because this news is too exclusive for her ears.'

'How did you know?'

'I know everything, Queen. Just be there.'

'Why don't you just tell me where Schoolboy is?'

'Because, Queen, even you would never believe where he is hiding.'

She clicked off, dropped the phone on to the blue tiles and ground her heel into it. She bent down, gathered the smashed pieces, swayed towards the bin and chucked the pieces into it. She looked at Ashara's present in her hand. Her gang mark on her nose-stud moved as her nostrils widened and beat back. She tipped the present into the bin, unopened, on top of the broken phone.

27

Schoolboy scrunched up the lower part of his face. What do you choose to wear with death possibly waiting around the corner to hold your hand? Silk? Linen? Good-time viscose? His facial muscles relaxed as he stared at the clothes in the wardrobe at Parkview. He felt the damp of the bedroom because he'd deliberately kept the curtains open throughout the night. He needed the moonlight, the daylight to remind him that he was now living in the light. He allowed his eyes to close as he let his hand brush each garment. The feeling had to be right. The body at the Junction flashed at him. Everything about that scene was so wrong – the blood, the absence of life, the wayward shoe, but those trousers had been so right. He smiled and shook his eyes open at the same time. Life must be hot if he was taking fashion tips from a corpse.

He let the humour take him, pump through him. He needed to feel that everything was going to be played his way today. He swept the after-life aside and concentrated on the world he did know. His fingers shoved inside to choose. Hand-made silk shirt, linen trousers. One was early morning blue, the other as blue as the unknown ending facing him. He was sad that he had to leave Parkview, just as he was appreciating the colours in the flat. But Death Row wasn't where he wanted to be when he was getting a second go at living. He checked his timepiece.

2 p.m.

Still a couple of hours to go. Then that left only another hour and a half to get the 17.30 train from Paddington. He stepped back, sat on the rumpled bed with Tammy's scent still hanging above, and prepared himself for what was to come.

Queen perused her collection. What gun do you choose to use when you're ordering your third death in a week? Slim and ladylike? Chunky and max destruction? Steady and reliable? Each lay in a line in front of her powder puff on the dressing table she had restored years ago. She let her palm trickle over them, feeling what each had to offer. Cool, hot, ridged and above all hard. She remembered the first time she had touched a gun. Back in '95, courtesy of Good Time Freddy, who told her to use it if anyone came crashing through the door. The grapevine had told him that his name was next on a list of dead men. No one had come to the door, except Freddy, who looked relieved when he saw her. He asked if the girls were OK, she'd nodded the way a good girlfriend should. She had hugged him, kissed him and welcomed him. Then she had shot him. Freddy had never understood that he should have taken his natural place behind her years ago. Never understood that she just didn't appreciate the various smells of perfumes cluttering up his skin. Never understood that he was last on a list of rivals she needed to get out of the way.

She chose steady and reliable, which was as quiet as blood spilling in the night.

Wahid slipped his gaze between the three women who stood before him in the back room. Which woman did you choose to screw before finally hitting the big time? White and peachy? Mixed and pouting? Good old-fashioned black and sensual? The odour of blocked drains came through the pores of the walls. He smiled at the white woman in the middle. There was only one big time and that was America. America didn't seem to take too kindly to the races getting it on so he'd better take a piece while he still could. The other two women left, leaving him with his choice. He stood, shaking off his jacket, and approached her. She remained, still knowing better than to take the lead. His fingers unbuttoned, unzipped, keeping his eyes on Peachy's face. Both his hands whipped up and pushed her breasts, making her stumble into the wall. Her chest heaved, making the tips of her blood-round nipples peep and play with him. He reached her, bowed his neck and moved his arms down. His mouth sucked her neck while he pulled her already rising violet dress.

Tammy stared at the three boxes of herbal tea in Evie's cupboard. Which tea do you choose to drink before savouring the tang of retribution? Vibrant orange smoothie? Soothing lemon harmony? Understated camomile tranquillity? She knew there was no contest really. She reached and pulled the box of camomile from the cupboard. She threw a teabag into each cup. She knew that Evie disliked herbals, but she knew her friend would need to be calm when the news about Schoolboy reached her. Tammy's mouth stretched and tilted as she poured the boiling water into the cups. She ran her nose above each cup, closed her eyes and inhaled. The poignant aroma reminded her of the wild grass near her grandmother's house that she and her brothers played in as children. Wahid always thought that he was leading the game, but she'd wink at Ashara to remind him who was really in charge. The cooling steam on her face and nose-stud made her curl her eyes open. She picked up both cups thinking that we've all got to die some time.

Schoolboy reminisced with his reflection in the Moorish mirror. The time he was the one to help Evie with some homework. The time Dad and his mates annoyed Mum by playing dominoes right through the night. The time he tasted his first really bad pattie. The good memories all came, one after another, to take their place near his image. Leaving both good and bad was not as easy as he once thought. He pulled up his neck, pulled down his shoulders and shook his locks so gently it was as if a breeze had taken hold of the room. The silk shirt was in place with added gold cufflinks and the trousers fitted like a tailor's dummy. He stuck on the old trilby, tipped it to the right and relaxed his head to the left. By catwalk standards none of his clothing matched, but this might be the last time he got to play the dude. He didn't suppose he'd get the chance to wear gear like this in Devon. The local Blues would be morally obliged to pull him over.

'Oi, Liberace, we want a word with you . . .'

No, he'd have to blend in. Get some polyester slacks and golfing sweaters.

That's if he ever made it. No point putting it off, the time was here. He bent to pick up his bag for life, strolled to the passage, doffed his trilby at the flat and left Death Row for what he hoped was the last time.

Queen sucked the cigarette until the butt was all that was left. Mr Frumpy, her daughter's sky-blue elephant, was her only company as she bent over the ashtray in her favourite room. She squashed the butt as she remembered the briefing with her men last night. She'd been clear: no theatrics, no flamboyance, just the bloke and the phone. A few of her guys had stared, mouths open, as if they were experiencing that make-or-break moment of cold turkey when she'd said flamboyance. She read their eyes – complete fucking incomprehension. What was she doing with a group of thickos who obviously had never seen the inside of a nursery much less a secondary-school classroom? That's why she was on diarrhoea drive, because they had messed up at Schoolboy's flat, cocked up at the church. She straightened, patted and smoothed back her tied hair, then shook her head. The warm air fanned away from her, but soon came back hotter than before. She checked herself in the mirror. She checked her gun in the mirror. Cuttie would be here at any minute to take her to the meeting point.

She swung around, catching Mr Frumpy's reflective plastic eyes. She didn't like the way he was staring at her as he guarded the French doors.

24/7 cabs was closed for the evening. No crack, no cars, no cocaine. No notice explained its early closure, but then who gave the people of Hackney an explanation for anything. The only downstairs room in the office was filled with a group of standing men, defined by their collective breathing. The sound came harsh, puffing, expectant, like Wahid and Peachy had been making an hour earlier against one of its walls. They waited for instructions from their leader. Wahid scanned the room, swinging and locking his neck from right to left, left to right, so that his eyes connected with each man standing in the room. Satisfied that he had them where he wanted, he placed his attention on the sports bag on the table in front of him. He gripped one end of the bag, unzipped it with the other. He drew the breath deep into his system, hugged the base of the bag with forearms and hands, let his breath out as he tipped it upside down. The contents banged down, each item creating its own tone as it resounded with the wood of the table. Number 1 ripped his eyes back on to his men. Some had stepped back, some had come forward, some stood still and the others waited with the discipline he had been trying to instil in them for the last two years. All eyes were fixed with the items on the table. Pistols, revolvers, sub-machine guns, two of which were the latest models on the street.

'This isn't our usual style, but we need to get it right this time. Our mission is to get our target quickly. We do not hang around, speak to anyone, just keep our eyes on the prize. If you have to use your piece to get his attention then do it, but remember all we need is the phone. If he will not give it up you know what to do.'

Schoolboy was biting the street again but this time the street was chewing him back. As soon as the congested air had hit him his confidence started to shift, started to walk away, started almost to disappear. The bad memories were back and wouldn't leave until they had had their say. They reminded him that some people were picked to atone for their sins and maybe he was one of the chosen few. He stretched his stride, trying to get his confidence back, but it kept outsprinting him. The sweat was building up, under his arms, behind his knees, pooling from the rim of the hat. He wanted to stop, to start this journey again, but there wasn't time for that. *Day and night done leave you behind.* Hadn't Mum told him that when he wouldn't get on and do something? He knew people were looking at him. Old man hat and young man style, who did he think he was? That's the type of speculation a dude died for. Yes, he was the dude, the one running tings. His confidence brushed him, jumped back inside him. He turned a corner as he tried to turn back the thoughts in his mind.

Tammy sat perched like a runaway who knew his time was up; on the sofa opposite, Evie was watching a taped episode of *The Bill*. Watching anything with the police in it made Tammy nervous. Her fingers threaded through her extensions, scratching her scalp, as she wished she was back in Lagos gazing at the sun going down. She twisted her wrist to check the time on her watch. 3.15.

'Tammy, why do you keep looking at the time?' Evie asked.

Tammy snapped her wrist back to its original position, surprised that Evie had been observing her.

'Just wondering if I've got time to go to the post office. Maybe we can go together now.'

'Now?' Evie shrieked, then checked the height of her voice, lowered it and continued, 'But I can't leave at this point in the programme.'

'Maybe I'll go on my own,' Tammy responded, kicking out her legs to stand up as a siren blasted from the TV. She swallowed.

'No. Sit and wait with me. When it's finished we'll go together.'

Another siren blared from the TV, making Tammy shudder.

Queen's mouth remained contorted as she stood next to Cuttie in the lock-up in Clapton. She didn't want to go, and shouldn't have needed to. The plan was a good one. But lately, every time she wasn't there things went wrong. It was like her kids. She should have been able to leave them to their own devices for an hour or two but she couldn't. Because they were kids. Same with her crew. They didn't have the intelligence or command in a difficult situation. She'd have to go too, but wrapped well back in the shadows. Some of the men were staring at the spot where Rufus had been begging for his life. That's exactly what she wanted. She needed them to know what might happen if they fucked up again.

'No more crap, OK? The plan's simple. Four of you go in and I follow. Keep your eyes peeled on the door. Remember, when he arrives let him get in and then, Thimble, you go up to him slowly, let him feel the chrome through your clothes and slowly take him outside. The rest of us get up and out. Simple, all right. Any stupidness and you're finished.'

Her men nodded.

The Numbers took to the streets of Hackney in a collection of mini-cabs, with pepped-up sports cars for the getaway smooching discreetly at the back. Inside each vehicle their breathing had intensified, becoming shallower, their expectancy focused on themselves and the part they had to play. Each steering wheel became hotter with the hands that squeezed it, more rushed with the control that jerked and twisted it. But anxiety had to be pulled back because they couldn't afford to be noticed.

So no lights were jumped, no other cars were cut up, no bus lanes invaded. The march of cars sharp-turned, slowed and extinguished their engines on Saffron Street, which was on the left side of the town hall. No one got out of the cars. Everything was to be done by radio control. Men in the back leaned forward, while fingers remain bonded with steering wheels. Ashara's voice filled each car, like a teacher on a trip with some unruly pupils.

'You know what to do . . .'

Each man nodded, checked that his metal piece was hidden, and piled out of the cars. The rest of the route to the canal was to be taken on foot.

The temperature had dropped, the way it does in London when you're near open water.

Schoolboy pressed his nostrils together and then used his fingers to wipe his nose.

'Oi, Mister, you got the time?'

Schoolboy pulled his head up to the voice and let his eyes take in the body standing in front of him. A girl with natural honey hair and blue glass eyes that jerked into his. She was at the best years of her teenage life but he knew she was out to screw him. He had never done this trick but he knew it well. As soon as you lifted your arm to look at the hands on your timepiece someone would jump you from behind and take everything they could get. He stepped up to her close so that she felt his don't-fuck-with-me breath in her face.

'I know the time all right. It's time for you, little one, to take your little poom-poom back to Mummy. Unless, that is, you're ready for me to slice you, brutalise you, take you home to meet my friends or why don't I just drag you into an alley and do you there?'

Her face dried as she rushed back and then ran.

The spit squirted behind his lips. Fuck the street. He emptied the liquid in his mouth on to the pavement. This time when he moved forward he started pounding the street with an energy he hadn't felt for a long time.

This was the final time Queen hoped that she was going to use the silver Jeep. The Jeep was now a witness and she didn't need the police crawling over all the clues inside. Its destiny was a fire and hers was the cross. Her eagerness made her shift.

'Cuttie, get your foot moving. We need to be there early. My girls swear there's nothing like a surprise party.'

28

The Liquid Fetish bar was situated on the corner of Cardamom Close and Guava Road by the edge of the canal near Broad Street. It had two entrances, the most popular being on Guava Road. Wahid was the first to go in, using the entrance on Cardamom Close. Four of his crew followed behind, each told to wear the face of someone who needed a drink. They headed for the south side of the bar while Number 1 found a table. He took the seat, checked his watch and settled back with five minutes to go. He thought of Disneyland, dollars and decaffeinated coffee. The land of opportunity. He already felt like wetting his lips to celebrate.

'Excuse me, sir, can I take your order?' a female voice interrupted him, bringing him straight back to business.

He stared at her dull face, took in her thin and straight body. No bum, no belly, definitely not his type.

'Yes, one of your cocktails. Something that has the taste of New York.'

Mal, Rob, Glass-eye and Thimble drifted into the chatter and smouldering salsa beat of the bar using the Guava Road entrance. They headed for the north end of the bar, closely followed by Queen, who found a corner table wrapped in the dark. She hated wine-bar joints. All house white, blended with bland oranges and reds. A place for tossers to meet and drink. She leaned back into the shadows, waiting for her tosser to come through the door.

Schoolboy's breathing followed the twitching of his heart as he came face to face with the door. He ripped off the hat and jammed it into the bag. He shook out his locks and waited for each dread to fall into its natural position. His tongue tipped out and moistened his aching lips. He lifted his hand, shaped into a fist, and banged the door.

Both the north side and the south side of the bar clocked the Dread as he came through the swing doors. A Dread that was smiling, rocking, rubbing his palms together, not to rejuvenate them from the cold but because life was sweet. He was nodding his head around the room as if he knew people, but no one acknowledged him back. The lead man in each group eyed their leader. Their leader eyed them back. The job was on.

As the newcomer jangled closer to the liquid refreshments, the south side and north side of the bar got closer. The Dread got to the bar, shuffled his feet apart and took pleasure in his balance. The human heat around him grew strong. He leaned into the bar.

'Hey, maestro,' he addressed the bar man, 'I-man would like one of them hot-shots . . .'

The words stopped coming, his eyeballs gaping wide when he felt the nozzle in his right side. His skin started to tremble when he felt another nozzle in his left side.

'Look, what the hell . . .' He screamed as his gaze swung up and took in both the men on either side of him.

But the men didn't hear him, as they looked hard into each other. The guns were whipped up as the men strained their pieces at each other. The Dread dived low as he realised that the only hot-shot coming his way was the explosion of noise around him.

Tammy watched the last seconds of the hour trip by on her watch.

57,

58,

59,

4 o'clock.

She beamed as the programme credits came up. She beamed, knowing that all their problems were behind them. Now it was just her and Evie as it should have been from the beginning. She leapt up with the spring of life driving her every move.

'Evie, life can be so good sometimes. Let's get a drink to celebrate,' Tammy screeched, taking in the sour look on Evie's face. That was the trouble with her friend, she just didn't know how to let herself go. But Tammy would show her. As she swung to leave the room, the front door started pounding.

'Get that for me, Tammy, I've just got to get something,' Evie called behind her.

Tammy skipped forward, extensions swaying around her. Her fingers gripped the door handle, turned and started to pull the door back.

Schoolboy kicked the opening door backwards, loving the gritty shock on Tammy's face, hating the position she had put him and Evie in. He rushed forward, locked his hand around Tammy's neck and slammed her against the wall. He thrust his sweating face above her nose-stud.

'You don't smell so clean close up, Tammy baby.'

'What are you doing here?' she croaked, fighting for air between each word.

'Try another question, babe, because that one's too easy.'

He tightened his grip, feeling the bone of her windpipe carve into his palm. He lifted her, drawing the weight of her body on to the tips of her toes. Tammy swung out her leg, trying to kick him. He raised his trainer and then stamped it down on her foot. She groaned, he held her in place.

'Tammy, what's that noise?' Evie's voice drifted to them from the main room.

Tammy didn't answer, instead she strained her hands out, trying to scratch his face with her nails. The nail art on her thumb touched his face, making him rear back as if a brand had kissed his skin. His hand dropped away from her throat, letting her fall.

He watched as she crouched, coughed, licked air back into her lungs as her fingers soothed her throat. She pushed herself up, shook herself back and put her smile back on. A smile he had once mistaken for a sign of peace. Her eyes wandered over him as if they were trying to scar him for life.

'Why couldn't you have just come and told me what the situation was.' Schoolboy gulped with anger. 'You're meant to be my sister's friend . . .'

'Oh, don't get all moral on me.' Her smile twisting into a sneer, so that each word jabbed him. 'You seem to have forgotten how you got yourself in this mess in the first place. Teefing phones from dead people . . .' she finished the sentence by kissing her teeth at him. 'Besides, I don't like you.'

Schoolboy shoved his face back into her space.

'What do think Evie's going to say when she finds out what her faithful friend has been up to?'

Tammy pushed herself and her smile up against him.

'Who do you think Evie's going to believe, me or you?'

'Why don't you tell me, Tammy?'

Evie's dead-toned voice joined them. Tammy's smile sunk in. Disappeared. Her tongue tipped out, lubricated her lips, shot back in to allow her smile to spread back. Then she gently turned around as she opened her mouth to answer. But when her eyes found her friend they widened, making her step forward lose its stride. Her legs bent as if a higher hand was forcing penance on her for the first time. Her hand seized the wall to steady herself as her gaze pulsed into the object hanging around Evie's neck.

'So Eli was right,' Evie cried out, her mouth now full of emotion.

Schoolboy thought it was a shame that the cross had to go back because it looked radiant against his sister's thunderous skin. Tammy jerked off the wall towards Evie, speaking at the same time, arms outstretched.

'Don't believe him. How many times have his lies stabbed your life?'

Evie shook her head, making Tammy stop moving.

'I don't understand, Tammy, how you could do this to us . . .'

'Not to us, to him, O! I tried to save you from him.' Tammy's arms fell as she reasoned.

'By trying to get my little brother killed . . .'

'He wasn't meant to be involved in any of this, O. He's just another brother trying to screw his sister up.'

'But murder, Tammy? What kind of person are you?'

'I don't need to answer that because you know what type of person I am.'

'But how could you bring all this shit into my home?'

'The only stench in here at the moment is your darling brother. You know the brother you said you wanted out of your life for good . . .'

'I never once said that I wanted to get rid of Eli.'

'Didn't you? How many times have I had to sit here and listen to you say how worthless he is? What a sponger he is? Why God didn't just take him so that you could get on with your life?'

Evie took an unsteady step back.

'But I didn't mean those things . . .'

'We always mean those things, Evie. I just did what you really wanted to do.'

Schoolboy moved to intervene, but Evie flicked her palm face up in his direction, stopping him.

'You're wrong,' Evie's voice strung back, her extensions wriggling free from her scrunch.

'Remember what Mother Dorinda always says,' Tammy shifted closer to Evie, taking her first opportunity to appraise the cross. 'Strong women go for what they want, women whose minds are neither here nor there are just waiting for other people to carry their load.'

Her eyes caressed the cross once more, then she turned her back, glided past Schoolboy and made her way to the door. Schoolboy saw more of Evie's extensions falling out and he knew what was coming. Just as Evie leapt forward to grab her former friend he chained his arms around Evie's chest and hauled her back. Her fury fought with him.

'No, let her go, Evie.'

His sister's struggles rippled against his body.

'Leave her. Shake her out of your life. She'll find her justice one day on the street.'

As soon as the door banged shut Schoolboy felt Evie fold into him and start to cry. He looped her around, squeezed his arms across her back. The cross dug into him as he smoothed her hair, rocking her gently. She raised her head to gape at him.

'She was so wrong. I never meant any of those things.'

'Well, you should've. I haven't been the greatest brother on earth.'

He hugged her closer while bending his arm back to look at his watch.

4.15.

'Evie, sorry babe, but if we don't get those other two jobs done I'm going to miss that train.'

29

Composure stepped out with Schoolboy and Evie as they left Nutmeg Wharf.

'There's Window,' Schoolboy said quietly as he spotted his friend's BMW-XS on the other side of the road.

'You people and your names,' Evie threw into the wind.

As they briskly walked towards him, Window's immense body filled the street as he jumped out of his Jeep. Schoolboy heard Evie's intake of breath as she saw his friend for the first time. A bicycle weaved past them as they reached Window. Window and Schoolboy greeted each other in the usual way.

'Evie, this is my mate . . .'

'Alexander. My friends call me Alex,' Window blew in.

So that was his name.

'Good to meet you, Alex. Does your tattoo say Alex?'

'Yes, in Thai. My great-grandmother was from Thailand,' Window replied, his eyes twinkling into Evie's.

'Sorry to disrupt the family tree club, but we need to keep moving because there are one or two things I still need to do if I'm going to make the train for 5.30.'

'I got all your stuff from Jay-Jay and put it in some of my travel bags,' Window informed him.

'Is that it?' Window continued, his eyes pinned to Evie's neck.

'Yes. Absolute beautilicious, ain't she?' Schoolboy answered, his eyes following his friend's.

'Don't get too attached, Eli, because she's going,' Evie reminded him.

'What you planning to do?' Window uttered as his eyes melted over the cross.

'Little-miss-too-good-to-be-true here is taking it down to the river police station right here in Wapping.'

Window's eyes burned away from Evie's neck.

'Don't worry, Alex, I will drop it in but ensure it's done anony mously.'

'Just the same, I think I'll wait with my four wheels around the corner.'

As Schoolboy opened his mouth to speak, the same bike that had weaved past them earlier rushed into him and Window. Window tripped back while the front wheel cut into one of Schoolboy's trainers. Schoolboy cried out as he bent over with his pain. The girl tilted the bike next to Evie as her foot tipped down on to the pavement to steady herself.

'Oi, don't you know it's against the law to ride on the . . .'

Schoolboy's sentence broke off as he saw the girl's hand, as quick as a drug deal done on a street corner, flash out and grab the cross around Evie's neck. Window rushed forward. Schoolboy rushed forward. Evie stumbled in surprise. The lean fingers yanked the cross.

'You little bitch,' Schoolboy bellowed as his hand touched the teenager's tracksuit bottoms.

Schoolboy was close enough to smell the soap she'd used that morning. She wouldn't remain clean for long doing this type of work. The leg snapped back, hitched up on to the pedal and twisted with the surge of the bike as it bobbed away. The cross and shoelace sailed in the wind behind the bike as a female voice laughed out, 'Who's a poom-poom now then, wanker?'

Schoolboy ground his eyes into the biker's glass blue ones, real- ising it was the girl he'd been trying to save earlier. Try and help someone, what do they do, rob you the first chance they get. Window had his arms around Evie and one of those frightening faces Schoolboy remembered from the old days.

'Fucker. Come on, let's go after her,' Window blew, already opening the Jeep door.

'No, leave it. Let it go.' Schoolboy's weary voice stopped him 'It's someone else's problem now. Evie, you all right, girl?'

She nodded, her extensions flopping in a disorganised way. As Window helped Evie into the back seat, Schoolboy pulled out his MB and checked the time.

4.30.

Schoolboy smiled. More than enough time for that one last stop before heading to the station. He slid into the front seat, feeling the rasp of freedom for the first time.

Schoolboy stood, his thumb and middle finger see-sawing together outside Jackie's flat. The door was open, as it always was from four to five during the kids' play-out time. The video inside was loud, making his sadness grow stronger. He banged the black door-knocker once.

'Ryan, is that you? You better not have broken another window,' Jackie's voice came, high and furious.

The video clicked off. He heard her slippers flapping and dragging against the carpet. When she appeared in the living room doorway, her slippers stopped as she saw him. Her green eyes defiantly brushed him, swept down, lifted, then brushed him again. She slowly walked towards him, until they stood with their body heat mingling together. She was on the inside, he remained on the outside.

'Thought you would be long gone by now.'

'I'm just going.'

'I get it. You came for your parcel.' As she spoke she flipped around.

Schoolboy stepped forward as his hand thrust out to clutch her arm. That stopped her. Still holding on to to her, he walked gently to stand behind her back. His hand dropped. She swivelled her slippers around. Schoolboy angled his neck down to her. Leaned into her. Took her lips. His mouth smoothed over hers, not sure what he was giving. She must have known what it was because her lips started fusing with his. He propelled her towards the wall so that he could really taste her emotions. Their mouths widened. Pulled into each other. Claimed what the other had to give.

'Mister Schoolboy, what you doing with my mum?' a young voice asked from the doorway.

Schoolboy and Jackie rushed apart, each breathing strongly. Jackie ran her hand through her hair as she faced her son.

'Your tea's in the oven. Don't forget to use the oven gloves.'

Ryan skipped past them into the kitchen. Jackie turned back to Schoolboy, who was looking straight into her eyes.

'I like your style of saying goodbye,' she rasped.

'I was hoping that this wouldn't be goodbye.' The words shoved out of him as if he couldn't really believe he was saying them.

'But you said . . .'

'I'm still leaving, but I just wanted to know whether you still wanted to taste cocoa-butter on my lips.'

Her small teeth came out to pinch her bottom lip, making her look so vulnerable.

'Schoolboy, if you feel gratitude because I helped you the other day . . .'

'No, it ain't that. I keep thinking of myself in Devon without your loud mouth, without your interference, without your who-gives-a-stuff behaviour and I know I don't want to let you go.' His last words were a rush, as if he was learning to speak for the first time.

Her flushed cheeks competed with the colour of her hair.

'So maybe we can keep in touch and the next time I come up I'll have that cocoa-butter ready just for you.'

'I'd like that.'

Three simple words, that was Jackie. She didn't ask for any promises, didn't ask him to make sure he kept his tush to himself in Devon.

'I see ya, Jackie.'

He moved out of her heat, reached the door, stepped over the threshold and began walking along the balcony.

'Oi,' her voice boomed behind him.

He turned to see her holding his parcel.

'I ain't gonna hold this for ever, you know,' she whispered as she passed the parcel to him.

He took it, surprised by its weight. He took a breath. Deep. He turned from her and started thinking of Devon, a place no doubt that had never even heard of cocoa-butter.

Schoolboy dwelt in the ridges of his thoughts as Window and Evie talked about South-East Asia, North Africa and other issues that didn't interest him. A local radio station played softly in the background. The words of the announcer on the radio started to penetrate his mind. He leaned forward sharply, at the same time saying:

'Window, turn it up.'

As Window followed his command they all started listening.

The rising tide of gun violence in East London claimed another four victims tonight in what police are describing as one of the worst incidents in the area for many years. Four people are believed to have died in a gun battle near a bar in Hackney after what some residents described as a Wild West style confrontation. Police have cordoned off the area and begun an investigation. They are keeping an open mind on the motive . . .

Evie's voice broke in, high, almost crying.

'That could have been you, Eli, that could have been you.'

He didn't respond because he knew she was right. He let his head rock back on his neck as the relief pumped air out of his body. He'd so nearly become another victim, another foolish statistic.

'At least Queen won't be on your case any more,' Window breathed.

'Queen?' Evie asked.

Neither Schoolboy nor Window answered her.

'You got your ticket?' Evie asked quietly.

'Yes, Mother,' he replied as his hands felt in his jacket pocket.

He could feel his MB, but nothing else. His hands dived out and one ran into his inside pocket. Nothing. He searched his trousers pocket. Nothing.

Fuckrees.

'Schoolboy, what's wrong?' Window asked as he felt his friend's movements beside him.

'Bullocks, I can't find the fucking ticket.'

Window's car eased by the silver Jeep as he drove to the end of road opposite Parkview. As soon as Schoolboy had realised that he couldn't find the train ticket Window had stopped the car so that he could search through his bag. The ticket had been a no-show. Window cut the engine outside Parkview.

'I wish I could drive you to Devon, but I can't. The reason I wasn't available until Saturday was my mum slipped away and died. Her funeral is tomorrow in Forest Gate so I need to be there,' Window said.

Schoolboy looked at him with surprise misting his eyes.

'Sorry, I didn't realise, mate. There's no way I'd ask you to drive me. I know exactly where this ticket is, so we'll make it to the station.'

'Just get on the train and bunk the fare,' Evie added.

He looked at Evie a bit shocked that she of all people was telling him to do something criminal.

'I can't start off my new life like that, Evie. No more illegals all right. I've left it under the pillow, so I'll be back in a flash.'

'You better be because it's already 4.45,' Window explained beside him.

'Don't worry, I'll be back before you know it.'

Schoolboy knew time was sprinting by as he jammed the key into the lock of the flat on Death Row. He tried to turn the key but the lock wouldn't move. He tried again, but the lock wouldn't budge.

Fuckrees.

He tore the key out of the door and looked at it. Definitely the right key. Typical Yale key. He pushed it in for the third time, rotating the key gently, and felt the lock finally turn. He pushed the door and plunged inside. He wasn't planning to stay so he left the door open. He ran along the passage and whipped into the bedroom. He kept his speed up as he got to the bed. He scooped down and shifted the pillow. He let out a long, easy breath. The ticket was exactly where he'd left it.

'Yes!' he whispered triumphantly.

He plucked up the ticket, folded it and crammed it into the side pocket of his trousers. As he began to fold up, the sting of expensive perfume crept into the room. Apple, iced with another fragrance he couldn't quite identify. He felt the flush of someone behind him. Bloody Evie. Couldn't she just have followed his instructions and waited with Window?

'Evie, I told you I'd be down . . .' His words lifted as he stretched his body.

He turned around, inhaled his remaining words and jumped back when he saw who the perfume belonged to.

'Mister Schoolbwoy, I'm sorry I'm not your sister, but I know a place where we can play happy families,' Queen sneered, as she screwed her mouth and aimed her .22 calibre at him.

30

Schoolboy knew that one step back meant becoming the eleventh victim to drop to their death from the roof of Parkview. The heels of his trainers hugged the rim of the roof. The wind scratched against his back with the malicious power to send him into free-fall. Queen stood a metre away, an angry silhouette against the hard London skyline, with her gun pointed at his chest. He noticed that her grip on the trigger seemed loose, while her lips trembled.

'So where is it?' Queen's question cut into the wind, as the abandoned shopping trolley on the far side spun in a half circle.

'I don't know.'

'Stop trying to jerk me off because . . .'

'I'd never do that, Queen. I thought we were getting tight, you know, rude bwoy and rude gal in this together . . .'

'What? After you tried to set me up and gob in my face today . . .'

'Me? Spit in your face? Got the wrong geezer, girl. I'm just some street hood who's a victim just like you, Queen.'

Queen's neck hiked back as she opened her mouth to laugh. The sound was quick, crazy, as it echoed in the wind. Her mouth snapped closed, cutting the echo dead. She raised the gun and fired.

Schoolboy ducked down as the heat of the bullet hurtled past his head on one side, while a gust of wind tugged him on the other side. He jammed his knees out and down grinding the soles of his feet into the bottom of his trainers. His mouth opened, gasping into the unfriendly air as his arms shot sideways to balance his body. He swayed, gulping harder, eyes closed, knowing this was where he'd join all the other unfortunates who smashed into the daffodils below. He stopped breathing. Tilted. Rocked. Waiting. Waiting for Hackney to claim his soul. The wind picked up urgency, squealed, grabbed his back, punching him.

The air punched Schoolboy a second time, dragging him forward. He stooped, body curved, as his trainers skated on the wet roof. He steadied himself and started breathing again with the strength of a newborn coming into life. He shoved his head up and screamed,

'I ain't got it.'

Queen quick-stepped towards him, bringing the rush of the wind with her, making Schoolboy bend his head and grip the concrete with his hands. He felt her harassed breathing comb through his locks. The nicotine of her breath added a new perfume to his skin. The force of cold steel touched his forehead. Even before he raised his head he knew that the gun was back into his life. Just like before, with him kneeling, with the 'why me?' curse of a victim whispering in his ear.

Queen eased herself and the gun back as her voice pummelled into him.

'You might as well throw yourself over because that's where your tongue is pushing you to go.'

'You've got the wrong guy,' Schoolboy yelled, as he eased himself up. 'Look at me. I'm just your average Hackney street fool. A phone here, a wallet there, that's my MO. I'd never tangle with a don like you. You know that. You need to be talking to other people who think they're bigger than you . . .'

'What people?'

'Come on, Queen babe, you don't need a 32-inch wide-screen TV to see what's been going on here . . .'

'If you've got something to say, just say it and stop pissing so slowly.'

'Queen, I thought you were smart enough to know when you're being played.'

'I found you, didn't I, so my brain cells must be working.'

Schoolboy's heart shivered as his toes squeezed forward in his trainers. So much for Evie's idea of a safe hiding-place. A bullet pumped into the ground between his legs, making him leap sideways. Another bullet struck the side of his trainers, making his movements look like a full-blown dance routine.

'Work it out, Queen.' His words were thick with the spit pooling in his mouth. 'Take the pieces and rearrange them and then think about who's been stringing you along. It ain't me. Do I look like I've got the clout to set up both you and the Numbers crew? Do I look like I could organise that level of play-off?'

He let the questions soak into her as the wind pulled her a step back.

Pulled him a step forward.

'That ain't what your sister told me . . .'

'Of course it ain't because that weren't my sister.'

'You'd say any old bollocks to get this gun out of your face.'

'By the looks of your gun I'm falling anyway so why would I lie?'

His statement was soft, breathless, lacerated with the weariness of someone who wasn't going to finish the race.

The wind jived around them, in between them, over them.

'Come on, tell me if I'm wrong here, Queen, but the person you spoke to had a nose-stud and gold hair-cuffs?'

Queen's eyebrows slashed down as her eyes began to blink rapidly.

'That ain't my sister . . .'

'Let's stop this foolishness . . .'

'Tammy or Number 8 ring a bell?'

Queen sucked in her breath. Her trigger-finger become looser as tiredness began to drip into her eyes, speeding up her blinking. Schoolboy moved one step into the ground that Queen had claimed as her own. Abruptly his Jim Reeves ringtone started waltzing in the wind from his pocket.

'Don't answer it,' she commanded.

'Think it through, Queen.' Schoolboy ignored the mobile ringing in his pocket. 'Shooting people is business, but it has to be good business. You know shooting the wrong guy is bad business. Very bad business. Twenty-five to life in prison for the right guy, well, that's a chance you take. Same sentence for the wrong guy – well, that's just stupid. How you gonna explain that one to your kids? You gave up seeing them grow up because you decided to take a chance on the wrong person?'

The gun punched forward, but Queen's finger remained still.

'What are you gonna tell your kids when the Social come to take them away?'

The gun started shaking in the wind.

'What you gonna tell them when they start calling someone else Mummy?'

The gun shook, then tilted towards the ground.

'Can I go now?' Schoolboy whispered.

A huge wall of wind swept between them. Queen's gaze strained into him. But she didn't answer. She shifted her weight on to her back foot. He felt the shift. From her to him.

Schoolboy took up the rhythm of her silence and began to move forward. He raised his hands to show he wasn't a threat, drawing the wet air into his mouth as he moved. He took his second stride, straining his back towards his chest as if that would save him if a bullet hit. He took his next stride feeling the sweat deepen the colour of his clothes. He could feel every layer of his skin as he waited for steel to tear into it. He waited for the sound of thunder. Waited for the crippling unbelievability of pain.

On the fourth stride he heard Queen's heels scratch against the floor, but he kept moving.

He felt the violence of the gun, but he kept moving.

He heard the skid of the shopping trolley, but he kept moving.

Finally he came face-to-face with the open roof shaft. He half-turned back to gaze at Queen. Her clothes, her hair, were blowing in the wind, her gun hanging at her side. His breathing became easier as he reached the roof shaft. He bent his trembling knees, gripped the metal around the shaft with his hands and lunged down until his trainers hit the ladder's third step. Instinctively he raised his arm to grab the lid of the shaft to close it. He stretched up and turned his hand back until it found the handle. As his numb fingers curved around it he screamed in pain as something sharp pierced the middle of his hand. The pressure propelled his chest out, his body up, as he tried to relieve the pressure. His head shot back up into the life of the roof. His face opened up to stare above him, expecting to find the black sky, but finding a sour-faced Queen. Gazing at her from toe to head made him really feel the power this woman had. Her legs were flexed wide, making him realise that she had her heel stuck in his hand.

'That,' Queen twisted her heel to the left as she spoke, 'is for putting your hands on me outside the church.'

She twisted her heel to the right, making a whimper and blood spurt from Schoolboy at the same time.

'And this is to remind you that you really should have listened to your mum when she said you must never steal from the dead.' Abruptly she pulled her heel out of his hand making him chant out in pain.

She dropped down and breathed into his crumpled face, 'If you were one of my girls I'd kiss it better for you. I don't want to see you anywhere on my soil any more, Schoolbwoy.'

She uncoiled herself to stand up, turned her back on him and moved towards the roof's edge to stare at the sky. Schoolboy jerked his arm inside the shaft and slid down the ladder.

31

Schoolboy didn't need a watch to tell him that time was clicking by. Exactly how much time he had left he didn't know, but he couldn't stop to check. His hand was soaked with pain, but he didn't have time to study that as he pelted down Death Row. As he swung into the lobby, a powerful hand grabbed his arm from the lift's entrance. He cried out with more pain. He back flipped his other arm ready to attack.

'What the hell are you doing, Schoolie, man?'

Window's question made his arm freeze in mid-air, but he continued to wince in pain.

'Sorry, I got held up,' he answered as he entered the lift that Window stood in.

'Your sister was getting worried so I said I'd check it out.' Window's eyes connected with the blood on Schoolboy's hand. 'What's been going on, dread?'

'Nothing you need to know. Don't mention my hand to Evie. What's the time?'

Window checked his watch.

'We got twenty-five minutes.'

'I ain't gonna make it,' Schoolboy cried as he leaned on the metal of the lift's back wall.

'Have faith, Schoolie, have faith.'

The lift doors closed, taking them down.

'Eli, just go, we'll try and catch you,' Evie belted out, checking her watch as they stood on the pavement near Window's car.

He snatched up his bags and ran like a refugee with danger on his back. Four minutes, that's all he had. His breathing was short, rough, as he weaved and dodged around people. Heart rumbling, he dived into the station. It was large, unfamiliar, not his territory. He stood under the glass-and-iron arched roof of as his eyes darted wildly around looking for information. His eyes were skimming and blinking so much he couldn't find it.

He let his eyes do the rounds again, skipping up and down, down and up until he finally found what he was after. He lunged towards the information screen, already feeling that the train had come and gone. His eyes peeled across the screen, hunting information on the train for Exeter. He couldn't find any. His eyes scrolled again. And again. Absolute zilch.

Life was so full of fuckrees.

Schoolboy almost collapsed as the bags fell from his loose fingers. He rammed his fingers through his locks knowing he just hadn't made it. But when had he made anything in his life. He sighed, defeated, a touch lost. There was no point standing here like a stand-up comedian being booed on stage. But he couldn't move. Couldn't believe that this just wasn't meant to be. His head stooped as he shook it. He raised his head just as new information flashed on to the screen.

Exeter 17.30, new departure time 17.40.

Schoolboy's mouth opened as he gulped in air, starting to laugh.

'Quaintness, coves and cooking,' he tickled out loudly to himself.

A woman with a child in a pushchair began to look at him. He grinned at her and affirmed, 'Life's good, ain't it.'

The woman wheeled the pushchair further away from him. He grinned at the toddler sucking a lollipop in the pushchair. He remembered the child in the church calling out to him:

Sweet Lord, redeem me.
Sweet Lord Jesus, save me.

His smile faded, as he knew that getting on the train was the start of a long way to go. He turned as he heard Evie's voice next to him whisper:

'This is meant to be, Eli, this is meant to be.'

He turned fully to her, inspecting her face as his hair flicked back.

She stretched her palms towards him. He stepped forward, just one step, and placed his good hand into hers. He slipped the keys for cell 95 Death Row into her hands. Their fingers meshed and clung over the coolness of the keys. He didn't feel her flesh, but felt all the things she had been to him. Stroppy wise woman, reluctant temporary mum, caring and tell-it-as-it-is sister. Could he really let go of all of this and stand on his own Tims-covered feet? He opened his mouth to speak, but her voice cut him off.

'You don't need me, Eli. Well, not that way.' Her hands withdrew from his as she continued, 'You make sure you tell your friend that I'm going to send the money for the knives.'

A voice came on the loudspeaker announcing the arrival of the train.

'Let's load those bags up,' Window said softly beside him.

When the bags were loaded, Schoolboy felt the power of his sister melt through him as they hugged. He pulled back and inspected her face, expecting to see tears. But her face was back to being Evie, representative of middle London, professional, in control. She took one step back from him, allowing Window to stand in front of him. Their index fingers came out, tapped, joined, squeezed and then each reached across to tap the other's heart twice. Schoolboy mouthed, 'Remember to look out for Evie.' Window nodded back. Window eased back and Schoolboy knew it was time to finally leave. He turned his back on them, on Hackney, on London, and stepped up into the train.

He found his seat and sat down like a soul just leaving the body of someone who had died. His friend and sister nodded their heads and waved from the platform. He waved back with a hand so heavy he knew he would feel pain very soon if he didn't put it down. The train began reeling, rocking, running away, taking him with it. His eyes and nose were filling up but he wasn't going to let them fall. He felt eyes on him and quickly looked at the woman opposite him. Flared trouser suit, square manicured nails and as stiff as they came. Not another wannabe plantation mistress?

He needed a distraction so he felt in the holdall beside him for Jackie's parcel. He pulled it out, heavy in its blue paper. He stuck his fingers in, pulling the top layer away. Inside was a simple white cotton cloth folded over like the parcel of a pastry. He peeled the cloth and unfolded it back. He stared at the items inside, his bottom lip flopping down as the tears started to fall. He cried, because the most wonderful knives he had ever known lay in his lap sitting pretty in their purple velvet box. He cried because Mr Prakash had thought of him while he was dying. He cried because he realised that he had been such a fool. All this time he had been running hot Jackie had held the answer to his future on top of her Corrie tape. He wanted to let out the demented laughter that was burning inside his mouth but Scarlett O'Hara's gaze was openly grazing against him.

'Are you OK?' her concerned voice asked. The type of voice that could sing a solo on its own easily.

He looked over at the woman opposite him. How could he have ever said that she was stiff? He wondered if her backside was as arched as her eyebrows. He knew Jackie's was. Jackie. He had made a promise to her and he was going to keep it. He pushed the knives back into his bag, shook his locks, breathed in deep and strong and let his dimples smooch and stretch out to enjoy the ride.

32

Schoolboy sat in South-West Devon's number one exotic restaurant to dine. The Likc was two doors up from the local post office and three minutes down from the beach. Some said the Likc was sultry, others claimed it was in-your-face-package holiday. Either way was right because it wanted customers to remember what the heat felt like on their backs and to dream of being somewhere other than England. The restaurant was willowy long with a bar designed for liming and bamboo chairs loosely fitted around smoked glass tables for eating and pure chat. The gold-tinted walls provided the sun for pictures of pale beaches that lined one side of the walls. But it was the fragrance of limes, crab and home-made bread mixed with dark and light rums that made people come back.

'Hey, MD – ten minutes till opening . . .'

It was a few seconds before Schoolboy looked up. He was still getting used to his new nickname – MD, short for Maître D'. His new name had almost been Coconut because of the light pastries he made. When he'd declared that he'd rather take his chances back in Hackney than be called Coconut, everyone had laughed. That's what he loved about the Likc, the gentle chuckles and softly spoken words that reminded him of how Mum said life was meant to be.

It had been a month since he'd left London and three weeks since anyone had called him Schoolboy. Michael was standing near the blue shutters on the front window getting ready to open the door while MD perched at a table skimming through a tabloid. Some restaurants on the Torbay Circus junction only opened when there might be customers coming but Michael was strict. The closed sign was turned around on the dot of 1 p.m. regardless of whatever weather was brewing outside.

Today it was rain, waves of it falling across the beach and making tiny dents in the sea. MD stood up, stretched as he gazed through a window watching a few holidaymakers who were determined to make the most of their week or two on the English Riviera. The rain and wind bent the palm trees on the seafront. They'd looked so out of place when MD had arrived, but he'd grown to like them.

MD began to stroll towards the bar, still clutching his newspaper. Although the restaurant was closed, its first customer was already at the bar. Colonel Rourke, dressed in his blazer, regimental tie and the rigid authority that he hadn't exercised in years, was reading a broadsheet. He'd been a colonial administrator in the Caribbean in the 60s and had retired to Torquay. Back in the old days he'd acquired a taste for the local food he'd never lost. Now he was in Michael's restaurant every morning. After the Colonel had brought in a collection of yellowing recipes for old-time Grenadian food, they had struck up a deep friendship. In return for the recipes, the Colonel was allowed in half an hour before opening and an extra portion of coconut tarts.

As MD approached the bar, the Colonel took off his glasses and folded them away in his top pocket.

'Colonel, fancy doing a swap?' MD held out his newspaper.

'Certainly, old man,' the colonel agreed, giving MD the paper he'd been reading. 'Pass me the *Daily Star*, will you?'

MD took the paper and spread it out on the bar. He lazily thumbed through it. On page 7 he stopped, spit curling in his mouth when he found something he wasn't expecting to see. In the background he heard the Colonel say, 'My word, she's a big girl.'

MD didn't respond, caught by a headline in bold type.

Priceless Cross Recovered

Today's discovery of a thirteenth-century cross in a bedsit in London's East End has focused attention on the illegal trade in African art. The police were called to the bedsit in Homerton this morning when neighbours reported a foul smell coming from inside. The cross was discovered next to the body of a young woman, who is believed to have died from an overdose.

The police have issued a statement saying that the cross is believed to be one of the seven crosses of Lalibela, Ethiopia's most famous collection of church crosses. Ethiopian tradition has it that anyone who removed any of the crosses from the church would be cursed . . .

MD quickly closed the paper, trembling. That life was over now. Nothing could touch him.

Michael called across the room as he opened the restaurant for business. 'Come on, MD, your knives are waiting for you.'

Also available from
THE MAIA PRESS

Merete Morken Andersen OCEANS OF TIME £8.99 ISBN 1 904559 11 5
A divorced couple confront a family tragedy in the white night of a Norwegian summer.
'A beautiful book' (Jostein Gaarder, author of *Sophie's World*), and a European bestseller.

Michael Arditti GOOD CLEAN FUN £8.99 ISBN 1 904559 08 5
Twelve stories from the award-winning author of *Easter* provide a witty, compassionate yet
uncompromising look at love and loss, desire and defiance, in the twenty-first century.

Hélène du Coudray ANOTHER COUNTRY £7.99 ISBN 1 904559 04 2
A prize-winning novel, first published in 1928, about a passionate affair between a British
ship's officer and a Russian emigrée governess which promises to end in disaster. •

Lewis DeSoto A BLADE OF GRASS £8.99 ISBN 1 904559 07 7
A lyrical and profound novel set in South Africa during the era of apartheid, in which the
recently widowed Märit struggles to run her farm with the help of her black maid, Tembi.

Maggie Hamand, ed. UNCUT DIAMONDS £7.99 ISBN 1 904559 03 4
Unusual and sometimes challenging, these vibrant, original stories showcase the huge
diversity of new writing talent coming out of contemporary London.

Linda Leatherbarrow ESSENTIAL KIT £8.99 ISBN 1 904559 10 7
The first collection from a short-story prizewinner – lyrical, uplifting, funny and moving,
always pertinent – 'joyously surreal . . . gnomically funny, and touching' (Shena Mackay).

Sara Maitland ON BECOMING A FAIRY GODMOTHER
£7.99 ISBN 1 904559 00 X
Fifteen new 'fairy stories' by an acclaimed master of the genre breathe new life into old
legends and bring the magic of myth back into modern women's lives.

Anne Redmon IN DENIAL £7.99 ISBN 1 904559 01 8
A chilling novel about the relationship between Harriet, a prison visitor, and Gerry, a serial
offender, which explores challenging themes with subtlety and intelligence.

Henrietta Seredy LEAVING IMPRINTS £7.99 ISBN 1 904559 02 6
Beautifully written and startlingly original, this unusual and memorable novel explores
a destructive, passionate relationship between two damaged people.

Norman Thomas THE THOUSAND-PETALLED DAISY
£7.99 ISBN 1 904559 05 0
Love, jealousy and violence play a part in this coming-of-age novel set in India, written
with a distinctive, off-beat humour and a delicate but intensely felt spirituality.

Adam Zameenzad PEPSI AND MARIA £8.99 ISBN 1 904559 06 9
A highly original novel about two street children in South America whose zest for life
carries them through the brutal realities of their daily existence.